HATE TO LOVE YOU

JENNIFER SUCEVIC

ALSO BY JENNIFER SUCEVIC

Campus Heartthrob

Campus Player

Claiming What's Mine

Confessions of a Heartbreaker

Crazy for You (80s short story)

Don't Leave

Friend Zoned

Heartless

If You Were Mine

Just Friends

King of Campus

King of Hawthorne Prep

Love to Hate You

One Night Stand

Protecting What's Mine

Queen of Hawthorne Prep

Stay

The Boy Next Door

The Breakup Plan

The Girl Next Door

Chapter One

BRODY

"Dude, I thought you'd be back earlier." Cooper, one of my room-mates, grins as I walk through the front door. There's a half-naked chick straddling his lap. "We had to get this party started without you." He shrugs as if he's just taken one for the team. "It couldn't be helped."

I snort as my gaze travels around the living room of the house we rent a few blocks off campus. Even though there are only four of us on the lease, our place seems to be a crash pad for half the team. By the looks of the beer bottles strewn around, they've been at it for a while. I'm seriously thinking about charging some of these assholes rent.

Although, I guess if I were stuck in a shoebox of a dorm, I'd be desperate for a way out, too. I played juniors straight out of high school for two years before coming in as a freshman at twenty. I skipped dorm living and went straight to renting a place nearby. There was no way I was bunking down with a bunch of random eighteen-year-olds who'd never lived away from home. Not to mention, having an RA up my ass telling me what I could and couldn't do.

That sounds about as much fun as ripping duct tape off my balls.

Which is, I might add, the complete opposite of fun. Hazing sucks. And for future reference, you don't rip duct tape off your balls, you carefully cut it away with a steady hand while mother-fucking the entire team.

My other two roommates, Luke Anderson and Sawyer Stevens, are hunched at the edge of the couch, battling it out in an intense game of NHL. Their thumbs are jerking the controllers in lightning-quick movements, and their eyeballs are fastened to the seventy-inch HD screen hanging across the room.

I can only shake my head. Every time they play, it's like a freaking National Championship is at stake.

I arch a brow as the girl on Cooper's lap reaches around and unhooks her bra, dropping it to the floor. Apparently, she doesn't mind if there's an audience. Cooper's lazy grin stretches as his fingers zero in on her nips.

I'd love to say this scene isn't typical for a Sunday night, but I'd be lying through my teeth. Usually, it's much worse.

Deking out Luke with some impressive video game puck handling skills, Sawyer says, "Grab a beer, bro. You can take over for Luke after I make him cry again like a little bitch."

"Fuck you," Luke grumbles.

I glance at the score. Luke is getting his ass handed to him on a silver platter, and he knows it.

"Sure." Sawyer smirks. "Maybe later. But I should warn you, you're not really my type. I like a dude who's packing a little more meat than you."

My lips twitch as I drop my duffle to the floor.

"Hey, you see that bullshit text from Coach?" Cooper asks from between the girl's tits.

I groan, hoping I didn't miss anything important while I was out of town for the weekend. I'm already under contract with the Milwaukee Mavericks. My dad and I flew there to meet with the coaching staff. I also got to hang with a few of the defensive players. Saturday night was freaking crazy. Next season is going to rock.

"Nah, didn't see it," I say. "What's going on?"

"Practice times have changed," Cooper continues, all the while playing with the girl's body. "We're now at six o'clock in the morning and seven in the evening."

Fuck me. He's starting two-a-days already?

"You think he's just screwing around with us?" I wouldn't put it past Coach Lang. I don't think he has anything better to do than lie awake at night, dreaming up new ways to torture us. The guy is a real hard-ass.

Then again, that's why we're here.

But six in the morning...that sucks. Between school and hockey practice, I already feel like I don't get enough sleep. And it's only September. That means I'll need to be up and out the door by five to make it to the rink, get dressed, and be on the ice by six. By the time eleven o'clock at night rolls around, I'll fall into bed an exhausted heap.

Sawyer shrugs, not looking particularly put out by the time change.

Cooper pops the nipple out of his mouth and fixes his glassy-eyed gaze on me. "Can't you have your dad talk some freaking sense into the guy?"

Luke grumbles under his breath, "I can barely make it to the seven o'clock practice on time."

"Nope." I shake my head. I'd do just about anything for these guys, except run to my father with anything related to hockey. Coach and my dad go way back. They both played for the Detroit Redwings. I've known the man my entire life. He helped me lace up my first pair of Bauers. So, you'd think he'd have a soft spot for me. Maybe take it easy on me.

Yeah...fat chance of that happening.

If anything, he comes down on me like a ton of bricks *because* of our personal relationship. I think Lang doesn't want any of the guys to feel like he's playing favorites.

Mission accomplished, dude.

No one would ever accuse him of that.

"Then prepare to haul ass at the butt crack of dawn, my friend." With that, Cooper turns his attention elsewhere, attacking the girl's mouth.

Luke eyes them for a moment before yelling, "Hey, you gonna take that shit to the bedroom or are we all being treated to a free show?"

Not bothering to come up for air, Cooper ignores the question.

Luke shakes his head and focuses his attention on making a comeback. Or at least knocking Sawyer's avatar on its ass. "Guess that means we should make some popcorn."

I pick up my duffel and hoist it over my shoulder, deciding to head upstairs for a while. I love hanging with these guys, but I'm not feeling it at the moment.

"Hi, Brody." A lush blonde slips her arms around me and presses her ample cleavage against my chest. "I was hoping you'd show up."

Given the fact that this is my house, the chances of that happening were extremely high.

I stare down into her big green eyes.

"Hey." She looks familiar. I do a quick mental search, trying to produce a name, but only come up with blanks.

Which probably means I haven't slept with her recently.

When it comes to the ladies, I've come up with an algorithm that I've perfected over the last three years. It's simple, yet foolproof. I never screw the same girl more than three times in a six-month period. If you do, you run the risk of entering into the murky territory of a quasi-relationship or a friends-with-benefits situation. I'm not looking for any attachments at this point.

Even casual ones.

I'm at Whitmore to earn a degree and prepare for the pros. I'm focused on getting bigger, faster, and stronger. The NHL is no place for pussies. If you can't hack it, the league will chew you up and spit you out before you can blink your eyes. I have no intention of allowing that to happen. I've worked too hard to crash and burn at this point.

Or get distracted.

In a surprisingly bold move, Blondie slides her hand from my chest to my package and gives it a firm squeeze to let me know she means business.

I have no doubts that if I asked her to drop to her knees and suck me off in front of all these people, she would do it in a heartbeat. Other than a thong, the girl grinding away on Cooper's lap is naked.

My first year playing juniors, when a girl offered to have no-strings-attached-sex, I'd thought I'd hit the flipping jackpot. Less than five minutes later, I'd blown my load and was ready for round two. Fast forward five years, and I don't even blink at a chick who's willing to drop her panties within minutes of me walking through the door. It happens far too often for it to be considered a novelty.

Which is just plain sad.

When I was in high school, I jumped at the chance to dip my wick.

Now?

Not so much.

It's like being fed a steady diet of steak and lobster. Sure, it's delicious the first couple of days. Maybe even a full week. You can't help but greedily devour every single bite and then lick your fingertips afterward. But, believe it or not, even steak and lobster become mundane.

Most guys, no matter what their age, would give their left nut to be in my skates.

To have their pick of any girl. Or, more often than not, *girls*.

And here I am...limp dick in hand.

Actually, limp dick in *her* hand.

Sex has become something I do to take the edge off when I'm feeling stressed. It's my version of a relaxation technique. For fuck's sake, I'm twenty-three years old. I'm in the sexual prime of my life. I should be ecstatic when any girl wants to spread her legs for me. What I shouldn't be is bored. And I sure as hell shouldn't be mentally running through the drills we'll be doing when I lead a captain's practice.

I pry her fingers from my junk and shake my head. "Sorry, I've got some shit to take care of."

And that shit would be school. I have forty pages of reading that needs to be finished up by tomorrow morning.

Blondie pouts and bats her mascara-laden lashes.

"Maybe later?" she coos in a baby voice.

Fuck. That is such a turnoff.

Why do chicks do that?

No, seriously. It's a legitimate question. Why do they do that? It's like nails on a chalkboard. I'm tempted to answer back in a ridiculous, lispy-sounding voice.

But I don't.

I'm not that big of an asshole.

Plus, she might be into it.

Then I'd be screwed. I envision us cooing at each other in baby voices for the rest of the night and almost shudder.

"Maybe," I say noncommittally. Although I'm not going to lie, that toddler voice has killed any chance for a later hookup. But I'm smart enough not to tell her that. Chances are high that she'll end up finding another hockey player to latch on to and forget all about me. Because let's face it, that's what she's here for.

A little dick from a guy who skates with a stick.

Just to be sure, I run my eyes over the length of her again.

Toddler voice aside, she's got it going on.

And yet, that banging body is doing absolutely nothing for me.

Which is troublesome. I almost want to take her upstairs just to prove to myself that everything is in proper working order. But I won't.

As I hit the first step, Cooper breaks away from his girl. "WTF, McKinnon? Where you going?" He waves a hand around the room. "Can't you see we're in the middle of entertaining?"

"I'll leave you to take care of our guests," I say, trudging up the staircase.

"Well, if you insist," he slurs happily.

My bedroom is at the end of the hall, away from the noise of the first floor. As a general rule, no one is allowed on the second floor except for the guys who live here. I pull out my key and unlock the door before stepping inside.

My duffel gets tossed in the corner before I open my Managerial Finance book. I thought I'd have a chance to plow through some of the reading over the weekend, but my dad and I were on the go the entire time. Meeting people from the Milwaukee organization, hitting a team party, checking out a few condos near the lakefront. Just getting the general lay of the land. On the plane ride home, I had every intention of being productive, but ended up sacking out once we hit cruising altitude.

Three hours later, there's a knock on the door. Normally an interruption would piss me off, but after slogging through thirty pages, my eyes have glazed over, and I'm fighting to stay awake. This material is mind-numbingly boring, and that's not helping matters.

"It's open," I call out, expecting Cooper to try cajoling me back downstairs.

When that guy's shitfaced, he wants everyone else to be just as hammered as he is. I've never seen anyone put away alcohol the way he does. It's almost as impressive as it is scary. And yet, he's somehow able to wake up for morning practice bright-eyed and bushy-tailed like he wasn't just wasted six hours ago. Someone from the biology department really needs to do a case study on him, 'cause that shit just ain't normal.

When I suck down alcohol like that, the next morning I'm like a newborn colt on the ice who can't keep his legs under him.

It's not a pretty sight. Which is why I don't do it. Been there, done that. Moving on.

The door swings open to reveal Blondie-With-The-Toddler-Voice. And she's not alone. She's brought a friend.

I raise my brows in interest as they step inside the room.

In the three hours since I've seen her, Blondie has managed to lose most of her clothing. The brunette she's with appears to be in the same predicament. They stand in lacy bras and barely-there thongs with their hands entwined.

My gaze roves over them appreciatively.

How could it not?

Their tummies are flat and toned. Hips are nicely rounded. Tits jiggle enticingly as they saunter toward the bed where I'm currently sprawled.

I should be a man of steel over here. I haven't gotten laid in three weeks. Which is almost unheard of. I haven't gone that long without sex since I first started having it.

But there's nothing.

Not even a twitch.

Which begs the question—What the hell is wrong with me?

It must be the stress of school and the skating regimen I'm on. Even though I'm already under contract with Milwaukee and don't have to worry about the NHL draft later this year, I'm still under a lot of pressure to perform this season.

National Championships don't bring themselves home.

I'd be concerned that I have some serious erectile dysfunction issues happening except there's one chick who gets me hard every time I lay eyes on her. Rather ironically, she wants nothing to do with me. I think she'd claw my eyes out if I laid one solitary finger on her.

Actually, all I have to do is stare in her direction, and she bares her teeth at me.

Maybe these girls are exactly what I need to relieve some of my pent-up stress. It certainly can't hurt.

Decision made, I slam my finance book closed and toss it to the floor where it lands with a loud thud. I fold my arms behind my head and smile at the girls in silent invitation.

And the rest, shall we say, is history.

Chapter Two

NATALIE

I grit my teeth in silent aggravation.

Brody McKinnon and Kimmie Sanders are at it again.

I've spent the last twenty-five minutes listening to Kimmie giggle her way through class along with the hushed whispers of Brody McKinnon. These two make it impossible to concentrate on the material that will most assuredly be on next week's exam.

For the hundredth time, I wonder how either of them are passing this class.

I almost snicker at the thought and shake my head. Well, I know *exactly* how Brody is passing. He's the captain of the Whitmore Wildcats hockey team. Him attending class is purely for show. It's doubtful he does any of the required work.

He's more of a...pretty decoration.

Man candy for the ladies of Whitmore to fawn over.

Managerial Finance meets every Monday, Wednesday, and Friday at ten o'clock in the morning at Brighton Hall, which is the business building on campus. It takes an extra-large caramel mocha to get through this class without coming unhinged and losing my shit on them. Since we don't have assigned seating, I'm strategic about choosing a different desk each class session in the hope that Brody will park himself elsewhere. Preferably on the other side of the room where I can't be distracted by the deep timbre of his voice.

He never does. Somehow, he always ends up right behind me. I swear he does it on purpose. Other than to mess with me, I have no idea why he would bother.

Whitmore is a private university where hockey reigns supreme. Not even football can compete with hockey at this school. Every year, there are a handful of players that end up drafted to the NHL. That alone makes Whitmore a premier school for rising hockey talent in the country and Canada.

I'm sure the university rakes in a ton of revenue from ticket sales and merchandising. Two years ago, they built a brand-new, state-of-the-art arena on campus. So, it goes without saying that the hockey players are treated like royalty around here.

It's annoying, but you get used to it...after a while.

Or, like me, you simply ignore it.

Personally, I don't understand all the fandemonium. It's just a game. Sure, hockey is a fun spectator sport. The pace, the action, the adrenalin. It's easy to get swept away by the frenzy. I'll admit to enjoying my fair share of games during the three years I've attended Whitmore, but that doesn't mean I understand the culture of hero worship that surrounds it. Nor am I one of these idiot girls who wants to sleep with as many of the guys on the team as I can.

Ummm...No, thank you. I enjoy being STD-free.

When it comes right down to it, these guys are just a bunch of over-muscly jocks who have mastered the art (snort) of slapping a black rubber disc at a net and getting into fistfights on and off the ice at the least provocation.

Let's keep it in perspective, people. They're not exactly curing cancer or solving world hunger. And thusly, shouldn't be treated as such.

There are about forty hockey players who attend Whitmore. And Brody McKinnon is probably the most talented—and talked about—player on the team. Even in high school, he was on the NHL radar. He made a name for himself playing juniors before gracing us with his esteemed presence. As much as it pains me to admit it, he's exploded at the college level. The chatter around campus is that he's already under contract for an NHL team.

Is that true?

Who knows.

Better yet, who cares?

I try not to pay attention to the constant gossip that churns where he's concerned, but it's impossible to ignore. Being at Whitmore is like being held prisoner in a hockey-obsessed bubble. You're inundated with the information whether you want it or not.

Even though it's perfectly clear that an extraneous conversation is taking place behind me, Dr. Miller ignores it and continues with her lecture on capital budgeting techniques. Far be it for her to reprimand one of our star athletes. Normally, I would tune Brody and his groupies out, but it's not working today.

I woke up late and didn't have time to stop at Java House for my usual extra-grande cup of caffeine.

So, I'm cranky and out of sorts.

Which is never a good combination. Especially for Brody.

When I can't stand another moment of their incessant chatter, I spin around on my chair and give Brody a perfectly honed death glare. It's not difficult. I can't look at him without my face contorting into that expression. This guy has rubbed me wrong from day one. And it's only gone downhill from there.

Our eyes collide, and Brody's brows skyrocket into his hairline before a knowing smirk moves across his face at a glacier pace.

He mouths one word.

Jealous?

I huff.

As if...

My guess is that he's taken one too many slapshots to the head. It's sad, really...

His eyes sparkle with mischief as he deliberately rims the edges of his lips with his tongue.

In your dreams, I mouth back and whip around again to face the front. My teeth are clenched so tightly, they're in imminent danger of shattering.

This is exactly what Brody McKinnon does to me.

Every.

Damn.

Time.

The remainder of class drags. The subject matter doesn't help. This unit is a killer. I find myself repeatedly glancing at the clock, antsy to get out of here. Which sucks. Usually, I enjoy Dr. Miller's lectures. The majority of the professors in the business department are old and stodgy. Dr. Miller has only been teaching for a few years. She's like a breath of fresh air. I've already exhausted all of her course offerings.

As soon as she wraps up her lecture and dismisses the class, I pack up my bag and beeline for the door. I need to put as much distance between myself and—

I don't make it more than five steps before a thickly muscled arm is thrown over my shoulders, halting my progress.

I grunt under the heavy weight of it.

What does this guy eat for breakfast?

Lead?

"Davies, why so angry this morning?" Before I can snap out an annoyed retort, Brody continues. "Wait, wait, don't tell me. Let me see if I can guess." He taps his chin with a finger in contemplation. It's an interesting look on him. Not one I've seen too often. I'm about to tell him this, when he says, "Your favorite vibe died just as you were getting to the kinky part of your self-love session."

One side of my mouth curls up in disgust, and I shove at the arm anchoring me to him. It doesn't budge. Not that I expected it to. "Nailed it. How'd you figure it out?"

Brody has the rare ability of making me feel like a rabid dog on a choke chain. If I could rip him to shreds with my bare teeth, I would in a heartbeat. I wouldn't even give it a second thought.

I'm in no way a violent person, but Brody McKinnon brings out the worst in me.

The chuckle that escapes from his lips is warm and sultry. Even though I fight against it, it still manages to strum something deep inside me.

"Well, you're even more pissed off than usual. Which is really saying something." He tugs me closer so that I'm inundated by the scent of his cologne. Something that smells unbearably like beachy sunshine overwhelms my senses. God, why does he have to smell so delicious? Why can't he reek of BO? That would be so much easier to deal with than this.

How can I detest someone so much and yet still want to devour them? It's not the first time I've wondered this. I can only hope it'll be the last.

His voice dips until it vibrates somewhere in the vicinity of husky and sumptuous. "Tell you what, if you've got some time to kill, I'll remedy that situation for you." He wiggles his eyebrows and purrs, "Take the edge off, so to speak." Even though I'm pressed against his hard, unyielding body, he somehow manages to give me the once-over. It feels very much like a physical caress. Heat floods my panties in response. Damn him for making me feel this way. "I bet I could get you off in ten minutes." He narrows his eyes in a thoughtful manner. "Probably less. You seem wound pretty tight, Davies. Ever have a multiple orgasm? I think it would do wonders for your disposition."

If any other guy on campus were stupid enough to say the same thing to me, I'd probably slug him. Even though it goes against my better judgment, I withhold any kind of response from him. This isn't the first time we've verbally sparred with one another, and it won't be the last. This, unfortunately, is the kind of demented relationship we've developed over the years. He loves to give me shit, and I do my best to pretend he doesn't exist.

Which isn't easy. Even though it kills me to admit it, Brody McKinnon is a lot to take in. Tall. Muscular. Athletic. Broad shoulders. Narrow, tapered waist. Long, dirty blond hair streaked with gold that grazes the collar of his shirt. Whiskey-colored eyes that are always crinkled with laughter. Usually at my expense. Damnable dimples that are capable of making grown women turn into babbling idiots.

I, however, am the exception.

It's like I have a superpower where Brody is concerned. He might be hot...Actually, there's no *might be* about it. The guy is off-the-charts smoking. Girls follow him around campus in droves, drooling and giggling while trying to catch his wandering attention.

But he doesn't affect me the way he does every other female at this school. I'm immune to his charms.

Okay.

Not immune *exactly*.

I'd have to be dead not to feel *something* when he's near. But there's no way I would ever act on the unwanted heat generated between us.

Good Lord, I'm not a masochist.

Brody's reputation as a manwhore preceded him before he ever stepped foot on Whitmore's ivy-covered campus. There are legions of women who have already punched their ticket for that ride. They could, if they were so inclined, form their own support group.

I have zero interest in joining their not-so-illustrious ranks.

If you're stupid enough to fall under his spell and into his bed, then you deserve to suffer the consequences of your stupidity. Which probably means getting swabbed regularly for a variety of STDs.

Reminding myself of his reputation is all it takes to stomp out the heat that had flared to life in the pit of my belly. All right, damn it, lower...*much lower*. I give him my best dead salmon look. "Thanks, but I'll be taking a hard pass on that generous offer."

He shrugs as if it's no skin off his back. And it probably isn't. He could get laid within a matter of minutes if he wanted to with any number of willing participants. "Suit yourself, Davies. It's your loss. I'm just trying to help a friend out."

I laugh. "Ahhhh. That's where you went wrong, McKinnon." I shake my head and give him an expression full of faux-sympathy. "We're not friends. We'll never be friends. Unsurprisingly, your thinking was flawed from the very beginning."

He places a hand over his heart as a wounded look flits across his handsome face. "Ouch. That hurts."

"Doubtful."

I exhale a breath when Brody holds open the door leading out into the bright sunshine. I'm not sure how much more of this intimacy I can take. I mutter my thanks as the warm wind hits my cheeks and we step on the wide stone stairs before descending. The last dregs of summer are still hanging on. Soon all of the trees on campus will change. Fall will be in the air. Which means one thing...

Hockey season.

Ugh.

A group of about six or seven girls at the bottom of the steps catch my eye. As soon as their hungry gazes fall on Brody, they start clamoring en masse. It's like a rock star has just stepped into their midst.

I roll my eyes at their ridiculousness. Are they unaware that women have been marching all over the world demanding gender equality, and here they are chasing down some hot dude? They seriously don't have a more productive way to spend their time? Maybe empower themselves with the education they're supposedly here to get?

As if to answer my silent question, a few actually squeal and wave their hands in the air. Yep, this is what I'm dealing with.

Instead of feeling irritated, I should thank them because they've created the perfect opportunity for me to make a hasty escape.

"It would seem that your adoring public awaits," I comment.

Slipping from beneath his arm, I hustle down the steps. The more distance that stretches between us, the easier it is for me to breathe. With any luck, I won't see Brody until Monday.

At ten a.m., to be exact.

And not a moment sooner.

I'll need at least that long to decompress.

"Aww, Davies, come on. Don't run away." Humor simmers in his voice as he shouts at my retreating backside. "I promise, there's plenty of me to go around!"

Without turning, I sense the full-blown grin on his lips. I'm sure his dimples are out in full force. I don't break stride as I flip him the bird.

His laughter follows me as I slip into the crowd.

Chapter Three
NATALIE

"Hey, girlie, what's the word?" Zara smiles up at me.

With a sigh, I drop my bag on the bench across from my roommate and slide in on the other side of the booth with my tray.

Zara has the appearance of a wood sprite. She stands a few inches over five feet and is slender as a wand with mink-colored hair that is short and pixie-like. Not many women could pull off the look, but Zara totally owns it. She may give off the delicate and tiny vibe, but she'll kick your ass if the occasion calls for it.

I've been on the receiving end of her foot more than a few times. It never feels good.

We met the summer before fourth grade when her family moved in down the block from mine. By the time school started, we'd become thick as thieves. I'm lucky to have Zara in my life. She's a good friend who has been there for me through hell and high water. When my parents' marriage fell apart nine months ago, it was Zara who picked up the shattered pieces. One month after that, when I discovered that my boyfriend, Reed Collins, was cheating on me, she threatened to cut off his junk. I declined the offer but appreciated the sentiment. Any friend who's willing to do that is one you hold onto for dear life.

Boys will come and go, girlfriends are forever.

"Annoying," I huff. Normally I'm able to shake off my run-ins with Brody. But my blood is still boiling from our exchange. "The word for today is 'annoying.'"

She laughs and spears a piece of lettuce and a cherry tomato with her fork. "Uh-oh, should I even bother to ask?"

"It's probably better if you don't." Plus, I don't really want to spend time talking about Brody. I pick up a fry and dredge it in ketchup before popping it in my mouth. If I have one weakness, it's French fries. Coffee is a very close second. "I'm doing my best to forget the entire unpleasant episode." Which isn't easy. Brody lingers like a bad stench that's stuck in your nostrils.

Luke, Zara's newly-minted boyfriend, slides his big body in next to her.

This is their first public appearance. At least in front of me, it is. I'm not going to go so far as to say they were hiding their relationship from me...

Fine, I'll say it. They hid their relationship from me.

Zara knows how I feel about the hockey players at this school. *Especially* after the whole Reed debacle. In fact, I was under the impression we were of one mind on this topic.

Apparently not...Because now she's dating one.

Luke meets my gaze from across the table. He gives me a chin lift in greeting like I'm one of the guys and us meeting up for lunch is a normal, everyday occurrence. "What's up, Natalie?"

Ha! As if I would let him off the hook that easily...

I don't think so.

"You mean, other than my best friend sneaking around behind my back with her new boyfriend?" I bat my eyelashes and give him an innocent look. "Not much. What's up with you?"

Zara chokes on a laugh, and the edges of Luke's lips curve into an easy grin.

"Does the fact that you haven't climbed across the table and strangled me mean we have your stamp of approval?" he asks.

Narrowing my eyes, I point a fry at him. "The jury is still out on that one, buddy." As I take a sip of my Coke, I give him the hairy eyeball. When I'm finished, I threaten, "Just know that if you screw around on her, I'll break both your kneecaps. Hockey will be nothing more than a distant, yet fond, memory."

He gives Zara a sidelong look from the corner of his eye. She shrugs her shoulders as if to say *what can you do?*

"Consider yourself warned," I add evilly.

He cocks his head as he picks up his burger. "You're kind of a scary chick, Davies."

"Good." I nod approvingly. "That's exactly what I was going for."

Even though I'm giving Luke shit, I do like him. Out of all the hockey players Zara could have fallen for, he's the nicest. Unlike most of his teammates, he doesn't consider sleeping with the girls on campus to be a competitive sport.

That being said, he does have one fatal flaw that's difficult to overlook.

Just as I shove another fry in my mouth, a hard body slams into me from the side. I grunt as the force of impact scoots my butt across the wood bench. I'm lucky that I don't come away with splinters.

"Slide it on over, Clyde," a deep voice says.

For one dazed moment, I stare in horror.

No. No. No. This can't be happening.

He isn't supposed to sit at my table while I'm trying to enjoy lunch with my friend. I'm not supposed to see him until next Monday. At ten o'clock. And not a moment sooner. It's an unwritten agreement between us. Like a peace accord. And he's flat-out disregarding it.

"Why in God's name are you here?" Before he has a chance to respond, I hiss, "Are you stalking me? Is that what's going on?"

"That depends, would you like me to stalk you?" One side of Brody's mouth hitches in amusement. "I've got a bit of free time I was looking to fill. I could probably slot you in."

Harnessing all of my energies, I glare and wait for him to burst into flames. I'm disappointed when nothing happens.

"Should I take your silence to mean that you're in agreement with this plan?" he drawls, looking perfectly at ease.

My eyebrows lower and my shoulders tense. *See?* He's only been here for thirty seconds, and already I'm starting to foam at the mouth.

This day nosedived in finance class and is now proceeding to explode on impact.

"Why are you here?" I ask again.

Brody lifts his chin toward the only other guy at the table. "Came to hang with my boy."

My eyes shift to Luke, and I shoot him a sour look.

I may reconsider leaping across the table and strangling him after all.

Luke's grin intensifies as if he knows exactly what's running through my head. "So...this is fun, all of us getting together."

"Sure, it's as much fun as plucking out my own eyelashes one by one," I grumble.

Not bothering to ask permission, Brody reaches over and helps himself to a few fries from my plate.

"Um, hello, that's my lunch."

He grins and filches another.

I shake my head at his audacity and wave a hand in the direction of my tray. "Please, by all means, help yourself."

"Thanks, I thought you'd never ask."

If I've learned anything over the three years I've known Brody, it's that I have to stop responding to him or the back and forth will continue indefinitely. He's like a needy child. One who doesn't care if it's positive or negative reinforcement he receives, he just wants attention.

I growl as he steals yet another fry. His dimples flash as he aims a full-wattage smile in my direction. On any other guy, I find dimples adorable. But not on him. As far as Brody McKinnon is concerned, there's not a damn thing he can do to soften my feelings for him. They're etched in stone for all of eternity.

Plus, he delights in pissing me off.

How perverse is that?

"Riddle me this, how do you eat this crap and stay so thin?" Even though I'm sitting next to him, his eyes wander up and down the length of me. His perusal brings a sharp sting of heat to my cheeks. "You must have one hell of a metabolism, Davies."

"My metabolism," I bite out, "is none of your beeswax. I'm sure you've got more pressing matters to think about. Like the number of parties you can hit tonight timed by the number of girls you can mislead into making you a drunken mistake they'll regret in the morning when they're racing to the pharmacy for the Plan B pill." I bat my eyelashes at him. "You know...the important stuff."

Rather than respond to my insults, he sweeps them aside and ignores them. Looking serious, he points a fry in my direction. "You should treat your body like a temple. It's the only one you've got. Maybe we should get together sometime and go over the importance of proper nutrition."

I snicker. "Sure, McKinnon. Now, would that involve me showing up at your house and playing a game of hide-the-sausage?"

A huge grin lights up his face, and his shoulders shake with barely contained laughter. "Sure, we can play that while I explain the basic food groups. I always like when you can hit two birds with one stone."

"The only thing around here that's going to get hit—"

"All right you two," Zara snaps. "I've had just about enough!" Her glare encompasses both of us. "If you don't stop this incessant bicker-ing, I'm going to turn this car around, and you'll both be sorry!"

I give Zara a sullen look and jerk my thumb in Brody's direction. "He started it."

"I don't care who started it," she says. "I'm gonna end it. Do you understand me?"

"Yes, Mom," I grumble.

"Good." She waggles a finger between us. "You two need to learn how to play nice with one another."

Brody holds up his hands. "Hey, I'm trying to play nice. I'd like to play nice all damn day with her."

He leers, and I shoot him another hard-edged look.

As much as I like Luke, I could do without his trusty sidekick. When Zara confessed that she was involved with the blond-haired hockey player, I never considered the possibility that Brody and I would occasionally be thrown together.

So, unless I want to stop hanging out with Zara, I'm going to have to find a way to deal with him.

My friend clears her throat. "About this weekend..."

The shift in topic makes me glance expectantly at Zara. When she doesn't continue, my gaze bounces to Luke and then back to Zara again. For some reason, all three sets of eyes are now focused on me. A sinking sensation fills my belly.

"What?" I tense and meet each of their gazes in turn with a frown. No one says a word. It's crickets. "What's going on this weekend?" My current plans include yoga pants and a comfy sweatshirt, binge-watching Netflix, and ordering a large pizza with extra cheese. Other than that, I got nothing.

"Well..." Zara's voice trails off, and she glances at Luke.

"Just spit it out," I say. My nightmare just so happens to be sitting next to me. So, how much worse can this get?

"The guys are having a huge blowout at the house on Saturday, and I want you to come with me."

"Nooooooo," I moan and slump on the bench.

I should have realized this conversation was going to happen. I'd heard through the grapevine there was going to be a massive party at the hockey house. It's been plastered all over social media.

"Yeeeeeeees," she responds.

"Come on, Zar," I whine pathetically. "Please, don't make me go. You know how much I hate those things." I'm not a total stick-in-the-mud. I've been to my fair share of parties over the past three years. But hockey parties are a madness all their own. It's debauchery and binge drinking at its finest. It's like they've ripped a page out of Hugh Hefner's playbook. All someone needs to do is start wearing a yacht captain's hat and a burgundy velour bathrobe, and it would resemble the Playboy Mansion during its heyday.

Zara's voice gentles as if she's trying to reason with an overtired child in the midst of a full-on tantrum. "I know, sweetie. And I totally get it, I do. But—"

"Then don't make me do it," I cut in. She doesn't need me there. She has Luke. He'll stick by her side.

"But I need you," she says.

"*Need* is an awfully strong word."

"You're my best friend and I need you there with me. You know what those girls are like."

She doesn't have to specify which girls she's talking about. The puck bunnies at this school don't take well to other females honing in on their action.

Zara gives me her best trembly lip and blinky-eyed look. Her technique is perfectly honed from countless years of manipulation. My shoulders slump. I'm moments away from caving. How am I supposed to say no to that face? God, but I hate when she brings out the big guns.

"That's not fair," I tell her.

She grins and asks, "Who said life was fair?"

"Now you sound like my mother."

"I always thought Karen was a smart woman. Anyway, I need my posse by my side when I walk through that door," she adds after another bite of salad.

"I'm pretty sure people aren't saying that anymore. I believe the new term is 'squad.'"

"Fine," she agrees easily. "I need my *squad* next to me when I walk in there. Say you'll come." She presses her palms together as if in prayer. "Pretty please?"

I don't want to give in.

I *really* don't want to.

"Okay," I finally relent. "Just don't give me the trembly lip anymore. I can't take it."

"You've always been a sucker for that look."

I pluck the fry from Brody's fingers and throw it at her. "You're a manipulative brat, and I hate you."

She laughs, batting away the potato. "Oh, come on. You love me."

True. But I'm not going to tell her that.

"Hey," Brody complains. "I was eating that!"

Picking up another fry, I pelt it at him. I'm tempted to throw the entire plate.

Chapter Four

BRODY

I stand so Natalie can slide out of the booth. Luke and Zara swap some spit before they get up. My eyes zero in on Natalie. Because I know it'll piss her off, I give her a cheeky grin. "Hey, thanks for buying lunch today, Davies. I'll pick up the tab next time."

A deep, growly noise vibrates in her throat. It's kind of sexy. "If I have anything to say about it, there won't be a next time."

My grin intensifies. She's way too easy to rile up. I barely have to do anything, and she loses her shit. I have no idea why her response is so gratifying, but it is. I can't think of another girl I enjoy annoying as much as her.

Luke and I drop back down into the booth. As I do, I keep my gaze firmly glued to Natalie's round backside. It really is a work of art. I could watch that girl's ass sway back and forth all day long and not grow tired of it.

Luke, who has already polished off his burger, grabs a fry from Natalie's unfinished plate and pops it in his mouth. His eyes flicker to where the girls are, and he asks, "What's up with you two? You guys bicker like an old married couple."

I shrug. Natalie Davies is probably the only female on campus who can't stand the sight of me. I don't want to sound like a conceited prick, but usually I have the opposite effect on women.

"You sleep with her?"

"Nope."

He narrows his eyes. "You sure about that?"

I hold up my hands. "I've never touched her." Trust me, if I'd slept with Natalie, even back in freshman year, I'd remember. Something like that would be permanently singed into my brain.

He shakes his head like he doesn't understand it either. "Normally girls are falling all over themselves to get to you. That one would be happy to rip you to pieces with her bare teeth."

I drag my gaze from her backside as she disappears through the crowd. Even though I don't believe it for a minute, I say, "Don't let her crusty exterior fool you. Deep down, she's in love with me. She just has a funny way of showing it."

He chuckles. "Yeah...I don't think so, dude. I've never seen anyone hate on you more."

He's probably right. I've known Natalie for three years, and her opinion of me has never changed. We had a business class together freshman year where she first caught my eye.

She's a beautiful girl with long, thick hair the color of teak that falls to the middle of her back. I can't deny that I've been tempted to sift my fingers through those dark, silky strands a couple dozen times. Maybe more. Have I actually attempted it?

Hell, no.

I enjoy having five fingers on each hand. It makes playing hockey easier.

Then there are her wide eyes that match the shade of her hair. Even though she's tall and slim, she's got a nice set of tits on her. They look to be the perfect handful. Anything bigger would be too much for her slender frame.

I know this because I've spent a good amount of time staring at her from the corner of my eye whenever we've had class together. Her perky breasts make my mouth water. Excellent peripheral vision isn't just useful for playing hockey. It's also advantageous for scoping out girls when you don't want to get caught ogling. While some chicks enjoy an appreciative look cast in their direction, others will claw your eyes out.

Natalie unequivocally falls into the claw-your-eyes-out category. I saw her deck some dude last year for giving her the once-over. Now, there's a girl who knows how to throw a punch. That probably shouldn't be so hot, but it is. I sported some major wood just watching her take care of business.

Although that's nothing new around her. Anytime she's in the vicinity I get a semi.

"You know she was with Reed Collins last year."

I shrug like I'm not keeping tabs on her.

"That's why Zara and I had to sneak around for a while," he says. "Guess Collins left a bad taste in her mouth."

Because we're both immature assholes, we snicker.

"That's not an image I need in my head," I say. I don't want to think about that guy being anywhere near Natalie's mouth. Much less *that*.

Luke grins. "I couldn't resist."

Did I know she was with Collins last year?

You bet your damn ass I did. It aggravated the hell out of me to see her with that douchebag player. Thank God, it didn't last more than a couple of months because he was hooking up behind her back.

Which only pissed me off more.

I may enjoy giving Natalie shit, but I don't care to see anyone else mess with her. And Reed Collins screwed her over big time.

Here are my thoughts on the matter: If you want to nail all the pussy you want, then by all means, have at it. Just don't have a girl-friend while you're doing it.

Simple enough, right?

Reed had other thoughts on the matter. Which isn't a surprise. The guy is a total tool. I've always thought so. We came in together as freshmen and played against each other a number of times during juniors. Of course, he's a center. Puck hogs who are glory hounds usually are. The guy isn't a team player and that, I have a problem with.

But that's just my opinion.

I'm pretty easygoing and laid-back. I get along with all of my teammates. He's the exception. We just rub each other the wrong way. I've got no love for the guy. Reed thinks he's a better player than what he really is. I bet it chafes his ass that I was picked up by an NHL team straight out of high school, while he'll enter the draft later this year.

Finishing off his drink, Luke says, "You take a strange amount of joy in riling that girl up."

I grin at his assessment of the situation because it's pretty much spot-on. I keep telling myself that I should lay off because I'm in no way endearing myself to her. But then she'll walk through the door, and I can't resist pulling her attention to me. It's just too damn easy. Anytime I have the opportunity to mess with her, I take it. And now that Luke is dating her roommate, I'll be seeing a lot more of her, which works out perfectly for me.

I lean back against the bench and grin. "Life's short, man. You gotta take your pleasure where you can find it."

Luke shakes his head, although the smile is still there. "That's so twisted."

I shrug.

Most definitely.

Chapter Five

NATALIE

"I can't believe I let you talk me into this," I shout at Zara as Megan, a friend who lives in the apartment next to ours, pushes open the front door of the hockey house. It's only ten o'clock, but the place is already packed with people. Music blasts from the speakers, making the walls vibrate. It's so loud and raucous that I can barely hear myself think.

The best thing I can say is that everyone appears to be wearing clothing. I've been here a few times when there were games of strip beer pong going on. But let's be honest, most of these girls don't need an excuse to shed their clothing.

As soon as I pause, Zara loops her arm through mine. My guess is that she's making sure I don't attempt a jailbreak. Which, I'm not going to lie, I was considering. I want to be here about as much as I want extensive dental surgery.

Given the choice, I'd opt for the surgery. It would be a far more pleasant way to spend the next couple of hours.

"You came because you're one of my best friends and you're always here when I need you."

I hate when she plays dirty. There's very little I wouldn't do for Zara, and she knows it.

"I'm giving this two hours and then I'm out." I level her with a hard stare so she knows I mean business. "Got it?"

Grinning, she kisses my cheek. "Yep."

"Good." I glance around, watching the chaos as it unfolds.

The hockey players at this school seem to live by one rule: Play hard on the ice and party even harder off of it. It's not uncommon for the police to get called when they have a massive blowout, although the cops do nothing more than slap the guys on the wrist. The whole town kisses their proverbial asses. If one or more of the hockey players got busted, they'd end up getting benched. And who knows how that would affect the team.

Without winning seasons and National Championships, Whitmore wouldn't be the sought-out hockey haven it is today. No one in their right mind is willing to mess with that. Not the president of the university or the town that prospers from all the hockey fans who descend and spend their money here.

"Hey, babe."

Within minutes of our arrival, Luke wraps his arms around Zara and pulls her in for a hug before attacking her face for an intense game of tonsil hockey.

Megan glances at me, and I roll my eyes. These two are incorrigible. Now that their relationship is out in the open, they're constantly mauling each other in front of whoever is around. It's PDA all the way.

Trying to look anywhere but at them, I let my eyes wander until they collide with amber-colored ones.

Son of a monkey.

I came here with the intention of avoiding two guys tonight. And I just made eye contact with one of them. No matter where I go lately, I can't seem to avoid Brody McKinnon. It's like some cosmic joke is being played on me. He's the last person I want to see and the first one I run into.

I give him my trademark scowl, and a huge grin lights up his handsome face. His dimples pop in tandem. It wouldn't surprise me if it's a calculated move.

There's a girl tucked under each brawny arm and a red Solo cup in his hand. He looks in his element surrounded by his adoring public.

Which suits me perfectly. I hope he stays on his side of the room, holding court. The last thing I need is to get into another verbal sparring match with him.

He crooks a finger at me.

Is he serious?

Lowering my brows, I send a look of disbelief in his direction. Then I shake my head just to make sure he understands that I'm not a horny puck bunny at his beck and call. He grins again and untangles himself from his groupies.

I just walked through the door and already this evening is nosediving like a plane shot down over enemy territory that's now in a death spiral. I'm not sure how I'll last—I glance at my phone—an hour and fifty minutes if this is what the first ten minutes have been like.

I throw a desperate glance over my shoulder, hoping I can slip away before he makes his way over. Unsurprisingly, Zara and Luke are still fused at the lips. Sheesh. Are they going to come up for air anytime soon? I hunt around for Megan, but she's been swallowed up by the crowd.

Looks like I'm on my own. Which is precisely why I didn't want to come here in the first place. Damn Zara and her trembly lip. She owes me big time for this. Searching for options, I spin back around. But it's too late. He's here, standing before me in all his massive glory. My eyes linger on biceps that are showcased rather nicely by the snug graphic T-shirt he's wearing. I really hate myself for being able to appreciate anything about this man.

"Davies!" he exclaims as if thrilled to see me. "You made it!"

"Yep," I drawl, hoping that one word is enough to convey my unhappy state.

He glances at Luke and Zara and shakes his head. "Those two are like a couple of cats in heat. Someone needs to turn a hose on them."

I chuckle. Brody's right. They are. Realizing I've just agreed with him—which has to be a first—I slap a hand over my mouth, trying to rein the noise back in.

His eyes widen with exaggerated shock. "Holy shit, did you just agree with me? Has hell officially frozen over? Should we break out the ice skates?"

I shake my head, trying to backtrack. "No. That's not what I—"

"Oh, yes you did," he cuts in smugly. His eyes dance with glee.

God, he is so loving this.

"I heard it with my own two ears." He folds his thickly corded arms over his well-defined chest. The cottony material stretches so tautly that I'm surprised it doesn't shred right off his body like the Hulk. Most of the girls at this party would swoon if that happened.

Okay, that does it. I need to get away from him. I'm obviously losing my mind because all I can think about is the hard, sinewy muscle he's packing beneath that shirt. And what those thick slabs of power would feel like against my fingertips.

Is it hot in here?

Right...I need a drink.

Latching on to an exit strategy, I gesture toward the kitchen where the keg will be set up. "Well, it was great running into you, McKinnon, but I'm in need of liquid refreshment." I take a hasty step away, wanting only to flee his presence.

I don't like the way Brody makes me feel. There's this unwanted push and pull of attraction that constantly flares between us. Half the time, I'm not sure what to make of it. It's just easier to avoid him and hope it goes away. Although, it's been three years and it's still there, humming insistently beneath the surface. Bubbling up when I least expect or want it to.

"Of course. Where are my manners? Let's get you something to drink." He holds out his hand. "Come on."

I stare at his wide palm as if it's a hissing snake and shake my head emphatically. "No, that's okay. Your entourage has been waiting ever-so-patiently for your return." I point to the bevy of girls he stepped away from who are openly staring with longing in their eyes. "You wouldn't want to disappoint them, now would you?"

"Davies." He chuckles. "You're hilarious."

With one swift movement, he swallows up the little bit of distance I've managed to put between us and grabs my fingers before I can pull them away. Awareness zips through my body when we make contact. He glances sharply at me. Questions hover in his eyes as our gazes lock. When I stare silently, his fingers tighten possessively around mine.

Like Moses parting the Red Sea, a path magically forms in front of him.

Even if Brody weren't Whitmore's star hockey player destined for NHL greatness, people would still scurry out of his way. He's tall. At least six foot three and two hundred and twenty pounds. His chest and shoulders are broad. I can only imagine what it must feel like on the ice when he drops his shoulder and slams into a forward driving for his net.

It takes only a minute before we find ourselves in the kitchen. Had I gone it alone, it probably would have taken me three times as long to push and shove my way in here. It's on the tip of my tongue to say thank you, but I bite the words back at the last second.

Even though it's the polite thing to do, I just can't force them out.

Rather than look at Brody, I focus on the bar that has been set up at the far side of the kitchen. Every possible kind of liquor has been set out on the counter. There's a dizzying array of options if you want to get your drink on. If you're looking for something a little tamer than shots or mixed drinks, there's a silver barrel near the sink.

"Pick your poison, Davies." He smirks, his eyes gleaming. "How about we start off with some body shots? I'll go first."

"Not in this lifetime," I retort.

Body shots...as if.

He laughs. "You're such a killjoy. I think you need to loosen up."

"I'm loose enough, thank you very much," I say primly. This isn't the environment to let your guard down. Anything under the sun could happen, and I prefer to have my wits about me.

He eyes me with interest. "Not from where I'm standing."

I glance dubiously at the assortment of alcohol. I'm not one for hard liquor. It hits me too fast, and then I'm drunk. I don't like the feeling of being out of control. Nor do I enjoy worshipping the porcelain god in the morning.

"I'll just have a beer."

"One beer coming up." Not budging from my side, Brody holds up a hand and raises one finger. The younger guy manning the keg gives him a quick nod in response. Even though there are a ton of people waiting in line, he fills a plastic cup and passes it to Brody.

Once Brody has it in hand, he passes it to me with a flourish. "Your drink, milady."

Now that he's played the part of gallant host and procured a beverage for me, I'm hoping we can go our separate ways. I mean, it's not like we're going to spend the entire night together, right?

I almost shudder at the thought.

"Thanks." Just as I'm about to take my first sip, someone steps into my line of vision. Before I can yank my eyes away, our gazes collide. Instead of taking a small drink, I end up downing half the glass. I need all the liquid courage I can garner to deal with this situation.

Forgetting about Brody, who hasn't moved from my side, I groan, "Oh, great."

"Davies?" He shoots me a confused look. "What's going on?"

"Nothing." Feeling agitated, I shift from one foot to the other wishing there was a place to hide. But it's too late for that. Reed has already seen me. If I turn tail and run, he'll only take pleasure in being able to scare me away and that, I will not have. I'd much rather stand here and endure a conversation with the asshole than allow him to believe he wields any kind of power over me.

Brody searches the surrounding vicinity. It only takes a moment for his eyes to land on Reed. "Fucking Collins," he mutters under his breath in much the same tone as I'd just used. It's enough to bring a small smile of commiseration to my lips.

Even though I'm looking everywhere but at Reed, I feel his gaze on me the entire time. Since he's blocking the exit, there's no way to avoid a confrontation. I straighten my shoulders and brace myself for impact.

Is it too much to ask that he simply ignore me?

Apparently so.

With a smirk twisting his lips, Reed beelines for me. People turn as he knocks into them with his shoulders. A few of them look ready to start something until they realize who it is. Then they bite their tongues and go back to their conversations.

"Well, look who it is. Natalie Davies." His gaze runs down the length of me and lingers unabashedly on my chest. I'm not embarrassed by my body or my attributes, but his blatant perusal is humiliating. Instead of squirming, I stand my ground. I'll be damned if I let him win.

When his gaze meanders back to mine, he says, "I'm surprised to see you here. Didn't think this was your scene."

I dig my nails into the palms of my hands and shrug nonchalantly. "Guess that makes two of us."

Ignoring Brody, Reed steps closer. "Have you missed me, baby?" He grins, and I'm tempted to smack the smile right off his face. It would be *so* satisfying.

"About as much as I'd miss having crabs," I say sweetly. "Or lice."

The corners of his lips tip upward and a glimmer of malice enters his eyes.

It's been about eight months since I told him to go to hell and we've barely spoken since then. Our breakup was not what one would refer to as amicable. We did not "uncouple" the way mature and sophisticated people apparently do and remain the very best of friends. Once I found out he was hooking up behind my back, I lost my shit the way any self-respecting girl would and kicked his ass to the curb.

Brody throws an arm around my shoulders and tugs me to him. Reed's blue eyes sharpen as they bounce between us as if he's surprised to see him standing next to me.

Reed and Brody have some sort of childish rivalry going on between them. Reed constantly bitched and complained about Brody when we were together. At that point, we were in complete agreement because I didn't care for Brody McKinnon either.

Thinking back on our conversations, I realize that it's more of a jealousy issue for Reed. Up until coming to Whitmore, Reed had always been the most talented hockey player out on the ice. Brody knocked him down a few pegs and Reed doesn't like it.

Before my ex-boyfriend can ask any questions, Brody cuts in. "Davies is here with me."

Wait...What?

Reed's brows shoot up. "Really?" He drawls out the question as if he finds that hard to believe.

"Yup, that's right." Brody glances at me from the corner of his eye.

I'm like a deer caught in headlights. "Ummm." I have no idea what to say. My brain has suddenly gone on the fritz. So has my mouth. I stand motionless, gaping like a smallmouth bass freshly reeled from the water.

Reed spears a finger in our direction and waggles it back and forth. "Are you telling me that you two are a couple?"

I need to put an end to this madness.

Unfortunately, Brody beats me to the punch.

"That's what I said, isn't it?"

Reed cocks his head and skewers me with a pity-filled gaze. "Things must have really changed, huh?" He laughs. "Can't say I pegged you for a puck bunny, Natalie. Too bad it wasn't that way last year. We could have been more of a one-and-done kind of thing." He shrugs. "But then again, you were a virgin, so I figured I had to put in the time and effort to get the goods."

His ugly comment knocks the air from my lungs. Heat floods my face.

It was only after I broke up with Reed that I realized what a self-centered asshole he was. To be completely honest, I had my suspicions. My only excuse is that, at the time, I was blinded by him and only saw what I wanted.

But this is hitting below the belt. Even for him.

Brody balls his hands into fists and takes a step forward. Snapping out of my stupor, I slap my hand across his chest to stop him from getting in Reed's face. Although, I'm hardly going to be able to stop someone the size of Brody if he wants to get to Reed.

"What'd you say, asshole?" Brody growls.

The intensity of his tone sends goosebumps skittering across my flesh. Very rarely have I seen Brody lose his temper. He's usually laid-back and easygoing, constantly joking around and poking fun at me.

This guy is a different animal altogether. The thickly corded muscles of his body have tensed as if he's on high alert, just waiting for the signal to attack.

"You heard me." Seizing on Brody's reaction, Reed smirks. "What? You gonna do something about it, McKinnon?"

Nausea swirls in the pit of my belly. The last thing I want is a fight breaking out. Especially over me. Brody and I aren't together. He doesn't need to defend me or take it to the next level. Hearing raised voices, people in the vicinity turn and stare. Everyone loves a good fight when they're drunk. Hell, they love a good fight when they're completely sober.

"You say anything like that again about Natalie, and I'm going to shove my foot so far up your ass you'll be tasting leather for weeks."

"Fuck off," Reed sneers. "You think you're such hot shit because your dad pulled some strings to get you where you are today. You're nothing but a hack. You always have been."

I expect Brody to come unhinged, but he doesn't. Somehow, he manages to rein himself in. Even though his lips curve into a tight smile, the flash of white teeth is chilling.

"Whatever you say, Collins." Brody takes a step toward Reed and grits out, "Natalie's with me now. You want to talk crap about her, I'm going to have something to say about it."

Reed claps Brody on the shoulder and shakes his head. "Shit, man, good luck with that. She's one lousy lay." His glittering gaze lands on me, and he shrugs. "You couldn't hold my interest, babe. Like I said before, one-and-done. But I've always been a sucker for a pretty face." His eyes skim down my body, zeroing in on my breasts. "Amongst other assets."

Chapter Six

NATALIE

I blink, and all hell breaks loose as Brody yanks back his arm and punches my ex-boyfriend in the face. Reed howls in outrage and lunges at Brody. I scream as people rush forward to break up the fight.

There's nothing unusual about scuffles breaking out at a hockey party. These guys seem to enjoy a good brawl. I may avoid these parties like the plague, but the aftermath usually makes the rounds on social media the following morning. There are always a ton of pictures and video clips. The only difference here is that the guys from the team don't usually get into it with each other.

I shout Brody's name a few times to get his attention, but he's intent upon fending off Reed's blows and landing a few more hits of his own before they're ripped apart. It takes two guys to hold Reed and just as many to pin Brody. Both glare, their breath coming out in harsh pants. Reed's nose is bleeding, and it looks like Brody will have a shiner in the morning.

How did everything fall apart within a matter of seconds?

I knew coming here was a mistake. I should have listened to my intuition and stayed home. Netflix and pizza sound so good right now.

Brody shakes off the guys holding him. He scowls at Reed and barks, "If you come anywhere near her or I hear you talking shit, you'll answer to me. Got it?"

I stand rooted in place, unable to believe what I'm hearing.

"Fuck off, McKinnon!" Reed shakes off the guys holding him and glares at the gathered crowd until his eyes come to rest on me. "Just know that he's dumber than a bag of bricks. It won't take long for him to bore you."

Even though I've thought the same thing myself a time or two—maybe more—it pisses me off to hear the insult roll off Reed's lips. Clenching my hands into fists, I step forward. Brody grabs me by the shoulders to halt my progress. "Go to hell, Reed! You're an asshole."

He smirks. "If you've gotten any better in bed, just give me a holler. I'd be willing to give you another try."

Brody lunges, and Reed melts through the crowd before he can get his hands on my ex again. Unable to believe what just happened, I stare at Brody in complete shock.

The party, which had been pumping only moments ago, is strangely silent. Only the sound of hushed whispers can be heard. People stand around and openly ogle us. In a stupor, my gaze slides over the crowd. Heat scorches my cheeks as humiliation floods through every pore of my body.

Everyone heard what Reed said.

That I was a virgin.

That I'm lousy in bed.

I just want the sticky floor beneath my feet to open up and swallow me whole. I want to flee, but stand rooted in place, paralyzed by all of the eyes focused on me.

Brody grabs my hand and drags me out of the kitchen and through the living room. I'm too stunned by the situation to question where he's taking me. The crowd parts as I struggle to keep up. Another ripple of whispers follows in our wake. I stare down at the gawking party-goers as Brody pulls me up the staircase.

My heart sinks.

This is exactly the kind of attention I don't want. When people talk about the fight that broke out between Brody and Reed tomorrow morning, I don't want my name associated with it. But even I know that's unrealistic.

I'm going to be plastered all over this story.

Once we reach the second-floor landing, he leads me down the dimly lit hallway as the revelry downstairs fades. My mind races, trying to process everything that transpired in roughly ten minutes of time. It never occurs to me to untangle myself from Brody's grasp.

Pulling out a key, he unlocks the door and yanks it open, towing me inside. Once he slams it shut, my eyes find his, and we stare at each other. The mental fog I'm cocooned in shows no sign of dissipating.

"What just happened?" I whisper.

"I just punched Collins in the face," he says calmly. "You're welcome."

Oh crap. That's what I thought.

"Why?" Coming to my senses, I tug my fingers free of his. Does he have any idea what he's just done? "Why would you do that?"

Brody stares at me like I'm crazy. And maybe I am. Maybe I'm in the midst of a total mental breakdown. The stress of school, graduation, and my parents' divorce has finally caught up with me. It's official. I've lost it.

"He was talking shit about you, Davies." His brows pull down. "What was I supposed to do? Just stand there like a puss and let him do it?" He scowls. "Hell no!"

Both of my hands fly to my temples. Gently I massage the sides of my head as if that will ease the ache growing inside. "I don't know. But you don't lie and tell him that we're going out." I slide my fingers into my hair and shake my head. "Why do you even care?" My voice climbs as hysteria sets in. "You talk shit about me all the time," I remind him, in case he's forgotten that our typical exchanges consist of barbs and darts thrown in one another's direction.

He folds his arms over his wide chest. "That's different," he snaps, looking offended. "I would never say crap like that to you or any girl."

The hurt that flashes across his face makes me feel guilty. He's right. Say what you want about Brody, I've never heard him humiliate anyone. He would never be that mean.

Aggravating? Without a doubt.

Infuriating? To be sure.

But he's not vicious.

The guy likes to needle me. But it's nothing more than that.

Filled with remorse for lashing out, I mutter, "I'm sorry. You're nothing like Reed." I swing away from him and gravitate toward the window overlooking the lit-up street below. Tons of people are milling around on the front lawn. Strolling up and down the sidewalk without a care in the world. Laughing, drinking, cutting loose on a Saturday night.

And I'm up here... Feeling like my life just imploded.

"I don't know how to make this better," I whisper. "Everyone heard the horrible things Reed said."

Even thinking about it makes me cringe with embarrassment.

I don't realize that Brody has come up behind me until his hands settle on my shoulders.

"I'm sorry, Natalie. Reed is an asshole. He shouldn't have said any of that to you."

The fact that Brody is referring to me by my first name just proves how dire the circumstances have become. He never calls me anything other than Davies. I bury my face in my hands. "But he did."

How am I going to show my face around campus Monday morning? This may be college, but it's more like high school on steroids. People love to talk. What happened tonight will be juicy gossip to be salivated over for days to come because not only is Brody McKinnon involved, but Reed Collins as well.

"It's my senior year, and I'm going to have to transfer schools."

"Look, I know this seems like a huge deal right now, but it's not. Certainly not enough for you to consider leaving Whitmore. Come on, Davies. I never took you for a drama queen."

I gasp and spin around, not realizing how close he is. My breasts graze his chest. Awareness skitters through me. Ignoring it, I focus instead on the insult. "A drama queen! I'm hardly a drama queen." I point toward the door. "You heard what Reed said. By Monday morning everyone on campus will know that I suck in bed."

"You never struck me as a girl who cared what other people thought of her."

True. But still… "I certainly don't need people talking about that," I grumble.

"How about I start spreading rumors that you're the best, most amazing sex I've ever had," he says. "Like you're doing things I never dreamed existed before. Would that help?"

I give him an exasperated look. "I don't need the kind of attention that would generate either."

We're both silent before he asks, "What if I knew of a way to fix this?"

"Unless you're able to travel back in time, I have no idea how you could possibly do that. From here on out, I'm going to be known as the lousy lay who dated Brody McKinnon for one hot minute."

"My plan is a little less complicated than that. You and I pretend we're going out. We stay together long enough for the situation to blow over. I'm sure it won't take more than a few weeks."

My brows scrunch as I process his words. "Are you serious?"

"As a heart attack. If we're together, no one will mess with you." He smirks. "You may not realize this, but I wield quite a bit of clout on this campus."

For the first time since seeing Reed downstairs, my chest loosens, and I roll my eyes. "Only you would say something like that."

His expression transforms into a wolfish grin. "Ah, there she is, the Natalie Davies I know and love."

"Please." Love…I almost snicker at the idea.

"So, what do you think?" he asks.

"That you've lost your mind," I quip.

Brody chuckles, and his eyes stay locked on mine. "That goes without saying."

I don't think I've ever seen him look so serious. It's frightening. A little shiver of apprehension scuttles through me. Uncomfortable with the sensation, I rip my gaze from his and mutter, "I don't know. It seems ridiculous for us to go to such lengths." I swallow past the growing lump in my throat. "We don't even like each other," I add, trying to throw up a roadblock as a way to divert the runaway train barreling down the tracks at me.

We're constantly at each other's throats. He makes a comment, and

I strike back tenfold. Look at what happened at lunch earlier today. Brody's main mission in life seems to be to aggravate me. But, I have to give credit where credit's due—he's awfully good at it.

And now he wants to pretend we actually like each other? For a few weeks? I'll end up killing him with my bare hands in less than twenty-four hours.

My words seem to throw him off. His expression falters.

"Of course, I like you, Davies. I wouldn't mess with you if I didn't."

I cock my head at such a ridiculous explanation. "Are you sure you're not really a fifth-grade boy masquerading as a senior in college?"

One side of his mouth quirks into a half-smile and a dimple winks at me. My heart flutters in response, and I glance away, trying to wrangle my emotions under control. There's no way I should seriously consider this idea. It has disaster written all over it.

"You can't sleep with anyone during the time we're together," I blurt, wondering if it'll be a deal breaker. Brody isn't exactly known around campus for his monkish ways. Hockey comes first. Girls a close second. Academics a distant third. "I'm not going to play the part of dumb, cheated-on girlfriend twice," I bite out.

Holy crap! Did those words just pop out of my mouth?

"Done. I won't even look at another girl," he promises.

"It's not the looking part that concerns me."

"You have my word that I won't touch another woman for the duration of our coupledom. You can trust me, Davies."

Trust Brody McKinnon...

Ha!

The very notion seems ludicrous.

Contemplating my options, I suck my lower lip into my mouth and chew on it. This can go one of two ways. The first is that we go downstairs and pretend the last thirty minutes never happened.

Fight?

What fight?

I have no idea what you're talking about.

Then I pray really hard that the people who witnessed the fight didn't overhear Brody tell Reed that we're together. Or hear Reed say that I'm lousy in bed.

My heart plummets.

The other choice is to pretend that Brody and I are going out for a couple of weeks. Maybe a month. Certainly not longer than that. It won't take long for someone else to become Whitmore fodder. It could be next weekend when someone else's life falls apart at the seams and then we can quietly part ways.

Would that really be so bad?

"What's it going to be, Davies? You in or out?"

"I..." There's nothing easy about this decision. Tying myself to Brody in any way feels dangerous. But what other choice do I have? None. Squaring my shoulders, I say, "I'm in."

A slow smile spreads across his face that makes both dimples pop. Even though I don't want it to, my heart skips a beat.

He arcs his hand in front of him and pretends to look out into the distance. "Can you picture it now? McKinnon and Davies, Whitmore's new golden couple." He wiggles his brows at me. "This is definitely going to be interesting."

"Oh hell," I mutter, burying my face in my hands. "What have I gotten myself into?"

He chuckles. "I'm just joking around. Everything will be fine."

"Nothing will ever be fine again," I moan.

At this point, I just want to slink home, crawl under my covers, and pretend this night never happened. If I'm lucky, when I wake tomorrow morning, this will have all been a horrendous nightmare.

"I think I've had enough for one night." I may have promised Zara I would stick around for a couple of hours, but that's not happening anymore. "I'm going home."

He nods. "Okay. Just follow my lead."

Before I can question what he has in mind, he grabs my hand and drags me out of the room, through the hall, and down the steps. Brody stops on the landing of the staircase and sticks two fingers between his lips. The whistle comes out sounding like a high-pitched screech. I'm not sure what I was expecting—maybe that we would sneak unnoticed out the door—but it definitely wasn't this.

If we didn't already have everyone's attention, we definitely do now.

The music is abruptly cut off, and silence descends. A crampy feeling settles in my belly as I reluctantly survey the crowd.

I try to tug my hand free, but he has a death grip on me. He raises his other hand in the air. More people pour in from the kitchen to find out what's going on.

"Hey!" Brody tugs me closer until I'm tucked against his side and his arm can slip around my shoulders. "I just want everyone to know that we've made it official. Davies and I are together!"

I wince as a loud roar tears through the crowd. Brody's grin widens. Did I seriously think the fiasco with Reed was the most embarrassing thing that could happen tonight?

This feels worse.

I'm going to strangle Brody as soon as I get him alone. This will be the shortest-lived relationship Whitmore has ever witnessed. Just as I'm about to whisper something scathing, he repositions me in his arms and his lips crash into mine.

I gasp in surprise, and his tongue slips inside my mouth, tangling with my own.

It's like I've entered a parallel universe. If you'd told me yesterday that I would be Brody McKinnon's fake girlfriend, I would have laughed my ass off and told you to seek psychological help.

Immediately.

And yet, here I am. Doing exactly that.

He pulls away, only an inch or two, and whispers, "Well, this is certainly going to be a perk."

Not knowing how to react, I can only stare. This night has turned out to be eerily similar to that old black-and-white TV show, *The Twilight Zone*. How did this happen?

"Come on, Davies. I'll drive you home." His lips curve. "You look like you're on the verge of stroking out."

I need to get away from all these people and think about what I've just agreed to. Then I need to figure out how to undo it. Because there's no way I can go through with this.

Maybe having everyone think I'm a lousy lay isn't the worst thing in the world.

Chapter Seven

NATALIE

The door to our apartment swings open and in strolls Zara doing the walk of shame. Her dark hair is mussed. Her clothing, which had been in perfect order last night, looks askew. Eyeliner is smudged under her eyes, giving her a raccoonish appearance, and her lips are puffy.

She halts in her tracks when she finds me perched on the kitchen counter, digging into a big bowl of Lucky Charms, and stabs a finger in my direction. "You, my dear friend, have a hell of a lot of explaining to do." Tossing her purse on the small table, she places her hands on her hips and gazes expectantly at me.

I give her a blank stare and shovel in another spoonful.

When I say nothing, both of her brows shoot up. "Well?"

"Well, what?" I ask.

"Well, what?" The words explode from her mouth at a decibel that could send dogs within a mile radius into a barking frenzy. "That's all you have to say for yourself?"

"Ummm..." I'm stumped. "About what?"

"About you and Brody! That's what!" She throws her arms wide and rapid-fires questions at me. "Oh my God, you two are together? You're dating? When did this happen? Have I been asleep for twenty years or something? Because the last time I checked, you two hated each other!" She amends her statement. "Well, you hated him. I've always suspected that he had a thing for you."

"What?" I shake my head. "No. You had it right the first time, we can't stand each other."

Looking confused, Zara massages her temples with her fingers and takes a few more steps toward me. "I think I'm still drunk, because you're not making a damn bit of sense."

"Brody and I are most definitely not going out," I say emphatically.

She gives me a strange look. One that says she doesn't believe a word coming out of my mouth. "And yet, he told the entire party last night that you two were dating."

"Oh, that." I wave a hand dismissively. "That was a joke. He was just goofing around." My new tactic is to downplay what happened last night. If I don't pay attention to it, no one else will either, right? In a few days' time, the entire situation will have blown over.

It could already be forgotten as we speak.

"Goofing around?" She stares at me like I've lost my mind. And I have to admit, it's beginning to feel that way. I'm hanging on by a thread. "Why on earth would he do that?"

I sigh and launch into the whole sordid story from last evening. "After you abandoned me—thank you very much for that, by the way —" I give her a sharp look. Oh, I haven't forgotten her part in this debacle. That girl is in deep doo-doo with me. "I ran into Reed, and he started talking crap. Brody was there and told him to knock it off." I'm not going to repeat what Reed said. I still don't understand why he would deliberately try to hurt and embarrass me.

It was a dick move on his part.

I could kick myself for wasting so much time on him. Not to mention, giving him my virginity. I'd waited to have sex because I never found the right person and I wanted it to be meaningful. At the time, I'd thought Reed was a good guy. Turned out he was the furthest thing from it.

"I never liked that douchebag," Zara says baldly. "But that still doesn't explain why Brody told everyone you guys are together."

I shrug. "He told Reed that to shut him up. That's it. Brody and I are not a couple. Our relationship is exactly what it's always been, and that's nonexistent. I doubt anyone paid attention to what he said anyway. You know how those parties are. Everyone was trashed. Half of them probably can't remember who they slept with last night." I'm deliberately choosing to forget about the dead silence in the room when he shouted the announcement or the cheer that went up when he kissed me. "As far as I'm concerned, it's no big deal."

Both of her brows shoot up, and she laughs. "You're joking, right?"

I shovel another spoonful of cereal into my mouth and chomp it a few times before swallowing. "Nope. Not even a little bit."

She shakes her head. "Natalie, it's all over the place. That's all anyone at the party could talk about after you two took off. Together, I might add."

I shift on the counter as an arrow of unease slices through me. "I think you might be exaggerating just a bit." Contrary to what Brody said last night, I'm no drama llama. For the last three years, I've kept my head down and worked hard in my classes. I have no interest in the popularity game or making a name for myself. "No one knows who I am. And furthermore, they don't care." Which is exactly how I like it.

Zara's tone softens. "It's all over Facebook." Sliding her phone from her back pocket, she taps the screen a few times and shoves it under my nose. I pluck it from her fingers and stare at her Facebook page. A sharp breath hisses from my mouth as I see a picture of me and Brody locking lips on the staircase.

Son of a monkey.

All right.

Calm down.

One picture isn't a huge deal. I mean, I've seen photographs of Brody making out with other girls before. Tons of them. It doesn't mean a thing.

As I scroll through her feed, my heart sinks. The majority of posts are pictures of me and Brody.

There's one of us standing on the landing.

Another of us holding hands as he drags me up the staircase.

Here we are kissing again.

Oh, look...There are numerous photos of us in the kitchen where Brody is all up in Reed's face.

Perfect.

Here's a video clip of Brody and Reed brawling for everyone who wasn't able to witness it in person last night.

I lock my jaw as I come across a meme.

This is so much worse than I allowed myself to believe.

Zara nips the phone from my fingers and taps the screen before shoving it back at me. "Now check out Instagram."

I shake my head and push it away. No. I don't want to see anymore.

Ever since opening my eyes this morning, I'd convinced myself that what happened with Brody wasn't a big deal. Easily forgotten. Obviously, that's not the case. Operation Forget-All-About-What-Happened-Last-Night is a no-go. Now I'm going to have to figure out another way to tackle this problem.

Zara rubs my back in soft, comforting circles. "You need to see what people are saying."

Steeling myself, I force my eyes to the screen again.

It's just more of the same.

A.

Lot.

More.

What have I done by agreeing to this madness?

It's weakly that I say, "I'm sure it'll blow over." Because deep down, I need to believe that's precisely what will happen.

Zara squeaks and claps a hand over her mouth.

I groan. Do I even want to know? Nope. Don't think so. But still, the question tumbles from my lips, "Now what?"

Whatever she's found can't be any worse than all the posts blowing up Facebook and Instagram.

"Well, it's official, Nat. You and Brody are exclusive."

"What are you talking about?" I mutter.

She turns her phone around, and I glimpse Brody's Facebook page. When I shift my eyes to hers in confusion, she huffs in exasperation and points to the bottom corner of his page.

"It's Facebook official. Brody McKinnon is in a relationship with Natalie Davies."

Aw hell.

Chapter Eight

BRODY

While my roommates are still sleeping off last night's drunken festivities, I'm up and out the door by five. The sun has yet to rise as I get in my truck and drive over to the community rink. Ever since I started at Whitmore freshman year, my dad has rented out extra ice time on Sunday mornings so we can run through drills and work on conditioning. Around eight, we head to my father's house, and I hit the weight room he installed in the basement. It has all the bells and whistles, including a sauna which I relax in for about twenty minutes before hitting the shower.

Since this is the only time during the week I'm able to stop by for a visit, my dad's wife, Amber, prepares a huge brunch for the three of us. By the time I sit down at the table with them, I'm physically exhausted but feel good. My endorphins are buzzing and I'm ready to tackle the week. Usually, we discuss any new developments with the Milwaukee franchise or potential endorsement deals that are in the works. Around noon, I head back to campus and hit the books for the rest of the day.

You know that old saying about how there's no rest for the wicked?

It's absolutely true.

My dad, John McKinnon, played for the Detroit Redwings for a decade back in the day. After retiring from the NHL, he opened a sports management company to represent professional athletes. He started out with a couple of hockey players and has since branched out with twenty-five agents working for him. He reps guys from the NHL, NBA, NFL, and the MLB. My game plan is to play in the pros for as long as I can and then join my father at his company, which is why I chose to major in business with a minor in finance.

Since Dad played professional hockey, he knows what I'll be up against when I make the move to the pros next year. It's an entirely different level—faster play, higher skill set, and a hell of a lot more physical and rigorous—and some guys can't hack it. You're no longer a big fish in a small pond. Everyone playing in the NHL is the best of the best. Because of this, he works me harder than any coach ever has. And I appreciate it. I'm a better player for it. So even though I only grabbed a few hours of sleep last night, you won't hear me bitching and complaining about hauling ass at five to get here.

Eggs, bacon, pancakes, sausage, hash browns, and a bowl of fruit have been laid out in the sunroom where the three of us sit down to eat. Famished from my workout, I dig in, loading my plate with a lot of everything.

Amber and Dad recently celebrated their three-year anniversary. She's fifteen years younger than he is and used to work for him. I've never actually sat down and counted out the months, but I suspect there was a rush to the altar because she was pregnant with my two-year-old sister, Hailey.

The fact that my father married again after so many years doesn't bother me. Maybe I'd feel differently if I were still in the house, but I'm not. Plus, Amber has always gone out of her way to make me feel included. And Hailey is a pretty cool kid. She's always smiling and happy to see me when I stop by on Sunday mornings.

"What happened to your face?" Amber asks as I dig in.

I shrug. "Took an elbow to the eye fooling around with Sawyer. No big deal."

I'd almost forgotten about the shiner Reed gave me last night. I should have been quicker and blocked him. At least I bloodied his nose and gave him a black eye in return.

You're welcome, asshole.

"It looks painful." Her brows draw together. "Maybe you should ice it after brunch. I think there's a bag of peas in the freezer."

"Nah, it's fine. But thank you," I add. I really do like Amber. As far as stepmoms go, my dad could have done a lot worse.

Dad's cell rings, thankfully interrupting our conversation. Neither Amber or I say a word while he's on the phone. Once he wraps up the call, she asks, "Are classes still going well?"

"Yeah, they're going pretty good." School started mid-August, and we're a few weeks in. Practice for the season is already underway but it'll become more rigorous once we start playing games which involves travel. I'm trying to stay on track with my classes because once that happens, I'll have a lot less time on my hands.

I'm not going to lie—balancing hockey and school has always been a struggle. Sometimes there doesn't seem to be enough hours in the day to get everything done. I chose to major in business because I knew it would be helpful after I'm done playing hockey. I could have picked a bullshit degree like some of the other guys on the team— something less demanding—but how would that help me in the long run?

"One of my finance classes is a little tough, but I'm working through it," I say as soon as I swallow down my eggs. I'm not sure what she adds to them, but they're delicious. "Thanks for making brunch. Everything's great."

"You're welcome. I love when we get together like this." A smile pulls at the corners of Amber's lips, but it's tinged with sadness. "It's going to be lonely without you stopping by on Sundays or us going to watch your games." She glances at Dad. "I'm not sure what he's going to do when you leave for Milwaukee."

"I'll work more," he replies before shoving a piece of bacon in his mouth. The man works a minimum of seventy hours a week and is constantly flying off to meet one client or another. I don't know how he could possibly work more than he already does unless he starts living at the office.

Amber worked for my father for about five years before they married. It's not like she didn't know what she was getting herself into.

By all outward appearances, she seems to accept that work comes first. "Maybe we'll get Hailey into skating."

Dad shrugs before changing the subject back to school. "I spoke with your advisor."

"Dr. Miller?"

He nods. "She said you didn't do so hot on the last exam and now you've fallen from a B to a C." He gives me a look. One that's chock-full of meaning. "The last thing we need is for you to get benched going into the season."

"I know." There are actually two classes that have fallen into the C range, but if he doesn't know that, I'm not going to mention it. All I can do is keep working my ass off in those classes and hope it pays off. When I have questions, I stop in for office hours. It's not like I'm sitting on my duff, twiddling my thumbs.

"Look, Brody, I know school has been a challenge. You have one year left, and then you're done. You're ahead of the game with Milwaukee already being lined up. There are a few endorsement deals that are being considered. Once May rolls around, you'll be able to focus on hockey full-time. You just have to push yourself a little harder."

Push myself a little harder.

I'm not sure how much harder I can continue pushing myself. Every moment of my day is spent either on school or hockey. I'm genuinely stumped at how some of these guys party the way they do.

Who the fuck has time for that?

I know people around campus assume I'm just coasting through school waiting to get to the NHL, but that couldn't be further from the truth. My degree matters. Yeah, maybe I should have picked something a little less rigorous. It's not like Dad wouldn't hire me afterward without majoring in business, but still...

This is what my mother wanted and fulfilling her wish is my gift to her.

"I'm working as hard as I can," I say.

"You can't afford to get benched," he repeats.

Does he seriously think I'm oblivious? Of course, I'm aware of that!

The very idea of riding the bench for even a few games this season is enough to induce nausea.

"John," Amber says softly as she lays a hand on his forearm.

Not that my father and I get into it often, because we don't, but Amber doesn't like tension or raised voices. She's one of those Zen human beings. I'm not sure if it's an overabundance of Xanax or yoga, but my hat's off to her on achieving inner peace.

I'd like some of that, please.

As soon as she senses Dad getting ramped up, she immediately steps in to smooth things over. Sometimes I feel like I should pull her aside and tell her that she doesn't have to get in the middle of it. I'm a big boy. I can handle my father. I've been doing it for twenty-three years.

Just as he turns to his wife, Hailey lets out a loud cry over the baby monitor sitting on the buffet.

Setting her napkin aside, Amber rises to her feet. "I better check on her. She was up a lot last night with an ear infection. The doctor just called in a prescription." She looks at my dad expectantly. "You'll need to run over to the pharmacy after brunch and pick it up."

Dad nods and waves her off. "Sure. Fine. I have to swing by the office for a couple of hours anyway."

Once Amber is safely out of earshot, Dad mutters under his breath, "She wants another one."

My brows pull together as I ask, "Another what?" I have no idea what he's talking about. I'm just glad we've veered away from the topic of my grades.

He shoots me an exasperated look. "Another baby. Amber would like us to have another baby."

The expression on his face is priceless. I chuckle and shrug my shoulders. "What's wrong with that? Hailey's a cute kid. It would probably be good for her to have a sibling."

"She has you," he points out, not looking the least bit swayed.

"That doesn't really count. I think Amber wants Hailey to have a playmate closer to her own age. And I'm not around very much as it is." I'd love to visit more, but there just isn't time for that. Whenever I walk through the door, Hailey grabs my fingers and drags me up to her playroom. There aren't many people I'll admit this to, but I'm well-versed in changing her baby dolls' diapers, feeding them bottles, and wrapping them in blankies. "Next year, I won't be around at all. She needs another kid to play with."

"We'll see," he grunts, sounding none too pleased with the prospect. "I've got a lot on my plate with the management company. We're thinking about expanding and opening an office in New York within the next six months." He pinches the bridge of his nose and adds, "I'm fifty years old. I'm not sure I want another baby at this point in my life."

I can't resist the smirk that settles around the corners of my mouth. "What'd you think was going to happen when you married a woman fifteen years younger than you without kids?" Seems like a no-brainer to me.

He takes a sip of his coffee. "When the hell did you get so smart? Guess you better keep that information tucked away for future reference."

Is he crazy? "Kids aren't part of my ten-year plan."

"Good. Let's keep it that way." Using his fork, he points to my face. "So, how'd you really get that shiner?"

I shrug and continue shoveling in my breakfast. "I told you. I was just fooling around at the house."

He raises a brow. "Fooling around, huh?" He sits back on his chair and stares at me for a long, ponderous moment.

I hold his gaze and say nothing. I'm not about to admit what really happened. If I know my dad, he'll blow it out of proportion.

"Since when does getting into a fistfight at a party with one of your teammates constitute roughhousing?"

I groan. "It's not a big deal."

He sucks in a deep breath and releases it slowly as if he's trying to rein in his temper. "Actually, it is. The fact you're even saying this tells me you don't see the severity of the situation. Do you really want Milwaukee getting it in their heads that you're not a team player? Or that you're a troublemaker? A loose cannon? Or worse, that you can't get along with your own teammates?"

His response seems a little overblown, but I'm smart enough to keep that opinion to myself. This is exactly why I didn't tell him the truth.

He throws his hands in the air in frustration. "It's one thing to get into it with players from an opposing team out on the ice in the heat of the moment and quite another to get into it with one of your own. The latter, if you hadn't already guessed, is unacceptable." He leans forward and steeples his fingers together on the table. "Do you really think you'll be a good sell for prospective advertisers if there's video of you knocking the shit out of someone? Is that an image any company wants representing their brand?"

Fine...maybe he has a point. It's not like I was considering future endorsement deals when Reed mouthed off. The only thing I'd been concerned about was shutting him up.

And that's exactly what I did.

Do I regret it?

Not one damn bit.

I won't, however, admit that to my dad. It'll only send him over the edge.

"I'm sorry." I run a hand through my still-damp hair and say with the proper amount of contrition, "It won't happen again."

The apology may take the edge off his anger, but he still looks exasperated. "We've talked about this, Brody. You need to keep your nose clean. That means no fights. No binge drinking. No baby mamas coming out of the woodwork looking for a payday. Nothing that's going to tarnish your image. In my day, there wasn't all this social media crap floating around. People weren't taking pictures or video every time you left the house. It was a lot easier to keep a lid on shit." Dad shakes his head. He's had to clean up more than one client's PR nightmare thanks to bad decisions and social media. "Now, the moment you fart, it goes viral. When you're a professional athlete, people can accuse you of almost anything—even if there's not a grain of truth to it—and ruin your career. I've seen it happen. You need to be careful."

This time when I mutter an apology, I actually mean it. Sometimes I forget that my dad has my best interests at heart. He's on my side, trying to steer me in the right direction. "You're right. I'm sorry." Last night got out of control. I let my emotions get the better of me. I'm usually more careful about that.

"You're too damn close to having everything you ever wanted to fuck it up now. You need to remember that your behavior has consequences. You're not a kid anymore. So, don't act like one."

"It was a momentary lapse in judgment," I add for good measure, wanting to smooth things over before I head back to campus. Looks like I'll be taking a page from Amber's book on how to handle my father. Maybe there's something to that Zen crap after all.

"Momentary lapse in judgment, my ass. Who's the girl who caused the ruckus?"

Fuck.

I should have known none of this would get past him. He's always been vigilant where my career is concerned. And most of the time, I'm appreciative of that. I wouldn't be where I am today—with a contract signed and endorsement deals rolling in—if it weren't for this man. But sometimes, he can be a little intense and overbearing. I wish he would give me some breathing room and let me figure things out on my own. He said it himself—I'm not a kid anymore. So, let me handle my own shit like an adult the way most twenty-three-year-olds do.

When I say nothing, he raises a brow and pulls out his phone. He taps the screen a few times and says, "I assume that this," he pauses and squints, "Natalie Davies is the reason a fight broke out between you and one of your teammates?"

I huff out a breath. "Yeah."

He frowns and tosses the phone onto the table. "Why would you get into a fight with a fellow player over a piece of college ass? I've been on campus. I've seen the girls at your games. There's more than enough to go around. You don't need to fight over the same piece of tail."

I glare, annoyed by the turn this conversation has taken. "Natalie isn't some piece of ass." Even using that term leaves a bad taste in my mouth.

He points to the phone and the lit-up Facebook screen. "If I've told you once, I've told you a thousand times that getting involved is a mistake. The last thing you need is to lose focus. Everything you've been working for is finally in reach. Don't fuck it up now. Not over something like this."

I plow my fingers through my hair again, feeling agitated. "It's not like that, okay? You're making a big deal out of nothing." I knew he would blow this out of proportion.

"Really?" He arches a brow. "So you and Reed are all good?"

Reed Collins and I have never been good. And I don't see that changing at this point.

"No," I bite out.

He shakes his head, and his eyes fill with disappointment. "I've always told you to go out and have fun. Enjoy as much pussy as you want."

I roll my eyes and grumble, "Jesus Christ, Dad. I seriously don't want to have this conversation with you over Sunday brunch." Everything I've just inhaled feels precariously close to revolting.

"What?" He smirks. "You think I didn't do the same thing when I was your age? I boned every girl who would let me." His look is knowing. "You and me, we're not so different. You work hard on the ice, you earn the right to blow off a little steam and play just as hard off of it." Getting serious again, he jabs a finger at me. "But you play smart. That means not getting serious about a girl at this stage of the game."

Even though I've only plowed my way through half of the eggs and pancakes, I push my plate away. When I remain silent, he continues.

"End whatever's going on with this girl before it gets out of control. You don't need the distraction. Especially now. You have enough to focus on with classes and hockey." He waves a hand in the air. "You want some pussy, be my guest. No one is stopping you. But that's all it is. There will be plenty more when you hit the pros."

I rub my forehead, just wanting to put an end to this conversation. "Natalie's a friend. That's it. This isn't something you need to worry about, okay? Just chill out."

And for the love of God, stop saying "pussy."

Before I left for juniors, my dad sat me down and had a very similar discussion about not getting involved in relationships and the necessity of keeping my focus on hockey and my NHL dreams.

Have there been girls I would have liked to get to know better?

Yeah. A few.

But I didn't pursue them. I've done exactly what he wanted and kept women at a distance. I can't say that he wasn't right. I see what most of these girls are like. They want a piece of you because of who you are and where you're going. I don't need that.

"Just make sure you keep it that way," Dad says in a stern tone.

The legs of my chair scrape against the tile floor as I push away from the table. "Well, this has been a real slice, but I need to get back to campus and study."

"Fine."

As I walk away, he adds, "And square things up with your co-captain. You don't need to bring bad blood out onto the ice with you. Not when your season is just about to get underway."

I wave a hand over my shoulder while walking toward the front door.

Yeah...that's not going to happen.

Reed can suck it, as far as I'm concerned.

Chapter Nine

NATALIE

"I need coffee," I moan, feeling blurry-eyed as Zara and I set out across campus. "Please tell me we have time to stop." I didn't sleep well last night. All I could think about was the ridiculous situation with Brody that I've become embroiled in. It's frightening how quickly it's taken on a life of its own. Clearly, it needs to be snuffed out before it grows any larger.

Zara glances at her phone. "As long as there isn't a huge line, we should be fine."

We stop at Java House, a coffee shop in the middle of campus. As I open the door and step inside, I'm not surprised to find a longer-than-usual line. My guess is that everyone is still hungover from the weekend and needs a little extra shot of caffeine to jumpstart their Monday morning.

I may not be hungover, but I feel the same pain.

A few customers glance our way, some doing double takes as a wave of murmurs moves through the crowd. Uncomfortable with the amount of attention I'm drawing, I pause over the threshold, causing Zara to slam into my back.

"What the hell, Nat?" she grumbles in irritation.

"Sorry." Ignoring the looks and hushed voices, I step inside the shop and take my place in line. I do a quick count. Looks like there are seven customers ahead of us.

"I don't know if we have time for this." Zara murmurs, glancing at her phone again. "We're cutting it close, and I can't afford to be late."

I bounce on the balls of my feet, jonesing for a caramel mocha. "I'm not sure I can make it through the next hour without some help." I need caffeinated fortitude in order to deal with Brody and the situation that is spiraling out of control.

Not wanting to acknowledge the looks aimed in our direction, I stare straight ahead. I'd told myself that what happened with Brody would blow over. In the grand scheme of things—war, politics, world hunger, disease—this isn't a big deal. But still, the rumor that Brody and I are now Whitmore's golden couple has spread like wildfire across social media in less than forty-eight hours.

Zara leans in close to my ear. "Is it my imagination or are these people staring at you?"

It's not her imagination. I can literally feel eyes crawling over me. For someone who enjoys her anonymity, it's a strange sensation. "It's your imagination."

"I don't think so." She sounds perplexed. "How are you not noticing this? It's even making me uncomfortable."

"No one is paying attention to us," I repeat. "It's a normal Monday morning. Nothing out of the ordinary is happening." It's like I'm reading from a script that I'm unwilling to deviate from.

She snickers. "Oh, sweetie, are you hoping if you say it enough times, it'll be true?"

"That's the plan," I admit tightly. "And so far, it's working." Not really. I noticed people staring as soon as I stepped onto campus ten minutes ago. A few even waved and said hi like we knew each other. The first time it happened, I actually swung around and glanced behind me figuring the greeting was meant for someone else. But there wasn't anyone there.

Creepy.

"Well, this should be interesting," Zara murmurs under her breath.

We're still four deep when a barista yells, "Extra-large caramel mocha with extra whip for Natalie."

With a frown, I glance at Zara from the corner of my eye. Then I look around the tiny shop waiting for someone with the same name to grab the drink I was planning to order. Thirty seconds tick by and the cup remains unclaimed on the counter.

Looking straight at me, the barista enunciates the order with more care.

Zara nudges my arm with her elbow. "Okay, this is going to sound strange, but I think she's talking to you."

That's not possible. I haven't made it to the counter yet. "It can't be mine."

"I know, but—"

"Natalie?" Again, the girl snags my surprised gaze. "Your name is Natalie, right?"

I jerk my head in the affirmative.

Again, she talks all slow-like. "You're dating Brody McKinnon?"

Oh, for fuck's sake.

Seriously?

"Ummm…" How am I supposed to respond to that question? I am most definitely *not* dating Brody. This entire fake-dating fiasco is a gigantic mix-up. One that needs to be rectified ASAP.

"Yep, that's her." Zara grabs my hand and forcibly drags me to the front of the line. More people turn to stare.

The barista beams as she hands over the coffee with a flourish. "This is what you usually order, right?"

"Ummm…" I'm confused. What's happening here?

"Yup," Zara supplies in my silence. "It is. Extra-grande and whip. Just the way she likes it."

"I thought so. You're a regular here." She leans toward me and whispers, "I'll have it waiting for you every day at quarter to ten."

When I continue staring in befuddlement, Zara jabs me in the ribs with her elbow and whispers under her breath with a smile, "Say thank you."

"Thank you," I mumble like an idiot.

"You're welcome. Just let McKinnon know that we absolutely love him here at Java House." The way she says "love" makes it sound more like *loooooove*.

"We'll definitely do that. Your support is appreciated." Zara pumps her fist in the air. "Go Wildcats!" Then she leans across the counter and asks, "So...any chance I can get a frap with no whip?"

"Of course, coming right up!"

With a delighted grin lighting up her face, Zara turns back to me. I'm sure my expression is more *what-the-fuck-was-that*. I frantically shake my head at her.

"This is freaking awesome!" she whispers giddily.

Finding my voice, I mutter, "This is weird! I don't like it. Not one bit."

Less than two minutes later, the barista is back. "Here you go! Frappuccino with no whip."

Thrown off by the whole bizarre exchange, I dig through my pocket for cash and pull out a few folded-up bills. "How much do we owe you?"

She takes a step away from the counter, holds her hands up, and shakes her head. "Don't worry. It's on the house."

"What? No!" My eyes slide to Zara, silently begging her to back me up on this. "We can't accept these drinks without paying for them."

"Are you kidding? Of course, we can!" Zara interrupts. When she elbows me for a third time, I glare. There's a perma-grin plastered across her face that makes her look slightly manic. Okay, it's more than slightly. "Thank the nice girl again and let's get to class before we're late."

I don't have the chance to argue because Zara pulls me away from the counter. Before I get too far, I stuff the wadded-up bills into the tip jar. I can't just *not* pay these people. It would be wrong. I feel bad enough for cutting in front of the customers who were already waiting in line.

I stumble out of the shop and grind to a halt. "What the hell was that?"

Zara grins and takes a sip of her drink. She closes her eyes and sighs with exaggeration. "That, my love, is one of the many perks of dating Brody McKinnon. And you know what? I love it. Dare I say that the coffee tastes a little better because of it?" She squeals. "All right, I dare.

It tastes *so* much better." Her eyes dance. "Told you this wasn't going to blow over anytime soon."

I hate to admit it, but Zara might be right. Which means that I need to speak with Brody immediately. This farce needs to end before it spins any further out of control

Chapter Ten

NATALIE

I arrive at Dr. Miller's class with a few minutes to spare. On the way over, I was bombarded with more people calling out my name and waving. After a while, I just waved back. A few even stopped and told me how much they love my boyfriend.

My boyfriend...

What am I supposed to say to that?

Ummm, thank you?

This episode has thrown off my entire morning. I'm a fidgety mess as I wait for Brody to make his grand entrance. I'm in the middle of taking my agitation out on my gnawed-to-the-pulp thumbnail when Kimmie Sanders walks in.

I do a double take.

Well...I think it's Kimmie.

Even though it's a ten a.m. class, and most of us usually look like we've just rolled out of bed and sprinted across campus like we're contestants on *The Amazing Race*, Kimmie usually sweeps into the room wearing full makeup with her hair perfectly styled. She favors tops that reveal way too much cleavage and skirts that barely cover her butt cheeks.

That's not the case this morning.

I can't help but stare. I don't think she's wearing a drop of makeup and her hair has been thrown up in a messy bun. Her outfit consists of leggings and a boxy sweatshirt. Not even a cute midriff-baring top.

Is that...a stain on her chest?

In the three years I've known Kimmie, I've never seen her dressed like this.

Since she's a finance major like me, I usually end up having at least one class with her a semester. That being said, we're more acquaintances than friends. Kimmie is all about the Delta Zetas, and I have zero interest in Greek life. But still, this departure from the norm has me concerned.

When she plops down at the desk behind me, I turn in my seat. "Kimmie? Are you okay?"

Maybe she's not feeling well. Although I'm not sure why she would bother showing up if that were the case. All she does is yap at Brody during class. Academics have never been her top priority.

As soon as her baby blues focus on me, her entire body deflates and tears fill her wide eyes.

Jeez.

Whatever is going on is much worse than I originally suspected.

"What's wrong?" I ask gently. I'm always willing to help a sister out. Pussy power and all that, right? "You seem upset."

She blinks. Her normally pretty face takes on a pinched quality as she glares at me.

"What's wrong?" Her voice rises with each syllable. A few students swivel on their chairs to see what's going on. "How can you ask me something like that?"

"What?" My spine stiffens in confusion. Clearly, I should have kept my big mouth shut.

Lesson learned.

Today has been weird enough without adding a Kimmie Sanders meltdown to the list. But it's too late to backtrack. I see the impending storm brewing in her eyes. Any moment it's going to rain down on me.

An innocent bystander.

A concerned acquaintance.

Kimmie leans toward me. Her hands have balled into fists on the desk. If she tries to crawl over it, I'm out of here.

"I really can't believe you, Natalie!" she snaps, her voice shaking with unspent emotion.

My eyes widen, and my hand flies to my chest in shock. "Me? What did I do?"

I think this chick has lost her mind. Maybe she's inhaled too many hairspray fumes. I'm no psych major, but this isn't normal behavior. Not even for Kimmie Sanders.

Her eyes narrow. If looks could kill, I'd be a pile of ash. "I'll tell you what you did! You stole the man I love right out from beneath my nose!" She wails the last part, and I cringe as more classmates turn in their seats, craning their necks to stare at the unnecessary drama she's creating. "How could you?"

The accusation has my jaw falling open and hitting the desk.

Stole the man she loves?

What is she talking about?

Before I'm able to wrap my brain around words and even try to sort out this mess, she continues. "I thought we were friends! Well, not anymore! Friends don't steal each other's men."

Oh my God, she's totally delusional. That's the only rational explanation for her unhinged behavior. I've heard about young adults in college having nervous breakdowns. I've just never witnessed it for myself. Poor Kimmie. I hope she finds the necessary help she needs to get better.

"Kimmie," I say carefully. "We've never been friends." Why would she think that? I can't think of one time she's even acknowledged me outside of class.

She folds her arms over her ample chest. "Well, we certainly aren't anymore!"

I'm afraid of what she'll do if I try rationalizing with her. It might make the situation worse. And I don't need that. Not on top of everything else going on this morning. Maybe I should just play along. "Who exactly did I steal from you again?"

Two fat, crystal-looking tears trek down her pale cheeks. "You know exactly who you stole, you conniving little bitch!"

More people have trickled into the room and are staring at the spectacle she's making of herself. I just want to melt into the floor. Is it too late to transfer to a different section this semester? I'm sure Dr. Miller would be sympathetic to my plight.

I keep my voice pitched low. "I really don't. Why don't you just tell me."

"Brody!" she wails. "He's the love of my life."

Son of a monkey!

I should have known.

Dr. Miller enters the room and shuffles through a few papers at the lectern. More people fill up the seats until all of the desks surrounding me have been taken.

Thankful that class is about to start, I say, "Look, Kimmie, there's been a misunderstanding. Can we discuss this after class?" I glance around, meeting a sea of curious stares. "Alone?"

Hope kindles in her tear-filled baby blues and her bottom lip trembles pathetically. "A mistake?" she repeats in a hopeful tone.

"Yes." I smile in relief as her anger magically melts away. "A huge mistake. I'll explain everything after class, okay? You have nothing to worry about in regards to Brody, trust me."

Her lips curve as she nods. "Yeah."

Turning toward the front of the room, I rub my temples in aggravation. A headache is brewing behind my eyes. It's only ten in the morning and already I'd like to wrap my hands around Brody's neck and strangle the life out of him.

Damn it. This is all his fault.

If he'd just kept his big mouth shut on Saturday night, none of this would be happening.

Brody saunters in as Dr. Miller launches into a lesson about nonprofit enterprises. He stops, his eyes scanning the small lecture hall. I slump in my seat, somehow knowing that he's searching for me. I need time to cool off before I talk with him. I flick my eyes toward him, hoping he's found a place to sit. He hasn't. The moment our gazes connect, he makes his way toward me. Unfortunately for him, all of the seats have been taken.

But that, apparently, isn't going to stop him. My brows draw together as he slips into the row I'm parked in.

What's he planning to do?

Sit on my lap?

When he gets to the occupied desk next to mine, he doesn't say a word. Just slants an eyebrow. The guy pales and scrambles to gather up his computer and backpack before hustling away.

For the umpteenth time this morning, my jaw drops. Looking relaxed, Brody slides into the desk next to me. Once he's taken out his computer, his eyes flick to mine as one side of his mouth hitches.

"Hey, babe," he says. "Thanks for saving me a seat."

I do the only thing I can.

I growl in frustration.

Every few minutes, I glance at Natalie from the corner of my eye. It's almost as if I can see the smoke pouring from her ears. My guess is that she's on the verge of busting a nut. I'm not sure what's going on, but I have a feeling I'll find out soon enough.

I'll say this about Natalie—she never leaves me guessing as to what her true feelings are. Particularly when those feelings have to do with me. And that, I find refreshing. I've been around enough females to know that they don't always tell you what's really going on inside their heads. Which can be tricky. I'd much rather be around someone who —good or bad—just puts it out there.

"Okay, everyone, I'll see you on Wednesday," Dr. Miller says. "Remember that the assignment on page two hundred and forty is due at midnight tomorrow. If you have any questions about the material, you can always email or text me. I do not, however, Snapchat."

A few chuckles erupt as people pack up their belongings and scatter like rats fleeing a sinking ship.

I'm trying to figure out the best way to approach Natalie when Dr. Miller says, "Mr. McKinnon, may I have a few moments of your time?"

"Sure thing." I glance at Natalie. "Wait for me?"

She nods. Her expression looks like it's been carved in stone. That, coupled with the fact that she hasn't spoken one single word throughout the entire fifty-minute class, has me concerned.

"I won't be long," I add.

Girls, as a rule, have never made me nervous. Maybe when I was fifteen they did, but certainly not since. There have always been too many clamoring for my attention to get hung up on anyone in particular. Nor have I ever had to work to gain a female's attention.

Natalie is the exception.

If I don't engage her, it's like I'm not even there. Which, I suppose, is why I start acting like a fifth-grade boy with his first crush and tease her mercilessly. What I said to her before is true. I wouldn't bother her if I didn't like her.

It might be time to reassess my tactics.

Gathering up her stuff, Natalie leaves the lecture hall without a backward glance. Guess nothing has changed in that regard.

With my backpack thrown over my shoulder, I head to the front of the room. Dr. Miller has been my advisor since I first stepped foot on campus. She has a laid-back demeanor, and the students love her.

"What's up, Dr. M?"

Her lips curve into a smile. "Hello, Brody. I wanted to check in with you and see how everything is going." Glasses sinking low on her nose, she shuffles around a few papers at the lectern.

"Everything's good." Could it be better? Hell yeah. But that's neither here nor there.

Her green eyes meet mine as she tucks a stray lock of blond hair behind her ear. "Did your father mention that we talked last week?"

"Yup." He sure did.

She nods, looking relieved. "Good. I don't want you to feel like I'm going behind your back when I discuss your grades with your father."

I shrug and state the truth. "He's been overly involved the whole time I've been here. Why would that change now?"

The edges of her lips curl with amusement. "That is certainly true. And while I understand his rationale, I want to make sure you're aware of what was discussed."

"I appreciate that."

Most people are intimidated by my father. Dr. Miller seems oddly unfazed by him.

"I looked over your test from last week more closely to see what kind of errors you were making and noticed that you had a hard time with some of the key concepts. I think it's because they're more abstract in nature. You do well with more concrete ideas. Your last test was a seventy-five percent." Her tone gentles. "The subject matter will continue to become more challenging in nature. You're hovering at a mid-level C. I'm concerned that your test scores will take a hit. You don't have much in the way of padding to allow for that."

She pauses and searches my eyes for understanding. The last two weeks of class have been more problematic. I stay on top of all the reading and assignments, but sometimes I don't absorb the concepts as quickly as I need to. I'm not in over my head yet, but if this class continues to become progressively more difficult at the rate it's going, then I might be.

"We're both aware of the standards Whitmore has set for its student athletes. If one of your classes drops below a C, you'll be forced to sit out until the grade is once again at C level."

"That won't happen," I cut in swiftly, mostly because I can't fathom the possibility. This is my last year at Whitmore. My last season playing with these guys. It's paramount that we bring home a National Championship. I'm also team captain. It would be a huge embarrassment to sit out for any period of time. My heart hitches at the thought.

Dr. Miller reaches out and squeezes my shoulder for a fleeting moment. "I know you're working hard, Brody. I can't say that about all the student athletes here at Whitmore. You and I are meeting as much as we can, but I believe it might be time to get a tutor. I took the liberty of checking with your other professors. You're borderline in your statistics class as well. I think at this point, it would be a proactive step to take." Opening a manila folder, she grabs the top sheet from her pile of notes and presses it into my hand. "These are a few names of tutors I think you would work well with. You'll need to email each one to check their availability and see if it works with your schedule."

A pit settles in my gut as I stare at the paper in my hand. "These are student tutors?"

"Graduate students, yes. I think it would be beneficial to work with someone twice a week. You and I will continue to meet during office hours, of course, but I think this would help."

I'm not opposed to working with a tutor, but I know how people love to gossip around here. Most of the time, there's nothing I can do about that, but I've always tried to keep my academic struggles under wraps.

So far, I've done my best to hold it together, but these upper-level courses are killing me. If I hadn't made a promise to my mom that I would finish college before entering the NHL, I would have gone straight to Milwaukee after juniors. But this is my last year. I'm in the homestretch now. I just have to work a little harder and I'll have my degree when I skate onto the ice with the Mavericks.

Dr. Miller is right. I need help. Getting benched isn't an option. An idea forms in my head. I stuff the list of tutors into the pocket of my khakis, hoping I won't have to contact them.

"Thanks, Dr. M. I'll look into it."

"There's no shame in asking for help, Brody," she reminds me. "Lots of students do."

I nod. It has nothing to do with me being embarrassed to ask for assistance. It's more about me wanting to control who knows about my issues.

Dr. Miller seems satisfied with my answer. "My plan is to check in with your other professors on a weekly basis. Then, when we meet on Wednesdays, we can go over your grade reports. We're going to get through this together, okay, Brody?"

Her words have everything within me loosening. Dr. Miller will continue working with me and if I can get Natalie on board, I'll be set. I'm just not sure how to convince her. Most days, that girl can barely stand to be in the same room with me.

I say goodbye to Dr. Miller and jog through the corridor, pushing out the main doors to leave the building. I hope Natalie didn't take off on me. I wouldn't put it past her. It takes my eyes a moment to adjust to the bright sunlight. There are a ton of students standing around shooting the shit.

Something instantly settles in me when my gaze lands on Natalie. Because all of my attention is focused on the long-legged brunette, it takes a moment to realize that she isn't alone.

She's standing with Kimmie.

Well, hell...

This is so not what I need right now.

Especially since Kimmie's arms are flailing wildly around her. Even though I'm a good ten yards from them, I can hear Kimmie's voice escalating in volume. She looks dangerously close to getting up in Natalie's face. I rush down the stairs. Every long stride propels me closer to them. A small crowd of bystanders has gathered around the girls.

As soon as I reach them, I slide an arm around Natalie and tuck her close to my body. Kimmie's eyes widen as hurt flashes through them. I'm not sure what Kimmie's deal is. There's nothing between us. We're friends. That's it.

We've never even hooked up.

I'm not saying that she hasn't come on to me, I'm just saying it's never happened between us.

It only takes one interaction with Kimmie to realize that she's the type of chick who has the ability to go stalker-girl on you. All the signs are there, flashing like the lights on the Vegas strip. I steer clear of women who tell you that they're cool with hooking up for a few hours but then end up sending you scathing text messages for months afterward and bashing you to every person they come into contact with.

Contrary to popular belief, I'm not a total dickhead. I'm always upfront about my intentions. If someone's not into what I propose, so be it. There are plenty of others who are cool with a casual situation.

Striving for nonchalance, I say, "Hey, Kimmie. What's up?"

I mentally groan when her eyes fill with tears. God, I hate when girls cry. Like any other man, it makes me feel helpless.

And, more often than not, ultimately responsible.

"So, it's true then?" she whispers huskily. "You two are going out?"

Natalie opens her mouth, and I quickly cut her off because I have the feeling she's about to blow us out of the water. And that, I just can't have. It doesn't surprise me that Natalie is having second thoughts about the nature of our relationship.

I get that.

I even expected it.

But here's the deal...Natalie has been on my radar for three years. Now that I've maneuvered her into this position, the last thing I'm going to do is let her slip through my fingers.

Plus, I need a tutor, and she fits the bill perfectly.

I just have to convince her that she needs me as much as I need her.

It shouldn't be all that difficult, right?

I'm a good-looking dude. I have a fairly decent personality. Most girls would chew off their own arms to date me. Even fake-date me. That being said, Natalie isn't most girls. She's the only one who would probably chew off her own arm to get away from me.

Go figure.

But first things first. I need to put the kibosh on the drama Kimmie is hell-bent on causing.

"Yep. Davies and I are together, all right." When Natalie tries to interrupt again, I squeeze her to me and smack a quick kiss on her lips. Once she's been effectively silenced, I pull back because I wouldn't put it past her to try biting me. She glares. "We finally decided to make it official. Right, babe?"

That's more of a rhetorical question. I don't expect an answer. In fact, I'd prefer not to have one. Natalie just needs to stand there and simmer quietly while I get rid of Kimmie.

"But-but," Kimmie sputters as if she doesn't know what to say. Which is a first. "You don't even like her!"

Natalie raises her brows as a smug expression settles on her face.

I shake my head. "Nah. It was never like that."

Kimmie sucks her pouty lower lip between her teeth as her confused gaze bounces between us. Her eyes have welled again with unshed tears. "I thought you and I..." Her voice breaks. "I thought we had something special."

Why would she think that?

Sure, I see her around at parties. But the only time we talk is during class. The girl yaps my ear off, making it difficult for me to concentrate. I've tried changing seats, but she follows me around like a lost puppy.

I glance at the growing crowd.

Don't these people have someplace to be?

The last thing I want to do is embarrass Kimmie. Whatever happens here will spread around campus in the blink of an eye.

"I'm sorry, Kimmie," I say gently. "I didn't realize you felt that way."

"I don't understand...I've never even heard of you going out with a girl before." She flicks her eyes at Natalie. "What makes her so special?"

Natalie's body becomes whipcord tight, but she doesn't say a word. I think she's waiting to see how I wiggle out of this predicament.

I shrug and keep Natalie firmly anchored to my side in case she gets any ideas. "She's smart and beautiful. Not to mention that sparkling personality of hers. Why wouldn't I want to get to know her better? I've had my eye on Davies since freshman year. And now that she's agreed to give me a shot, I'm taking it."

Kimmie's brows slide together. "Really?"

Her shocked tone annoys me. It's like I just told her that I enjoy eating my own feces. "Yeah, really. I like Natalie. She's a cool chick."

"Huh." My explanation seems to leave her flummoxed.

It's time to wrap this up. There's nothing more that needs to be said.

Again, Kimmie's eyes shift between Natalie and me. I sense she wants to continue arguing. Like she's going to talk me out of liking this girl. That isn't going to happen. After a few uncomfortable moments, Kimmie's shoulders sag, and she shrugs. "Okay. I guess I'll see you later, Brody."

"Yup." Relief zips through me that I've managed to detonate this bomb without blowing all three of us to oblivion.

With one last soulful look aimed in my direction, Kimmie stalks away. Realizing that a catfight is not about to break out, the gathered crowd disperses leaving Natalie and me alone.

"You can let go of me now," she growls.

I chuckle. "Maybe I don't want to let go of you." I realize there's more than a kernel of truth to that statement. I like the feel of her tucked against me. She fits perfectly. Although it's highly doubtful she thinks the same thing.

She punctuates my thoughts with a quick jab to the gut. I grunt and release my hold.

"You're one violent chick, Davies." I hate to admit it, but that quality is attractive as hell. *She's* attractive as hell. It makes me wonder if there's anything she could do to turn me off.

Looking relieved, Natalie steps out of my embrace. "You have no idea how violent I can be, McKinnon. But I have the distinct feeling you're going to find out soon enough."

I smile and rub my belly. "See? It's only been two days, and already you know me so well. That's why this is a match made in heaven."

She sucks in a breath and slowly releases it. "Right. About that. I was hoping we could talk about this whole...situation."

"Sure." Whatever she wants to discuss isn't going to be good. I can tell by the stiff set of her lips.

"Want to grab a coffee at Java House?" I ask.

Her eyes widen, and she shakes her head. "Absolutely not!"

I slant a questioning look her way, but she remains silent. "Fine, where do you want to go? I've got a few hours between classes. Want to head back to my place?"

That suggestion leaves her glaring.

"I didn't mean for that." I chuckle. Unable to help myself, I tease, "Although I'm not opposed to the idea if you're interested."

"We are not going back to your place," she says firmly.

"Fine. Tell me where you want to go."

She grabs my hand and pulls me along. "Off campus. I need to get out of here. Now. Before anymore weirdness can happen."

I have no idea what that means.

"All right. I've got my truck. Why don't we head over to Maples on Main? We can grab an early lunch." People check us out as we move through the crowd. I'm used to the attention, but I get the feeling that Natalie is uncomfortable with it.

"Fine."

Twenty minutes later, we slide into a booth across from each other. Bev, one of the waitresses who normally waits on me, stops by the table with menus and two glasses of water.

"Hey, sweetie," she greets with a grin. "Want me to set you up with the usual?"

Natalie cocks a dark brow at me.

This is my home away from home. I wink at Bev. "They take good care of me here."

Bev chuckles. She's a grandmotherly type of woman who I've gotten to know over the years. "You got that right. He and a few guys from the team stop in after practice. A hungrier bunch, I've never seen."

"That's because you got the best meatloaf in town."

"Lou makes it fresh every day with you in mind."

I hand her the menu. "I wasn't planning on the meatloaf for lunch, but you talked me into it."

A hearty laugh tumbles from her lips. "You got it." She turns expectantly to Natalie. "What about you, hon? What'll you have?"

Natalie skims the menu and says, "Just a plate of fries, please."

"Easy enough." She writes our orders down on a small pad of paper and sticks the pencil behind her ear. "Should be up in ten."

"Can we get two Cokes, please?" I glance at Natalie and ask, "Or did you want Diet?"

"Nope." She shakes her head. "The real McCoy is fine."

Now here's a girl after my own heart.

"Coming right up," Bev says and walks away.

As I sit back against the bench, my gaze is drawn to Natalie. But that's nothing new. I've felt the pull for years. Now that it's the two of us, I'm not sure what to say or how to start this conversation. Somehow, I need to convince her that this fake relationship is a beneficial arrangement for both of us. Sure, I know exactly how it benefits me. What I need to figure out is what I bring to the table.

"I want to apologize for what happened with Kimmie. I had no idea she would go off the rails like that." Although deep down, I suspected as much.

"It's fine." Natalie shakes her head and amends her statement. "Weird, but fine." Her eyes dart around the half-empty restaurant before settling on mine again.

"Look, Brody—" she begins.

"Uh-oh, I know it's serious when you opt for my first name."

Her lips lift a fraction. My eyes drop briefly to them as the memory of what her mouth felt like when mine slid over it flashes through my head. The urge to kiss her again pounds through me.

Can't say I see that happening anytime soon. If Natalie has her way, it'll never happen again.

"I appreciate what you did for me Saturday night with Reed," she begins again. "I really do. You didn't have to involve yourself." Her gaze slides over the bruised skin around my eye. "But I don't think it's necessary for us to pretend we're involved. Honestly, I think that will only stir the pot. All the gossip that's circulating will eventually blow over." She shrugs. "You know what it's like around here."

Of course, I do. But still...

I'm not ready for this to be over. Not by a long shot.

Stalling for time, I lift my glass to my lips and take a big gulp of water. My eyes never release hers. Natalie threads and rethreads her fingers as if she's nervous. Which is strange. She's not the fidgety kind. Certainly not around me. Setting the glass down, I lean forward, resting my elbows on the Formica table.

"I think we should stick it out for a few weeks," I say.

Looking adamant, she shakes her head. "Why would we bother doing that?'

"Because it's advantageous for both of us."

She arches a brow. "How so? I've already told you that I don't care if people talk."

"Well," I drawl, trying to come up with a few reasons on the fly why it would be in her best interest to date me. I really should have given this more thought, but I wasn't expecting her to try ditching me so quickly. In hindsight, I should have. "For one," I improvise, "everyone on campus already thinks we're dating."

"It'll blow over," she repeats. "It has to."

I raise a dubious brow. "Will it?" Before she can respond, I add,

"Because I'm not exactly known for my relationships. And maybe you noticed, but that's all anyone could talk about since I announced it Saturday night."

Her expression sours. "Yeah, I'm aware of that, which is part of the problem. Just walking across campus, I was bombarded with people trying to talk to me or give me free coffee."

I quirk a brow. "And that's a problem for you?" Because it certainly wouldn't be for most girls.

She shrugs. "I don't like all the attention. It's weird. People who don't even know me are stopping and talking to me or waving at me."

I sit back and snicker. "Welcome to my world, baby. Pull up a chair and stay awhile."

"Yeah...the thing about that is that I never asked to be dragged into your world."

"You do realize that if we part ways now—two days later—you'll be even more newsworthy than you were before." Because I sense that I'm losing her, I say, "Coupled with what Reed said at the party..." Words trailing off, I allow her to draw her own conclusions.

Maybe I'm a shit for bringing up that sensitive topic, but it can't be helped. Desperate times call for desperate measures.

Her eyes lower to the table. Christ...I really am a bastard. Even if she doesn't want to admit it, part of her realizes the truth of my words.

"The only reason people aren't talking about that right now is because we're together." I point to my blackened eye. "No one is going to say shit about you while we're a couple. If we break up, it'll be open season. You'll be all anyone can talk about."

Whatever color had been filling her cheeks, drains. It may be hard to hear, but Natalie needs to see reason. Sure, at the moment, people are focused on our dating situation. This is breaking news for a guy who's never been tied down before. We end things now, before they ever had a chance to heat up, and there will be a shit ton of speculation as to the reasons behind it. Reed's words will be resurrected.

"Hey," I say carefully. "This doesn't have to be a big deal. We make a few public appearances. We hang out a bit." A thought occurs to me. One that doesn't sit well. "Is there someone else in the picture? Is that the issue?"

Let's face it, Natalie's a hot girl. Prickly to be sure, but smoking hot nonetheless. A guy would have to be blind and stupid not to want her. My pulse kicks waiting for her response. For some reason, I never considered the possibility of there being another guy before. Maybe I should have.

After what feels like an indeterminable amount of time, she shakes her head. "No. I've got too much going on with school to worry about a relationship." She fiddles with the wrapper of her straw. Her brows furrow. "Why are you doing this?"

When I remain silent, she glances up, her eyes locking on mine. Suspicion laces her voice. "What's in it for you, McKinnon?"

I shrug, trying to downplay the situation. "It hurts that you think I'm looking for something in return. I'm just trying to look out for a friend."

Her eyes narrow and she tilts her head. "When have we ever been friends?"

I laugh. "Come on, Davies. We're friends. Have been for years."

Her look is skeptical.

"All right, all right, there is something you could do," I finally admit. "I could use a little of your expertise in our finance class."

Her brows draw together. Like I've thrown her a real curveball. "You want my help?"

"Yup."

"You mean like tutoring?" she clarifies as if I might be suggesting something far more nefarious.

My muscles tense. I don't make a habit of discussing my grades. Reed's words echo unwantedly in my head. *He's dumber than a bag of bricks. It won't take long for him to bore you.* It's nothing I haven't heard before, but still...it picks at a scab. It sucks that people assume I'm stupid because I struggle. It takes some effort to loosen the tension rolling through my shoulders so I can shrug casually. "Yeah, something like that. I have a C right now. If it drops below that, I'll get benched, and I can't afford for that to happen. Especially this season. I'm just trying to be proactive."

She watches me silently. "Let me get this straight. We'll pretend to date so people won't talk about me. In exchange, you'd like some help with a class."

"Two classes," I admit reluctantly. "The other three, I'm holding my own in," I add, not wanting her to think I'm a total dumbass. They're solid B's. I'm not worried about them.

The way she stares leaves me feeling stripped bare. Like she sees more than I want her to. More than I'm comfortable with. I shift on the seat, trying not to squirm under the heavy weight of her gaze. "Why don't you make an appointment at the tutoring center on campus?"

I glance away. "I'd prefer not to do that. You know what it's like around here. I don't need the hassle."

"You could hire a private tutor," she suggests, apparently trying to wiggle out of our agreement.

"I am." I grin. "And you get to be paid with my winning personality. Don't you feel lucky?"

She takes a sip of water and mulls over my proposal. "I don't know..."

"There's something else I can throw in to sweeten the deal," I interject before I can think better of it.

Her eyes narrow. I don't think I've ever had a female look at me with so much distrust and derision. I'm used to adoration and longing.

"I'm almost afraid to ask," she mutters under her breath.

I clear my throat knowing that I'm already skating on thin ice. It won't take much to push her away, and then I'll be screwed. And not in a good way either. "Just hear me out on this, okay?"

A jolt of awareness slices through me as her wary eyes fasten onto mine.

Chapter Twelve

BRODY

"Your inexperience...I can help with that."

Natalie pokers up in her seat as if someone just rammed a two-by-four up her ass. Her mouth falls open, and I have the feeling she's about to blast me into next week when Bev sets our plates down in front of us.

"Careful, they're hot." As if sensing the tension, her gaze bounces cautiously between us.

I give her a nervous smile, praying that Natalie doesn't flip her lid. I like this place. I'd hate to avoid it from here on out. I don't take my eyes off the girl sitting across from me. "Thanks. Everything looks great."

"No problem, hon. Anything else I can get for either of you?"

Natalie doesn't say a word.

"Nope, we're good. Thanks." I just want to hurry her along before Natalie explodes.

Once Bev is out of earshot, Natalie leans over her plate of fries and growls, "I'm not discussing my lack of sexual experience with you!"

"Hey." I hold up both hands in a gesture of surrender. "Settle down. I'm not trying to embarrass you. All I'm saying is that I can help." I'm trying to play it cool. Like I really don't care. But make no mistake, I do care. More than I want to admit. "If you're interested."

The fact that Natalie doesn't have much sexual knowledge probably shouldn't turn me on, but it does. I learned early on to steer clear of girls who lacked experience. They're the ones who equate sex to a relationship, which translates into needy and clingy.

It's almost comical the way Natalie's brows snap together.

"Help how?" she asks skeptically.

I'm tempted to reach across the table and smooth out her furrowed forehead, but I don't. She's liable to take the fingers right off my hand.

"Well," I shift on my seat. Tact is of the utmost importance here. This discussion is like walking through a minefield. I could be blown to bits when I least expect it. "I could, ah, assess the situation and give you some helpful pointers."

If her eyes widen any more, they'll fall right out of her head. "Are you suggesting what I think you are?"

I cock a brow. "If you think I'm suggesting that we make this relationship physical, then yes. That's precisely what I'm suggesting." She doesn't move a muscle. Just continues staring at me like I'm crazy. "I told you this could be a beneficial arrangement for both of us. I have the necessary skill set you require, and you have the necessary knowledge I'm looking for. Correct me if I'm wrong, but that sounds very much like a symbiotic relationship to me." I tap my finger against the side of my head.

Thank you very much, Biology 101. That's probably the only thing I remember from that class.

"Oh my God, you're not joking," she mumbles. "I thought you were just trying to be an ass. Because honestly, who says something like that?" She shakes her head and pops a fry into her mouth and then mutters, "But no. You're actually serious about this."

"Once you've had some time to think it over, you'll see the benefit to what I'm saying. Obviously, you have a few hang-ups where sex is concerned—"

She grips the edges of the table with her fingers until her knuckles turn bone white. "I do not have any hang-ups."

"You sure about that, Davies? Because your reaction to my proposal suggests otherwise." Striving for nonchalance, I fork off a huge hunk of meatloaf and shove it in my mouth as I watch her.

She drops her gaze to her plate and says with less force, "I don't have hang-ups. There are absolutely no hang-ups to speak of."

I sense there's more coming. When she says nothing further, I ask, "But?"

Her hair slides forward like a curtain as she drops her chin to her chest. Finally, she lifts her eyes, skewering me with them. "I'm not a prude or some born-again virgin. I just don't have a ton of experience. I've dated, but for the most part, I've been too busy with school to get wrapped up in guys. And I have zero interest in being a puck bunny." A look of anger crosses her face, and she snaps, "Is that what you wanted to hear?"

"Of course not."

Maybe.

Giving her explanation time to settle, I scoop up some mashed potatoes and lift the spoon to my mouth. Once I swallow them down, I say, "I'm not trying to embarrass you."

"Are you sure about that?" Instead of holding my gaze, she focuses on dragging a fry back and forth through the puddle of ketchup on her plate. "Because I get the distinct feeling you're enjoying this."

She's wrong about that. Making her feel like shit was never my intention. "Not being experienced isn't anything to be ashamed of."

"I'm not ashamed," she bites out. "I could have sex every weekend if I wanted. It's my choice, and I've chosen not to."

"Fair enough. All I'm saying is that I can help remedy the situation. Obviously what Reed said bothered you."

She shrugs and reaches for another fry. "It hurt because I never thought he'd throw that in my face in front of so many people."

Disgust burns a hole in my gut. "Reed is an asshole." And that's putting it nicely. "The guy has a major problem keeping it in his pants." People think I'm bad when it comes to whoring around, but Reed Collins is ten times worse. That guy is on some sort of quest to nail as much ass as he can. When I caught wind that he was going out with Natalie last year, I'd thought maybe he'd had enough and was ready to settle down and get serious about someone, but that didn't turn out to be the case.

"Yes," she replies dryly, "I know. That was part of the problem."

"Right." Growing serious again, I lean toward her. "Just think about what I'm saying, okay? You don't have to give me an answer right now."

She shakes her head. "I can't sleep with you, Brody. It would be...weird."

Weird isn't the first word that comes to mind when I think about having sex with Natalie.

Hot.

Sexy.

Amazing.

Those are just a few off the top of my head.

"Why would it be weird?"

"Because..." Natalie shoves another fry in her mouth, and I suspect she did that to buy herself some time to come up with an answer to my question.

My eyes fall to her lips. They're a perfect Cupid's bow. The urge to close the distance and slant my mouth over hers pounds through me. I've been thinking about those lips since Saturday night. The unexpected softness of them took me by surprise. Because we'd been in front of a crowd of people, I hadn't been able to explore them the way I'd wanted. It makes me wonder if I'll ever get another chance.

Getting a boner while sitting across from Natalie is not in the game plan right now, so I jerk my gaze back to hers. "Because?" I prompt. I can't believe how turned on I am just watching her eat a French fry. That's what this girl does to me. I can't explain it because I don't understand it. I've never experienced this kind of attraction before. In the three years that I've known her, it's only grown stronger.

Looking uncomfortable, she shifts on the bench. "I know this is going to sound antiquated, but I've never had meaningless sex before. All the guys I slept with, we were involved in relationships."

"We're involved," I remind her. "You can ask anyone, and they'll tell you we're going out."

That response gets me a fry pelted at my chest. I grin, relieved that the mood has been lightened.

"We're not really going out, Brody." She huffs out a breath. "I have no idea what this is between us."

We both fall into a comfortable silence before she clears her throat and flicks her eyes to mine. "Just out of curiosity, how many girls have you slept with?"

"You really want to know that?"

"You know a lot about my sex life. Seems only fair that you should share some details with me." A gleam enters her dark eyes. "What's the matter, don't you know?"

I do a rough mental calculation. I started having sex when I was sixteen. It's been seven years. Which means...

Fine, she's caught me. I haven't the slightest clue. It's not like I've been keeping track on my phone. Christ, is there an app for that? I'll have to check with Cooper. If anyone would know, it would be him.

"I'm not sure," I hedge, turning the question around on her. "How many guys have you slept with?"

"Three." She raises her brows. "Now you. Ballpark it if you have to."

Well, shit...My number is much higher than that. Even if you squared her number and maybe squared it again...It would still be higher.

"I don't know." I suck in a breath and admit carefully, "Maybe a hundred or so." There's no question about it...It's definitely the *or so*. All I can say is that juniors was a crazy time.

"You've slept with a hundred women!" she whisper-yells while giving me a disbelieving look. "Are you serious?"

The sound of her incredulous voice leaves me flinching. "Keep it down." I crane my neck to see if anyone's staring. Thankfully, no one is paying us the least bit of attention. "It's just a guess. You said to ball-park it."

"So, it's probably more than that," she points out.

Very possibly.

"I wasn't expecting it to be that high." She arches a brow. "You sure like to get around, don't you?"

I spear my fork in her direction. "Are you slut-shaming me, Davies? Is that what's going on here?"

"Maybe." She snickers and shakes her head. "How do you sleep with that many people and not know? Or care?"

I shrug. "You are aware that people have sex because it feels good, right? Not necessarily because they're involved in a relationship?"

"Of course, I am." She shifts on her seat as if uncomfortable by the concept.

I lean in, closing the distance between us. "You know, sex is a great stress reliever. Maybe you should try it sometime."

A blush blooms across her cheeks. "I do other things to relieve stress." Damn, but she's adorable.

"Such as?" I ask, unwilling to let the topic drop so easily.

"Working out."

I smirk. "If you do it the right way, sex can be a great workout."

She throws another fry at me, and I chuckle. "I don't want to talk about sex anymore."

"If you insist."

"I do," she sighs. "I totally insist."

Instead of talking, we dig into our food. It only takes five minutes for me to polish off the meatloaf and potatoes. Lou really nailed it today.

"Have you ever cheated on a girlfriend?" Natalie asks.

The question seems to come out of left field, but I take it in stride. "No."

She looks both surprised and mildly impressed. Can't say I've ever seen that look on her face before. "How many girlfriends have you had?'

"Including you?" I ask.

She rolls her eyes. "Sure, why not."

"One."

She blinks and drops her chin before asking, "You've never had a girlfriend?"

"Never wanted one. I've always been too busy to get involved. After high school, I played juniors for two years. We traveled a lot. There was no time for relationships." I cock a brow. "The same goes for Whitmore. My focus has been the NHL. The last thing I need is to get distracted." It doesn't escape me that I'm parroting my father's words back to her.

"Yeah, I guess that makes sense," she says thoughtfully.

After a few moments, I squirm beneath the intensity of her gaze. The way she pins me in place almost feels physical in nature. No one has ever taken the time to really look at me. They don't see past the hockey prowess and the pretty package. And up until this point, I've been fine with that. For the first time, I can't help but wonder what Natalie sees when she looks at me.

Breaking the heavy silence, I repeat, "I think this relationship can be a mutually beneficial arrangement for both of us. Just think about it."

She shocks the hell out of me when she says, "Okay."

I wasn't expecting such an easy capitulation. In all honesty, I wasn't expecting a capitulation at all. It wouldn't have surprised me if she threw her drink in my face. "Okay, you'll do it?"

Her shoulders sag, and she says begrudgingly, "Yeah, I guess."

This was the outcome I'd been hoping for but didn't think would actually come to fruition. To say that I'm relieved is a vast understatement. I want to pump my fist in the air but contain myself. Barely.

Looking dead serious, she says, "Don't make me regret this, McKinnon."

I grin and settle back against my seat. "Would I do that to you?"

"In a heartbeat."

I chuckle. "I'm going to be the best fake boyfriend you could ever ask for. You just wait and see."

Natalie groans and lays her forehead on the table. "You realize that this situation has disaster written all over it, right?"

"Have a little faith, Davies. This is going to be epic."

I wink and laugh when she groans again.

Chapter Thirteen

NATALIE

"Hey, Natalie, wait up."

Recognizing the voice, I groan and pick up the pace, hustling my ass down the path. With any luck, I'll lose him in the crowd of students moving like cattle across campus. Reed Collins is the last person I want to speak with. After Saturday night and the ugliness he hurtled in my direction, I don't know how he has the audacity to approach me.

But he does.

What a jerk.

As tempting as it is to lump Brody and Reed into the same hockey-playing-manwhore category, they're nothing alike. Until now, I hadn't realized it. Yeah, they're both players—that goes without saying—but there's an egotistical self-centeredness to Reed that I didn't notice until it was too late. He doesn't give a damn about anyone else's feelings but his own. And he doesn't care who he hurts in the pursuit of his own pleasure either.

Brody doesn't strike me that way. But that's something I'm still trying to figure out. And until I do, my guard is up, and I'll tread carefully.

Catching up to me, Reed slows his jog and gives me a smile full of charm and bullshit. It's the very same one that used to make my heart hitch and bring a dreamy smile to my lips.

Now it makes me want to throat punch him.

"I'm glad we ran into each other." He falls in line with me as I walk. "I was hoping we could talk."

"Yeah, I'm kind of in a hurry at the moment." Even if I had all the time in the world, I wouldn't waste a single minute of it on him. Hoping he gets the message, I give him a bit of side-eye and hasten my pace. "Maybe some other time?"

Or never.

Never works just as well. In fact, it's preferable.

"Where're you heading?"

"Brighton." I keep my eyes focused straight ahead. Even looking at him makes my blood boil.

"What a coincidence. I'm going that way, too."

"Awesome," I mutter under my breath.

Without any further preamble—which I can appreciate—he gets straight to the point. "So, what's up with you and McKinnon? Are you two really a thing?"

My mouth falls open as I stop in my tracks. This guy is unbelievable! "Seriously? You embarrass me in front of a ton of people Saturday night, and instead of apologizing like a normal human being, you want to know if I'm dating Brody?"

He blinks in confusion and gives me a *what's the big deal* look. "Yeah, that's what I asked."

I laugh.

Why?

I have no idea. The way this guy's brain works is impossible to understand. I'm not even going to try. And the fact that I wasted four months of my life on the asshole only makes me laugh harder.

A flicker of annoyance crosses Reed's pretty-boy features as the giggles roll off my lips. Deciding to ignore him, I walk away.

"Hey." He grabs my arm and hauls me over to the grass so we're no longer in the stream of student traffic. "I'm not done talking to you."

The laughter dies a quick death as my brows lower. "Wanna bet?" I try jerking my arm free. When his fingers tighten around me, I growl, "Let me go, Reed. You and I have nothing further to discuss."

All polite pretense falls away. "I want to know what's going on between the two of you."

"Excuse me?" Who does this guy think he is? The extent of his douchebaggery is almost mind-boggling.

"Why are you slumming it with McKinnon?" he snaps, eyes narrowing. "If you're doing it to fuck with me, it's not going to work."

I rear back like I've just been slapped. "You're insane to think that you have any bearing on the decisions I make. You stopped being a consideration a long time ago."

"Sure." Reed rolls his eyes. "Cut the crap, Natalie. I know you're still pissed that I dumped you."

I gasp and fire back, "If you remember correctly, it was me who dumped your ass. Not the other way around."

He smirks, and I'm tempted to slap the smile right off his face. "Only because you found out I was getting a little side action. Come on, admit it...we had a good thing going. You should have chilled out and overlooked it."

I fist my hands and try to rein in my temper so I don't explode. But that feels impossible. "Are you suggesting that the appropriate action would have been to turn a blind eye to your screwing around?"

He reaches out with his other hand and trails his knuckles over my cheek.

I scowl and bat it away.

"None of it ever meant anything. You're the girl I liked having by my side. I saw a future for us." He shrugs. "At the time, I wasn't ready to settle down."

The scary thing is, I think he's being serious. He wanted to have his cake and eat it, too.

Or maybe I should say, *he wanted to have his pie and eat it, too.*

"So, I was just supposed to stand there like a dumbass while you fucked all the puck bunnies you wanted?"

A cocky smile curves his lips. "Is that really such a big deal? It's not like you were into having sex."

The blood drains from my face as I choke out, "Excuse me?"

"I have a high sex drive." He shrugs. "You didn't. Plus, you didn't know what you were doing. Maybe you should have watched some porn and gotten a few ideas. If you had tried spicing things up, I wouldn't have gotten so bored."

I can only stare in shock that all of this nastiness is spewing from his mouth.

"You know what?" I jerk my arm away again and this time, he releases me. If he hadn't, I would have junk punched him. Hard. I'm not going to put up with his manhandling. "I can't believe I let you take my virginity," I hiss, stepping toward him. My hands are still balled. My nails dig into my flesh. "And I can't believe you're trying to blame me because you couldn't keep your dick in your pants. You're a real piece of work, you know that?"

He holds his palms up. "Look, we're getting off topic here."

"Off topic?" I shriek. "Are you kidding me?"

My elevated voice doesn't seem to bother him in the slightest.

"Yeah. What I'm trying to say is that if you're so desperate to have me back again, I'm more than willing to give you another shot. You don't have to stoop to dating McKinnon to get my attention."

I can only shake my head. "You're delusional."

Not taking my comments seriously, he chuckles. "Am I delusional or am I right in thinking that you're trying to make me jealous?"

"Delusional. And I sincerely hope you get the help you so desperately need."

"Why else would you be with McKinnon, huh? You couldn't stand that guy when we were together."

"My relationship with Brody is none of your business."

"Listen, babe, we both know that I'm the one you want."

"*You*," I emphasize, "are the last person I want."

"Whatever you say." He walks toward the crowd of people on the pathway. "Whenever you're ready to stop playing games, just shoot me a text."

"Don't hold your breath!" I shout.

He gives me a little wink and disappears into the crowd.

Chapter Fourteen

NATALIE

Two weeks before Christmas last year, my dad dropped the bomb that he was leaving my mother. After twenty-something years of marriage, he was walking away. I still remember coming home from college and finding my mom sitting in the living room, looking shell-shocked. She's the one who told me that my father was upstairs packing his bags.

He'd fallen in love with another woman. Life, he'd said by way of explanation, was too short not to be happy and if he didn't seize this opportunity while he still had the chance, he'd regret it for the rest of his life.

When Mom brought up the possibility of counseling, he told her his mind was already made up, and he wasn't interested in trying to fix the problems. He just wanted to be free to live his life.

I have no idea if he realized that when he walked away from my mother, it felt like he was walking away from me as well. I may have been twenty-one years old, but their separation cut me to the bone.

For the last nine months, I've avoided all contact with Dad. I've been so angry that he blew our world apart. And it's not that I'm any less mad, but I've decided that maybe it's time for us to sit down and talk. I'm not sure if we'll be able to resolve anything today, but I have to try.

Since I'm the first to arrive at the restaurant we chose to meet at, the hostess shows me to a table. This is the first time I've agreed to meet with him, so you'd think he'd be on time. He's not. Already it feels like we're getting off on the wrong foot.

After he walked out, Mom was a mess. She'd been a stay-at-home mom for twenty years. All of a sudden, she needed to rejoin the work-force and find a way to support herself. It took months for her to pull herself together, but she did it. I came home every weekend so that she wouldn't be alone in the house. A friend of hers, who owns a real estate company, talked Mom into taking a real estate class so she could get her license. Once she immersed herself in the course and helped out with a few open houses, she realized just how much she enjoyed selling real estate. It's been great for her self-esteem.

Taking a sip of water, I glance at my phone, feeling annoyed that Dad still isn't here. Ten minutes late and counting. If he really wanted to sit down and work things out, he'd make an effort to be on time. I have too much going on to sit around waiting for him to show up.

I'm giving it five minutes.

If he's still not here, I'm leaving.

Just as I start to gather up my purse and phone, I see Dad walk into the restaurant. He glances around the dining room, and I raise my hand in a half-hearted wave. Even though this is my father and we enjoyed a close relationship before he left, I'm still nervous. He smiles and moves in my direction.

"Hi, sweetheart," he says. "Sorry about being late, I got held up in traffic."

I stand, and he takes me in his arms. I can't help but notice that he's wearing a different cologne than he used to. As we break apart, my eyes slide over him.

He's wearing...jeans.

Not only are they fitted, but they're distressed as well.

I can't remember the last time I saw Dad in jeans. He's always dressed in a suit or Dockers during the week and sweatpants and T-shirts on the weekends. As he slips out of his leather jacket—another article of clothing I don't recognize—I notice he's wearing a patterned button-down with the sleeves rolled up.

It's like I'm sitting with a stranger. He doesn't look like the man I remember.

Not knowing what to say, I blurt, "You look different."

Instead of taking offense, he smiles. "New haircut."

Now that he's mentioned it...His hair is cut much shorter on the sides and is spiked with product in front.

I wave a hand toward the rest of him. "Your whole look is different." I try to keep the accusation out of my voice, but it's difficult. Dad spent twenty years dressing the same way and now he looks like some old guy pretending to be younger than what he is.

I can just imagine whose idea the haircut and clothes were.

He shrugs like it's no big deal. "Seemed like it was time to freshen up the wardrobe. Out with the old and in with the new."

A pang shoots through me.

Am I part of the old that needed to be thrown out? Whether he realizes it or not, that's the way it feels.

"You look nice, Dad," I say because I don't feel like I can share my true feelings with him. That it looks like he's trying too hard to be something he's not.

"Thanks." He looks sheepish. "I haven't worn jeans since college. It's taken a little getting used to."

"Then why are you wearing them?"

He shrugs and picks up the menu the hostess left on the table for us to peruse. "Just trying something new. Trying to get out of my comfort zone."

I nod, but don't say anything further.

He asks how school is going and what my plans are for after college. He tells me about his new apartment and that he'd like me to stop by sometime and check it out. I make the appropriate noises but remain noncommittal about it. Seeing his place would make the divorce more real, and I'm not sure if I'm ready for that yet.

Once the waitress stops by to take our order, it seems like we've run the gamut of superficial pleasantries. Silence falls over us.

Dad clears his throat. "I'm glad you agreed to meet me. I've been wanting to sit down and talk to you for a while now." There's a hint of reproach in his eyes. "We shouldn't have gone this long without communicating." When I don't respond, he sighs and pushes onward. "I know the divorce hasn't been easy for you, and I'm sorry for that. It was never my intention to hurt you."

I want to laugh. Or cry. My heart feels like it's beating a painful tattoo on my ribcage. Is he really naïve enough to believe that his leaving wouldn't affect me? That I was going to be ambivalent to my parents breaking up just because I'm twenty-one years old and out of the house? Honestly, it didn't make a damn bit of difference. Having your parents split up at any age sucks. It turns your whole world upside down.

"We've drifted apart over the last nine months, and I want to fix that. What happened between your mother and me had nothing to do with you." His eyes search mine. "We both love you more than anything."

"I know, Dad."

He reaches across the table and squeezes my fingers.

"I don't want to lose you, Nat. No matter how old you get, you'll always be my little girl."

Those words are like a much-needed balm for my soul.

I lick my lips, unsure if I should ask the one question that has been pounding through my head. "Now that you've had some time apart, do you think there's any chance you and Mom can work things out?"

Sadness washes over his expression. "I don't think so." He shakes his head and sighs. "I'm sorry. I know that's not the answer you wanted to hear."

Tears fill my eyes. I hadn't realized that I'd been holding out hope that they'd find a way back to each other. You hear stories like that all the time. Sometimes people just need some space to work things out in their heads, and then they come back and are better partners because of it.

"I know it feels like the divorce came out of nowhere, but it didn't. Not really. Your mother and I hadn't been happy for years. And it took me a long time to figure out that I didn't want to continue living like that. We were just getting on, day in and day out." He shrugs. "With you away at college, it seemed like my decision to leave would be less impactful. There wouldn't be any custody arrangements to deal with."

"It doesn't matter how old I was," I say quietly. "You walking away hurt."

Pain flashes across his face. His voice turns deep and husky. "I never left you, Nat. Not ever."

"That's what it felt like."

He glances away. "I'm sorry. I knew my decision would affect you, but I'd hoped you would be old enough to understand where I was coming from."

Air leaks from my lungs. "I think it's just going to take time for me to get used to all the changes. It's a lot to deal with."

"I can understand that. I don't want to push you, but I don't want to be iced out of your life either. Can we make a promise from here on out that we'll at least talk on a regular basis? If you're angry about something, tell me."

My lips curl, and I nod. "I can do that."

"Good."

Our dinner arrives, and the conversation once again turns light, which is a relief. There's been enough heaviness for one evening. I need time to digest everything we've discussed.

Every once in a while, his phone dings with a text. He glances at it and types out a quick reply.

"Sorry," he says after the third one.

"It's fine." I assume it's work and don't think much of it.

Once our plates get cleared away, he asks if I want dessert.

Duh. Of course, I do. I haven't changed that much in nine months. "Have you ever known me to turn down dessert?"

"Nope. Never." He chuckles. "Stupid question, right? Dessert has always been your favorite course."

It's totally true.

Once dessert arrives—chocolate lava cake for me and apple pie à la mode for him—it feels like old times. I can *almost* pretend nothing has changed. That our family is still intact.

I might have walked in here dreading this meeting, but I'm happy we did this. I wish I hadn't been so stubborn and agreed to sit down with him months ago to hash out our feelings. Not only have I been mourning the fact that my family is no longer together, but I've been grieving the loss of my dad. After he walked out the door, everything shifted between us.

But maybe now, moving forward, it can be different. Better. We can spend more time together. Next year, who knows where I'll live and how often we'll be able to see one another. It's important that I get our relationship back on track now, while I can still repair it.

I'm still mad and hurt. I haven't completely let go of my anger. But there's nothing I can do about my parents' marriage ending. I love them both. And that will never change no matter what.

Maybe that's what I have to hang on to right now.

Dad forks off a hearty chunk of apple pie and takes a bite. Once he's done, he says, "It means a lot to me that we're moving forward, Nat."

"I'm glad we are, too." I've managed to plow my way through half the lava cake, which is rich, gooey, and utterly delicious.

Taking a breath, he fiddles around with his pie instead of digging in. Right away my antenna goes up. I can tell there's more he wants to say.

Before he has a chance to speak, I cut in. "I'm sorry about freezing you out. I shouldn't have done that." I shrug helplessly. "I just felt so angry with you for leaving the way you did. For not trying to work it out."

"I know," he acknowledges gently. "And I understand. The separation has been hard on all of us, but especially you."

I nod and take a deep breath. We've talked through a lot over dinner. But we haven't discussed everything. We haven't discussed *her*. As difficult as it is to think about, it's a topic that needs to be forced into the light if we're truly going to move forward with our relationship.

"Dad, I—"

At the same time, he says, "Nat, there's someone I want to introduce you to."

My brows draw together as a woman materializes beside our table. "Huh?"

"This is Bridgette." Dad shoots out of his chair and wraps an arm around her waist. She leans her body into his.

Thrown off by the interruption, my eyes bounce between Dad, who looks like he's sweating bullets, and the curvy woman at his side.

"Hi, Natalie. It's so wonderful to finally meet you." Her voice is deep and rich. Sultry.

I blink in confusion. "Hello." Who is this woman? Why is she here at our table?

She beams a smile at Dad, who leans over and kisses her on the lips.

What the hell?

After they break apart, she lowers herself to the chair situated between us.

"Sweetheart," Dad says nervously. "I hope you don't mind that Bridgette stopped by to meet you."

I don't...

Oh.

Ohhhhh.

The chocolate cake I've just eaten feels like it's going to revolt and make an encore appearance. I do my best to tamp down the rising nausea.

So, this is the homewrecking whore. I should have known. She's got a sex kitten vibe to her. I narrow my eyes. There's no way she's more than twenty-eight or twenty-nine years old, and Dad is...

In his late forties.

She's closer to my age than she is to his. She could be his daughter.

Ewww.

I'm totally grossed out.

Unaware of the thoughts rampaging through my brain, Bridgette flashes a big, toothy smile at me. I hate her instantly. All the anger I've felt over the last nine months roars to life again. The sight of her is like waving a red flag in front of a bull.

"I'm so glad you and your dad were able to get together and work this out." She leans toward me, and I'm half afraid she's going to grab hold of my hand. "He's missed you so much. He talks nonstop about you."

Realizing that I'm clutching my fork in a death grip, I carefully set it on my plate and inhale a deep breath, hoping it will calm me. It doesn't.

"Bridgette, is it?" And yes, I damn well know that's her name. It is, unfortunately, singed into my brain for all eternity.

The happiness on her face falters. She nods, and the smile dims in wattage.

I angle my body toward her and say, "I agreed to meet with my dad and talk to him. I have zero interest in talking with the woman who destroyed my parents' marriage."

Her eyes widen before darting to my father as if she's unsure what to do or say. Which is hilarious. *Come on, girlfriend...What'd you expect was going to happen? That you'd waltz in here and the three of us would join hands and sing "Kumbaya"?*

Over my dead and decomposed body.

"Natalie!" Dad says sharply.

Glaring at him, I jerk my thumb toward Bridgette, who is squirming silently on her chair. "Why is she here?"

My father looks thrown by the question. He falters before finding his footing. "I thought it was important for you to meet Bridgette." There's a pause as I wait for the other shoe to drop. "We're getting married."

And there it is.

My mouth falls open. "Are you kidding? Please tell me you're kidding. You can't marry her!" I shake my head, trying to wrap my mind around his words and what they mean. "Oh my God, how old is she?"

Bridgette's face turns a dull red. She looks like she wants to sink right into her chair.

Good. I hope she's humiliated. She deserves it, the homewrecking little slut.

My father pokers up in his chair, his face turning stern. He used to trot out that expression when I was a kid and had done something wrong. Ironic that he's now the one doing something wrong and trying to give it to me.

I don't think so, buddy.

"It doesn't matter what her age is," he says calmly. "What matters is how we feel for one another."

"You can't be serious." Turning toward the interloper, I narrow my eyes. "Are you even thirty?"

Her cheeks pinken even more until she looks as though she's moments away from bursting into flames. I'd rejoice if that were to happen.

"Natalie, I'm appalled by your behavior. I think you owe Bridgette an apology. Maybe we shouldn't have sprung this on you, but I wanted everything out in the open so we could move forward."

For the first time since my dad's fiancée sat down at the table with us, hurt rushes through me like a river. Wetness stings the backs of my eyes, and I blink furiously, not wanting the tears to fall. I'll be damned if I allow either of them to see how upset I am.

Bridgette clears her throat. "I'll be twenty-eight next month. I know the age difference is a bit of a shock, but I want you to know that I love your father." She glances down at her hands, which are twisting in her lap. "We make each other happy, and we want to be together." Her eyes lift to mine again. "I'm sorry that it hurts you."

Precariously close to losing it, I bolt from my chair. "I'm sorry, I can't do this right now," I say hastily.

Both Dad and his fiancée rise from their seats.

"Natalie, please...Let's sit back down and discuss this like rational adults," my father implores.

My hands tremble as I swipe my phone from the table and my purse from the back of the chair. I shake my head. "No, I can't. I have to go."

Not bothering to say goodbye, I rush toward the exit. My dad doesn't try and stop me, which is a relief. I need to get out of here. Away from both of them.

I can't breathe.

After I push out through the doors into the warm evening air, my feet grind to a halt, and I suck in a deep breath. Then close my eyes and try to steady myself.

My apartment building is about a mile from the restaurant. Zara dropped me off earlier this evening. If I called her, she'd be here in a heartbeat. No questions asked. Next to Mom, Zara is the only other person in the world I can count on. But I don't want to do that. I think the walk will do me good. It'll give me some time to clear my head and process what just happened.

"Davies?"

I blink and focus on the guy who has appeared out of nowhere.

Feeling confused, I ask, "What are you doing here?"

I jerk my thumb toward a couple of guys from the team who are behind me. "We're just about to grab dinner." My eyes slide over her with more care. Even though I don't know Natalie all that well, I can tell something's bothering her. She seems off. And pale. "Are you okay?"

Not answering, she bites her lip, and her eyes jerk back to the restaurant.

"Natalie?" I say with a bit more force. This isn't the Natalie Davies I've known since freshman year. That girl is a bruiser and yeah, upon occasion, a real ballbuster. The quiet woman in front of me is nothing more than a paper-thin shadow of her.

She remains silent as a couple of guys pass us on their way inside.

There's no way I'm leaving her out here alone like this. Making a split-second decision, I tell them, "Hey, I'm going to run Natalie home. Just grab dinner without me."

Of course, a few of the assholes otherwise known as my friends can't just say *okay, catch ya back at the house*. They've got to get in a crack or two about me being pussy-whipped.

I roll my eyes.

Give me a break. It's been less than a week.

Ignoring them, I say, "Come on." I nod my head toward the lot. "My truck is parked over there. I'll take you back to your apartment."

Looking a little more like herself, she waves me away. "Go have dinner with your friends. It's not that far of a walk. I'll be fine."

The sun is just beginning to dip beneath the horizon. Sure, it'll be a while before it's dark out, but so what? I'm still not letting her walk home alone. She may not know this about me, but I can play the part of a gentleman pretty well.

"I'm sure you would be," I say. "But there's obviously something wrong, and I'd like to know what it is." Before she gets it in her head that arguing with me will do any good, I add, "I'm not taking no for an answer. We can stand here all night and discuss it, sweetheart. It's up to you."

She sucks in a sharp breath and slowly releases it. "Don't you think you're taking this fake-boyfriend thing a bit too far?"

I chuckle because it sounds like she's on the verge of relenting. Which, quite honestly, is very un-Natalie-like. My girl over here loves to get into it with me. That only reinforces my suspicions that whatever's bothering her is a big deal. "It's good practice for the real thing, right?" I give her a wink and the tension radiating off her in thick, heavy waves dissipates.

We fall in line together as we walk toward the truck. I open the passenger side door and make a grand sweeping gesture with my arm. "Your chariot awaits, madam."

She snorts and slides inside without a word. I close the door and circle around to the driver's side.

"Since when do chariots cost more than forty grand?" she asks as I turn the key and start the engine.

I shrug. "Dunno. Inflation?"

The edges of her lips pull up, and she settles onto the leather with a deep sigh as if she's bone weary.

Once we're both fastened in, I pull the truck out of the lot. When she remains silent, staring contemplatively out the window, I ask, "Are you going to tell me what happened or do you want to play a game of twenty questions?" When she doesn't immediately respond, I add, "I'll have you know that it usually only takes ten questions before I'm able to guess correctly."

Natalie rolls her head toward me. She looks a little unsure and a lot exhausted. "You really want to know?"

Electricity zips through the air as our gazes connect. My teasing tone falls away. "I wouldn't ask if I didn't."

She pulls her eyes from mine and focuses straight ahead. "My parents separated nine months ago. I met with my father at the restaurant for the first time since he walked out."

"I'm sorry to hear that." No wonder she looks upset. "It didn't go the way you thought it would?" Hearing this makes me realize just how little I know about Natalie on a personal level. It also makes me realize that I want to dig beneath the surface and get to know her better.

Her expression turns to one of sadness. "Not at all."

"What happened?" I have no idea if she wants to talk about it. I just know that I want to make her feel better.

Natalie chuckles, but the sound is scraped raw and full of pain. It makes me ache for her. "She showed up halfway through dessert."

My brows pull together in confusion. I feel like I missed something in the conversation. "Who?"

"His girlfriend," she bites out. "Actually, I was informed over dessert that the happy couple is now engaged to be married. Which is interesting because the divorce hasn't been finalized yet."

I let out a long, low whistle. "Shit, Davies. That sucks."

"Yeah, it really does." Looking deflated, she says, "We've texted a few times since he left, but I've been so angry about everything. This was the first time I'd agreed to sit down and talk about the divorce with him. I was hoping we could move forward."

I don't say a word. I just let Natalie talk.

"We make it through dinner and everything starts to feel normal again." She glances at me. "It was nice. And then he ambushes me. Suddenly there she is, standing at the table, smiling at me like some kind of lunatic."

I grimace at the picture she paints. "What'd you do?"

Her eyes dart to mine, and she whispers, "I lost it."

"Lost it like you leaped across the table and tackled her to the ground?"

The edges of her lips lift. "No. But I would have loved to do that."

I nod my head. "Yeah, I could see it happening. Chaos breaks out and the waitstaff has to pry you off her."

"Oh, come on." She chuckles and swats at my arm. "You could seriously see me doing that?"

"Hell, yeah." I glance at her again as we continue toward her apartment. "Don't forget that I saw you deck Nick Jacobs last year at a party."

She covers her face with her hands. "Oh God, I forgot about that."

"I think about it every time I see you." I refrain from adding what a turn-on it is to see a girl who can take care of business when it's called for. "So, if you didn't tackle her to the ground, what'd you do?"

She huffs out a breath and shakes her head. "I don't even remember. Honestly, it's all a blur. I think I might have called her a homewrecker. Or something to that effect, anyway."

"Oh, shit."

"Yeah..." She sighs. "My dad wasn't too happy."

"I can't imagine that he was."

"Did I mention that Bridgette—that's her name by the way—is only twenty-seven?"

Wanting to offer comfort, I reach out with my free hand and lay it on top of hers before giving her fingers a gentle squeeze. I'm not sure what else to do. Her eyes lock on mine as if she's surprised by the gesture. When she doesn't slip them free, it feels like we might just be making progress.

"I'm sorry, Davies. The situation sucks all the way around."

"Yeah, it does." She's silent for a beat. "These last nine months have been difficult. Even though I've been angry with him, I've still missed having him around...if that makes sense."

I get it. "He's your dad. Of course, it makes sense."

"I guess I was hoping we could," she shrugs, "I don't know...get back to where we were before he walked out."

"You could still do that," I say quietly.

Her expression hardens and her body tenses. "No, I can't." Looking resolute, she shakes her head. "I'm more pissed now than I was before, if you can believe that. Coming face-to-face with that woman, knowing she's the one who broke up their marriage...I honestly don't know what he was thinking when he invited her to join us."

"I don't know, Davies. Maybe he just wanted you guys to be okay with each other," I suggest. I'm grasping at straws.

"Well, that's definitely not going to happen in this lifetime. He made his choice." Natalie's voice breaks. "And it wasn't me."

I clench her fingers, wishing there was more I could do. "Maybe you just need to give it time."

Not saying a word, she stares out the window.

Just as we're pulling into the parking lot of her building, I realize that I don't want to let her go. Impulsively, I ask, "You want to go somewhere?"

Her expression immediately turns suspicious.

I can't resist the chuckle that escapes. "I'm not going to take you back to my house, okay? Sheesh."

She bites down on her lip looking as though she's trying to rein in a smile. "What do you have in mind?"

"You'll see." Considering how upset she is, an almost-there smile seems like a small victory. "Grab a jacket and let's go."

Her brows draw together, and I see the questions swirling in her eyes. Before she can ask them, I say, "It's a surprise, Davies. Just grab a jacket and you'll find out soon enough."

In a shocking turn of events, she does exactly as I say. Guess there's a first time for everything. Of course, I'm smart enough *not* to mention that to Natalie.

Fifteen minutes later we pull into the city ice arena parking lot. This is the place where I first started out playing Mini-Mites when I was four years old. I hope it'll take her mind off what's bothering her, if only for a little while.

"You brought me to a skating rink?" She shoots me a skeptical look as we exit the truck.

"Yep."

Confused, she asks, "So...what are we going to do here?"

I grab hold of her fingers and tug her along when she stops and stares at the huge white building. "We're going to do a little something called skating. Maybe you've heard of it before?"

"You're hilarious."

"I try." Especially around her. "We're strapping blades on your feet, and I'm taking you out on the ice." I raise a brow in challenge. "Do you know how to skate, Davies?"

"I took a few lessons." She pauses and adds, "When I was seven."

"Then you'll be fine. It's just like riding a bike."

"Yeah, I'm thinking it might be a bit harder than that. I seem to remember falling on my ass quite a bit."

With our hands clasped, I tow her through the automatic doors and into the arena. We head toward the rental booth and grab two pairs of skates. Then we move to a bench outside the rink so we can change. When we're both laced up, I stand and hold out my hand for her to take. There's something strangely natural about having her smaller one ensconced in mine.

I like it.

And I like her.

There are three rinks with full sheets of ice at the arena. One of the rinks has open skate for the next two hours. The metal door leading to the ice is open. I step out first and turn to Natalie. "You ready?"

She sucks in a lungful of cold air and nods. This time, she reaches for me. I steady her as she finds her bearings on the slippery sheet. When she doesn't immediately fall, a smile blooms across her face. Her eyes seek out mine.

"See? Easy as pie," I say.

"We'll see."

The first time around, we take it slow. A couple of kids who can't be more than eight years old whiz past us. Natalie is stiff, her body too upright. Every time she tips too far in one direction or digs the toe pick into the ice, she throws her arms out wide in an attempt to regain her balance. The second time around, she loosens up and we gain some speed. She finds her rhythm, alternating between pushing off and gliding. By the time we hit our third lap, we're moving at a good clip. The eight-year-olds are still passing us, but that's okay. Natalie's not as tense and awkward. Her cheeks are rosy from the cold and a huge smile lights up her face.

From day one, I thought she was beautiful. When she smiles like that, she's absolutely stunning.

And knowing that I'm the one who put it there makes it all the more better.

Chapter Sixteen

BRODY

I hoist a beer to my lips and glance around the room searching for Natalie, but I don't see her anywhere in the thick crowd. Before I dropped her off at her apartment the other night, I talked her into meeting me at the Kappa party. I figured it would be a good place to start our publicity tour.

We had a great time ice skating at the rink. At least I did. And if the perma-smile plastered across Natalie's face was any indication, so did she. I was just happy to take her mind off what had happened with her father.

Am I hoping something has shifted between us? Of course, I am. We actually conversed while skating without her taking my head off. And you know what? I like Natalie. I like being with her. I like her sense of humor. It only makes me more antsy to see her again. Which is definitely a first for me. Instead of fighting the feeling, I pull out my cell and fire off a text.

Where r u?

I stare at the phone in my palm, willing her to respond. Five minutes later, my hard work pays off.

Not there

Even though she can't see me do it, I roll my eyes.

Why does she have to be such a smartass?

Bigger question—why do I find that trait so freaking attractive?

Yes, I c that. When r u getting here? I miss my fake girlfriend. Having a hard time fighting off the chicks...

eyeroll that sounds terrible for u

It is

Wasn't in the mood 2 go out 2nite

Davies...

McKinnon...

All right. This isn't getting me anywhere, so I'm pulling rank. Not that I have any to pull, but whatever.

U have ten min 2 get ur arse here or I'm coming 2 find u

Good luck with that

I'm totally serious, Davies

No response...

"Brody!" a high-pitched voice squeals, interrupting my back-and-forth with Natalie. "I've missed you soooooo much."

A raven-haired girl with red-slicked lips and matching talons stares up at me as she strokes her hands over my chest. She has long, straight hair that hangs down her back and a slender body that is showcased in a tight, low-cut shirt and even tighter skinny jeans.

"I haven't seen you in so long!"

She looks familiar, but her name eludes me. There's only one chick on my mind tonight, and this isn't the one.

"Hey, how you doing?"

"Cassandra," she supplies when I don't say her name.

I nod. "Right. Cassandra. Got it."

When she tries snuggling against me, I gently, but firmly pry her hands off me. Whatever this girl is looking for, she's not going to get it from me.

Her brows wing up in disbelief. "So, the rumors are true? You have a girlfriend?"

"Yup. Totally true. I'm a taken man," I add in case she doesn't take the hint.

She pouts. "That's too bad." Her fingers go to the round scoop neck of her shirt and trail leisurely over the edge, which lies against the creamy skin of her chest.

I raise a brow.

Such an obvious ploy. I'm onto you, girl. Trying to get me to check out your tits by drawing my eyes there...Not happening today.

Her lips curve into a sly smile. "I won't tell if you don't," she whispers huskily.

I shake my head. "Sorry, if I wanted to fool around with other chicks, I wouldn't be in a relationship." I give her a penetrating look. "I'm sure you can appreciate that."

She sighs. "Natalie is a lucky girl."

I give her a little wink. "You be sure to tell her that the next time you see her."

"I will."

I chuckle at the image of Natalie flipping her lid if people actually start telling her how lucky she is to be dating me.

Just as I'm trying to come up with an exit strategy, I spot Luke coming through the front door. He and Zara have been attached at the hip lately, so I hope Natalie is with them.

"If you'll excuse me, there's someone I need to talk to."

"Okay," she says wistfully. "Bye, Brody."

I give her a wave and take off. I don't have to push and shove my way over to them. The crowd parts as I move through it. Once I reach Luke and Zara, I'm disappointed to see that Natalie's not with them.

Damnation, that girl vexes me.

"Where's your roommate?" I ask Zara.

"Well, hello to you too, Brody," she says in greeting. "Always nice to see you."

I raise a brow and wait impatiently for an answer. "I thought Davies would be with you."

Zara shakes her head as Luke slips an arm around her and pulls her close. "She needed some time to herself."

What does that mean? "So, she's at your place?"

Because if she is, then that's exactly where I'll be heading. My threat wasn't an idle one. I'm going to find that girl if it's the last thing I do.

"No." She bites her lip and glances at Luke. "I think she just wants to chill by herself. It's been kind of a shitty week for her."

Zara's giving me the runaround, and I don't like it one bit. I want to know where Natalie is. "If she's not here or at your apartment, where the heck is she?"

Not taking kindly to my tone, Zara narrows her eyes. She may be tiny and sprite-like, but she's an ass-kicker. It's not difficult to understand why she and Natalie are such good friends. They both subscribe to a take-no-prisoners mentality. "Why do you want to know?"

I shrug, trying to reel in my impatience. "We made plans. She's supposed to be here."

When she doesn't say anything, I glance at Luke for support.

He grins at his girlfriend. "Come on, babe, just tell him where she is. Otherwise, he's going to hound you all night. You really want that?"

Zara sighs. Annoyance is written across every line of her face. "I dropped her off at her mother's house a couple of hours ago, okay?" She rolls her eyes. "She's staying there for the weekend."

Something instantly loosens within me at the information.

"Thanks." I head for the door.

"You're not going over there, are you, Brody?" she calls after me.

I turn and flash her a grin. "Of course, I am."

This has officially been the week from hell.

It kicked off with Reed and his lousy-lay comments. Then it got worse when Brody told the world-at-large that we're now an item, which led to some pretty odd behavior from other students on campus. Not that I didn't enjoy my free caramel mocha, but it's definitely weird. I avoided Java House on Thursday and Friday, instead bringing a thermos of crappy coffee from home. In no way did it feed the need for my usual morning caffeine fix. It was so terrible, I could barely choke it down.

By the end of the week, I'd started wearing a ballcap low over my eyes so I would be less recognizable. That's ridiculous, right? I shouldn't have to live this way. I'm not famous or noteworthy. These people don't give a crap about me. They care about who I'm dating. Well, let's be real...fake-dating. I'm *fake-dating* Brody McKinnon.

Then there's the situation with my dad...

And his twenty-seven-year-old fiancée.

Ugh.

Come Friday afternoon, I'd reached my limit. Even though I was supposed to meet up with Brody at some off-campus Greek party so we could pretend to be enjoying blissful coupledom, I don't think I can plaster one more fake smile on my face. My quota for the week has been filled.

I'm done. Fed up.

Is it terrible that I hoped Brody would get mobbed by his adoring public at the party and forget all about me? Yeah, that didn't happen. Instead, he messaged me, demanding I haul ass over there or he'd come find me.

I chuckle.

Good luck with that, buddy. He can scour campus all he wants. He won't find me.

Zara dropped me off earlier this afternoon at my mom's house, which is about forty minutes away from school in a neighboring town. As soon as I'd pushed open the front door, I knew I'd made the right decision in heading home for the weekend. I need some time to chill and regroup.

Because this was an impromptu trip home, Mom wasn't able to be here when I arrived. She just got home about forty-five minutes ago from showing a house. I offered to make dinner, but she insisted on stopping at the store on the way home from work to pick up the ingredients for stroganoff, which is my favorite.

We're talking ultimate comfort food. Which is exactly what's required at a time like this.

Now that she's home and cooking dinner, we've migrated to the kitchen. I sit at the island, watching her slice a chunk of beef into thin strips before dredging them in flour and frying them up in garlic and butter. The aroma is dizzying. God, but I miss Mom's cooking while I'm at school.

Mom catches me staring and shoots me a smile as she continues prepping dinner. "This is such an unexpected surprise. I'm glad you decided to come home. It's been a couple of weeks since I've seen you."

Even though Whitmore isn't far away, I'm busy with school and Mom is busy building her career. We don't see each other as often as we'd like. That's why both of us appreciate this chance to spend some time together.

I nod, feeling the same. It's good to be here. "I needed a break from campus."

She flips the meat over in the pan and asks, "Everything okay?"

I shrug. "It's fine."

Her brows slide together. "Is there anything you want to talk about?"

There's no way I'm sharing all of this drama with her.

How cringe-worthy would that be?

Remember my ex-boyfriend, Reed? Yeah, well, he decided to announce at a party that I'm a lousy lay.

If I know Mom, she'd probably drive to Whitmore just to wring his neck. She has the tendency to be a bit of a mama bear when she feels someone is attacking me. Plus, she was never very high on him in the first place. I chalked it up to the divorce, which was so fresh at the time, but her instincts were spot-on. More so than mine were. The thought of her confronting Reed is almost enough to make me smile. "Nope. Just wanted to spend a little time with my mom."

"Aww, that's sweet. You know how much I love having you around."

Sometimes I feel guilty for living on campus when Mom is here all by herself. I offered to stay at the house and commute to school, but she was firm in her decision that I needed to live my own life and not worry about her.

But I still worry. I hate the idea of her coming home to an empty house at the end of a long day.

Now feels like a good time to change the subject. "How's work going?"

She transfers half the meat to a plate in order to fry up the rest. "It's going really well. I have a couple who is going to make an offer on their first home tomorrow, so that's exciting. I need to meet them at the property at ten so they can take one more look around and then we're going to write up the offer." She glances at me. "Maybe after that we can go out for lunch?"

I nod and take a sip of my water. "Yeah. That sounds like a plan."

She smiles. "Great."

As my mom and I continue chatting, all of the tension that had been filling me drains from my body. My shoulders no longer feel like they're up around my ears. It only makes me realize how much stress I've been holding inside.

I'm not sure if I can deal with another week of feeling like I'm living under a microscope. How long do I have to wait until I'm able to extract myself from this relationship? A week? Two? More?

Oh, God...

That sounds excruciating.

"Are you sure nothing's going on? Because I get the feeling you're not telling me something." She waves the kitchen tongs in my direction. "Your forehead is all scrunched up."

It takes some effort to smooth out my features.

It shouldn't surprise me that she's picking up on my mood. She's always had some kind of weird parental radar where I'm concerned. It was frustratingly annoying when I was a teenager and trying to slip things past her.

Which, trust me, didn't happen very often.

As tempted as I am to spill my guts, my recent developments aren't something I can share with her. "Nope. It's all good."

Hands going to her hips, she pins me in place with her gaze until I squirm on my stool. "Natalie Marie, I know when something's bothering you. Do us both a favor and spit it out."

In this kind of situation, deflection can be your friend. "Why do you think something's going on?"

She tilts her head and studies me for a moment. "Because I know you and can see it in your face. You looked stressed. And you're quieter than usual, more introspective. You know I hate when you keep things from me." She shoots me a look. "It makes me worry more than I probably should. So how about you just put me out of my misery and tell me what's going on?"

Now that the stroganoff is simmering on the stove, she takes a seat next to me. Her gaze combs over me with even more intensity. It won't take much prodding for her to break me.

When I don't respond, she asks, "Does this have anything to do with the dinner you and your dad had a couple of days ago?"

That's not a situation I want to discuss with her. Mom is still in a fragile state. In less than a year, her entire world has been turned upside down. Telling her about Dad's engagement will only hurt her, and I don't want to do that.

I focus my attention on a swirl of color in the tan granite and mumble, "No, dinner was fine."

"Really?"

I shrug and keep it vague. "Yep."

She sighs. "Natalie, you can be truthful with me."

My eyes dart to her, and she arches a brow. Not only does she sound skeptical, her face is full of it. Like she doesn't believe one word coming out of my mouth. And I hate that. Because I'm an only child, Mom and I have always been close.

"I am."

Almost gently she says, "Your dad called me yesterday and told me about his engagement."

My eyes widen. "He did?" I'm so shocked by this information that I feel like I'm going to fall right off my stool. I had no idea they were still in contact.

She nods. "He said you were pretty upset about it. That you walked out of the restaurant."

The air hisses from my lungs. "You guys aren't even divorced yet and he's already asking someone else to marry him?" Even thinking about it pisses me off. "Who does that?"

She reaches over and rubs my arm. "The paperwork has been filed, Natalie. It's going to happen, and you need to make your peace with it."

This conversation hurts my heart. It also strikes me as odd that I'm more upset about their divorce than either one of my parents are. I was afraid that Mom would be devastated when she found out about the engagement. I take a closer look at her. She certainly doesn't seem upset.

"I just didn't expect him to move on so quickly." My lip curls with disgust. "And with *her*, no less."

"I know. And I understand you're still hurt and angry. But this is what your father wants." She pulls her hand away from me and folds both of them in her lap before sitting up straighter. "I don't want to be with a man who doesn't want to be married to me."

"Mom..."

"I'm fine," she says quickly. "I really am. I found a career that I enjoy and I'm taking better care of myself. I haven't done that for a long time. And," she pauses, "I've started dating again."

I blink, shocked by her announcement.

"You're dating?" I wasn't expecting this at all. Of course, I want her to be happy. I don't want her sitting home alone on a Friday night, drowning her sorrows in a bottle of pinot grigio. At some point, I fully expected her to get back out there again.

Just not yet.

She nods. A smile simmers on her lips. "In fact, I had plans to go out tonight."

"You cancelled your date? Why?"

"I'd rather spend time with you. I thought we could rent a movie, maybe do a little spa night." She wiggles her brows. "I have a new charcoal face mask I want to try out. We can do mani pedis on each other. All the stuff we used to do."

"That sounds great, Mom." I chew my lower lip, feeling guilty that I'm getting in the way of her budding social life. When I decided to come home, it never occurred to me that she might have plans. I run a hand over my face. I'm not ready for this. Dad is engaged and Mom is dating. "I don't want you cancelling your date for me. We can always watch a movie and do a spa night tomorrow."

"I don't mind." Growing more serious, she says, "You come first. Always."

One side of my mouth hitches. She doesn't have to tell me that. "I know. But still, don't cancel your date. I'm pretty tired and was planning to hit the sack early."

Uncertainty flickers across her face. "Are you sure?"

"Positive." Reaching over, I give her fingers a little squeeze and search her face. "You seem a lot more Zen. I was afraid to tell you about Dad and Bridgette. I was worried that it might push you over the edge."

Like it did me.

Her expression turns thoughtful. "I haven't mentioned it before, but I've been working with a therapist for about a month, and it's really helped me to see things with more clarity. Our marriage didn't just fall apart overnight. It had been slowly eroding for years, and I chose not to repair it." She searches my eyes and adds, "He may have been the one who walked away, but I'm not sure I blame him for that anymore. I think he did us both a favor."

Her admission catches me completely off guard. I've always blamed my father for leaving. Not once did I ever think she brought this on. He fell in love with someone else and left us. I'm happy for her and glad she's moving on, but I'm not at that point yet.

And I'm not sure when I'll get there either.

"I've also started practicing yoga and meditation."

When I just stare, she cracks a smile. I'm having a difficult time imagining her meditating. Or doing the downward dog.

"In fact, there's a seven o'clock class tomorrow morning." Her smile widens. "You're welcome to join me."

"That sounds interesting, but I'm going to take a hard pass on that. I plan on sleeping in until at least ten."

She shrugs. "Maybe another time."

"Definitely." I've avoided yoga like the plague. I like high-energy cardio like kickboxing and Zumba. The thought of sitting quietly and holding poses doesn't appeal to me. Although, for Mom, I'd give it a try.

"You know, I wouldn't have thought that yoga and something as simple as meditation could help so much, but it does. I feel so much better when I'm finished. More centered. Like I'm letting go of all the anger and sadness that has been weighing me down and focusing on the future and all the positives in my life."

I blink. This woman is seriously starting to scare me. "You sound like a hippie."

Not taking offense, she chuckles. "I'm starting to think that hippies might be onto something. What I've learned through this experience is that you can't hold onto anger. It'll eat you alive if you do."

My mom is blowing my mind with all this insight, and I'm not sure how to feel about it. Both of my parents are morphing into people I no longer recognize.

"I know you're angry with your father, but he loves you. Even though a lot in our lives has changed, that's one thing that never will. Don't cling to the past, Natalie. Nothing good ever comes from it."

I glance down again at the swirling pattern in the granite countertop and sigh. "I don't know, Mom." When she opens her mouth to argue, I cut her off. "I'll give it some thought." Maybe.

"Good. I hate to see you so upset." Her eyes search mine. "Are you sure you don't want me to change my plans? I don't mind. I'm totally up for a girls' night."

"No." I shake my head. "I'll be fine. Maybe some time alone to think about everything will do me some good."

"It certainly can't hurt."

Thirty minutes later, we've finished dinner and are cleaning up the kitchen when the doorbell rings.

"Why don't you get that while I load up the dishwasher," Mom says.

I pad on stocking feet to the entryway and open the front door.

My eyes widen at the sight that greets me. "What are you doing here?"

Her response makes me grin. Which I'm sure she doesn't appreciate. I'd be lying if I didn't admit this is precisely the reaction I was expecting. Although, given the time we spent together the other night, I'd hoped for a warmer reception.

Guess not.

Looks like I'm back to square one with this girl.

I throw my arms wide. "Now, is that any way to greet your boyfriend?"

"Fake boyfriend," Natalie fires back.

When she doesn't invite me in, I angle my body against the doorframe. "You stopped answering my texts. Don't you know that it's girlfriend etiquette 101 to respond immediately to all calls and texts?" I reach out and casually flick the tip of her nose.

Eyebrows lowering, she bats my hand away like it's a pesky fly. "And you didn't take that as a hint? Most guys would."

I place a hand over my heart and give her my best wounded stare. "Ouch. That hurts."

"Doubtful." She slowly runs her tongue across the front of her teeth. "How did you find me?"

I grin and say lazily, "It wasn't all that difficult. I can be fairly resourceful when I need to be."

Her expression flattens as she crosses her arms over her chest. The cottony material of her shirt stretches taut, emphasizing the roundness of her breasts rather nicely. My eyes drop momentarily.

Natalie clears her throat, and my eyes jerk to hers. A slight blush stings her cheeks. Her fingers grip the door as she drags it shut. "Well, it was great seeing you. Thanks for stopping by."

I flatten my hand against the wood as she closes it in my face. "What? You're not going to invite me in after I came all this way to see you?"

"Nope." There's not even a drop of hesitation in her voice.

"Natalie? Who's at the door?"

A tall, slender woman with a medium-length, dark bob walks out of the kitchen with a dishcloth in her hand. A smile touches her lips when she sees me loitering in the doorway.

"Hello." Curiosity fills her eyes as they slide from mine to Natalie. Because there's such a striking resemblance between the two women, I'm guessing this must be her mother.

When Natalie remains stoically silent, the older woman asks, "Is this a friend of yours from school?"

"No," Natalie bites off. Her face tightens as she gives me the evil eye.

If I were more adept at reading subliminal messages, I'd have to wager that Natalie wants me to say that my unannounced appearance on her doorstep is a mistake. Wrong house or something along those lines.

Now, am I going to let Natalie off the hook and invent some cocka-mamie excuse before slinking back to my truck?

Hell, no.

This situation is much too tempting for me to resist.

"Actually, I'm the boyfriend." I give Natalie's mom my most charming smile.

Not only do Natalie's eyes widen to the point of looking like they might fall out of her head, but she squeaks out some unintelligible response that I can't make heads or tails of.

Pushing past my slack-jawed girlfriend, I thrust my hand toward the older woman. She looks equally shocked by what I've just revealed. "Brody McKinnon. Nice to meet you, ma'am." Of course, I'm going to trot out my best manners.

"Karen," she says, still looking surprised. "Natalie's mother." Her brow furrows. "Brody McKinnon?" She slants a questioning look at her daughter before her gaze pins mine again. "The same Brody McKinnon who plays hockey at Whitmore?"

I give her a full-wattage grin that makes my dimples flash. Besides Natalie, I haven't met a woman who doesn't go all soft and gooey at the sight of them. Hopefully, that's not a family trait. I want this woman to like me. "Yup, that's me."

Karen blinks a few times like she's trying to play mental catch-up. "And you're going out with Natalie?" She says this as if it can't possibly be true.

A chuckle slips out, and I sling an arm around Natalie, tugging her close. "Sure am."

"Well, that's very strange because Natalie hasn't mentioned a word about it. How long has this been going on?"

Natalie gives me a well-honed death stare—one that nearly shrivels my balls—and grits, "It's more of a recent development."

If the look on Natalie's face is any indication, I'm going to pay dearly for letting the cat out of the bag. Knowing this, I still can't bring myself to regret my decision to seek her out. It's not like I didn't give her ample warning about what would happen if she didn't get her ass to that party. So really, she only has herself to blame for this.

What can I say?

You mess with the bull, you get the horns.

And yet, somehow, I know that I'm the one who'll end up being gored.

Instead of trying to smooth things over, I dump more gasoline on the fire by adding, "But it's been a long time in the making. Right, sweetheart?"

She snakes her arm around me and sinks her fingers into my flesh, pinching me. Thank God, she's not one of those girls with manicured talons. Hers always look bitten to the quick. She'd probably be drawing blood if that weren't the case.

"Oh, I don't know if that's true, sugar-booger." She bats her lashes, and my chest shakes with ill-concealed mirth. "It seems like I told you where to shove it just last week."

She pinches me again, and I wince, keeping the smile firmly plastered across my face. "I suppose that's the beauty of love. You lose all sense of time."

Natalie bares her teeth as she agrees with the sappy sentiment.

I almost forget about Karen watching us until she murmurs, "Right." Although it comes out sounding more like *riiiiiiight*.

Karen's eyes bounce between us. I can't tell if she's buying this or not. If she's anything like her daughter, probably not.

"Why don't you invite your boyfriend in, Natalie. I'd like to get to know him a little better." Her eyes settle on me. I don't miss the assessing manner in them. "Have you eaten dinner already, Brody?"

I pat my flat belly. "I can always eat again." I make it a policy to never turn down a homecooked meal. Those are few and far in-between.

The tension fades from Karen's dark eyes, and she smiles. "I made Natalie's favorite tonight. Beef stroganoff."

"What a coincidence! That just so happens to be one of my favorites, too." I look adoringly down at Natalie, who is still wrapped in my arm. I'm surprised she hasn't stomped on my foot yet. "See how much we have in common, muffin? It's like we're a match made in heaven."

"Or hell," she grumbles under her breath so that her mother doesn't hear.

"Semantics," I agree jovially.

Together we walk into the kitchen. Behind her mother's back, Natalie glares and mouths, *I'm going to kill you.* She slashes her finger across her neck to add emphasis.

I grin at her antics. She's adorable all heated up like this. Luke's right—I really do take perverse pleasure in riling her up. It's oddly satisfying.

Her mother bustles around the kitchen, taking containers out of the refrigerator as we both take a seat at the kitchen island. Karen fixes me a plate with noodles and a heaping of meat-drenched sauce and pops it in the microwave. "What can I get you to drink, Brody?"

"Water's fine. Thank you, Mrs. Davies."

She grabs a plastic bottle from the fridge and places it in front of me. "Seeing that you're my daughter's boyfriend—the one I never heard of—you should probably call me Karen." She glances at Natalie and adds, "Don't think for a moment that we won't talk about this tomorrow."

Natalie groans and lays her forehead against the granite of the island.

When the microwave dings, Karen pulls out the plate and sets it in front of me with a fork. "Hope you like it."

"Thank you. And don't worry, I've yet to meet a homecooked meal that I didn't enjoy." Without further ado, I shove the first bite into my mouth. My eyes drift shut as I savor the flavors of garlic, red wine, sour cream, and mushrooms. Using my fork, I point to the plate. "This is delicious."

Karen beams at the compliment. "I'm so glad you like it. There's more where that came from."

"It's seriously amazing. I'm going to have to come home with Natalie more often." I wink at my fake girlfriend. "Right, babe?"

There's just a hint of a vibration that rumbles from her chest. It makes my lips curve.

Karen stands silently on the other side of the island. Her eyes continue to ping-pong between us as if she's trying to solve a puzzle in her head. I keep waiting for her to fire off more questions about our relationship, but she doesn't.

When I've plowed my way through half the plate, she admits, "I'm a little taken aback, Natalie, that you didn't mention you've been seeing someone. You haven't dated anyone seriously since—"

"We all know since who," Natalie says sharply.

That douchebag asshole otherwise known as Reed Collins is who I'm guessing they're talking about. I honestly don't understand how he could have had a girl like Natalie by his side and cheated on her. It defies logic.

Hurt and surprise flash across Karen's face. "You always tell me what's going on."

"Yeah, well..." Natalie trails off, looking uncomfortable.

Remorse pricks at my conscience for putting her in this situation. My intention had been to give Natalie a little crap. I never expected her mother to be hurt by it. Now I feel like an ass.

Natalie sighs. "The only reason I didn't mention it was because the relationship is so new."

Karen shrugs, seeming to accept her daughter's words at face value. "Okay." Her eyes fasten onto mine. "Well, I'm glad you stopped by tonight and that we had the chance to meet."

"Me, too," I say sincerely. "And thanks for dinner. It was great."

"I should probably get ready." Karen glances at her daughter and nibbles her lower lip. "Are you sure you don't want me to stay home? It's not too late for me to cancel."

Natalie shakes her head. "I'll be fine, Mom. I'm going to rent a movie and chill."

Karen's eyes light up. "Maybe Brody can stick around and keep you company while I'm gone."

Natalie looks thrown by the idea. "No, I'm sure he has—"

"I'd love to," I cut in smoothly. This couldn't have worked out more perfectly if I'd planned it myself. "Thanks for suggesting it."

On her way out of the kitchen, Karen calls out, "If you get hungry later on, there's more stroganoff in the fridge. I'm sure Natalie would be happy to fix you another plate."

If her glare is any indication, Natalie isn't pleased by the proposal. The comment muttered under her breath only confirms my suspicions.

"FYI— if you want more, you can fix your own damn plate. Contrary to the crap you just fed my mother, I'm not your little wifey."

"Get my own plate?" I pretend to be affronted and grumble, "Some fake girlfriend you are."

"Emphasis on the fake part. Which, again, begs the question of why you're here." She raises a brow. "At my house." Another pause occurs. "Bothering me." When I don't respond, her voice becomes even more irritated. "So, why are you here, Brody?"

I shrug.

Honestly, when she ditched me, I realized that I didn't want to be at the party without her. Weird, huh? So here I am. At her house. That being said, there's no way I'm going to tell her that. I know exactly how she'll react. And that would be to laugh her ass off before tossing me out on mine.

"We were supposed to make an appearance, remember? And then you went all MIA and wouldn't respond to my texts." That's about as close to the truth as I'm going to get.

She sighs. "I needed a break from all the Brody McKinnon craziness of this week. And I wasn't up for a party tonight. Nowhere in the contract was it stipulated that I was to be at your beck and call twenty-four hours a day, seven days a week."

"Really? 'Cause I thought it was pretty much implied," I quip easily.

"I'm sure you wouldn't understand because you're used to it, but it's been a weird week for me. It feels like I've been living in a fishbowl." She shoots me a look and admits, "I don't know how you do it."

I shrug. "After a while, you get used to it." I've lived in the spotlight for so long that I don't even think about it. Other people staring and pointing doesn't faze me. I don't miss a beat when complete strangers come up and tell me about how much they enjoy watching me or when they regale me with tales of their own hockey-playing days. I barely blink anymore when someone asks me to autograph something. Although I draw the line at body parts. That never leads anywhere good.

Okay, that's not necessarily true. I seem to vaguely recall a threesome that was pretty damn fun that started out with just such a request.

"Maybe I don't want to get used to it," she mutters. "Maybe I like being low-profile."

Most girls enjoy the celebrity status that comes along with dating an athlete. It shouldn't surprise me that Natalie is of a different mindset. She's not like anyone else I've ever met. And the more I discover about her, the more there is to like. "Well, you're no longer low-profile, baby. So, get used to it. Your days of anonymity are long gone."

"Yeah," she sighs, "I've already come to that conclusion." Looking resigned to the situation, she straightens her shoulders and waves her hand. "As you can see, my plan is to kick back for the weekend. I'll be back on campus Sunday night, where I'll resume all fake girlfriend duties. But until then..." her words trail off as she stares expectantly.

I raise my brows. If she wants to get rid of me, she's going to have to do a lot better than that. "No problem. I'm up for chilling out and watching Netflix or something."

She looks less than thrilled with the prospect of having me all to herself. "I thought you were just saying that for my mom's benefit. At least that was the hope I was clinging to."

"Nope, I'm all yours. You, me, and a movie. Maybe some popcorn. We can hang together. Just like an honest-to-goodness couple."

"Wow...that sounds like so much fun," she states flatly.

"See? Now that's the spirit." I have to rein in my smile before adding, "You know what I like about you? How special you make me feel."

Natalie opens her mouth to make some sort of smartass retort when Karen strolls into the kitchen looking all gussied up. She's traded her yoga pants and sweatshirt for a sexy dress and knee-high black boots. She also added a little curl to her hair and applied a bit of makeup.

The woman is a knockout.

Natalie does a double take and frowns. "You look nice." She says this as if she doesn't quite like it and after everything that happened with her father this week, I understand the reservations she has about her parents' social lives.

They're moving on, and she's not ready for it.

Karen smooths the dress with a nervous hand. "You think so?" She does a little turn. "It's not too much, is it?"

Natalie sighs. "No, it's perfect." She smiles as her voice softens. "You look really nice, Mom."

Out of view of her mother, I reach across her lap and squeeze her hand. She glances at me, and I wonder if she'll tug it free. She doesn't. Her fingers stay curled inside of mine.

"So, where's this guy taking you?" Natalie asks, sounding very much like a concerned parent. I don't point this out because it's doubtful my observation would be appreciated. And I'm not ready for her to yank her hand from mine just yet.

"We're driving separately and meeting at a bar downtown. There's a band playing."

"That sounds fun." Again, her tone implies that she doesn't want them having *too* much fun.

A hesitant smile lifts Karen's lips. "I think it will be." She adds, "This is our third date."

"You've been out twice with this guy already?" Natalie raises a brow. "Guess I wasn't the only one keeping secrets."

Her mother's cheeks pinken, and she glances away. "I didn't want to mention anything until I was sure it was going to lead somewhere."

Karen's excuse is a near echo of what Natalie said about our relationship.

"And is it?"

Karen shrugs. "We'll see. He's a nice guy, but I'm taking it slow." She glances at the thin silver watch adorning her wrist. "I should probably get going." She holds her daughter's eyes. "I'll be back in a few hours. Call if you need anything, okay?"

Before Natalie can respond, I say, "Don't worry about a thing, Mrs. D. I'll hold down the fort until you return."

The thinly veiled tension she'd been vibrating with dissipates as a gurgle of laughter falls from her lips. "Thank you, Brody...I think."

I see her to the door, telling her to have a good time. Once it's closed, I turn to Natalie, who has followed me into the foyer. Now I have her all to myself. This is so much better than being at an overcrowded party with a bunch of drunk assholes.

"I like your mom. She's cool." *And hot for being a MILF,* but I keep that part to myself.

Natalie settles her hands on her hips and arches a brow. "You'll hold down the fort, huh?"

"Yup." Before she can kick my ass to the curb, I rub my hands together. "Let's get this movie situation figured out." I head back to the kitchen, leaving her to stare wide-eyed at me. "I think I'm ready for round two of that stroganoff." With a grin, I toss an innocent look over my shoulder. "Want to fix me a plate, wifey?"

I hear her growl and can't resist chuckling.

Chapter Nineteen

NATALIE

I sneak a glance at Brody as we sit on the sectional in the family room. The lights are off, and we've got a movie playing. He's sitting so close that his hard, muscular thigh rests against mine.

It shouldn't be a distraction, but it is.

Had I been thinking about strategy, I would have allowed him to choose his seat first. Then I could have selected a different spot with a ton of space between us. Unfortunately, I plunked myself down and he practically sat on top of me.

Instead of enjoying the movie, I'm intensely aware of the point of contact between us. I don't think I've ever been more conscious of another person in my life. And I hate it. It's the last thing I want or need.

Especially with a guy like Brody.

It's like asking for trouble and being surprised when you get it.

I fled from campus because I needed a little distance from this guy. Somehow, my plan backfired, and now I'm spending the evening alone with him in a dark room. It doesn't make a damn bit of sense.

Then again, nothing has made sense since Brody opened his trap last weekend and told Reed, along with everyone else, that we were an item. My life has been flipped upside down ever since. And I'm not sure how to get it back to the way it was. The way it *should* be. I'm drowning in the deep end over here, and there's no lifeguard on duty.

My phone chimes with a message. Thankful to have something else to focus on besides Brody, I pick it up and glance at the screen.

Ugh.

Hard to believe there's someone else I want to deal with even less than the guy I'm with.

Dad.

He's texted a few times since our dinner went sideways. I haven't bothered responding. What's there to say?

Congratulations?

Go fuck yourself?

I'm partial to the latter. But for now, I'll hold my tongue.

Brody glances my way. "Anything interesting?"

My jaw tightens until it feels like it might shatter. I set the phone facedown on the couch next to me, refusing to text my father back. "Nope."

He raises a brow. "Your pinched expression says otherwise. If I didn't know better, I'd think you were constipated. Normally, I'm the only one who makes you look like that. I feel a little jealous over here." He scratches his chin thoughtfully. "You're not two-timing me with another fake boyfriend, are you?"

Those ridiculous comments dissolve the tension that had bubbled up inside me like a geyser. Even though I don't want to encourage him, the corners of my lips twitch. "I hate to break it to you, but you're not the only one capable of giving me that strained expression."

"Hmmm. Guess I'm going to have to step up my game. I thought we had something special between us."

Good Lord, I don't think I could handle that. I lay my hand on his forearm, which is—I might add—just as muscular as his thigh. *Sheesh.* Does this guy have a body part that isn't hard as steel? I almost choke as that thought flits through my head. I definitely *don't* want to think along those lines.

Our gazes catch, and I rip my hand away as if I've been burned. "I don't think that's necessary."

When I say nothing more on the topic, he nudges my shoulder

with his broader one. "Who was the text from? His eyes narrow and his voice hardens. "It wasn't Reed, was it?"

I shake my head. "It was my dad."

His voice softens. "Have you spoken to him since the restaurant?"

"Nope." It's easier to stare at the television than meet Brody's inquisitive gaze. It's weird to have this conversation with him. The other night he caught me at a weak moment after the restaurant incident. My defenses were down. I normally wouldn't share such personal information with someone I barely know. I don't even talk about the divorce with Zara, and she's my best friend. She's the one who was there to pick up the pieces when my dad blew our lives to smithereens.

My belly prickles. I hope my one-word answer will be enough to shut down any further questions.

"So, what are you going to do about the situation?"

I should have known better. Brody's not much into taking social cues. The guy does what he wants when he wants.

Uncomfortable with the direction of our conversation, I shift next to him. After a few silent moments, my gaze meanders back to his. The sincere interest in his eyes takes me by surprise. I'm not used to seeing that from him. What I'm used to is his merciless teasing and me sniping back. I'm used to us being on opposite sides of a fight.

This kind of behavior—even though I've seen more of it lately—knocks me off-kilter. I'm not sure what to make of it. I never expected him to defend me against Reed. Or try to make me feel better by taking me skating. I don't know if I'm ready for a shift of this magnitude in our relationship. Or to change my narrative about him. I've had Brody pegged from day one of our freshman business class three years ago, and nothing since has changed my opinion of him.

He's a conceited, womanizing, attention-whore who's biding his time at Whitmore until he moves on to bigger and better things. But the Brody I've caught glimpses of this week isn't like that at all.

The words spill from my lips before I can rein them back in. "I don't plan on doing anything. He's the one who walked out and left us. And now he's moving on with the woman who wrecked their marriage." Fury rushes through my veins like molten lava.

"Don't you miss him?"

I lay my head against the back of the couch so I can gaze up at the ceiling because I don't want to continue holding his eyes. The conversation we're having feels too intense. We're barely friends.

"I miss the way we used to be when we were all together." I think about how Dad was dressed at the restaurant, trying to act like something he's not. Hip and cool and young. "The guy I met a couple of days ago, I don't know him." The one who ditched my mom and has taken up with someone who isn't that much older than I am.

"Maybe you need to tell him that. Get it all off your chest so you can move forward."

I shrug, wishing I didn't care as much as I do. "I don't even know what more I would say."

"Any dialogue is better than none," he says quietly.

"It's complicated, Brody." I turn my head so our eyes can meet. A little zip of energy sizzles in the air between us.

He nods. "Family usually is."

"Yeah." What sucks is that it never used to be.

He slips his arm around my shoulders and hauls me close, dropping a kiss on the top of my head. My body stiffens. Like the conversation we're having, this is unchartered territory for us. I'm not sure what to make of it or how to react.

Brody doesn't say anything more about my dad, which is a relief. His eyes go back to the movie playing on the screen. Instead of releasing me, he settles in. I'm pressed against the hard lines of his body. There's nowhere for my head to go except against his chest. The fresh, clean scent of his aftershave batters my senses. I can't help but inhale more of him.

Why does he have to smell so good?

And why does being held in his arms feel surprisingly...nice?

Little by little, my rigid muscles loosen.

How can I feel so at-ease with Brody when we've always been at odds with one another?

Not wanting to dwell on that thought, I push it from my mind and focus on the movie. With my head nestled against his chest and my body pressed against his, I realize there's nowhere else I'd rather be.

Brody clears his throat and says, "My mom died when I was ten."

My breath catches as shock floods through every part of me. I scramble to find adequate words, but there are none. I'm left giving him platitudes. "I'm sorry. I didn't know."

Other than the snippets I hear around campus—which usually entail his antics on and off the ice—I don't know much about Brody's personal life. Certainly not something so important.

He shrugs as if it's not a big deal, but the tensed way he holds himself says otherwise. "It happened a long time ago."

Thirteen years is a long time, but not enough to take away the sting of that kind of pain. I'd be devastated if something happened to my mom.

"Do you have any siblings?" Again, I have no idea.

"I have a two-year-old sister named Hailey."

Like a kaleidoscope, my image of him shifts. No longer is Brody the one-dimensional, hockey-playing jerk I assumed him to be. He's a man who has suffered great loss.

Unsure what to say, I remain silent, and he continues. "My dad remarried a few years ago. His wife's name is Amber." He shrugs. "As far as stepmoms go, she's a pretty good one. I can't complain."

This is the first time I'm being allowed a true glimpse of Brody. I get the feeling he doesn't let many people inside. I can appreciate that. Most of the time, I feel the same way. But the difference is that Brody is constantly surrounded by people—teammates, girls, fans—who want to get close to him because of who he is and where he's going in life.

Forgetting about the movie, I turn in his arms so I can fully meet his gaze. "Are you and your dad close?"

"Yeah, we are. After my mom died, it was just the two of us. He didn't get together with Amber until I was already out of the house and doing my own thing, so I wasn't very upset about it. I meet with him every Sunday morning at the ice rink, and we run through drills for a couple of hours. Then we have brunch at the house with Amber and Hailey. Because of my schedule, it's the only time I have to spend with them." He adds, "My dad owns a sports management agency. He played in the NHL for a decade. When his hockey career ended, he decided to rep other athletes. He started out with a few teammates and made a name for himself, and now he owns a company with about twenty-five agents working for him. He mostly oversees the operational side of the company, but he's repping me."

"Wow." I had no idea. About any of this.

After a few beats of silence, he admits, "My dad wasn't too happy when he found out about you."

Surprise washes over me. "Really? Why?" I can't see what difference it would make. Brody's a twenty-three-year-old man. What he does is his own business.

"He wants to make sure I stay focused on school and hockey. This is my last year before moving up to the pros. He doesn't want me getting derailed."

A thought occurs to me. "Is he the reason you've never had a girlfriend?"

"I guess." He shrugs. "But it's not like I've ever met anyone either. Hockey takes up so much of my life. I don't have the time to devote to a relationship at this point."

What he says makes perfect sense. But still...It seems weird that his father would be so overly-involved in his son's personal life.

"I guess it's good that we're not really dating," I say lightly. For the first time, I'm not sure how I feel about that. There's so much about Brody that I'm only just discovering.

"I tried explaining the situation, but he didn't get it. I told him I was just helping a friend out."

I snort. "Friend..." Two weeks ago, I wouldn't have considered Brody McKinnon my friend.

He chuckles. "What? We're friends, right?"

"I don't know. We're more like," I pause, racking my brain for the right term, "frenemies." But even that doesn't fit anymore.

"Wow." His brows rise. "I had no idea you felt that way about me. I always thought we were just joking around." Looking surprisingly serious, his eyes lock on mine. "Has that changed this past week? Are we friends now or still frenemies?"

Knocked off balance by the change in conversation, I shrug. How am I supposed to answer that question? Strangely enough, our relationship *has* changed over the course of this week. I wouldn't have thought it possible. There's more to Brody than meets the eye and I would be lying if I didn't admit I want to dig deeper. To slowly peel back the layers of who Brody McKinnon is.

I'm starting to wonder if he's someone I could actually like.

As a friend. Nothing more.

"I guess we're slowly venturing into friends territory." When his lips lift, I add just so he doesn't get any ideas, "But I reserve the right to change that opinion at any time."

"Fair enough." Before I realize his intention, his hand grazes the side of my face until he's able to cradle my cheek in the palm of his hand. My breath lodges in my lungs. I can't breathe. I can't move. I can only watch with wide eyes and wait for his next move. "I don't want to be your frenemy, Natalie," he admits quietly.

He searches my eyes intently, looking for...I have no idea. Then his mouth slants across mine, leisurely brushing over me once, twice, three times. The movement leaves me wanting more. It's like he's teasing me.

When he finally presses his mouth against mine, it never occurs to me not to open for him. His actions are measured as if we have all the time in the world.

His tongue sweeps inside my mouth, mingling and playing with my own. Tasting and exploring at the same unhurried pace. Shifting me around in his arms, he changes the angle. This kiss is so different than the one we shared in front of everyone at the party. That was more of a show of ownership. This one is entirely different. It's more exploratory in nature and feels as if he wants to take his time and savor what's unfolding between us.

His fingers slide into my hair, holding me in place. Pushing him away is the last thing on my mind. I never imagined what it would be like to kiss Brody. Of course, I've heard the rumors. You can't be on campus for more than a week without being regaled with his sexual exploits.

If this display is anything to go on, then all the gossip is true. Brody knows exactly what he's doing. His kisses are enough to melt my panties.

And I'm at the opposite end of the spectrum.

As much as I hate to admit it, Reed's ugly words have taken up residence inside my head. They've wounded my confidence. Instead of enjoying the moment, I find myself wondering if Brody likes kissing me. If I'm doing the right thing. Is there—

I break away, pulling out of Brody's grasp. My fingers tremble as they seek out my lips. I suck in a greedy breath and push it out again, trying to regain my bearings. There's a drugged look in his eyes. I imagine it's mirrored in my own.

"Do you want me to stop?"

I shake my head.

Nope. On the contrary.

Now I just have to find the nerve to tell him what I want.

Chapter Twenty

NATALIE

It takes a moment—maybe five—to dig deep and find the courage to open my mouth.

There's a voice inside my head that screams for me not to do it. To abort the mission. Once I vomit out the words, there's no reeling them back in. For better or worse, they'll be out there.

Ignoring my instincts, I clear my throat. "What you said the other day at the diner...Did you mean it?"

I hold his gaze with a penetrating stare of my own, praying he'll understand what I'm referring to without me having to explain. Even though it's just the two of us, it's still embarrassing. The fact that I'm putting myself out there and asking him for help is difficult enough without coming off as totally pathetic.

"What I said?" He looks confused.

Heat scorches my cheeks, and I drop my gaze, avoiding eye contact. I gulp and push onward. "About my sexual experience being lacking."

He sits up a little straighter. His voice tightens. "You want to have sex?"

I sputter out a nervous laugh. "No!"

I'm nowhere near that point. Yet.

But now that I've had a little time to rethink our conversation, I see the merit of his suggestion to let him give me some bedroom advice. The kiss we just shared certainly proves that if there's a guy who can offer some assistance, it's Brody.

"I thought you could...I don't know," I mumble, wishing I'd kept my big mouth shut and we were back to kissing. That was easy. This, on the other hand, sucks. "Assess the situation," I finish in a rush.

Just kill me now before I say something else that will make the situation more unbearable. I can't stuff the words back into my mouth and pretend I didn't say them.

They're out there.

Sitting uncomfortably between us.

It's Brody's move to make.

My insides feel like they've been twisted into a series of painful little knots. My stomach roils. Any moment, I'm going to be sick.

His fingers slip under my chin and turn my face until I'm able to meet his sharpened gaze. I release a shaky, pent-up breath. One side of his mouth curves, making him look even sexier than he already does. I finally understand what the female population at Whitmore has been talking about. To have all of his attention focused on me is powerful.

I feel it straight down to my core.

"So, what I hear you saying is that you'd like some tips and pointers of a sexual nature from yours truly."

And just like that, the spell is broken. Which is for the best. It really is. I don't want to complicate matters between us. Nor do I want to feel anything that might confuse me in regards to the guy who now stares smugly at me.

Feeling like I'm once again back on even footing, I roll my eyes. I should have known he would enjoy this.

"Lessons," I correct, feeling more like myself. Which is a relief.

"Lessons," he repeats slowly as if tasting each syllable of the word. A slow smile spreads across his face. Another arrow of desire slices clean through me. "Yeah, I could definitely do that."

Before I can specify the terms of our arrangement, his lips are back to cruising over mine. Just like before, it doesn't take much for me to lose myself in the caress.

Brody pulls away enough to meet my gaze. "Lesson number one," he whispers as his eyes fall to my mouth. "Kissing isn't just about the lips."

Duh.

Who doesn't know that?

With an absurd amount of gentleness—more than I would have imagined possible—he presses his lips to the corners of my mouth. A little sigh escapes as he trails soft, butterfly-like kisses along my jaw and down the column of my neck. When I try to slide my hands into his hair, he pulls away and imprisons my wrists with his fingers.

I meet his gaze with a questioning look of my own. He stretches my arms above my head and lays them against the couch cushions.

"Those stay there. You just relax and enjoy what I'm doing."

His husky words send a thrill spiraling through me. As Brody trails his fingertips down my arms, goosebumps rise in their wake. The way his hot gaze licks over me feels like a physical caress. Heat explodes in my core and I shift restlessly under him, needing more.

"Do you realize how beautiful you are?"

My pulse kicks.

I quickly remind myself that what's happening between us isn't real. This is more of a learning experience. Something to help boost my self-confidence.

While Reed isn't the last guy I was with, it's been a while.

All thoughts of my ex disappear when he nips my bottom lip with his teeth, tugging it before releasing. A shiver of pleasure rushes through me. It's a sexy move. Using his tongue, he rims my mouth. I open for him and, without our lips touching, our tongues mingle in an erotic dance. What he's doing is exquisite torture.

"Does that turn you on?"

"Yes," I groan. How could it not?

"Good. It's important to know what excites you. You can't be afraid to tell your partner what you like or don't like."

His teeth sink gently into my lower lip before he sucks the flesh into his mouth.

When he releases me, I whisper, "I really like that." The pleasure flooding through me is dizzying.

"Me, too."

He presses more kisses against my mouth and makes his way to my throat. His warm breath feathers against my flesh, heating me from the inside out and making me feel needy and feverish. I wiggle beneath him, wanting to run my hands over every sculpted slab of muscle. And make no mistake, Brody is all carved strength.

I can't remember foreplay ever feeling so good. With Reed, it was always hurried as if we were racing toward the finish line. And the two guys after him weren't any different. No one has ever taken their time to simply explore me.

And that, I'm only now realizing, makes all the difference in the world.

Brody's mouth drifts toward my chest. I'm wearing a scooped-neck shirt, so he has easy access to my collarbone. His mouth dips to the valley between my breasts, nuzzling the sensitive skin.

When his hands cup my breasts, I nearly levitate off the couch. With careful fingers, he kneads the soft flesh until my nipples are hard little points. His lips hover over one of the tips, his warm breath feathering against me. Lowering his mouth, he gently bites my nipple through the thin material of my shirt. Pleasure tinged with pain floods through me.

"Brody," I groan, arching my back to get closer.

"You like that?"

"Love it," I admit on a breathy sigh.

Now that I've had a small taste, I'm greedy for more.

The feel of his mouth through my clothes isn't nearly enough to satiate me. Lust and longing swirl through me and settle in my core. I whimper when he fists the hem of my shirt and shoves it over my breasts, exposing the teal cheetah print bra I'm wearing.

He stares at it for a long moment before his gaze slices to mine. The heat filling his eyes nearly singes me alive.

"Now that's an unexpected surprise," he growls with appreciation.

My lips bow up at the corners. "Glad you approve."

"Oh, I more than approve." Lowering his head, he scrapes his teeth against the silk covering my breasts.

Unable to control my body's response, I writhe beneath him, wanting more contact. Wanting to feel his hands and mouth on me.

"As much as I love this bra, it needs to go."

I couldn't agree more.

I don't give myself time to consider the ramifications of my actions. If I did, this episode would come to a screeching halt, and I'm not ready for that to happen.

His fingers delve into the lacy cups and maneuver the soft flesh out of them. I shiver as cool air kisses my naked breasts. Brody strums his thumbs over the hard peaks. Lowering his mouth, he wraps his lips around one turgid point and sucks it deep inside his mouth.

The warmth disappears from one nipple only to descend upon the other. I gasp when he makes contact. Even though he told me not to, I lower my arms and slide my fingers through his thick hair, holding him in place as he draws upon my flesh. It's as if there is an invisible thread connecting the nipple in his mouth to my core. Every pull of his lips, every stroke of his velvety tongue against the stiff peak, sets off an avalanche of sensation within me.

Just when I can't stand another moment of his warm mouth, Brody pulls away and stares into my eyes. I imagine that mine look just as dazed and heated as his do.

"I should—"

"Yes!" I practically shout, wanting him to take this further. I've never felt this turned-on before. It's nothing short of a revelation.

"Go," he finishes lamely.

Wait a minute...what?

He blinks but remains silent.

"You're leaving?" I whisper dumbly, unable to believe I heard him correctly.

But I must have because he's already off the couch. The weight of his body, which had felt so delicious moments ago, disappears. He backs away like he just found out I'm contagious. Flummoxed by his abrupt shift in attitude, I stare mutely. I'm still sprawled on the couch cushions. My shirt is shoved against my chin, and my breasts look like two sunny-side up eggs being served on a platter.

With his eyes glued to my tits, he drags a hand over his face. "Yeah. I need to go. Now."

"But..." I have no idea what happened to make him act like this.

This is the guy known around campus for his one-night stands. The guy who has slept with half the girls at Whitmore. The guy who told me himself that he's never had a girlfriend and has slept with so many women that he's lost count.

And he's the one slamming the brakes and walking out?

He's got better things to do?

Oh my God, I'm going to die of embarrassment.

Coming to my senses, I slip my bra over my breasts and yank my shirt down before rolling to my feet. Brody stares at me in silence. Before I know what's happening, he reaches out and pulls me into his arms. His mouth crashes down on mine.

Unlike the kisses he showered on me earlier, this one is demanding. Insistent. When his tongue probes the seam of my lips, I open for him. I might be confused, but I still want him. His tongue claims my mouth, dancing with my own. He pulls my body flush against his hard one. Just when I think he's changed his mind and will take this further, he rips himself away and holds me at arm's length.

"I've really got to go."

None of this makes sense. "You do?"

"Yeah."

He sounds resigned. And I'm not going to beg. As much as I've enjoyed what just happened, I refuse to do that.

I blow out a breath and try to regain control of my clamoring hormones. "Okay."

"I'll see you later?"

I nod, still feeling muddled.

Brody flicks his finger across the tip of my nose. "And no more avoiding my texts. Got it, wifey?"

Instead of pissing me off, the nickname makes me smile. It diffuses the sexual tension simmering in the charged air between us.

"Got it."

With one last speculative look, Brody heads for the door. As soon as it closes behind him, I drop back to the couch and bury my face in my hands.

Did that just happen?

Did I really make out with Brody McKinnon?

Yeah, I did. And stranger than that, I can't wait for it to happen again.

Chapter Twenty-One

BRODY

That was a close one.

If I hadn't gotten the hell out of Dodge, there wouldn't have been any turning back. All I could think about was burying myself deep inside Natalie's hot little body.

And those breasts...

They're so much more spectacular than I allowed myself to imagine. And don't think for a moment that I haven't spent a good amount of time fantasizing about them. Natalie Davies has always been the go-to girl in my spank bank. I'll say this—my fantasies didn't do them justice.

I seriously have to pat myself on the back for deciding to slow my roll. I could have easily taken it to the next level, but I knew Natalie wasn't ready for that. I might have wanted to stay and continue playing with her delectable body but pulling the plug was the best thing for both of us. If I had screwed her, she would have regretted it in the morning. She probably would have regretted it before I pulled all the way out of her body.

I'm not under any grand delusions about her dislike or distrust for me. She may enjoy the way I make her feel, but she doesn't necessarily like *me*. There's a huge difference between the two, and I'm more than aware of it.

If I'd gone for instant gratification, I'd be back to square one. Actually, I'd be at negative twenty. I have no idea what I want with Natalie. But until I figure that out, I'm not going to do anything to fuck up all the progress I've made up to this point.

Which means I need to keep my dick in my pants.

By the time I make it back to my place, it's just after midnight. I thought for sure everyone would be out partying their collective asses off and I'd have the place to myself.

No such luck.

I adjust myself before walking through the door. I'm still a man of steel. Sawyer is sprawled out on the couch with two girls who are permanent fixtures at the house. There's one tucked under each of his arms. Cooper is settled on the recliner with a chick perched on his lap.

I'm not sure what it is about that leather recliner, but when Cooper is making out with a girl, that's where you'll find him. I would suggest against shining a black light on that thing. I'm sure it's covered in body fluids. Just thinking about it makes me queasy.

The dude has a perfectly private room upstairs. Now that I think about it, I've never seen him take a girl up there. We all know he screws them on the chair, which is precisely why everyone gives it a wide berth.

I'm happy to report that, for the first time in a long time, everyone has all their clothing in place. For the moment, anyway. I'm sure as the night wears on, that'll change. It always does.

"Where'd you take off to?" Sawyer asks, his eyes flicking to mine. "Thought you were hanging with us tonight."

I shrug, not wanting to mention Natalie. Neither Cooper nor Sawyer have any interest in settling down. I'm not even sure if *I* want to settle down. But I'm not ready to rule it out either.

"Had some stuff to take care of," I say nonchalantly, hoping he'll drop the subject.

"Oh yeah?" Looking blurry-eyed, he raises his brows. "Is that what we're calling it nowadays? 'Cause if so, I've had a lot of stuff to take care of, as well." He tightens his arms around the girls. "Right, ladies?"

They giggle as if on cue, and I roll my eyes while walking into the kitchen to grab a beer from the fridge. Yeah, I'm definitely over this. I'm tired of the constant parties and drinking. Of random people showing up at all hours of the day and night like I'm running a goddamn boarding house.

I almost wince.

Christ...I'm not eighty years old. Even though I'm doing a damn good impression.

I hadn't given much thought to living on my own last year when we renewed the rental agreement. I kind of wish I had.

"What happened with the Kappa party?" I ask, changing the subject.

"It ended up being a lame-ass sausage fest. So, we decided to come back here and chill for a while. I think a few more guys might show up."

The girl on Cooper's lap sheds her top.

It was really only a matter of time before that happened. I'm impressed she kept it on for as long as she did.

I jerk my head toward the staircase. "I'm gonna head upstairs and hit the sack."

Sawyer gives me a surprised look. "Really? It's still early. Here," he gestures to the girls snuggled up against him. "You want one? I don't need both." He smirks. "At least not right now, I don't."

Sawyer's words curdle like cottage cheese in the pit of my gut as Natalie's face flashes in my mind. I have zero interest in getting it on with a puck bunny. The sad thing is, two years ago—even last year—I wouldn't have given it a second thought. I'd have sat down next to one of them, and she would have happily crawled on my lap and did what-ever the fuck I wanted.

But random hookups don't seem to be doing it for me anymore. Somewhere along the line, they lost their luster.

I'm going to turn twenty-four in March. I've been partying my ass off for the last five years. And juniors, that was a crazy time. I don't remember half the shit I did. It was my first real taste of freedom, and I went off the rails in the beginning.

What guy wouldn't?

"Nah." I shrug. "It's been a long week. I'm tired."

Sawyer shakes his head. "When did you turn into such a pussy?"

This is typical shitfaced Sawyer. Instead of taking it personal and starting something, I grin and say, "Well, I guess what they say is true. You are what you eat."

On that note, I head upstairs, away from the soon-to-be orgy.

Chapter Twenty-Two

NATALIE

"Look who I found on our doorstep," Mom says. A huge smile lights up her face as she makes a ta-da gesture with her hands.

My gaze moves to the guy standing behind her. Dwarfing her, actually. Mom must be at least a foot shorter than Brody. It makes me realize just how tall and broad he is. At twenty-three, he's a man who has grown into his body. There's nothing boyish about him. A tingle of awareness zips through me. That never used to happen when I saw him before we began fake-dating. Normally all I feel is annoyance.

The forkful of pancake I was in the process of hoisting to my mouth stalls in midair as I meet Brody's eyes from across the room. His hair is freshly washed and is pushed away from his face. The ends curl slightly above the collar of his sweatshirt.

It doesn't escape me that guys with long hair have never been my type.

Apparently, that's changed.

Crap.

Crap.

Crap.

The last thing I want is to find myself attracted to Brody. That would be disastrous. Falling for a manwhore never ends well for any girl. I'm no exception to the rule.

In the cold light of day, I'm angry at myself for allowing this to happen. I'm smarter than this. I went through a similar situation last year with Reed. I don't want to stereotype, but I know what these guys are like. I've been witness to it for three years running. A countless number of girls have cried on my shoulder about Wildcats hockey players who lured them into bed (snort—more like they dove in there headfirst, but whatever) and then dumped them the moment they zipped up their khakis.

The good old pump and dump.

I have to remind myself that what Brody and I have is nothing more than a pretend relationship. There's nothing meaningful going on between us. There are absolutely no feelings involved.

See? Now I feel better. More in control.

The fork drops back to my plate with a clink as I frown. "What are you doing here?"

My reaction doesn't seem to faze him in the least. In fact, he beams a smile my way. "I thought you might need a ride back to campus."

"That is so considerate of you, Brody," Mom says. "Have you eaten breakfast already? I have a few extra pancakes and some bacon if you're hungry."

"Thanks, that would be awesome. I had an early practice this morning. Other than a protein bar, I didn't have a chance to eat."

My voice fills with irritation. "Don't you and your dad normally have brunch after practice?"

Mom grabs a dish from the cupboard and stacks three fluffy pancakes with a side of bacon onto a ceramic plate before setting it down in front of him.

"He had a meeting, so we skipped it." His eyes dance with ill-disguised humor. "I thought I'd stop over and see what you were up to." He bats his eyelashes and coos, "Plus, I missed my Pooh bear."

I nearly choke at the endearment. "Maybe you should have called first."

"Would you have answered?" he fires back in a singsong voice.

I grind my back teeth, saying nothing because we both know I would have gone into avoidance mode after what happened Friday night. Damn him for showing up out of the blue and forcing my hand. I spent all Saturday thinking about it and my physical reaction to Brody still mystifies me. If he hadn't put the brakes on our makeout session, I don't think I would have. Considering that I don't even like the guy, it's a real kick in the pants.

A superior expression settles across his face. "Hence me showing up unannounced on your doorstep."

"Syrup is already on the table," Mom cuts in, sounding shrill. Her eyes pinball between us as if she doesn't know what to make of our interaction. "How about some orange juice?"

I wilt in relief when Brody drags his eyes from me to Mom. "Thanks, Mrs. D. I'd love some."

"We're happy you could join us." Mom's questioning gaze darts in my direction as she arches her brows. "Wasn't it thoughtful of Brody to come by and pick you up?" The silent message written across her face is clear.

Be nice, Natalie Marie!

I'm tempted to roll my eyes but don't. Mom has no idea what's going on between us. Well, she's not alone. I haven't a clue either. "Yes, it was very considerate." Changing my tone, I say in an overly sweet voice, "Thank you so much for showing up on my doorstep for the second time without any warning. You're like a bad penny that keeps turning up at the most inopportune times."

He grins around a forkful of pancake. "Anything for you."

Mom shakes her head. "You two have a very odd relationship."

Brody's shoulders tremble with silent laughter. I can't help it, the corners of my lips twitch.

Mom's right. We have an odd relationship. He loves to give me shit, and I enjoy slinging it right back at him. Tenfold.

"That's one of the things I like about your daughter, Mrs. D. Her sharp tongue keeps me on my toes."

Mom's expression turns from confused to thoughtful before she carefully asks, "Do you come from an abusive home, Brody?"

He nearly spits out the mouthful of orange juice he's in the process of swallowing. He coughs and thumps his chest with his fist as it goes down the wrong hatch. Being the loving girlfriend that I am, I pound on his back extra hard until his eyes grow glassy with tears.

He chokes out the words, "No, ma'am. Why?"

Mom shrugs. "Just a theory."

I say with a straight face, "Brody knows I subscribe to the philosophy of treat 'em mean, keep 'em keen." I flutter my lashes at him. "Isn't that right, dear?"

Too busy trying not to cough, Brody nods his head emphatically. "Can't argue with that," he croaks.

Mom purses her lips and sighs. "I think the divorce has hit you hard, Natalie. Maybe you should see if they have yoga classes on campus. I think a little self-reflection would be good for you."

Before I can reply, Brody catches his breath and changes the subject. "How'd your date go last night, Mrs. D?"

The question seems to throw Mom off guard. I'd asked her the same thing this morning, and she'd brushed the query aside, saying nothing more than "it was good." And because it's weird to discuss dating with my mother, I hadn't pushed the issue.

But I'm curious as to what she'll tell Brody.

"We had a nice time, and the band was great."

Brody shoves another mammoth bite of pancake into his mouth before asking, "Think you'll get together again?"

I perk up, interested in her response.

She hesitates and glances away. "I think so."

"So, when do we get to meet the lucky fellow?" Brody gives me a wink. "Maybe we can double date. How fun would that be?"

Mom chuckles but looks uncomfortable by the suggestion. And I'll admit, it's not something I really want to do either.

"Oh, I don't think we're quite to that point yet. But maybe." She glances longingly at the door leading to the hallway as if plotting an escape. "I'm, ah, going to the study to finish up some work. Let me know before you leave, okay sweetie?"

Before I can open my mouth, Brody cuts in. "I'll be sure to do that, Mrs. D."

Mom purses her lips in an attempt not to smile. I think she's already figured out that it's a mistake to encourage him. "I meant my daughter. But it was lovely to see you as well, Brody."

He gives her a little wink.

Once she's gone, I wad up my napkin and throw it at him. "A double date, huh?"

He chuckles. "Did I go too far?"

"By like a mile."

He shrugs. "Seemed like a good idea at the time. Figured you'd want some backup while meeting the new guy your mom is getting serious with."

Something in my belly clenches at the idea of her dating one man exclusively. Ever since Dad left, it's been just the two of us. I'm not sure if I'm ready for some stranger to barge in and throw off the balance we've found after all these months.

"Davies?" Brody reaches out and touches my arm. "You okay?"

I force my lips up and lower my voice. "Yeah. I'm fine." I don't want Mom to overhear our conversation. "It's weird to see your parents dating. This is the first guy she's gone out with. At least, it's the first one she's mentioned. It's not that I don't want her to find someone, but..." I'm not sure how to finish that sentence without sounding like a selfish jerk.

"You don't necessarily want to have a stranger dropped in the middle of your life," he finishes for me.

My body wilts as he voices my silent concern. It's a relief that he gets it. That I don't have to justify my feelings to him.

"After everything that happened with my dad, I'm not ready for that. I'm not ready for both of my parents to be in relationships. To introduce new people into my life."

His fingers brush against mine and wrap around them. "It took a little bit of time to get used to the idea of my dad dating again. It sucked thinking someone might come in and try to take my mom's place, but," he shrugs, "I wanted him to be happy." He gives my hand a squeeze. "It'll get easier. I promise."

For the first time since the divorce, I feel like someone understands what I'm going through. The fact that it's the guy I spent three years hating on makes it even more bizarre. Or a cosmic joke. Even though his mother died and my parents are separated, we still have to deal with extraneous people involved in our lives.

"I hope so," I whisper. Because right now, it feels excruciating.

"Just give it some time. Let the dust settle."

I nod.

Who would have ever thought I'd be taking life advice from Brody? It's enough to make me wonder if I've entered a parallel universe.

Chapter Twenty-Three

NATALIE

Brody and I are camped out on the third floor of the library. Books and papers are spread out across the table. We have a test on Friday in our Managerial Finance class, so we've been hitting the library to study when time allows. Which, with Brody's hockey schedule, is no easy feat.

I never realized that playing a sport at the college level is like having a full-time job. I hate to admit it, but Brody's schedule is grueling. I'm not sure I would want to have it. He's usually up by five and doesn't fall into bed until eleven. Tonight, he looks especially exhausted. I feel a little guilty for assuming that he's been coasting his way through school. Obviously, that's not the case.

There's something else I've noticed this week.

The books Brody uses are large-print texts, which make me suspect that something's going on, but I have no idea what.

Vision problems?

But that doesn't make sense when he's such an amazing hockey player.

Sometimes I watch him from beneath my lashes. Where I can skim over the page of a textbook in a matter of minutes, Brody takes a lot longer to read through and digest each section. He highlights passages or important concepts and types them on his laptop. The entire process seems painstaking and slow.

I'm beginning to suspect that Brody has a learning disability. He hasn't mentioned anything and I've been too afraid to ask. I don't want to offend him. A couple weeks ago, I wouldn't have cared about hurting Brody's feelings, but something subtle has changed between us. Somehow, we've managed to strike up a tentative friendship, and I'm loath to ruin it.

After about an hour, I pull out a stack of index cards from my bag and silently slide them across the table.

Brody stares at the pile held together by a rubber band. There's a guarded expression on his face when his eyes lift to mine. "What's that?"

An unexpected burst of nerves wing their way to life inside me. "I made some cards for you to study with."

He seems taken aback. "You made me flash cards?"

Only now do I wonder if I've made a mistake. Unfortunately, it's too late to snatch them off the table and pretend this never happened. I gulp. "I thought it might make studying a little easier. That way you have something small and portable you can pull out when you have a couple of minutes of downtime." I don't want him to think it's a big deal. "Even if you spend five minutes flipping through them a few times a day, it might help." I shrug, wishing this didn't feel so awkward. "Zara sometimes makes notecards for herself. It helps her to memorize the material."

When he remains silent, I repeat miserably, "I thought it might help." Shifting on my chair, I reach out, ready to slip the cards back into my bag. As I make a grab for them, he covers my fingers with his own. I stare down at our clasped hands.

Brody clears his throat. "Thank you."

"It's not a big deal," I say quickly, just wanting to drop the subject.

"It is," he says. His voice is low and scratchy. Full of emotion. "I appreciate it."

I suck in a breath and force it out again. The question tumbles out of my mouth before I can stop it. "Is memorization an issue?"

Silence stretches between us. It seems like forever before he says,

"I have dyslexia. Pretty much everything school-related is an issue for me."

"Oh." Once again, I feel like Brody has thrown me for a loop. I've spent three years in class with him and it never occurred to me that he might struggle academically. Now that I think about it, the signs were there. But for some reason, I assumed the worst about him from the beginning. "I didn't know," I say stupidly.

He shrugs like it's not a big deal, but I can tell it is. It's there in the stiff set of his shoulders. The way he refuses to hold my gaze for more than a moment or two. The tension radiating off him in thick, heavy waves is another indicator that I've unearthed something raw and painful.

Our hands are still clasped. I shift mine around until I'm the one holding him. I want to offer comfort, but I'm not sure how and that makes me feel helpless.

"My professors know, and for the most part, they've been great about making accommodations. They give me notes prior to class so I can focus on the lecture. Instead of taking written exams, sometimes I can take an oral one. I do better when I don't have to read long sections and answer questions. That's always been a killer for me. I also buy large-print books because it helps make reading easier."

I shake my head in wonder. I would have never suspected.

"Look," he says gruffly. "I've been dealing with this for a long time. I've figured out strategies to help myself."

"Is there anything I can do?" God, I feel like such an asshole right now.

"Actually, the cards are great. My handwriting is pretty messy, so these will make it easier."

"I can make cards for your other classes, too," I say quickly. "It's not a problem."

He nods. "Quizzing me verbally on the information helps as well."

A piece of the puzzle slides into place. "Is this the reason you didn't want to work with a tutor?"

A look of guilt flashes across his face before he pulls his gaze from mine. "I've managed to get through three years of college on my own.

But we're only a month into the semester and it's already challenging. I'm struggling more than I have in the past."

My heart feels like it's being cracked wide open. I've never felt anything like it. "I'll help you as much as I can."

The corners of his lips lift. "Thanks. And I appreciate the cards."

"You mentioned going over the information verbally. Is there anything else we can do?"

He takes a breath. "If we could discuss the concepts, especially in finance, so I have a better understanding of them, that would help a lot. I have a difficult time memorizing for the sake of memorizing. If I have a better working understanding of the ideas, then it's easier for me to commit them to memory."

"We can do that." I make a mental note to do a little research on dyslexia. Maybe if I have a better understanding of Brody's struggles, I can figure out other ways to support him.

"I appreciate your help, Davies." His eyes drop as he shifts on the chair. "Do me a favor?"

"Anything." And strangely enough, I mean it. I'd do just about anything he asked right now.

His whiskey-colored gaze pierces mine. "Don't mention this to anyone, okay?"

"Is that what you think? That I'm going to blab this all over school?" It hurts that he feels the need to say that to me. "I would never do that to you."

Some of the tension drains from his shoulders. "I'm sorry. I know you wouldn't. It's just..." He shrugs as if at a loss for words. "I've learned over the years to keep my guard up. Whitmore is a cesspool for gossip. I don't want this getting out. It's no one's business but my own."

"You have nothing to be embarrassed of. You've obviously found strategies that work for you."

He nods. "Yeah, I have. But school has always been a struggle. I've had to work my ass off just to get B's." He cocks his head. "Do you have any idea how much it sucks to work that hard and not see a payoff?"

I'm ashamed to admit that I don't. School has always come easy for me. I've never had to study very much. I'm blessed with a good memory.

"I spent a lot of years hating school, hating how difficult it felt, hating that everyone seemed to pick up stuff easier than me. They watched me struggle and thought I was lazy or stupid, or a trouble-maker because I would get so frustrated and lash out."

His words break my heart. Especially since I'm guilty of thinking the same. I've never felt so ashamed of myself as I do at this moment.

"I'm sorry, Brody. That sounds miserable."

"You know what saved me?" He pauses for a beat, and I shake my head. "Hockey. As much as I struggled in the classroom, I was a natural on the ice. If I didn't have hockey growing up, I'm not sure I could have gotten through all the other bullshit."

"If school was so difficult, why go to college? Why not go straight to the NHL?"

"I signed a contract with Milwaukee during my senior year of high school. They wanted me to play juniors. I was eighteen years old and needed time to mature physically. Attending college was my decision. I could have turned pro after the second year of juniors, but it was important to my mom that I get my college degree, so that's what I'm doing. I've focused on a business degree, because after I'm done playing hockey my plan is to join my father at his management company."

I feel like everything I've ever thought about Brody is wrong. Okay...maybe not *everything*, because he's still a manwhore. But the importance he's placed on school even though he clearly struggles is proof enough that there's more to Brody than I allowed myself to believe.

It makes me realize that I was quick to judge him on outward appearances. My impression of him was that he was an arrogant jock coasting through college, so I placed him neatly into that category without examining it any closer.

With our fingers locked together, he reaches over with his other hand and slips it under my chin. "I'm not telling you this because I want you to feel sorry for me." He shakes his head. "Your pity is the last thing I want."

I lower my eyes. "It's not that." After Friday night, this glimpse into who Brody is only makes me feel more confused.

"Then what is it?"

I shrug, still feeling like an asshole. "I've always thought you were just here biding your time before going to the NHL. But that's not the case at all."

"Don't feel bad about it. I'd much rather have people think that than find out I'm dyslexic."

My brows draw together. What he's saying doesn't make sense. "But no one would judge you for it."

"They already have." His voice takes on a sharp edge. "When people find out you have a learning disability, they treat you differently. They don't expect as much from you. They assume you're not as smart because your brain works differently. Or that you're somehow damaged. I don't need that."

"But you just told me," I whisper.

His eyes singe mine. "Maybe I wanted you to know the real me."

Those words bring a thick lump to my throat. "Thank you. And I'm sorry for misjudging you."

Surprising me, he gets to his feet and pulls me up with him. "Come on."

It takes a moment for me to mentally switch gears. "What are we doing?"

"Taking a much-needed study break." He doesn't let go of my fingers as he snakes his way around the stacks.

I glance at our table. Everything is still strewn across the top of it. "We're just going to leave our stuff there?"

"Don't worry, it'll be fine."

The third floor of the library is always quiet since most students prefer to study on the first two floors. I've only seen a few other people in the two hours we've been here tonight.

"Where are we going?" I ask.

"You'll see," he says, tugging me behind him.

We walk around a few more corners before Brody grinds to a halt. My breath catches as he pins me against a tall bookcase filled with doctoral theses.

"What are you doing?" I squeak in surprise.

He smirks. Both of his dimples pop. "I think it's time for another lesson."

"Another lesson," I repeat stupidly. What is he—

Oh.

A *lesson.*

My eyes widen, and he chuckles. The sound is low and rough. It scrapes against something buried deep inside me. His mouth hovers dangerously over mine. My heart pounds with anticipation. I want him. My lips part of their own accord. I'm hungry to feel his mouth crushing down on mine. Instead of doing what I expect, he runs the tip of his nose across my cheek. The touch is subtle.

I release a shaky, pent-up breath.

He nips at my chin with his teeth, and I melt against the shelving unit I'm pressed against. His mouth trails across my jawline, teasing my flesh until I groan with need.

"Are you ready for your second lesson?"

God, yes...I'm desperate for whatever he wants to show me. Whatever he wants to do. I've never felt this way before. I've always been contained, removed. No one has ever made me lose my mind or forget myself.

Brody does that to me. All I'm aware of, conscious of, is him. His hands. His mouth. The position of his body as it aligns with mine.

"Yes," I moan.

Not once does it occur to me to put a stop to what we're doing. We're making out in a public place. Anyone could stumble across us. But that's not even a thought in my head. The only thing that matters in this moment is the feel of his hands branding my body. His lips coasting over me. The pleasure blooming in the pit of my belly. And lower.

So much lower.

"Good, because after Friday, all I've thought about is touching you again."

With that, he flips me around so that my front is pressed against the stacks.

"What—" I gasp.

"Shhhh."

Any protest bubbling up in me dissolves when he presses his hard body against my backside. He grabs my hands and stretches them high above my head.

"Leave them there," he whispers in my ear.

"You've got a real thing for that, don't you?" I breathe out in a shaky voice.

He chuckles. "I like the idea of having you at my mercy. All these years, you've been sharpening your claws on me. I hate to admit it, but all it's done is turn me on. Now you're going to do what I tell you to. Understand?"

"Yes."

His fingers trail along my arms and down my sides. Shivers scamper across my spine as he grips my hips and pulls me flush against the lower half of his body. The feel of his erection pressing into me nearly makes my knees buckle. His hands slide around to the button of my jeans and flick the metal disk from its hole.

"Brody..." My teeth sink into my lower lip. As much as I want him to touch me, we can't do this. Not here.

"No talking," he whispers harshly. "Only feeling."

"But—" my voice rises in panic.

"I said no talking, Davies."

My heart thunders as his fingers draw the zipper down. Parting the material, he traces lazy circles across my lower abdomen. I turn my cheek so that it rests against the spines of the books. My eyelids feather closed as he dips his fingers into my jeans, grazing the edge of my panties.

As wrong as I know this is, there's a growing part within that doesn't give a damn. When Brody lays his hands on me like this, all rational thought disappears.

"What do you want me to do?" His fingers dip inside the band but don't descend any further.

Even though I shouldn't, I groan out the words. "Touch me."

"I am touching you." His voice is silky soft. Almost playful.

"You know what I mean." I wiggle against him, trying to get his fingers to slide inside my panties.

"You're right, I do," he whispers against my ear. "I know exactly what you want."

With that, his fingers slip under the band and stroke over my naked flesh. My knees quiver as he glides over me, caressing the seam of my lower lips. I widen my stance wanting him to sink deep inside me, but he doesn't. He toys with me instead. When I can't stand another moment, when I feel like I'm going to scream with the need building inside, his fingers slide through my folds and zero in on my clit, rubbing slow circles as if we have all the time in the world. It's nothing short of exquisite torture.

I bite my tongue to keep quiet when he sinks a thick finger inside me.

"Mmmm, you're so fucking tight," he murmurs.

A second digit joins the first. He pumps them a few times before dragging his fingers from my body. Just when I think he'll pull all the way out, he drives them back inside. I moan as he buries his fingers to the hilt. His other hand snakes up my body until he's able to cup my breast. He squeezes the softness and plays with the pebbled tip.

More nerve endings spark to life. An orgasm brews as he finds a rhythm, stroking in and out of my body. I arch my pelvis, wanting to pull him in deeper. Wanting these intense feelings of pleasure to go on forever.

The hand that had been touching my breast trails down my rib cage and delves into my panties, zeroing in on my clit again.

The low murmur of voices cuts through the thick haze of pleasure cocooning me. My eyes fly open in alarm. We can't be discovered in such a compromising position.

"Relax," he breathes against my ear. "They have no idea we're here." Instead of releasing me, his grip tightens. His fingers thrust in tandem, never ceasing their assault on my flesh.

"We have to stop," I whimper as pleasure crashes through me.

Even though I said the words, I think I would die if Brody stopped what he was doing. Any moment now, the orgasm that has been building is going to streak through my body.

Instead of answering, the intensity of his touch becomes more focused until it's almost unbearable. I bite my lip to stifle the scream rising within.

The voices grow louder.

Closer.

They must be on the other side of the bookshelf. If I weren't so out of my head, I would push him away and straighten my clothing, but I can't bring myself to do that. I'm so close to coming. It's all I'm able to focus on. Everything in me tightens.

"Come for me, baby." He nips my neck and growls, "Right now."

That's all it takes to push me over the edge. His lips capture mine, swallowing the moans that fall from them as he thrusts his fingers inside me while the other hand plays with my clit.

It takes a moment for me to come back to my senses. For me to realize that I'm still pinned against the stacks with Brody's big body pressed against my back, his hands continuing to strum my body.

"Fuck, that was amazing," he mutters.

His breath is just as labored as mine. I strain to hear the voices that had been just on the other side of the shelf, but there's nothing. They've obviously moved on, away from us.

I can't believe we just did that. That I allowed Brody to finger me in the library.

"Stop thinking." His teeth bite down on my ear, pulling gently on the lobe. "Just enjoy how I made you feel."

He's right. I don't want to ruin this moment with regret. I need to enjoy whatever this is between us for what it is.

Instead of separating myself and feeling awkward about what just happened, I say, "I think I'm going to enjoy your lessons."

He relaxes against me and chuckles. "Damn right you are."

Chapter Twenty-Four
NATALIE

"Got anything special planned for the big twenty-two?" Zara asks, fingering the fabric of a shirt she's thinking about purchasing at Olive + Ashley, one of our favorite stores.

I shrug. Birthdays have always been special occasions in my family. Since I was an only child, my parents would go all out. For the first time in my life, I'm not looking forward to it.

Normally, the night of my birthday, my parents and I go out for dinner at my favorite Mexican restaurant, La Fuente. It's been a tradition for as long as I can remember. For obvious reasons, that won't be happening this year. Dad texted a couple of days ago asking if he could take me out for lunch so we could talk, but I politely declined the offer.

I'm still pissed about what happened a few weeks ago. I have no desire to see him or his fiancée. They can both go to hell as far as I'm concerned.

"I'm not sure yet," I admit reluctantly. "I thought my mom and I would hit the restaurant alone, but she texted yesterday and said a showing came up that she can't get out of."

Zara's brows shoot up, and a look of sympathy settles across her elfin features. "Oh, that sucks." She picks up a long, flowing bohemian-style shirt and looks it over with a critical eye. "What about your dad? Have you spoken with him since the incident?"

That's what we're now referring to it as...*the incident*.

More like *the incident where I lost my shit*.

I shake my head. "Nope, and I don't intend to."

When your parents go through a breakup, you realize how meaningful all those little traditions you didn't appreciate during your childhood become. It makes you want to hang onto them tightly with both hands and never let go. Somehow, having a little bit of normalcy makes life feel as if it hasn't been completely yanked out from under your feet.

So, my mom cancelling at the last minute stings. In her defense, she did ask a bazillion times if I'd be okay and offered to rearrange her schedule. I, of course, said no. I'll be twenty-two years old on Saturday and didn't want to act like a big baby. Even though I kind of feel like a big baby at the moment.

Now that she's a single parent and reliant on her own income, if a showing comes up, she has to jump on it. She's just starting out in this business and can't do anything to jeopardize her budding career.

But it sucks.

Big time.

"What about Brody?"

I give her a blank stare. "What about him?"

Zara rolls her eyes. "Did you mention that it's your birthday on Saturday?"

Why the heck would I do that?

I shake my head and focus on the rack of tops I'm perusing. Unlike Zara, I'm not in the market for something new. "Of course not. It's not like we're actually going out."

"You two have been spending an awful lot of time together lately," she says nonchalantly.

My eyes narrow and she suppresses the smile hovering around the edges of her lips.

"Please. We've been studying at the library." Heat fills my cheeks as I think about all the times we've snuck around the corner of the stacks and made out. I can't think of another guy I've enjoyed kissing more than Brody. He has the best lips. And his hands...

I really need to stop thinking along these lines. It's dangerous.

"Sure," Zara snickers. "Brody's well known around campus for his academic prowess."

I open my mouth, ready to blast her, but catch myself at the last minute. I promised Brody I wouldn't tell anyone about his struggles with dyslexia. And that includes Zara. I'm almost taken aback by how quickly the need to defend him rises up within me.

The relationship we've become embroiled in is messing with my head. I should do myself a favor and end it. It's been a few weeks. We could quietly part ways without too much commotion. No one would even notice.

The idea of doing that leaves a sick knot in the pit of my belly.

When did I start to develop feelings for him? It's a shocking revelation.

Almost offhandedly, I say, "Brody cares about his grades. He's getting a business degree. After the NHL, he's going to join his father's management company." How many people my age have a ten-year plan in the works? I certainly don't. I don't think Zara does either.

Her eyes cut to mine in surprise. I bite my tongue, wishing I'd kept my big mouth shut. What do I care what Zara thinks about Brody?

Only recently have I come to realize that Brody isn't the guy I always thought he was. And he isn't the guy Zara thinks he is either. It bothers me that she can't see him for who he really is. Which is ridiculous. It took me long enough to scratch beneath the surface.

"Huh." A slow smile spreads across her face. "Is that so?"

I shrug and turn my attention to a shirt I have zero interest in purchasing because it's easier to focus on that than acknowledge the growing curiosity in Zara's eyes.

If I were smart, I'd change the subject before she figures out what's really going on. That I'm actually falling for this guy.

Unfortunately, my lips start moving before my brain has time to pull the plug. "Brody could have gone straight to the NHL after juniors, and he chose to come here and work on his degree first. It's important to him."

Even though I'm tempted to tell her about the promise Brody made to his mother before she died, I don't. For all Brody's party-boy, manwhore ways, he's turned out to be infinitely deeper than I gave him credit for. I wish other people could see that side of him.

But that's not my decision to make.

It's his.

And I would never break the promise I made to him.

Zara's eyes narrow as she considers me. "I can't believe I'm hearing this from you. For three years all you've done is hate on that guy."

Her words make me wince. She's right. "Hate is an awfully strong word," I murmur. "I don't think I ever hated him."

She gives me an *are-you-crazy* look. I can't blame her for being confused at my sudden about-face. "Yes, you did. In fact, I specifically remember you saying that you hated him and wished Brody's penis would shrivel up and fall off. That was like a month and a half ago."

All right. Fine. I said it. I wanted his penis to shrivel up and fall off.

But clearly, that's no longer the case. I'm not sure what to do about these strange feelings growing inside me. I have to remind myself more and more often that we're acting out a charade. That's all.

No longer wanting to dwell on the Brody situation, I change the subject. "How about we grab dinner Saturday night? Maybe see a movie? We can keep it low-key."

A look of guilt flashes across her face. "Oh. I can't." She bites her lip. "I'm sorry, Nat. I just assumed you'd be with your mom on your birthday. I've already made plans with Luke. His parents are coming into town for a visit. We're going out to dinner."

"That's fine," I say hastily, trying to backtrack. "It was just an idea. No big deal."

After a moment she says, "I'll cancel if you want and we can go to dinner and a movie. Now I feel terrible. I don't want you to spend your birthday alone."

I shake my head. "No way are you cancelling on Luke. I'm happy things are going so well for you guys." I was nervous when she first told me about getting together with him. Most of the hockey players are douchebags. But not all. Luke is definitely one of the good guys.

Zara smiles and her entire face lights up as she confides, "I told him that I loved him."

"Wow." Setting aside my own disappointment, I say, "You two are amazing together. And for the record, I was wrong about him. Luke is a great guy. Nothing like Reed."

What I'm starting to realize is that Luke isn't the only hockey player I was wrong about.

Chapter Twenty-Five

NATALIE

I slant a look Brody's way as we walk through the parking lot of La Fuente. Which is weird, since he didn't even ask where I wanted to go. He just showed up at my door thirty minutes ago and told me to change out of my yoga pants and T-shirt because he was taking me out.

I peppered him with questions on the car ride over, but he wouldn't tell me who let the cat out of the bag.

"It was Zara, wasn't it?" I ask for the tenth time.

I should have suspected she would do something like this. She didn't want me getting all sad-bastard on my birthday, knuckle-deep in a carton of chocolate peanut butter chunk. Which is exactly what my big plans consisted of.

Brody shrugs, looking all cagey. "You'll never know, will you?"

Who else could it have been? Mom? Or, as he likes to refer to her as, Mrs. D? I almost snort. "I think we both know it was my bigmouth roommate."

He winks, and I'm secretly glad to have narrowly avoided the ice cream portion of this evening. How depressing would that have been?

"Why didn't you tell me yourself?" he asks as we hit the walkway.

I shrug, keep my eyes focused straight ahead, and lie. "It didn't seem important."

There's a teasing lilt in his voice. "Didn't think I needed to know something like that about my girlfriend?"

"Fake girlfriend," I correct because it feels like I should. Not necessarily because I want to point it out. Maybe I'm trying to remind myself of it. Who knows? It's my birthday, I'm not going to think about it tonight.

Brody holds the glass door open as we make our way to the hostess station located inside the restaurant.

"Hi. I have a reservation under McKinnon," he says, flashing his trademark smile at the girl working behind the desk.

Her eyes widen as she drinks him in like a tall glass of lemonade on a scorching hot August afternoon. Not once does her gaze deviate from him. I'm tempted to roll my eyes. His effect on the opposite sex is ridiculous. I've never seen anything like it.

No wonder he's slept with so many women. All it takes is one look aimed in their direction—one flash of his dimples—and they're putty in his hands, willing to do whatever he wants.

Thank goodness, I've never felt that way about him. I'd be in so much trouble if I actually gave a damn about this guy.

She perks up at the last name. You can almost see the lightbulb going off in her head. Although I'm not going to lie, the wattage seems dim. Okay, now I'm just getting bitchy.

"Oh my God, your Brody McKinnon!" she gasps. "You play defense for Whitmore!" She leans across the desk, looking as though she might crawl over it to reach him. "I'm your biggest fan! I was at every single home game last season and all of your preseason scrimmages this fall!" Her hand flutters to her heart. "You are so completely amazing!"

Brody takes a small step back but keeps the smile firmly in place. "Thanks. We always appreciate our fans coming out to support us."

Her smile grows impossibly wide as she bounces on the tips of her toes like an overexcited child. "Would you mind signing this menu for me? Then we can hang it on the wall." She gives him a sly look from beneath her lashes. "Or maybe I'll take it home and hang it on my bedroom wall."

My brows skyrocket across my forehead. I don't even want to think about what she'll be doing while staring at that menu. *Ewwww.*

"Sure, no problem," Brody says, looking like he doesn't mind at all.

She opens a drawer and hands him a black Sharpie. Hostess-With-the-Mostest looks completely starstruck as Brody scribbles his name across the plastic.

"Feel free to write your number on there," she adds huskily.

And he does. I feel like I've been slapped as he scrawls something across the bottom.

I look away and fight back the sting of hurt and jealousy blooming throughout my body. In all honesty, I have no right to feel this way where Brody is concerned. We're not together. He's not my boyfriend. We're friends. Sort of.

I shouldn't be surprised by this. The hostess is cute. Actually, she's more hot than cute. She has raven hair and gray eyes. And a curvy body. This is *exactly* the kind of girl I'd expect him to be with. Someone with big boobs, tight clothing, and a highly excitable personality.

Unwilling to have a front-seat view of her shameless flirting, I take a step back, away from them. Letting Brody talk me into going out tonight now feels like a mistake. I just want to go home and dive head-first into that carton of ice cream that's sitting in my freezer. The happiness that had zipped through me on the ride over feels like a distant memory.

I keep my gaze focused on them, forcing myself to watch the interaction. If anything can kill the budding attraction I feel for Brody, it's him flirting with this girl right in front of my face.

Hostess-With-the-Mostest is all giddiness and smiles until she peers more closely at the menu. As she stares, her brows beetle together in confusion before she glances up again.

"Oh, I meant your other num—"

"Yeah," Brody says, his voice hardening. The easiness that had threaded its way through his tone earlier is now long gone. "I know what you meant."

His smile is strictly polite as he slips an arm around me. "We're here for my girlfriend's birthday."

For the first time since I've been standing at his side, her eyes swivel to me. Color floods her cheeks as she snaps to attention. "Oh, of course! Let me show you to your table." She grabs two menus from the holder. "Right this way."

Brody glances at me as we follow her into the restaurant. *Sorry*, he mouths behind her back.

I shrug, pretending that what happened doesn't bother me in the least. But it does. My gut is still burning. I can lie all I want to him, but I can't deny my feelings to myself.

Watching other girls flirt with Brody is maddening.

When did that change? For three years, I've watched girls fawn all over him and never felt this way.

My mind spins as we walk through the main dining room. When I was younger, this was our go-to place to eat. The food is delicious, and it's always crowded. So, I'm not surprised to see all the tables filled and servers rushing around with trays of food and drinks.

As much as I hate to admit it, what just happened a few minutes ago has brought my relationship with Brody into sharp focus. I'm not going to dwell on the ramifications right now. I'm going to enjoy dinner. But later, when I'm alone, I need to think about what's going on between us. Obviously, feelings are coming into play. And that, I can't allow.

I think it might be time to pull back. To protect myself before I fall any deeper. Because that's the way this is headed.

And sleeping with him...while it sounded like a good idea in the beginning, now has disaster written all over it.

"Surprise!" a loud chorus of voices ring out, knocking me from my thoughts.

I stumble to a halt as my eyes widen and fly around the table in the semi-private room we've been shown to.

Zara rushes forward to give me an exuberant hug. "Happy Birthday!" she shouts. "Are you totally surprised?"

Surprised is an understatement.

"Shocked," I say, continuing to glance around at the table filled with my friends.

Luke beams and waves from the other side. Megan and Anna, who live in the apartment next door, wave as well. Mom—the very same

Mom who lied to me about having to work tonight—sits near the end of the table. Her grin is ear-to-ear.

The room has been decorated with pink and black balloons. There's a fancy cake on a small table off to the side. A sign that reads *Happy Birthday Natalie* has been taped to the wall in the back.

And I'm...speechless.

Brody, who still has his arm wrapped around my waist, leads me to the head of the table, next to Mom. Glass bowls filled with my favorite candies are strategically placed on the long, rectangular table. Colorful confetti has been sprinkled across it.

As soon as I sit down on the chair, Mom leans over and envelops me in her arms. "Happy Birthday, baby girl!" She gives me a big squeeze. "I felt so bad lying to you. Forgive me?"

I shake my head, still trying to process what's happening. "Thank you." I meet her eyes. "Did you arrange this?"

Her grin intensifies. "Nope. Brody did!"

She beams at the man who has taken a seat next to me, across from her.

Brody planned this?

Why would he go to all this trouble?

My eyes swing to his in surprise. "You did this?"

He shrugs like it's no big deal. "I had some help with the planning. Your mom and Zara gave me lots of ideas."

Unwilling to let Brody brush aside the praise, Mom interrupts, "It was all Brody's idea. He wanted to do something special for you. Isn't that sweet?" Her gaze softens as it fastens on him. Admiration shines brightly in her eyes. Any reservations she might have had about me dating a guy like Brody have clearly been swept away. "He really nailed it, don't you think?"

My mind continues to cartwheel. Not in a million years would I have expected this from him. "Yes, he did."

I stare at Brody as confusion rushes through me. But it's more than that. Feelings I've only begun to recognize and tamp down are hurtling to the surface.

But I don't have time to dwell on them because the waitress stops at the table with a round of tequila shots. Even Mom takes one, which is hilarious. She never drinks anything stronger than an occasional glass of wine in the evenings. And yet, here she is belting it back like she does it every Saturday night. The chips and salsa flow, and dinner is amazing. I order my favorite dish—cheese enchiladas swimming in a red mole sauce.

Afterward, I'm forced to wear a huge sombrero that swallows my head as the waitstaff serenades me with "Happy Birthday." Normally I'd be melting into my seat at all the attention, but I'm buzzed from the shots. Everyone is laughing and having a great time.

We devour the cake and decide to head over to a bar to keep the celebration going. After Mom cancelled our plans, I'd thought for sure this birthday would suck. But that hasn't turned out to be the case at all. I've had the best time. I'm surrounded by the people I love most. Mom and all of my friends are here helping me to celebrate.

And then there's Brody...

The guy I've spent my entire college career avoiding. The very same one who I believed was only attending Whitmore to burn time until he moved up to the NHL, falling into any and every vagina along the way.

But Brody has turned out to be a completely different guy than I pegged him to be.

"Okay, sweetie," Mom says. "I'm going to take off. There's no way I'm tagging along to a college bar at my age."

I'm so glad she was here tonight. This dinner has meant so much to me. Again, it blows my mind that Brody is the one who arranged it.

"Oh, come on, Mrs. D," Brody cajoles teasingly. "You should join us. It'll be fun."

Not looking swayed in the least, Mom shakes her head. "Nope. I'm going home. But you kids have fun, okay?" She pulls me in for another hug. "I love you, Natalie. And I'm so proud of you." She kisses my cheek and whispers in my ear, "I think you have a real keeper here. Brody's a wonderful guy. The best one so far."

"He is," I agree, gulping down the riot of emotion her words unleash in me.

"He likes you a lot," she continues. "I can tell."

I blink, unable to muster a response as a thick lump rises in my throat.

Only now do I wish I'd told her the truth from the beginning. Then she would know that Brody can't possibly have feelings for me because our entire relationship is a sham. This isn't real. He doesn't like me. And I don't like him.

"Ready to go?" Brody asks, interrupting my turmoiled thoughts.

I smile and say, "Yup," while shaking off the strange emotions coursing through me. This is my birthday, and I want to have fun. With Brody, I realize. I enjoy spending time with him. There's an easy give-and-take to our relationship. With him, I'm never worried about being anyone other than myself.

We all head to a bar a few streets over from campus. Rowdy's is a hole-in-the-wall dive bar where they serve cheap pitchers of beer and shots. Every once in a while, they kick it up a notch with a local band. A lot of hockey players from school hang out here, which means that there are a ton of puck bunnies floating around looking for a guy to latch onto. Since I've gone out of my way to not be one of those, this isn't my usual scene.

We get to the door, and Brody fist bumps the bouncer as they exchange small talk. Other than flicking his eyes in my direction, the guy doesn't say a word to me.

It may only be nine o'clock, but the bar is already jam-packed. There are back slaps and chin lifts of acknowledgement as Brody grabs my hand and tows me through the crowd. Plenty of girls smile and wave, greeting him by name. He waves back but keeps it moving.

In the past, whenever I'd see Brody out at a party, he'd be surrounded by a bevy of females. Usually there's one tucked under each brawny arm. And it's never the same girl. More like a revolving door of them. Even on campus, he has an entourage.

And yet, since we've gotten together, I haven't seen him with anyone else. For some reason, the girls have been keeping their distance. He doesn't encourage or flirt with them. Even with the hostess from earlier.

That was all her doing. *Bitch*.

Whenever we're together, my hand is firmly tucked in his. It's almost like he's afraid I'm going to take off if given half a chance. Which in the beginning—I'm not going to lie—had been the plan. If he's not holding my hand, his arm is casually slung around my shoulders, anchoring me to him. For a guy who never wanted a girlfriend, he sure does enjoy having someone at his side.

Brody grabs us each a beer, and we join the table with everyone from the restaurant, along with a few of Brody's teammates who meander over. We do a couple more shots, and when Zara's favorite song comes on, she jumps up, pulling me onto the dance floor. We carve out a small space in the middle of the chaos and let loose. Normally I'm not a drinker. Sure, I'll have a beer or two, but usually not more than that. Tonight has been an exception. I feel light and happy. Every time the chorus plays, Zara and I throw our hands up in the air and shout out the lyrics.

One song bleeds into three or four. I catch a glimpse of Brody from across the room. He's taller and broader than most guys. Unsurprisingly, there's a girl at his elbow. Her gaze is pinned to him. Her lips are moving, trying to engage him in conversation, but his eyes are firmly locked on mine.

Satisfaction floods through me because he's not paying her the least bit of attention.

Zara moves a little closer. "What's going on between you two?"

I shrug. My eyes stay fastened to Brody as the tempo of my heartbeat picks up. "I have no idea." I never expected for our arrangement to morph into something else. But I think that's what's happening.

"Are you two sleeping together?"

Surprised by the question, my eyes cut to hers, and I shake my head. "No. We haven't."

It's not that I don't want to. I just don't think it's a good idea. It'll only end up confusing matters between us.

She glances toward the table again. "I've never seen Brody into a girl before." Her lips quirk. "I think you have a smitten kitten on your hands."

My gaze reluctantly slides back to his. A little zing of pleasure slices through me when I find him watching me.

Sounding devilish, Zara says, "Let's drive the boys crazy."

Even though I groan, my lips twitch upward. I know *exactly* what she has in mind.

Without waiting for agreement, Zara grabs my hand and dances around me until her front is aligned with my backside. She grabs my other hand and holds them both over my head. Slowly she traces her fingertips along my arms and ribcage until they settle on my hips.

I throw a glance over my shoulder to see if Brody's attention is still focused on me. I almost laugh at the way his eyes have widened and his jaw has gone slack. Such a typical guy response. It's ridiculous the way two girls dancing, laying their hands on one another, can bring most men to their knees.

Closing my eyes, I sway my hips and feel the beat of the music as it pours through me. Once the last chords have faded, Zara and I separate. Instead of heading back to the table, we stay out for a few more songs until we're both in need of liquid refreshment. We push our way back to the table. As soon as I'm within three feet of Brody, his arm shoots out, and he nabs my fingers, reeling me to him until I'm flush against his rock-solid body.

"You," he growls in my ear, "are in so much trouble."

I laugh and lean back, putting a bit of distance between us. I flutter my lashes. "I have no idea what you're talking about."

The simmering heat in his eyes is enough to scorch me alive. Fire ignites in my belly.

"You just wait until I get you alone," he whispers harshly. "Then I'm going to give you a little taste of your own medicine."

"Promise?" Even thinking about his kisses is enough to leave my panties flooding with heat.

"You bet your damn ass, I do."

Chapter Twenty-Six

BRODY

My arms are wrapped possessively around Natalie. After that little stunt on the dance floor with Zara, there's no way in hell I'm letting her wander around this bar on her own. My eyes may have been locked on her while she was dancing, but I was more than aware of all the other drunk cocksuckers salivating over the girls.

This is the first time I've ever felt the sting of jealousy whip through my body. I swear to God, if one of those assholes had even tried making a move, I would have went apeshit all over them.

Luke must feel the same way, because Zara is perched on his lap.

Watching the two of them out there...

I don't think I've ever seen anything hotter in my life. And—just to be clear—I've seen my fair share of sexy shit out on the road travelling for hockey.

I'd like nothing better than to hustle her sweet little ass out of here.

What am I going to do when it's time for this farce to end?

The possibility that our relationship could shift back to the kind of interaction we used to have scares the crap out of me. I like where we are, what's slowly developing between us. I'll fully admit to taking advantage of the situation with Reed. I saw a way in, and I took it. Can't blame a guy for going after what he wants.

And I wanted Natalie.

Only now do I realize just how much I want to keep her.

Every time I see that girl, I find myself holding my breath, waiting for her to pull the plug on this fake relationship.

I can't allow that to happen. I have to figure out something fast otherwise she'll cut me loose and move on without so much as batting her eyelashes. Natalie isn't like any girl I've ever met. She intrigues the hell out of me. She challenges me at every turn.

And fuck...she's so smart. God, that's sexy. She doesn't give a crap about all the meaningless social bullshit. She doesn't get wrapped up in it like most of the girls I know.

I lean down and whisper in her ear, "You ready to get out of here?"

I don't care where we go or what we do, but I'm done sharing for the evening. I want Natalie to myself.

She glances up, and our gazes collide. Her eyes are bright and shiny. She looks happy and relaxed. The way her lips curve...Something undefinable shoots through me, punching me right in the gut, nearly knocking the breath from my lungs.

"Yeah, let's go."

Has she ever looked at me like that?

It's addictive. There's not much I wouldn't do to have her stare at me like that every damn day.

Those thoughts filtering through my brain are the precise moment when I realize I'm in deep with this girl. Acknowledging those feelings should terrify me. Oddly enough, it doesn't. It feels right. As if something has fallen into place.

The ride back to her apartment is a quiet one. I have no idea how to go about winning Natalie over. For the first time in my life, I don't have a game plan in mind. I'm flying by the seat of my pants. And it's scary as fuck.

Once I turn into her building's lot, I park the truck and cut the engine.

She turns toward me. "Are you coming up?"

"Yeah. But only for a few minutes." With the way I feel, it's probably not a good idea for me to stay. I want this girl too much. I can't remember when I've wanted someone more.

It only takes a few minutes until we're inside her apartment. She hangs up her jacket and lays her purse on a small table by the door.

"Want something to drink?" she asks, heading to the kitchen and filling up a glass of water. She downs half of it.

"Nah, I'm good."

I don't think I've ever seen Natalie have more than a drink. Maybe two. Tonight, she's had two or three shots and just as many drinks. She's not drunk, but she's definitely buzzed. Maybe a little more than that. Wherever that happy place is between the two, that's where Natalie is hanging.

I'm happy that I could make her birthday a good one. Especially considering that it's the first one since the divorce.

I settle on the couch and watch as she kicks off her heels and runs her fingers through the long strands of her hair. Her dark waves tumble around her shoulders. There's a glint in her eyes as a smile curves her lips. Her hips sway as she walks toward me. I'm mesmerized by the sight of her.

"I had a great time." Placing her hands on my shoulders, she straddles my lap. "Thank you for dinner. For everything. You have no idea what it means to me."

Our faces are scant inches apart. My breath catches, becoming trapped in my lungs. For the first time in my life, I have to think about releasing the air from my body and sucking it back in again. It's just as scary as it is exhilarating.

"You're welcome."

She leans forward and presses her lips against mine. A sizzle of electricity zips through me at the contact. I want to grab hold of Natalie with both hands and never let go, but I have no idea if she wants me the same way. I'm afraid she likes the way I make her *feel* but she doesn't actually like *me*. All I can hope is that what I'm feeling isn't totally one-sided, that she feels the chemistry and the growing feelings and friendship, as well.

It doesn't escape me that this is the first time Natalie has initiated physical contact between us. It takes everything I have inside not to haul her body against mine. Not to run my hands greedily over every inch of her.

But I don't.

I want her to set and control the pace.

The kiss that unfolds between us is deliberate and measured. She takes her time nibbling at my mouth. Sucking on the top and then the bottom. Pressing kisses against the corners. Her arms twine around my neck, pulling me closer.

When her tongue licks at the seam of my lips, I open. Her fingers tunnel through my hair, tugging at the strands. There must be an invisible thread running from my hair to my dick. Every time she tugs, my cock twitches in response.

Her tongue strokes mine before she draws it into her mouth. The urge to flip her over and take what I want pounds through me until it's all I can think about.

Natalie sits back and searches my eyes, the glassiness shining brightly in hers. "I want to sleep with you, Brody."

Hearing those words fall from her lips makes my cock stiffen. If I was hard before, I'm like steel now.

Her hands are still tangled in my hair. I feel the pull of it against my scalp.

"I don't think that's a good idea," I groan, unable to believe I'm turning her down.

Her brows beetle together. "Why?"

"Because you've had too much to drink." I stroke my fingers over her cheek. "I don't want you having regrets in the morning."

Given the way I feel, I don't think I could deal with that.

She purses her lips. It's the most adorable thing ever.

Christ... What's this chick doing to me?

"Will you at least stay the night?"

Sleep in a bed next to her, but somehow resist the temptation of her body? I don't know if I'm strong enough to do that. I've spent many years indulging my urges by gorging on women and booze. Whatever pleasure I wanted, I took.

"Please?"

"Okay," I grind out against my better judgment. "I'll stay." Even though it's a lousy idea, I'm unable to deny her what she wants. "But we're not having sex," I reiterate firmly.

Not in a million years did I ever think those words would come out of my mouth.

Looking pleased, she hops off my lap and holds out her hand. I slip my fingers into hers, and she tugs me to my feet before towing me to her room.

A queen-sized bed with a turquoise comforter takes up most of the square footage. A mirrored nightstand sits next to it and a matching dresser is shoved against the far wall. There's a framed picture of Natalie and her parents on the nightstand. She looks like she's just a kid in it.

Everything in here is neat and more girly than I would have expected. Is it possible that under Natalie's hard candy shell lies a soft nougat filling?

It's an interesting concept.

I pick up the silver-framed picture of her and her parents. This is the first time I'm seeing a photograph of her father. When I'd met Karen, I'd thought Natalie bore a striking resemblance to her, but now I see that she also looks a lot like her father. They both have the same dark hair and eyes. She's a perfect mix of the two.

"Did your dad call to wish you a happy birthday?" I ask out of curiosity.

The lazy smile falters from her lips as a cloud passes over her eyes. "He texted when I didn't pick up his call."

"Are you going to talk to him anytime soon? Try working things out?" I know she was pissed after the night at the restaurant. What I feel for Natalie isn't just physical. I want her to open up and let me in.

Which is yet another first for me. I've never made an effort to know a girl. Sex was all I was looking for. The women were inter-changeable. There's been more than a few times that I've been buried balls-deep in a chick and couldn't remember her name.

I'm not proud of it. But whatever is happening with Natalie is different. It's light-years away from some nameless one-night stand where I'm just dipping my wick and blowing my wad.

Natalie shrugs. "I wasn't planning on it."

She fingers the hem of her sweater. In one swift movement, she yanks it over her head and tosses it to the floor, standing in front of me in a silky black bra with white cherries printed on it. My mouth dries as I greedily take her in.

That bra...

It's entirely possible my tongue is hanging out of my mouth and I'm drooling.

Racking my brain, I try to pick up the thread of our conversation. Right...Her dad. "Maybe you need to give him another chance to make things right." The more I stare at her, the harder it becomes to concentrate on the discussion I'm forcing us to have.

Her fingers hover over the waistband of her jeans before slipping the metal disk from its hole and pushing the material down her hips and thighs. She bends at the waist, and her long, wavy hair falls like a curtain around her as she removes the denim and her socks.

I want to sift my fingers through all those soft strands and gather them up in my hands. It doesn't take much effort to conjure up an image of Natalie on her knees, pouty lips wrapped around my thick cock.

When she straightens, revealing skimpy panties that match the bra, I hiss out a breath.

Motherfucker!

I knew this wasn't a good idea and I was right.

She slips the thin black straps off her shoulders and asks, "Do you really want to continue talking about my dad?"

Ummm...

"No," I mutter.

"Good." She reaches around and unhooks the bra. The material slides down her arms and falls away from her chest before dropping to the floor. "Because he's the last thing I want to think about right now. Especially after having such an amazing night."

My eyes are fastened to her breasts. We're talking utter perfection. Firm and perky with tiny, blush-colored nipples. My fingers ache to play with them.

She slips her fingers under the elastic band of her panties and starts to slide them over her hips.

"Leave them on!" I shout, breaking the silence.

Her eyes widen, and her fingers freeze. "What?"

My heart feels like it's going to explode right out of my chest. "Leave them on," I grind between clenched teeth.

She cocks her head, her brows drawing together in confusion. "You don't want me to take my underwear off?"

I shove my hands into the back pockets of my jeans and shake my head. "Nope." *Fuck no.* I'm barely keeping it together as it is.

If she removes the thin scrap of material barring her sweet pussy from me, I'm done. Right now, I have the best intentions in the world. But if those are gone...all bets are off. There's no way I'll be able to resist her.

This girl is my kryptonite. She always has been. I just never realized it until now.

Natalie shrugs and turns toward the bed. My eyes drop to her barely-covered ass. I have to bite back a groan.

I yank my T-shirt over my head and throw it to the floor before tearing my jeans from my body. When I'm in nothing more than a pair of black boxer briefs, Natalie's eyes rove hungrily over the length of me and I feel my dick harden to the point of pain.

"Not taking off your boxers?" she asks.

They stay on no matter what.

"Nope." Much safer this way.

Once we slide between the sheets, I pull Natalie into my arms. She rests her head on my chest. Her breasts are crushed against me. I push the hair away from her face as our legs tangle.

Even though it feels like the tip of my dick is going to explode, a strange kind of contentment washes over me. This is the first time we've laid together in bed, but already I know it's a feeling I'll never get enough of.

Natalie closes her eyes and sighs as if she's just as happy as I am. "Tonight meant a lot to me. Thank you."

I sift my fingers through her hair. "You're welcome."

I've never cared enough about someone else to want to make them happy. The way Natalie looked at me tonight with light shining in her eyes...I want more of it.

I want her to always look at me like that.

Now I just have to figure out a way to make it happen.

Should be easy enough, right?

My first realization as I drift into consciousness is that I'm not alone. I'm plastered against a warm body. With my eyes closed, I trail my fingers over a muscular chest and tight, washboard abs. I crack an eye open. It's still early. The sun is just starting to stretch its fingers across the eastern horizon.

Brody and I are so tangled together that I'm not sure where he begins and I end. My head rests against his chest. The steady rise and fall of it soothes me. The rhythm could easily lull me back to sleep if I let it. Instead of allowing that to happen, I lift my head and glimpse his stubble-covered jawline. A bolt of awareness shoots through me and explodes in my core.

One look.

That's all it takes to send lust and need careening through my system.

At every turn, he surprises me. I've always taken Brody for a manwhore, and yet I'd offered myself up on a silver platter last night and he refused to lay a finger on me. He wouldn't allow me to take off my panties. He did nothing more than hold me in his arms the entire night.

And I've never slept better.

I feel like I've spent the last couple of years protecting myself. Building walls and keeping people out. Reed may have bruised my ego, but he didn't break my heart. After last night and the surprise birthday dinner Brody planned...I think I'm falling for him. My heart clenches as that thought flashes through my brain.

How can this be happening?

Sitting up, I study him more carefully. This is really the first opportunity I've had to look my fill. If he caught me staring like this, I'd never hear the end of it. Brody has a massive ego. I'm surprised he's able to stand upright with it.

It's not that I didn't realize Brody was good looking before—you'd have to be blind not to notice how smoking-hot he is—but he's even more so than I allowed myself to acknowledge. A mop of tawny hair streaked with gold brushes his broad shoulders. Heavy eyebrows arch across a strong forehead. And thick eyelashes feather against chiseled cheekbones that flank a long, straight nose and full, kissable lips.

And those dimples.

Don't even get me started on them. They're nowhere in sight at the moment, but every time he grins, my panties melt.

I'm beginning to suspect that all the dislike I'd harbored for him was really lust and longing masquerading as aversion. I'd convinced myself that Brody was nothing more than a dumb jock coasting through college, screwing his way through the female population at Whitmore while helping to bring home three National Championships.

I never bothered to scratch beneath the surface. And now that I have, I realize there's so much more to Brody than I allowed myself to believe.

More shocking than that, I actually like the man I'm discovering him to be.

I blink as that thought resonates through my brain.

What am I supposed to do about this?

It's not like this is a real relationship. Brody did me a favor by protecting me from Reed and the ugliness he'd hurtled at me. At some point, this farce will end and we'll go our separate ways. Our relationship will revert back to what it was before this started.

Is that what I want?

I...don't know. I'm not sure about anything anymore.

But what I do know is that I want him.

I stare at my hand as it rests against the hard ridges of his abdominals. He's touched me. Several times, in fact...Hello, library. But I haven't dared to do the same. I've held back. But I'm done doing that.

Isn't it about time I explore his body just as thoroughly as he's explored mine?

My belly trembles in anticipation.

I slide my hand lower, slipping it beneath the elastic band of his boxer briefs. My heart trips as I trail my fingers over the hot length of him. Already he's hard. I guess the rumors are true—the man is definitely more than a handful. Gripping his cock, I slowly slide my palm over his thick shaft.

Brody arches against me. A groan slides from his lips and his eyes jerk open, colliding with mine.

Chapter Twenty-Eight

BRODY

I'm having the hottest freaking dream ever. We're talking the stuff wet dreams are made of. Natalie is fisting my dick, pumping me slowly. My balls stir in response.

Only...it's not a dream. She really is stroking my cock.

My eyes spring open, and I blink furiously, trying to focus. The first thing I see is Natalie leaning over me. The blankets have been pushed aside, and her hand is inside my boxers.

"Morning." An innocent smile curves her lips. "Sleep good?"

Her tone is so fucking nonchalant. Like we're just shooting the shit and her hand isn't wrapped around my cock for the first time, making me impossibly hard.

I blink a few more times, wondering if maybe I'm still dreaming. If so, this is the best dream I've had in a while. Unable to resist, I reach out and cup her warm breast. Her nipple pebbles in my hand. Goddamn, but I love her nipples.

Nope, definitely not a dream.

She leans over and presses her mouth against mine. I nip her bottom lip with my teeth and pull. If she keeps touching me like this, I'm going to blow my load. That's not something I've done since high school. Sophomore year, to be exact. Before I got laid on a regular basis. I don't even want to talk about how humiliating of an experience that was.

With my free hand, I cover hers, stilling the movements.

She frowns. "You don't like that?"

"I like it too much," I grunt.

Her forehead smooths out as she tilts her head to the side. "And that's a problem why?"

"Because I'm not fourteen and I don't want to come on your sheets." What's this girl trying to do? Kill me?

Her lips lift into a sly grin as she pulls her hand away. I expel a deep breath in relief. As much as I love her touching me—and make no mistake, I love it—I wasn't kidding. She's going to make me come all over the place and that, I don't need.

Before I realize what's happening, she shimmies out of her panties and crawls on top of me.

My gaze drops to her bare pussy, which is nestled against my erection. Even through the thin material of my boxers, her heat radiates against me. I try to remain still, but that's impossible. Within moments, my hips start moving and I'm thrusting against her softness. I'm mesmerized by the way her pussy slides against the black cotton. After a few more gyrations, her lower lips glisten with arousal, soaking my boxers.

All I want to do is sink deep inside her silky warmth and bury myself to the hilt.

My hands grip her hips, locking her in place. I still my movements and stare at her sitting astride me naked like a goddess. Her lips are parted, her pupils are dilated, and her dark hair tumbles in a tangle of waves around her shoulders. Her breasts are soft, firm globes topped with dusky nipples that I long to suck into my mouth. She has a narrow ribcage, flat tummy, and gorgeous, plush pussy lips that I'd give my left nut to sink into.

She's driving me insane.

"What are you doing?" I rasp. Weeks of pent-up need crash through my aroused body. I'm barely able to rein in the lust. She's pushing me past my limits. Any moment I'm going to snap and then all control will be lost.

Her lips curve into a smirk.

Do you believe this girl?

A fucking smirk...

"With all your worldly experience," she says, "I'd think that would be obvious."

The groan that slides from my lips turns into a deep chuckle. I can't stand much more of this sweet torture.

But still...

I'm trying to take this slow. I'm trying to do the right thing where she's concerned. There's no need to rush this. For once in my life, this isn't a race to the finish line before moving on to the next conquest. What's happening here means something. Natalie means something. I want her to realize that.

"I'm trying to be a good guy, and you're making it impossible. I don't want you to regret anything we do together."

She leans over and kisses my lips. "I won't regret this," she whispers. "I promise."

I grit my teeth and flex my hips, sliding against her. I'm hovering over the point of no return. If Natalie changed her mind and decided to shut this down right now, I'd roll off the bed, throw on my clothes, and race home to take an icy cold, thirty-minute shower. Because that's exactly how long it would take to deflate this hard-on.

But she's not saying that. In fact, she keeps giving me the green light. I'm the one who's pumping the brakes. It's an unusual position for me to be in.

Last night she'd had too much to drink. There was no way I could take advantage of the situation, no matter how tempting she'd been while standing there in all her fucking glory.

But this morning is different.

She's the one initiating this sexual encounter.

"Brody?" My name comes out on a breathy sigh full of need. "Please?"

Christ. Did I ever think I'd hear Natalie Davies begging for my cock outside of my fantasies?

Nope. Definitely not in this lifetime.

"Okay," I say, giving in.

I raise my hips and hastily shove my boxers down my legs until I can kick them away. I groan when she nestles her slick heat against me. My eyes are glued to the place where our bodies are connected. With my fingers digging into her flesh, I move her lower half so that she slides against my hard length. Her pussy is pure nirvana.

"You feel so good," I bite out. I'm not even inside her yet, and I'm about to lose it. Which is ridiculous. I should be embarrassed, but I'm not.

I've spent the last couple of months feeling not much of anything as far as sex was concerned. I could take it or leave it. I've stared at naked women and haven't felt the slightest twinge of arousal. My roommates are nailing as much ass as they can. Once upon a time, I'd been the same way. There wasn't enough pussy to plow my way through.

But somewhere along the line, that changed.

And sex became mundane.

This feels anything but.

How am I ever going to get enough of this girl?

Natalie throws her head back and a low moan slides from her lips as I flex my hips again. Slow and controlled is the name of the game. I want her to be just as needy and turned on as I am. Is that even possible? I doubt it.

"Brody," she whimpers. "I want you inside me."

Even though my brain is clouded with pleasure, I know we can't do anything more without protection. I won't put either one of us in that situation.

"Do you have a condom?" There's one in my wallet. I'll certainly get it if necessary, but the thought of moving her delectable little body is an unpleasant one.

Displaying an impressive amount of flexibility—something that will most definitely be explored in the near future—Natalie leans over and opens a drawer on her bedside table. She pulls out a foil packet and tears into it.

With her teeth.

Fuck...that's hot.

I'm wondering if there's anything she could do that I wouldn't think was a turn-on.

I gulp as she tosses the wrapper onto the table. "You want me to do that?"

A gleam enters her eyes. "Nope."

Sitting back, she slowly rolls the latex over the tip of my dick. Let's face it, condoms aren't sexy. But watching Natalie unfurl it onto my cock is sexy as fuck. My eyes flick to hers. There's a look of utter concentration on her face. Her teeth nip her bottom lip as if she wants to get it just right. When she rises to her knees, I groan at the loss of warmth as she slides the rubber over my shaft.

She grips the base of my dick with one hand and aligns it against her opening. My eyes are focused on the erotic sight. Still poised over me, she strokes the head against her lower lips.

Unable to stand another moment of this exquisite torture, I arch my pelvis, needing to bury myself deep inside her.

I glance up. Her teeth are still nipping her lower lip, and her eyelids have fallen shut. Her cheeks are stained with color. Sitting astride me like this, Natalie takes my breath away.

By the time she slides her pussy lips around my hard length, I'm on the verge of exploding. I have to grit my teeth against the pain radiating from my cock. She moans and seats herself completely.

I close my eyes as I immerse myself in her body. She's so hot and tight, it feels like my dick is being strangled. Fuck...I don't think I've ever felt anything like this before. It feels like heaven.

My fingers bite into her hips as I slide her up and down my hard length. "Christ, you feel amazing."

Natalie sighs in agreement.

"I'm not going to last much longer." I grit in warning.

"Me, neither."

I thrust my hips, and she finds her rhythm, the pair of us moving as one. Everything about this moment feels right. I want it to last forever, but I'll be lucky if I can hold on for sixty more seconds.

She arches against me, her head lolling back. When her inner muscles convulse, I lose it and we both come at the same time.

She yells out my name and I chant hers feverishly as an orgasm streaks through my body. I feel it all the way from my head to the tips of my toes.

When the last little spasm dissipates, she collapses limply against my chest. Her harsh breathing matches my own. I wrap my arms around her body and hold her anchored to me so that she can't escape. And then I close my eyes and enjoy the aftermath. Even though I've softened, I'm still buried deep inside her body.

This, I realize in an odd moment of clarity, is exactly where I belong.

Here.

With Natalie.

And I'll be damned if I let her slip through my fingers.

Chapter Twenty-Nine

BRODY

I slam into a forward, stealing the puck and racing toward the net. My skates dig into the ice as I cross the blue line, moving the puck seamlessly between the blade of my stick. The two defensemen I'm scrimmaging against come at me, trying to block my path. I drop my shoulder, hitting one and deking out the other. Once I'm in front of the net, I wind up and take a shot, aiming for the top left corner. Jack, our goalie, slides and catches the rubber disc in his glove before falling to his knees.

I circle back around as he says with a smirk, "Just an FYI—my grandma takes harder shots than that." There's a pause. "And she's dead."

I grin and skate back down to my side of the ice.

Maybe I didn't make the shot but I feel like I'm on top of the fucking world.

I'd be lying if I said my life hasn't been good up until this point. It has. Sure, I've had some shit times. Who hasn't? The loss of my mother blew my world apart. Nothing was ever the same after that. And most of the time, school sucked major ass. Even after being diagnosed with dyslexia, it didn't get any easier. I worked with tutors and special education teachers, but for the most part, I had to figure it out for myself. There wasn't a magic pill that fixed it.

Hockey has always been there to balance out the bad shit. When my mom died, I spent hours on the ice or in the driveway hitting pucks at the net. When there were issues at school, I could lose myself in practice. I took my aggression out on the teams we played against. I worked myself over until I fell into bed at the end of each day too exhausted to think about any of the problems that threatened to swallow me whole.

And the girls...there has never been a shortage of them. If anything, they came too easily. There was no challenge to it. If I wanted pussy, all I had to do was crook my finger. It was mine for the taking.

The best day of my life was when I signed a contract with the Milwaukee Mavericks. I don't think my father has ever been prouder of me. The only tinge of sadness had been that my mom hadn't lived long enough to see me make it to the pros.

The two years I spent playing juniors were fucking fantastic. I worked my ass off on the ice and played harder off it. With no school to worry about, I could pour all of my energies into elevating my game to the next level.

Playing at Whitmore for Coach Lang has been the icing on the cake. I've made friendships that will last for the rest of my life. My teammates are like family. No matter where we end up, they will always be my brothers. Come spring, I'll have fulfilled the promise I made to Mom and will graduate from college with a degree before heading to the NHL.

So, yeah, my life has been good.

All right...Better than good.

It's been fucking amazing.

I'm living the dream.

And this is only the beginning.

That being said, who would have ever guessed that something was missing?

Certainly not me.

But it was.

Until Natalie came into my life, I wouldn't have realized it either. Somehow, she makes everything better. She's the first girl who has ever meant something to me.

The fact that I could lose her—lose this feeling—scares the shit out of me. Now the challenge is to convince Natalie that what we have is real. That I'm worth taking a chance on. I've got some time to figure it out. But not much. Possessiveness rushes through me. I need to lock that girl down. I want to know Natalie is mine. Then I'll be able to relax and enjoy the season when it starts in a few weeks.

I'm jarred out of my thoughts when someone rams into my shoulder, knocking me off balance. I don't fall, but it's damn close.

First rule of hockey—don't skate with your head down. You're just asking to get knocked on your ass. And if I didn't weigh two hundred and twenty pounds, that's exactly where I would have ended up.

"Watch where you're going, McKinnon."

I snap to, my eyes narrowing on Reed fucking Collins, who has skidded to a halt a few feet from me.

My jaw locks. It's a natural reaction. I can't stand the guy.

He's been a royal pain in my ass since day one, and it's never gotten better. At first, I thought it would eventually smooth itself out and that it would take some time to find common ground between us. But it's been three years and that has yet to happen. I'm sure Coach naming me Captain last year only intensified the animosity he feels toward me.

Well, tough shit. Find a way to man up and deal with it.

I straighten to my full height, lifting my chin. If Reed is delusional enough to think he can intimidate me, he's wrong. "What's your problem?"

There's an ugly twist to his lips as he skates a little closer, invading my space. "You're the one who wasn't paying attention, not me."

I knock my gloves against his chest to back him up. I'm not afraid to throw down. Although, I have to say, out of all the teams I've played on, Reed is the first teammate I've openly had a conflict with. This isn't the first time we've gotten into it, and it won't be the last.

When I don't say anything, he keeps running his mouth. I swear, that's the only thing he's good at.

"Must have pussy on the brain."

I shake my head. The guy is a major douche. "Whatever you say, Collins."

This isn't the time or place to start something. If Reed wants to have a conversation, I'm more than happy to do it off the ice. Where Coach can't see me kick his ass into next week. Because that's exactly where this is headed if he keeps flapping his gums.

When I attempt to skate past him, he slides over, blocking my path. "Well, it can't be Natalie you're thinking about. That girl is like a starfish in bed. Bored me out of my fucking mind."

I clench my jaw until it feels like it's going to shatter. I curl my fingers inside my gloves, trying to calm the rage brewing inside. I'm this close to throwing a punch. And by the look on his face, he knows it. The little prick is just trying to set me off. I see it in his eyes.

"Shut your fucking mouth, Collins," I growl. "You don't know what you're talking about."

His smirk widens into a grin as he taunts, "Just remember, that pussy belonged to me first. Do us all a favor and teach her what to do with that pretty little mouth of hers. I could deal with a lousy lay if a girl can give a decent blow job. Maybe when you're finished with her, I'll have another go. She can't be any worse than before." He shrugs like we're just shooting the shit, having a normal conversation. "You know what virgin pussy is like. Takes awhile to break in. Didn't have the patience for it."

And just like that, my temper ignites like a fucking powder keg. All rational thought disappears. I don't think about what I'm doing. Or the consequences of my actions. I throw my gloves to the ice and swing. I land two solid punches to his face. I'm going for a third when someone steps in and pries me off him.

Reed touches his nose and looks down at the blood soaking his fingers. I huff and puff, struggling against the hold they've got me locked in. All I want to do is hit him again.

"Settle your ass down, McKinnon," Luke growls in my ear.

"What the fuck is wrong with you?" Sawyer demands from the other side.

Coach blows his whistle. It's sharp and short. Everyone freezes. The sound of my labored breathing is all that fills my ears.

"Fuck," Luke mutters. "You've really stepped in it this time. Hope it was worth it."

I glare at Reed, taking in the blood smeared under his nose and on his practice jersey. "It was."

"Get your ass over here, McKinnon," Coach bellows. His voice echoes off the walls of the arena.

"What the hell did Collins say to you?" Luke asks.

He knows me well enough to realize that if I went after Reed, there was a reason for it.

I shake my head. I don't even want to repeat the words. *Goddamn it.* I should have skated away instead of standing there and listening to the shit spewing from his pie hole. I made a tactical error, and now I'm going to pay the fucking price.

I jerk out of Luke and Sawyer's hold and pick up my gloves before skating over to the benches where the coaching staff stands huddled together. I glance at the defensive line coach and see the disappointment swimming in his eyes.

"Get off my ice, McKinnon. You're done for today," Coach barks.

Head hanging, I don't say a word. I just leave.

There's a knock on the apartment door. Launching myself from the couch where I've been studying, I jog over and open it. I'm surprised to find Brody on the other side. He usually texts before showing up.

Energy zips through me as my eyes run over the length of him. I can't help myself. Everything feels different between us now that we've slept together.

He looks, in a word, delicious. I can honestly say I never thought there'd come a day when I would lust after Brody. And here I am, totally doing just that.

His hair is wet and shiny like he's come straight from practice. My fingers itch to run through the long strands. My eyes drop to his mouth. Gah...those lips. I've never met a man who knows how to use his lips the way he does. They're sinful.

It's only then that I notice how tightly clenched his jaw is. As if he's pissed off about something. More often than not, Brody is laughing and joking around. There's usually a perpetual smile curving his lips upward. Sometimes it's more of a smirk. It used to get on my nerves. Now it makes my tummy tremble.

This time, there's no smile in sight.

His whiskey-colored eyes normally dance with mischief. Unless they're smoldering with heat. But neither of those emotions are present. Instead, they flash with barely-suppressed anger.

Unease prickles at the bottom of my gut. "What's wrong?" I swing the door wide, allowing him inside. Zara isn't home, so we have the place to ourselves.

His body vibrates with pent-up agitation as he stalks past me into the living room. Closing the door, I silently pad after him. For just a moment, he stands in front of the window overlooking the street before dragging a hand over his face.

"I'm sorry to just show up like this." His shoulders are hunched. There's a closed-off look about him. One that tells me to keep my distance.

"It's fine." Unsure what to do, I stay frozen in place. Something is coming, I'm just not sure what. Unconsciously, I hold my breath and wait.

"I was kicked out of practice today," he mutters.

"What?" Out of all the things I was expecting to hear, that wasn't one of them. Shock floods through me, and my eyes widen. Hockey means everything to Brody. I can't imagine what could have happened to cause him to reach a breaking point.

His eyes fasten onto mine before he pulls them away. Heaving out a breath, he says, "I threw a punch."

My head swims with confusion. "Why would you do that?" That kind of behavior doesn't sound like the Brody I've gotten to know over the past month. My opinion of him has done a complete one-eighty.

His eyes become hooded. "It doesn't matter."

Ahhh. There's only one person who could cause this kind of havoc.

I force the question through stiff lips, "Does Reed have something to do with this?"

Brody jerking his shoulders into a tight shrug is answer enough.

Why is Reed so intent on causing problems for me?

Needing to understand what happened, I push for answers. "What did he say?"

Brody's expression turns stubborn. He closes the distance between us with four long strides. Reaching out, he sinks a hand into my hair.

His thumb gently strokes over my cheek. I'm tempted to close my eyes and lean into his touch, but I don't.

"It's nothing worth repeating," he bites out.

My shoulders fall. Whatever happened between them is my fault. And I hate that. "I'm sorry."

His demeanor softens. I hadn't realized just how rigidly he'd been holding himself until his entire body loosens. With his hand still in my hair, he pulls me against him. Once his arms are wrapped protectively around me, he drops a kiss on the top of my head.

"You have nothing to be sorry about," he murmurs. "The guy is an asshole."

I rest my head against his chest and squeeze my eyes shut. "I don't want to cause problems between you two."

He chuckles, but it's tinged with aggravation. "Collins and I have always had problems. That started way before you came into the picture."

"How much trouble are you in with your coach?" The thought of it makes me sick.

"Other than getting my ass chewed out, it's fine. I don't want you to worry. There's nothing to be concerned about." He rubs light circles against my back as if I'm the one who needs to be consoled, which is ludicrous. His arms tighten around me, and I burrow into their comforting strength.

"Just do me a favor and stay away from Reed, okay?" Brody says.

I tilt my head until I can meet his eyes. Concern swims around within their golden depths. "I don't want anything to do with him."

"Good." Again, he relaxes. "Keep it that way."

He walks us over to the couch and I fall onto his lap as he takes a seat in the middle of it. My arms are still wrapped around him. I just want to hold Brody close. I want to be the balm that soothes his soul.

He sucks in a breath and expels it with measured movements. "We need to talk."

And just like that, my world tilts sideways.

He's going to end this. I can feel it. And after what happened at practice today, I can't blame him for wanting to put a little distance between us. This charade has gone on long enough. The last thing

Brody needs going into the season is to be on his coach's shit list or have bad blood with another player.

If I hadn't gotten all gooey-eyed, I would have expected it sooner.

I nod and steel myself for the inevitable.

Wait a minute...

What am I waiting for?

That's when I decide to pull the plug myself.

"I get it," she says abruptly.

"Get what?" What's there to get? We haven't even begun to delve into this conversation yet.

My brows draw together as I stare at Natalie.

My gaze drops to her lips.

I'm tempted to wrap my fingers around her neck and bring her mouth to mine. As soon as she opened the door, I wanted to gather up her into my arms and kiss her. It showed great restraint on my part that I didn't do exactly that.

Unfortunately, this conversation needs to happen. And it needs to happen now. Especially after what that douchebag said on the ice. Every time I think about it, it pisses me off. I need to know where Natalie and I stand. I don't want to dance around my feelings anymore.

She drags her gaze from mine and says woodenly, "That this needs to end."

Even though I'm sitting on the couch and she's perched on my lap, I rear back. What's she talking about?

This isn't how I envisioned this conversation unfolding.

Like at all.

My brows jerk across my forehead and nearly slam into the ceiling.

"You want to end this?" I don't give her time to respond before clarifying, "Between us?"

Well, fuck.

This isn't good.

Sharp white teeth sink into her lower lip, and she jerks her head in the affirmative. "It's probably time, don't you think?" She avoids eye contact, looking everywhere but at me. I have no idea what's going on in that head of hers.

Fed up, my fingers settle under her chin. I gently turn her face until she has no choice but to meet my gaze again. "What the hell are you talking about, Davies?" Even though I don't mean to snap out the words, that's exactly what happens.

"When we got together, we agreed this relationship would last for a few weeks. After the whole thing with Reed died down, we'd go our separate ways." She looks at me for confirmation.

"I know what we said," I mutter, feeling annoyed by the way this is going. I went into this arrangement knowing that a relationship with me would be a tough sell, but still...I didn't expect Natalie to drop me like a bad habit. I'd been holding out hope that things had changed between us.

Maybe I was wrong to assume she felt as strongly as I do.

She shrugs. "Well, it's been a month. We should probably move on." Something flickers in her eyes. "Right?"

Now I'm getting pissed.

Scratch that...I'm already pissed.

"Is that what you want?"

Remaining silent, she jerks her shoulders.

I wrap my hand around the back of her neck and bring her face close to mine until our foreheads can touch. "Is that what you want, Natalie?" I repeat.

Dodging the question, she turns it on me. "Isn't that what you want?"

I inhale a deep breath. One of us needs to dive into the deep end of the pool first, and I guess that someone is going to be me. "No, it's not."

"It isn't?" A look of shock slides over her features.

I shake my head. "I know this started out as some fake, bullshit relationship, but that's not what it is anymore. At least not to me. My feelings for you are real. And I don't want to throw that away."

"Really?"

"Really," I confirm. If I'm going down, it'll be in a blaze of glory.

Her lips curve sweetly. "I don't want to either."

"Thank fuck," I say as a tidal wave of relief washes over me.

Her shoulders shake for a moment before she gets serious again. "Are you sure this is what you want, Brody?"

"I've never been more certain about anything in my life," I say with complete honesty. "I like you. I want the chance to explore it."

Her smile widens right before she leans forward and brushes her lips against mine. "I want that, too."

My arms tighten around her, holding her close.

I'm never letting this girl go.

Chapter Thirty-Two

NATALIE

"Are you sure this is a good idea?" I ask nervously.

I smooth a hand over my skirt for the hundredth time since Brody picked me up this morning. We're on our way to his father's house for Sunday brunch. This is the first time I'll meet his family.

Any moment, I'm going to throw up. I'm not ready for this.

Brody squeezes my hand and glances over at me from the driver's seat. A reassuring smile tilts his lips upward. His smile gets me every time. I used to grit my teeth whenever I saw him. Now my belly flips and desire sparks to life in my core.

It's amazing how much something can change in one short month.

"I told you, it's going to be fine," he says, trying to comfort me. Which, of course, I appreciate, but it's not doing much good. I've heard a lot about Brody's dad. He sounds... *controlling*. Brody told me in the beginning that he wasn't happy about us being together and at that point, we weren't really even together. So, I can't imagine anything has changed on that front.

If given the opportunity to back out of this brunch, I would do it in a heartbeat. I don't know what I was thinking when I agreed to it. Oh, right. I was over-the-moon-happy that Brody wanted me to meet his family. That he's serious about us. How could I refuse?

But still...

I voice my deepest fear. "Your dad doesn't want you dating. He wants you focused on school and hockey." Not necessarily in that order.

A shadow crosses over Brody's handsome face. "I'm not worried." He shrugs, and the darkness that had been clouding his features disappears, leaving me to wonder if it was there in the first place. "He'll get over it."

Not saying another word, I nibble on my bottom lip and watch the scenery pass by outside the truck window. We're about twenty minutes away from school when we turn into a high-end residential area and stop at a small brick building that blocks the entrance to a gated community. Brody rolls down his window and waves to the guard sitting inside. Then we're once again on the move, slowly rolling down a street with multimillion-dollar houses sitting in the middle of massive lots. My eyes widen as I take in house after house. We're talking huge stone and brick structures with perfectly manicured lawns, neatly trimmed trees, and flowering garden beds. A few have small ponds with water features in the front areas.

These aren't houses. They're palatial estates. More butterflies wing their way to life inside the pit of my gut.

Of course, I realized that Brody grew up with money. His dad was a professional hockey player and now runs his own company. But this kind of wealth is beyond what I could have envisioned.

It's a little overwhelming.

Scratch that, it's a lot overwhelming.

I clear my throat and try to keep the awe and nervousness out of my voice. "This is where you grew up?"

He shoots me a concerned look. "I know it looks intimidating, but you have nothing to worry about. My dad grew up poor, playing pond hockey in Minnesota. He doesn't judge people by what they have, only by how hard they work."

We meander our way through the sub until we reach the very furthest edges backing against the woods. The properties are more spread out, each one sitting on a few acres of rolling land. The very last mansion looks like a fairytale castle with turrets spiraling into the sky.

Brody turns into a driveway made up of concrete squares edged with bright green grass, set in a diagonal pattern.

He parks in front of the massive stone house, and we exit the truck. By the time I slam the passenger side door closed, Brody has already made it around the hood and is at my side. He must sense my anxiety because he pulls me into his arms and holds me close. I inhale a big breath of air and slowly release it.

"Everything will be fine," he whispers. "I promise."

I nod against his chest. I just want to stay like this forever.

"Ready?" he asks.

As I'll ever be.

He separates himself and reaches for my hand. "You're important to me. I want you to meet them."

His words melt my heart and give me courage to enter the lion's den. How can I deny him anything when he says such sweet things to me?

"Okay," I say with a firm nod.

Hand in hand, we walk up the wide stone stairs leading to the front door. Brody doesn't bother knocking, just turns the handle and pushes it open. We step inside an enormous three-story foyer with a gigantic crystal chandelier hanging overhead. The floors are white marble, and there's a gorgeous curving staircase with a fancy iron bannister that looks like something out of the movies.

"Dad?" Brody calls out. "Amber?" His voice echoes throughout the cavernous entryway.

There's the click of heels coming from the hallway before a striking blonde with a warm smile greets us. "Hello, Brody." She turns green eyes to me. "And you must be Natalie. We're so happy you could join us!"

Her friendly demeanor instantly puts me at ease. Maybe this won't be so bad after all. It makes me feel silly for getting so caught up in my own head and psyching myself out. My first impression of Brody's stepmom is that she's really nice.

"Your father is in his office on a conference call. He'll be out short-ly." She nods toward the back of the house. "Why don't we move into the sunroom and get started before everything turns cold? I'm sure he won't mind."

Amber spins on her heels, and we fall in line behind her. I glance at Brody, who is still holding my hand. He gives me a wink and mouths, *Told you so*.

I nod. He was right. I overreacted.

We move from the entryway through a long gallery into a two-story family room. A massive stacked-stone fireplace occupies an entire wall. We continue walking through the family room into the kitchen. Everything is white marble, stainless steel appliances, and chandelier-type lighting. Three glass vases filled with lemons are strategically placed on the massive island.

Mom would have a field day wandering around this place. Even before she got involved in real estate, she would drag me to open houses and get decorating ideas for our own house.

Brody tugs on my hand, and I realize I've stopped to take everything in. We pass through the kitchen into another room that is all floor-to-ceiling windows with a set of French doors that overlook a spacious backyard that has a pool and formal gardens.

The table is centered in the middle of the room. Brody pulls out a chair for me and then sits down at my side. Amber has been very gracious, chattering the entire time, but still...I feel out of my element. I hate to admit it, but it's a relief that Brody's dad is occupied for the time being. I need a few moments to find my bearings. It's important that I make a good impression on him. Other than his dad and step-mom, Brody doesn't have any other family.

Amber flutters around the table, making sure everything has been laid out before taking a seat across from us. It's hard not to notice how warm and kind her features are. "Brody mentioned that you two have known each other since freshman year."

I nod, thankful she's opening up the dialogue and trying to put me at ease. "Yes, we met in a business class first semester." My throat feels dry and scratchy. I pick up my glass of orange juice and take a large swallow.

"It was hate at first sight," Brody says almost conversationally. "It took three long years for me to grow on her."

I nearly spray the juice from my mouth before forcing myself to swallow it down. Once I do, the coughing and sputtering begins.

Oh my God! I can't believe he just told his stepmom that! I'm trying to make a good impression so that his family likes me. And he just shot that to hell.

"Brody!" I hiss.

He laughs. His eyes dance with a mischievousness I've come to expect from him. "It's the truth, right? I'm just giving Amber a little background story."

I shake my head furiously and peek over at his stepmom. I'm almost afraid of what I'm going to see. "No..." I hesitate, trying to backpedal my way out of this. "It wasn't like that exactly..."

I really hope Brody enjoys his brunch because it's going to be the last meal he gets.

A smile hovers around the edges of Amber's lips. "I think you're going to be good for my stepson, Natalie."

Just as we begin passing around platters of French toast, eggs, fruit, bacon, and hash browns, a man who bears a striking resemblance to Brody enters the room. He stops as his gaze connects with mine and I rise from my chair, holding out my hand for him to shake.

Unlike his wife, his smile is more guarded. Polite, but not overly friendly. "It's nice to meet you, Natalie. I'm John. Sorry for not being able to meet you when you arrived."

"It's no problem. And it's nice to meet you as well." I gulp and push out the rest. "Thank you so much for inviting me to brunch with your family."

The easy feeling that had permeated the air changes, becoming stifling. He hasn't said or done anything to make me feel uncomfortable. And yet, I do.

John moves to the head of the table and takes a seat. Amber passes him a few platters and trays as he loads his plate with breakfast fare. "I hope everything is to your liking," he says.

I glance at Brody's stepmom. "Everything is delicious."

Amber smiles at the compliment. "Please, help yourself to as much as you want."

All of the tension that had previously drained from my body is back in full force. Brody's father is an imposing man. He's just as tall and broad as his son. Although his hair is dark where Brody's is golden.

Where Brody has a playfulness about him, this man does not. He's all business. He spears his food with his fork, chewing methodically. When our eyes meet across the table, I quickly lower mine to my plate. The manner in which he watches me is assessing.

I'm not sure what to think of him. And I have no idea what he thinks of me. Although, if I had to take a stab, I'd guess that he doesn't think much. It's not anything specific. Just a vibe I'm getting.

One that could be wrong.

"Brody tells us that you'll be finishing up at Whitmore in the spring," John says.

Grateful for the lifeline he's throwing me, I latch onto it with both hands. "Yes, I'll be graduating with a degree in personal finance. I'm trying to decide if I should apply to graduate school right away or take a few years off and work."

It's gruffly that he says, "Getting real-life experience is always beneficial. You can learn all the theory you want in the classroom, but when it comes down to it, you have to know how to apply everything you've learned in the real world. As someone who has a staff of over forty, I would never hire someone who doesn't have at least some experience."

I nod. "That's what my mom says as well. She thinks I should work for a while and then apply to grad school."

"I know it's still early, but have you started searching for jobs? Do you have any idea what you're looking for?"

"Last summer, I interned with a personal finance company. They've offered to hire me once I graduate."

He nods. "Getting your foot in the door is oftentimes the hardest part. Did you work in the area?"

With every question he volleys at me, my nerves continue to escalate. "Yes, I was lucky enough to find something local through school, and I lived at home for the summer. I'm still planning to put my application in at other companies, but it's nice knowing I already have something I can count on if nothing else pans out. And what's nice about the company I interned with is that they have offices all over the country, so I can stay here or transfer somewhere else."

Everything turns silent again as John spears a piece of cantaloupe with his fork and lifts it to his mouth. His eyes stay focused on me to the point of discomfort. I have to squelch the urge to squirm on my chair. I get the feeling that he doesn't want me with his son.

"Much like Brody, it sounds like you have everything mapped out for yourself." Releasing me from his penetrating stare, his gaze shifts to his son. And just like that, I'm dismissed. "We need to set up another weekend trip to Milwaukee and take a closer look at housing options for next year. I thought we could check out a few more condos near the lakefront. I'll forward the listings Dana sent over." He pulls his phone out and glances at the calendar that pops up. "It needs to happen soon. There won't be time once the season gets underway."

Brody nods, working his way through his loaded-down plate of food. It still amazes me how much he can pack away. "Once I get back to the house, I'll look at my school and hockey schedules and get back to you."

John glances at him and adds, "I want to have something on the books by the end of the week." His tone doesn't brook any arguments.

Nerves hum along my skin, but Brody seems unfazed by it. "Okay." I get the feeling that it's John's way or the highway.

Amber regales the table with stories about Haley and what a little devil she's turning out to be as she slams headfirst into the terrible twos. Brody slips his hand around mine under the table. When I sneak a peek at him, he winks and smiles. I don't know why that simple gesture is able to dissolve the building tension in me, but it does.

I jump as a loud wail pierces the quietness of the sunroom.

"It appears that our little ray of sunshine has woken from her nap." Amber rises smoothly from her chair and glances at me. "If you're finished eating, Natalie, you're welcome to join me upstairs. Hailey likes to play in her room for about ten or fifteen minutes before coming downstairs."

"Thank you, I'd like that." I try to keep the relief from my voice. I don't want to offend Brody's dad, but I'm grateful for the chance to escape his intimidating presence. Even though he hasn't necessarily been staring, I feel like he's been watching us closely. Brody holding my hand beneath the table has not evaded his notice.

I give Brody a small smile and follow Amber out of the sunroom. I don't realize just how stifling the room has grown until I leave it behind.

"We'll be back in about fifteen minutes," Amber says.

"Take your time," is John's response.

When I glance over my shoulder, I catch Brody's eyes and blow him a little kiss. He grins as I turn the corner.

I'm happy that he brought me here, but I'll be equally glad when we leave.

As Amber and Natalie climb the staircase to the second floor, Dad clears his throat and says, "She's a lovely girl."

Something sours in my gut, and I almost laugh. "But?"

Because there is most definitely a *but* coming.

He sighs and sets his fork on his plate. "Buuut," he says, drawing out the word. "You have enough going on without getting wrapped up in a girl. This is your last season before moving to the pros. Your focus needs to be on hockey and school, not getting into the pants of some pretty girl."

Maybe I was naïve, but I'd hoped that once Dad met Natalie, he would understand that she's not some puck bunny I spent Saturday night with. Natalie is different. She's smart, gorgeous, amazing. She has her shit together. And for some odd reason, she wants me.

Unfortunately, I now see I made a mistake. Dad isn't interested in getting to know the girl I'm falling for.

He's concerned she'll get in the way.

Annoyed with the way he's starting out this conversation, I say, "Natalie isn't a distraction. If anything, she's helping me with the classes I'm having trouble with." I shift on my chair and quietly admit,

"I told her about the dyslexia. She's making copies of the notes she takes in class—"

"Your professors already do that, don't they?" He doesn't look impressed.

"Yeah, but hers are more detailed. She's made notecards for me to study from and has researched other methods that can help me."

Does he have the slightest fucking clue what that means to me?

I don't make a habit of discussing my learning issues with anyone. I hide it like a dirty little secret. Natalie is the first person I've been completely open with. Not even Sawyer, Luke, or Cooper know, and they're my closest friends.

He disregards my words, shrugging them off. "You can hire tutors for that. Hell, you can even fuck them if you want." His voice hardens. "What you don't do is get emotionally attached to them." He shakes his head like I'm a child who refuses to see reason. "Now isn't the time. There's too much at stake to risk fucking it up."

I crush the paper napkin in my hand until it's nothing more than a tight ball.

Dad and I rarely butt heads. After Mom died and before Amber came into the picture, it was just the two of us. His life revolved around me. I realize that he has my best interests at heart, but still...I want him to give Natalie a fair shot. I want him to see just how good she is for me.

I sit back on my chair. "Look, I didn't plan for this to happen, but it did. Natalie is important to me. I won't let her go. I can handle everything, it won't be a problem."

Changing tactics, he says, "I spoke with Lang the other day."

Aw, hell. I know what's coming. My father has always been two steps ahead of me.

When I remain silent, he continues. "You got into a fight at practice with Reed Collins?"

I lock my jaw. "Yep."

He angles his head. Anger brews in his eyes. "Correct me if I'm wrong, but that's the same guy you punched at a party about a month ago, right?"

I slump on my chair. Since he already seems to be privy to every-thing, there's no point in trying to cover it up. "Yeah, that's him."

"Why?"

I arch a brow. "Why did I punch him?"

Dad leans forward, resting his elbows on the table. "What I'd like to know is if Natalie had any bearing on your decision to punch him."

Fuck.

I shrug. "Does it matter? Reed is an asshole. I can't tell you how many times I've wanted to hit him."

"But you didn't, did you?" He stabs a finger at me. "You were able to contain it and channel the energy elsewhere."

I grit my teeth.

"I think we both know the reason behind it matters. And my guess is that you hitting him has everything to do with that girl."

Backed into a corner, I snap, "So what if it does? Reed and I have never seen eye to eye, and that's never going to change."

"Maybe not. But you've never gotten into a physical altercation with him before she came into your life."

I shake my head and repeat stubbornly, "Reed is a douchebag—"

"That might be true, but he's your teammate. And you don't fucking get into it with your teammates, because that shit always bleeds over onto the ice. You're trying to bring home a National Championship this season. How does the animosity you feel for one another help to achieve that goal?"

I blow out a measured breath and try to wrangle my feelings under control. "Natalie has nothing to do with Reed Collins."

"Lang sees a difference in you. He's concerned. You're not looking as sharp as you did last year."

Shocked by his words, I fall back on my chair. "There's no reason to be concerned."

"I'm not going to argue about this. Natalie seems like a nice girl, but she needs to go."

I stare as his words reverberate in my head.

"There'll be plenty of time after you make your move to Milwaukee for relationships, if that's what you want. You have seven and a half months left at Whitmore and then you'll be moving on.

And from everything she said, so will she. There's no point in pouring your energies into something that has little chance of working out. Not when those energies could be better served by focusing on your career."

Unwilling to listen to another word, I bolt upward. The chair scrapes along the marble, nearly tumbling backward as I do. "I care about Natalie. She's the first girl who has ever meant something to me. I'm not going to break up with her."

Everything about this conversation pisses me off. All I wanted was for Dad to give Natalie a chance and he's unwilling to do that.

Well, fuck him.

Dad rises so we're eye level. "You need to calm down and think about what I've said." He lowers his voice, trying to sound rational. "I only have your best interests in mind, Brody. I want to see all these years of hard work pay off." He adds in a softer tone, "Your mother would be so proud of everything you've accomplished. It's important that you finish your last year strong. I want you to be a force to be reckoned with out on the ice. This isn't the time to let up on the gas." He reaches out and lays a hand on my shoulder.

Even though I want to shrug him off, I don't.

"Think about what I've said. I don't want to see you make a mistake you'll end up regretting for the rest of your life."

"I won't." With that, I walk out of the sunroom. Just as I reach the foyer, I hear Natalie's voice. My feet grind to a halt as she walks down the staircase. Our eyes catch. She smiles, looking a lot more relaxed than she did when we arrived at the house. I'll have to text Amber later and thank her for putting Natalie at ease. She has no idea how much I appreciate it.

I hadn't realized just how much Natalie's come to mean to me until Dad told me she needed to go. I'm not breaking up with her. If Coach thinks my game is slipping, that just means I need to work harder. I can handle hockey, school, and a relationship with Natalie.

Even though I don't feel like smiling, I force my lips into some semblance of one. "You ready to take off?"

"Sure." Natalie's gaze roves over me. Her eyes sharpen as if she realizes something is wrong. The last thing I want is for her to catch a whiff of the conversation I had with Dad. It would only upset her. And that, I'm not willing to do.

When I threw the invitation out there for brunch, I knew she was nervous. Her mother is easygoing and laid-back which is the opposite of my father. He has a foreboding presence. He spent years honing that persona on the ice and then in the conference room, using it to his advantage. I don't think he was rude to Natalie, but I felt her discomfort as if it were my own.

At this point, I'm sorry I brought her home to meet him.

It's not a mistake I'll make again.

"Oh, you're leaving already?" Amber seems genuinely disappointed to see us go. Hailey squirms in her arms.

As I smile at my little sister, some of my anger dissipates. "Yeah, we both have work to finish up before Monday."

When Natalie comes to stand by my side, I slip her hand into mine.

Our eyes meet and hold, a silent communication passing between us. I've never experienced that with anyone else.

I squeeze her fingers.

Dad joins us in the entryway. He turns to Natalie, and I stiffen, half-afraid he'll say something to her himself. That he'll try to reason with her since I refuse to listen.

As he extends his hand for her to shake, Natalie steps forward with her own.

"It was nice meeting you, Natalie," he says. "We enjoyed getting to know you."

"Thank you for inviting me," she replies.

"Good luck with your job search. We wish you all the best."

"Thank you."

When Dad meets my gaze again, he merely gives me a nod. "Let me know what your schedule looks like."

"I'll text you," I reply stiffly.

I'm pissed that at twenty-three years of age, he thinks he can tell me to get rid of someone I want in my life. Hopefully, he realizes that it's not going to happen. Natalie is here to stay. Whether he likes it or not.

Chapter Thirty-Four

BRODY

The next week flies by. I blink and almost miss it. There are tests to study for and assignments to finish typing. I swear I spend as much time hunkered down on the third floor of the library with Natalie as I do busting my ass in the arena. I make sure that when I skate off the ice at the end of each practice, I'm leaving everything I have out there.

Contrary to what my dad thinks, it's important for me to finish this year strong. I know exactly what hinges upon it. I haven't lost sight of my goals and what I need to do to reach them. The only difference is that Natalie now factors into those plans.

Reed and I haven't had any further run-ins. I'm not looking to start shit with him, but I'm also not hiding out in a corner hoping to avoid that asshole either. If he needs another beatdown, so he better understands his place in the pecking order, I'd be more than happy to deliver it.

Fuck that guy.

I don't want to waste another brain cell thinking about Reed Collins.

So, I'll focus on Natalie instead. I spend as much time with her as I can, but it's not nearly enough to satisfy the growing need I have for her.

Without us discussing it, I end up at her place every night. I know she doesn't want to be at the hockey house. And I can't blame her for that. Most of the time, I don't want to be there either. Every night is a party with people passed out on the couch and beer cans strewn about the tables. I'm over it. Cooper and Sawyer have given me some shit about being pussy-whipped, but Luke gets it. Half the time, he's hauling ass out of Zara's bedroom at five in the morning to make practice like I am.

I wish Dad could understand that Natalie has changed everything for me. We've spoken a few times on the phone, and the Milwaukee trip is in the works, but he hasn't brought up the subject of Natalie again. We're both avoiding the issue.

I'm hopeful that if I give it a little time and don't push matters, he'll see for himself that I'm not going to fuck everything up because I'm dating someone. That's the plan. This thing with Natalie has taken me completely by surprise, and now that she's in my life, I can't imagine one without her.

I turn my head and stare at her. Fuck, she's gorgeous. Like seriously, take-my-breath-away gorgeous. All that long silky hair is fanned out against the ivory pillowcase. Her lips are full and pouty, ripe for kissing. I'm tempted to lean over and nip them.

Sometimes I can't believe she wants to be with me. Natalie could have any guy she wants. She's smart and gorgeous. And that fucking mouth of hers...

God, but I love that sassy-ass mouth.

It's always been a turn-on. Looking back at all the shit we used to give to each other, I think it was all foreplay leading up to this.

I roll toward her and gently press my lips against hers, wanting to wake her with a kiss. Is that cheesy as hell?

You bet your ass, it is.

But I don't care.

I'm that guy now, so deal with it.

I press soft butterfly kisses across her face until her eyelids flutter and she focuses on me. A smile spreads across her face.

"Morning," she says. Her voice is all low and husky.

"Morning," I whisper in return.

I playfully snag her bottom lip between my teeth and tug it until she giggles.

My hands glide across her naked breasts until I'm able to cup their warm weight in my palms. A purring noise rumbles from deep in her throat as she arches her body against the hold I have on her. God, but I love how responsive she is.

"Get a condom," I groan. "I need to be inside you." Watching her writhe under my touch has my cock rock-hard.

She glances at the clock on the nightstand. "We don't have time. You need to leave for practice in five minutes."

I shake my head, making a split decision. "I'm skipping it this morning." I'm going to spend the next couple of hours making love to her.

Her brows slide together. "Brody, I don't want you getting into any more trouble with your coach."

I kiss one corner of her mouth and then the other. "Don't worry about it. I won't get in trouble." All right, so maybe Coach will be pissed, but I don't give a shit right now. I've got more pressing matters to contend with.

Her hand comes up to stroke the side of my cheek. "I'm not going anywhere. Go to practice. I'll be here waiting when you return."

I groan.

Goddamn it. I don't want to leave her, but she's probably right. I should get my ass to the rink. "Promise you won't move?"

A sleepy smile curves her lips. "I promise. I'm all yours. Now, go." She makes a shooing gesture with her hand as she cuddles into the covers. She looks so sexy all tousled and warm. "Get. I don't want you to be late." The smile turns seductive. "And when you get back, I'll make it worth your while."

My brows rise at the enticement, and I throw the comforter back, high-tailing it from bed.

Natalie chuckles.

I point at her and narrow my eyes. "You move from there, and you'll be in big trouble."

"I won't move a muscle," she says.

I lean over and press my lips against hers. She twines her arms around my neck and opens her mouth when I lick at the seam. Our tongues tangle for a moment before I reluctantly pull away.

"Just remember," I murmur. "You've made promises, and I'm going to hold you to them." With that, I smack another kiss against her lips and throw my clothes on with record speed.

Just as I'm heading out the door, she says, "Brody..."

I glance over my shoulder, and Natalie tosses the covers back, revealing her naked body. Her legs fall open so that she's spread wide. She trails her hand from her ribcage, moving down her belly until she reaches her pubic bone, where her fingers linger.

And just like that, I'm at full wood.

I gulp. My gaze is fastened to her gorgeous pussy, so soft and velvety smooth.

Her fingers descend, gently tracing her parted lips before stroking over her clit in lazy circles. She arches her back and closes her eyes.

I groan, "You're killing me, Davies." I can't take my eyes off her because she's so beautiful.

"That's a little preview of what you'll find waiting for you upon arrival." A small smile curves her lips. "We'll just call it motivation."

"The only thing you've done," I growl, "is give me a raging hard-on."

She giggles. "Well, no one will mess with you when they see that thing."

I narrow my eyes. "You're a little demon, you know that?"

"See you in two hours, sugar-booger," she singsongs gleefully. With that, she flicks the covers back over her body and burrows into them.

Goddamn, but I lov—

Shocked, I catch the words right before they explode in my head.

But you know what?

I think I do.

I'm supposed to meet Brody at the library in twenty minutes, and I'm running late. I grab my bag from the table and am flying out the door of my apartment when I smack into a hard body. I bounce back a step as large hands reach out and grab my arms, steadying me before I can tumble backward.

My eyes land on the man holding me and widen. John McKinnon is the last person I expected to find on my doorstep. Once I have my balance, I quickly step away from him.

He inclines his dark head. "Hello, Natalie."

"Hi, Mr. McKinnon." I gulp down the rising nerves. "Are you looking for Brody?" I ask, hoping that's all his presence signifies.

I'm about to tell him that he's not here, when John says, "No, actually I came to speak with you. Do you have a few minutes for us to talk?"

I shift from one foot to another, intimidated by him. "I was just on my way to meet someone," I say evasively. The last thing I want is to have a conversation alone with him. Already I know that whatever he wants to discuss won't be good.

Even though he smiles, the expression doesn't reach his eyes. "I'm sure my son will understand if you're a few minutes late."

When I don't move from the door, he quirks a brow as if amused by my behavior. "May I come in?"

I glance behind me and gnaw my lower lip. Zara is at class, and I'm here by myself.

"Natalie," he says impatiently. "It's important that I speak with you about Brody. Give me ten minutes of your time, and then I'll be on my way."

I jerk my head into a nod and step aside, allowing him to pass. He walks in and settles himself on the couch. I trail stiffly behind him into the living room and remain standing. I keep about ten feet of distance between us. If I need to dart to the door, I think I can make it.

Which is ridiculous. This is Brody's father we're talking about. Not some thug in a dark alleyway. And yet...I feel just as vulnerable and ill-at-ease.

He points to the chair situated across from the couch. "Wouldn't you be more comfortable if you sat down?"

I shake my head. There's nothing that will make this impromptu visit comfortable. "If you don't mind, I'd prefer if you just tell me why you're here."

He nods his head, a touch of respect entering his eyes. "I can appreciate that." He leans forward until his elbows rest on his knees. He holds my gaze with a penetrating stare just long enough to make me squirm. "I think you and I have the same goal in mind."

"What would that be?" His odd words have my brows pulling together.

His gaze is relentless. "To see Brody reach his full potential."

Feeling confused, I say, "Of course, that's what I want. Brody is a talented hockey player." I may not know much about the sport, but I know he's ranked one of the best college players in the country. He's poured his whole life into making it to the NHL. "He's going to go far," I say with conviction.

John's eyes soften. "Yes, he will. But he needs to stay focused. This is his last college season before making the jump to the NHL. Do you have any idea the strength and conditioning it takes to compete at a professional level? It's brutal. And it's just as much a mental game as it is a physical one."

I shake my head. "Mr. McKinnon, I don't understand why you're telling me this."

He sighs and folds his hands in front of him. He stares at them for a moment before meeting my eyes again. "Natalie, you seem like a smart young woman. It's easy to understand what my son sees in you. But—"

The reason he's turned up unannounced at my apartment dawns on me before he has a chance to finish the sentence.

"—I'm a distraction," I whisper, my heart pounding harshly under my breast.

"I'm sorry to state it so baldly, but yes, you are." He pauses for a beat. "Am I correct in assuming that you and Brody have grown close?"

"Yes," I admit miserably. In a little more than a month, Brody has come to mean so much to me. More than I could have imagined.

"And he's been candid with you about his struggles."

"If you're talking about the dyslexia," I say, "then yes, he told me about it."

"I've watched my son struggle his entire life. I hired all the best tutors, and it didn't make a damn bit of difference. There were no magic bullets that eased the pain. Do you have any idea what it's like as a parent to watch your child struggle just to get C's and B's?"

"No," I say softly. "I don't."

His lips twist bitterly as he rasps, "Hopefully, you never will. There's nothing more painful than sitting helplessly by as your child struggles to achieve something others can do without any effort at all."

A thick lump rises in my throat because I can't imagine what it was like, not only for Brody, but his father as well. Needing to sit down, I fall onto the chair.

"Brody needs to get through this season and continue to elevate his game. Next year, no matter how good he is, will be a transition. He needs to stay mentally committed to that."

"He is committed," I murmur.

John sits back and arches his brow. "Is he?"

"Of course."

"And yet, he's gotten into two fights since you've come into the picture. One of them was at practice, where he was kicked off the ice."

Folding in on myself, I wrap my arms around my waist. Every word he hurtles feels like a poisonous dart. I'm not sure what to say because the same guilt gnaws at me now as when Brody first told me about the fight with Reed. I'm to blame for it.

"My concern is that Milwaukee will get it in their heads that Brody isn't a team player. Even though he has a contract, they can always release him if they feel he isn't a good fit for their organization. Or sit him for the season and then he'd only see a minute or two of ice time each game, if that."

My belly spasms at the possibility. Brody loves hockey so much that not playing would kill him.

"You seem to have his best interests at heart," John says. "I can't imagine you'd want to see that happen."

"Of course not. I would never do anything to hurt Brody."

"I can see that, Natalie." He leans forward. "I'm not saying any of this is your fault. Brody is the one who made the decision to get into a fight with Reed Collins. But that's the problem—he's not making good decisions with his future in mind."

When I say nothing, he continues. "I think we both know what needs to be done, don't we?"

I bury my head in my hands. "I...I'm not sure," I say unhappily. I care about Brody so much. How can I just let him go?

When John stands, I hope he'll quietly let himself out of the apartment. Tears burn the backs of my eyes. Instead of leaving, he closes the distance between us. When I don't look up, he lays a hand on my shoulder. "If you truly care about my son, you'll do what's best for him." He squeezes my shoulder until I meet his gaze. "I trust this conversation will stay between the two of us."

Sick to my stomach, I nod.

The hand gripping my shoulder disappears, and then he's gone. The door closes softly behind him.

I don't know how long I sit on the chair, everything Mr. McKinnon said swirling through my brain. It's only when a text from Brody flashes across the screen of my phone do I remember that I was supposed to meet him at the library.

I find Brody on the third floor, tucked into the corner that has become our spot. His books are spread out, and he's looking over another set of flash cards I made for him. Each chapter is color-coded and I made sure to use big, block writing so he's easily able to decode the words.

All I'm trying to do is help.

And yet, according to Brody's dad, I'm a liability. I still feel shaken from the conversation. Dropping onto the seat across from him, I avert my eyes and lay my bag on the table.

"I thought we were meeting at four?" Brody asks with a slight frown.

"I'm sorry. Something came up," I say evasively.

Even though I'm focused on pulling out my books and computer, I feel his eyes on me as if he's waiting for an explanation. But I can't give him a truthful one. I can't tell him that his dad just paid me a visit. That he wants me to end things between us.

It's all I could think about on the way over. If I tell Brody about his father stopping by for a private conversation, it'll just cause problems between them. How can I do that? Brody doesn't have any other family. It's always been him and his dad. I can't, in good conscience, do anything to jeopardize that relationship. No matter how much I care about him.

Mr. McKinnon wants the best for his son. I want that as well. The difference is that he doesn't see me as the best thing for Brody.

And that hurts.

The last thing I want is to hold Brody back.

"Nat?" Brody asks, jolting me out of my thoughts.

He must sense something is off with me, because he didn't refer to me as Davies like he usually does. It's enough to make the backs of my eyes burn. When I have my emotions firmly under control, I glance up. Concern darkens his golden-colored eyes.

I lift the corners of my lips into a thin smile, one that will hopefully reassure him. "Um, Stacy, my boss from the internship last summer, called, and wanted to know what my plans are after graduation."

"Oh?" Looking interested, he perks up.

I nod. "We ended up talking for about fifteen minutes. Sorry."

He reaches out and snags my fingers. I stare at our clasped hands, realizing just how affectionate he is. We hold hands at every opportunity. Brody often slings an arm around my shoulder when we're walking around campus and holds me in his arms when we're standing in line.

"That's great. What did you tell her?" He sounds genuinely happy for me.

"I told her that I was interested." I clear my throat and force out the rest of the lie. "And that I'd like to meet with her to speak at greater length about the opportunity."

His gaze sharpens. "You mentioned they have offices all over the country, right?"

I glance away. "Yeah, I think they have offices in every major city." I have spoken with Stacy, but I'm nowhere near making a decision. It was the first excuse that came to mind.

"Good to know." He gives me a little wink. "That could come in handy down the road."

The implication of his words brings a lump to my throat. I need to change the subject before this conversation goes any further. Until I figure out what I'm going to do, I'm not going to mention his dad's visit. "You've been going over the cards I gave you?"

"Every chance I get, I pull them out," he tells me.

"How about I quiz you?"

"Sure."

We spend the next hour going over the cards. The upcoming test covers a lot of ground and some of the concepts are tricky. I gave him the materials more than a week ago so he would have enough time to study instead of trying to cram it in at the last moment.

Leaning back on his chair, Brody lifts his arms over his head and stretches his body. The graphic tee he's wearing rides up his belly, showing a tantalizing strip of tight abs. My eyes arrow to the sun-kissed flesh.

"I think we could both use a study break right about now," he says, closing his textbook.

My eyes snap to his. A sexy smirk curves his lips upward. He obviously caught me staring at his perfectly chiseled body. Before I can respond, he grabs my fingers and pulls me up and around the table until I tumble onto his lap. Brody wraps his arms around me and slants his mouth over mine.

Unable to resist, especially after the brutal conversation with his dad, I open immediately, and his tongue slips inside my mouth before stroking against mine. His hands go to the sides of my face, holding me in place.

After a few breathless minutes, I break away.

Even though I could spend the rest of the night kissing Brody, I don't want to get off task. It's important that he does well on this test. So much is riding on it. If he bombs it or even gets a D, that will pull his grade down even further, and then he'll end up benched. "We should probably get back to studying," I remind him.

"Not yet," he grumbles. "I haven't seen you all day. I've missed you."

His words make my heart ache. "Okay," I give in. "But only a few more minutes. We have to make sure you ace this exam."

He huffs out a breath. "That's not going to happen. I'll be ecstatic if I pull off a B."

"If we study a little bit harder, you can do it. I know you can."

"I'd rather study you," he murmurs right before his lips coast over the column of my neck. As soon as his mouth makes contact, my eyelids feather closed. He nips at my throat before his tongue darts out to sooth the area.

"God, but I just want to get you alone," he growls as his hands delve under my shirt, zeroing in on my breasts.

I groan as he palms the soft flesh and teases my nipples.

"Brody, you need to focus." I'm barely able to get the words out.

"Trust me, sweetheart, I'm focused."

His father's words ring unwantedly in my head, leaving me cold. This is exactly what John was talking about. Instead of studying for an important exam, Brody would rather be making out with me.

Even though I would never do anything to intentionally hurt him, I can't help but wonder if that's what is going on. Am I nothing more than a distraction that pulls his focus from what's truly important? Am I jeopardizing his future?

I tug his hands from under my shirt and jump off his lap. My body trembles as I slump on the chair across from him. "You have to study," I repeat. "You need to do well on this exam. It's important."

Annoyance flashes across his face. "Chill out, Davies. You don't need to remind me that it's important. I know it is." He adds, "My dad rides me enough. I don't need to hear it from you, too."

I wince. His words feel like a slap in the face.

Unable to meet his eyes, I stare sightlessly at the book splayed open in front of me. "I'm sorry," I whisper. "I just want you to do well. That's all."

He sighs. His fingers slide across the table until they're able to tangle with mine. He brings them to his lips and gently presses a kiss against my knuckles. "No, I'm sorry. I didn't mean to snap at you. I know you're just trying to help, and I appreciate it. I'm under a lot of pressure right now."

I glance at him. "I know." My heart feels like it's about to crack wide open.

Maybe his dad is right.

Maybe I'm just in the way.

Chapter Thirty-Seven

BRODY

I grab Natalie's fingers as we leave campus and head to my truck parked nearby in a lot by Campbell Hall.

"Are you hungry?" I ask. "Want to grab something to eat?" I'm always starving. Between two-a-days practice on the ice and lifting in the gym, I burn through calories. I may not be eating the crazy amount that Michael Phelps does when he's training, but it's not that far off either.

When she doesn't answer, I glance over and squeeze her fingers. "Natalie?" She seems lost in her own world lately. I can't shake the feeling that there's something weighing on her mind that she's not telling me about.

As soon as I say her name, she jolts to attention. "Sorry." She gives me an apologetic smile that barely lifts her lips. "I wasn't paying attention."

"Do you want to grab lunch?" I glance at my phone. "We've got time to hit La Fuente."

"Oh." She shakes her head. "I'm not really hungry. But we can go if you want."

I know how much she loves that place, so I'm a little surprised she isn't jumping at the chance to go. I jerk my shoulders. "Nah, I'll just grab something at your place. It's not a big deal."

"Okay." She smiles again, but it's distracted. Like she's not fully here with me, and I hate it.

Once we reach the truck, I open the passenger side door and she slides in. I hustle around to the other side. As I start the engine and pull out of the parking lot, I glance over at Natalie. She's staring out the side window. Even though her face is tilted away from me, I'm able to glimpse the sadness in her eyes.

"Hey." I reach over and slip her hand into mine. I love touching her. I'm addicted to the constant contact and the connection between us. "What's going on?" I ask because it's obvious that something's bothering her.

She stares down at our clasped hands for a beat before raising her eyes to mine. "I've just got a lot on my mind with school."

I nod, understanding the pressure she's under. I feel it myself. Senior year is stressful, and I know Natalie isn't sure where she'll end up or who she'll be working for. "Do you want to talk about it?"

She shrugs and says, "Not really. It won't help."

Her odd response makes my brows tug together. I pull up in front of her apartment building and cut the engine. Even though it's the last thing I want, I ask, "Do you need some time to yourself? Would that help?" Maybe I'm crowding her. All this relationship stuff is new to me. I'm trying to figure it out as I go and strike a happy balance.

Natalie isn't one of those clingy girls who wants to glom on to you and never let go. That's one of the things I like about her. So, the last thing I want is for her to feel like I'm doing the same thing. Although, if I had my way, I'd be with her all the time. When we're together, I feel like I can finally breathe. Like I can be myself. She's one of the few people who see me for who I really am.

I don't want to lose that. So, if she needs me to back off a little, I will. I may not want to, but I'll do it anyway.

Natalie shakes her head, and I release the pent-up breath that has become trapped in my lungs.

Thank fuck.

I don't want to leave her. The time we spend together is precious.

A few minutes later, she opens the door to her apartment. Since we're greeted by silence, I'm guessing that Zara is at class or out with Luke. Now, those two are attached at the hip. Although, it's not like I can give Luke shit about it. Not when I feel much the same way.

Natalie sets her bag down on the kitchen table. I'm not sure how to play this. Do I push for more information or do I back off and pretend everything is normal?

Before I can make a decision, she wraps her arms around me and squeezes tight. I hold her against my body, and somehow her grip becomes even more constricting. This is the kind of hug you give someone at the airport before they leave the continent for a year.

I shake off the weird feeling that settles over me and laugh. "Hey, what's going on?"

She tips her head back and smiles. But again, there's something off about it. Almost as if the edges are tinged with sadness. I'm not sure what to make of it. If there's a problem, I wish she'd just put it out there. I'd much rather deal with an issue head-on than get blindsided by it down the road.

Instead of answering, she steps out of my embrace and pulls me toward the bedroom. Her eyes stay fastened to mine as she pushes me onto the bed and pulls at my shirt. Once that has been thrown to the floor, she starts on the button of my khakis.

Even though I love where this is headed, I lay my hand over her fingers, stilling their frantic movement. "Natalie?"

Her eyes lift.

"What's going on?" I rack my brain for an answer since she seems unwilling to give me one. "Did something happen with your dad?" I'm grasping at straws here. I need her to throw me a lifeline.

She shakes her head. "Everything's fine. I just want to be with you."

Whatever she's selling, I'm not buying. My gut tells me something's up, but I have no idea what. It's starting to drive me crazy.

Flicking open the button, she slides the zipper down until she can slip her hand inside my boxers.

All right...if she's trying to distract me from asking any more questions, she's doing a damn fine job of it. As soon as she wraps her fingers around me, I groan and recline against the bed, resting on my elbows to give her greater access.

She pumps my cock, sliding her hand up and down the shaft. It doesn't take much to get me going. *Christ.* All Natalie has to do is look at me, and I pop a boner. The chemistry we have is undeniable, but there's so much more between us.

I hiss out a breath when she takes me in her mouth. Her tongue swirls around the tip of my erection before she draws me in further. Even though I want to lay back and enjoy this, I force my eyes to stay open. There's nothing hotter than watching Natalie on her knees, lips wrapped around my dick, sucking me deep inside the warm haven of her mouth.

Fuck. I'm not going to last long.

Which bites, because I want this moment to last *for-e-ver*. Actually, I'd settle for five more minutes of this heaven, but that's not going to happen.

Two is pushing it. She has a choke hold on my cock as she slides her fingers up and down in the same rhythm as her mouth. When her other hand comes up to cup and play with my balls, I know I'm going to explode.

I've never come in Natalie's mouth. I'm more than aware that some girls don't like it. And I never wanted to make her feel like it was an expectation.

"Natalie," I groan, trying to pull her off me. "I'm going to come."

She opens lust-filled eyes and pops my cock out of her mouth. I hiss out a breath as the cool air of the room hits my sensitive flesh.

"I want you in my mouth," she murmurs.

Then she's back on me, sucking me down even further.

Fuuuuuuck.

I thread my fingers through the long strands of her hair and watch as she moves up and down my shaft. When she reaches the tip, she laps the slit before taking my length into her mouth again. The further she draws me in, the harder it becomes to remain in control.

The hand cupping my sac squeezes tight as her gaze locks on mine. An orgasm stirs in my balls, and I gently piston my hips.

And then I come.

Long and hard.

I can't rip my eyes away from Natalie as she continues pulling on my cock. Coming in her mouth...I don't think I've ever seen anything sexier. My orgasm lasts for what feels like days. Not once does she let up. Even when I collapse on my elbows, she's still there, milking every last drop from my softening dick.

Unable to stand another moment, I grab her under the arms and haul her against me as I lie back on the bed. I hold her, never wanting to let go. "Fuck baby, that was good."

A smile curves her lips as I kiss her, thrusting my tongue inside her mouth before rolling her over. Goddamn, but I love the feel of her body beneath mine.

"Turnabout is only fair play, right?" I growl.

She chuckles. "I sincerely hope so."

I sit up and practically shred the clothing from her body until she's naked. I can't help but sit back and admire just how beautiful Natalie is. We're talking absolute perfection.

With all this post-orgasmic satisfaction pumping through my veins, I'm tempted to tell her how I feel, but I'm afraid she's not ready to hear it. Maybe it's too soon. I don't want to spook her. Instead of giving voice to the words bubbling beneath the surface, I show her with my hands and mouth, wanting her to feel revered.

Moving down her body, I kiss her breasts, ribcage, and belly. Then I work my way back up until I can suck one pebbled nipple into my mouth. When she arches her back and writhes beneath me, I switch sides and suckle greedily from the other tight bud. She moans and plows her fingers through my hair, raking her nails against my scalp. The pleasure-pain of it feels good.

Everything we do feels amazing.

It feels right. Like I've finally found the one person who makes me feel whole. The one who sees me for the guy I am and accepts me, faults and all.

"Brody..."

The way she moans my name is music to my ears.

I pop her diamond-hard tip out of my mouth and gently press a kiss where her heart lies between her breasts before licking a hot trail down to her pelvic bone. Again, I feather soft sweet kisses on her inner thighs and lower abdomen.

"Brody, please..." she moans again.

Natalie spreads her thighs in invitation. It's all I can do to resist delving straight into that sweet pussy of hers. I want to. God, do I. But I want to drive her just as crazy as she makes me. I want her to realize that I'm the only one who can make her feel this way. I want her just as addicted to me as I am to her.

Is that even possible?

I have no idea. But I'm going to damn well try.

Moving between her parted thighs, I pick up one long, lean leg and gently nip at her calf before raining kisses all over her thighs. Then I do the same to the other until I reach the vee between her legs. I gently bite her mons, and she thrusts herself against me. My tongue swipes along her cleft before tracing lazy circles around her clit.

She moans as I back away, moving instead to the delicate skin of her inner thighs. My tongue dances along her outer lips, which have plumped with arousal. I pull back and stare at her pussy.

It's so fucking gorgeous. Pink, soft, and creamy. I could lose myself in the silky heat of her body.

"Brody, please...Stop teasing," Natalie says with a pout.

"I'm never going to stop teasing, baby," I mutter, glancing up at her.

And then I make slow love to her with my lips and tongue, relentlessly pushing her toward climax until she screams my name over and over.

It's the best fucking feeling in the world.

Something's up with Natalie.

She's been acting weird for a couple of days, and when I ask her what's wrong, she smiles and tells me everything is fine. But it's not. Far from it.

How can I fix the problem if she won't even admit there is one?

How much freaking sense does that make? What? Does she think I'm a mind reader?

Well, I'm not.

This is the first relationship I've ever been in. I have no idea what I'm doing. I'm like a blind man stumbling around in the dark...

All right, maybe that doesn't make sense, but you get the picture.

Feeling desperate, I go to the only person who might be able to offer some half-decent advice. I sure as hell can't ask Sawyer or Cooper. Those two are the guys you hit up if you've got questions regarding orgy etiquette.

Because, yeah, apparently that's a thing.

I rap my knuckles on Luke's door before pushing it open. "Hey, you got a minute?"

He pulls a T-shirt over his head, looking like he just got out of the shower. "Sure, what's up?"

Now that I'm here, I'm not quite sure how to delve into this conversation without sounding like a complete pussy. Shifting from one foot to the other, I scratch my chin, stalling for time.

Is it too late to back out the door and pretend this never happened?

Fuck. This is really uncomfortable. I didn't realize I would feel like such a horse's ass while asking a friend for relationship advice. It's not like I have a ton of friends who know what the hell they're doing when it comes to the opposite sex.

Okay, let me rephrase that. I have a ton of friends who know what they're doing when it comes to the ladies. I do not, however, have a lot of friends who know what to do in girlfriend situations.

Let's face it, my closest friends are hockey players. And most of these guys aren't in monogamous relationships. They'd much rather play the field and hook up whenever the urge strikes them.

Been there and done that.

It's completely understandable.

But that's not where I am anymore. And I don't want to fuck things up with Natalie. I like her way too much for that. So, I guess if that means I have to stand here feeling like a complete asshole, then that's what I'm going to do.

Luke is the only guy I know who has a couple of relationships under his belt. Which means he's the most knowledgeable one to seek out advice from. Right?

Quite frankly, it's slim pickings.

It's either Luke or Jack Schiff, our goalie, and I think Jack has a few screws loose. Unfortunately, that seems to be a requirement to be a decent goaltender. Who else would be crazy enough to stand there and get pelted with pucks by guys who have a ninety-five-mile-per-hour slapshot?

Exactly.

Plus, his girlfriend is just as loco as he is. Yeah, they've been together for two years. But they've also had the cops called on them twice for domestic disturbances because when that girl loses her shit, she goes nuclear.

Luke is my safest bet.

"Um..." I mutter.

When I continue standing there, saying nothing, Luke cocks his head and stares at me with growing interest. "What's up?"

I shake my head and drag my fingers through my hair. Spitting out the words is so much harder than I thought it would be.

He laughs. "Brody?"

"You're the only one I can come to about this, okay?" I lower my voice and shut the door. "And I don't want to hear any shit about it afterward, got it?"

Looking mildly baffled, but still highly amused, he says, "Um, all right."

"It's about Natalie."

"Shit." His amusement fades. "Have you fucked it up already? 'Cause there's a pool saying this won't last more than six weeks."

"I haven't done anything." Well, I don't think I have. See, that's the problem. I have no idea if I've done something or not. I draw myself up to my full height and frown. "Wait a minute...A pool?" My brows lower as I narrow my eyes. "What'd you bet?"

He looks sheepish. "Three weeks. Already lost my money."

I roll my eyes. "Seriously, dude?"

He shrugs. "What do you want me to say? You've always been a hit-it-and-quit-it kind of guy. Didn't you have some sort of schematic for sleeping with the same girl twice?"

It was three times in six months.

But, fine...I see where he's coming from.

"Can we please stay focused?" I snap.

"Sure." He shrugs. "What's going on with Natalie?"

I shake my head and plow my fingers through my hair for the second time in as many minutes. "I don't know. She's acting weird. Every time I ask her what the deal is, she brushes me off and says everything's fine. But it doesn't seem fine. You know?" I search his face for understanding.

Luke takes a seat at his desk and spins the chair around to face me as I plunk down on the bed across from him.

"Maybe there really is nothing going on with her." He leans

forward, his elbows balancing on his knees. "Maybe you're reading into something that's just not there."

At this point, anything's possible. But my gut tells me something's up. "I don't know. She just seems more distant lately. Sometimes I catch her staring at me, and she's got this look in her eyes. I keep waiting for her to drop a bomb, but she hasn't." And it's killing me. Every time it happens I find myself holding my breath and waiting.

We're both silent for a moment before he suggests, "Why don't you take her out for dinner—or better yet—cook something nice for her." He points a finger at me. "That shows effort and chicks love that. Get a bottle of wine, and then you can talk."

Hmmm.

That's actually not a bad idea.

I want Natalie to understand that even though I've been a player in the past, I'm not one now. She can trust me. I want this to work between us. I'm in it for the long haul.

I think Luke might be onto something here.

I nod. "All right, I'm going to do it."

"Just let me know when and I'll make sure Zara and I steer clear of the apartment. You'll have the place all to yourself."

I nod and hold out my hand for a fist bump. "Thanks man. I appreciate it."

"Anytime."

Just as I come to my feet, Luke says, "Natalie's been good for you. Don't fuck this up."

I nod. He's right. Natalie *has* been good for me. And the last thing I want to do is mess up and lose her.

Chapter Thirty-Nine

BRODY

I pour two glasses of wine and light the candle in the middle of the table in the dining area. A bouquet of wildflowers shoved in a vase that I picked up at the grocery store while I was out shopping for dinner sits next to the flickering flame.

With a critical eye, I take in the setting.

I want everything to be perfect.

Romantic, but not overly cheesy.

Unfortunately, I don't have time to fuss with the table setting because the timer for the noodles boiling away on the stove dings.

Believe it or not, I've never made spaghetti before. I had to read the directions. Then, just to make sure I didn't fuck it up, I YouTubed it. Seemed simple enough. I'd almost go so far as to say idiotproof. Except, I don't want to jinx anything.

I use a fork to fish out a noodle and test its readiness.

"Shit," I mutter, burning my fingers as I throw the pasta into my mouth and chew it quickly.

I check the sauce.

It tastes good.

Although it's from a jar. So...kind of hard to screw that up, which makes it the perfect dinner for a novice like myself. I need a culinary dish with training wheels. Something that shows I put in effort but nothing that would end up looking like a charcoal briquette.

Or make the fire department break down the door.

I throw the garlic bread in the oven for five minutes and pour a bag a chopped salad into a bowl.

For the fiftieth time, I scan the table taking stock of everything. It looks good, if I do say so myself. I don't want to be premature and pat myself on the back, but I am seriously crushing this whole dinner thing.

Natalie is going to be super-impressed with my mad culinary skills.

You know what?

I'm super-impressed with myself.

Just as I take the bread from the oven, I hear a key slide into the lock, and the door to the apartment opens. My heart, believe it or not, leaps into my throat and then beats in overdrive. I can't believe I'm this nervous. I need this night to go off without a hitch. The end game here is for Natalie to understand just how important she is to me.

If everything goes according to plan, I might even drop the L-bomb.

I almost shake my head at that.

Right now, I'm blowing my own mind.

Natalie comes around the corner, her feet grinding to a halt when she sees me standing in the kitchen.

"What's going on?" she whispers, looking stunned.

I state the obvious while pointing toward the pots and pans cluttering up the counter. "I made dinner for you." Then I correct, "For us."

Her eyes travel slowly around the kitchen before landing on the table. She sucks in a sharp breath and brings her fingers to her mouth.

"The candle isn't too much, is it?" I ask nervously, wishing I had opted for either the flowers or the candle, not both. Maybe it's overkill.

She shakes her head. "No, it's perfect. Absolutely perfect."

My entire body relaxes, and I realize how tense I'd become while waiting for her reaction. "Good. I want everything to be perfect for you."

Her eyes slide back to mine. "I can't believe you did all this."

Since she hasn't moved, I close the distance between us and slide the messenger bag off her shoulder, dropping it to the floor. Then I wrap her up in my arms. Hers slip around me and hug me so tightly that it feels like she's going to squeeze the air from my lungs. But I love it. Love that she's holding on for dear life.

I drop a small kiss at the crown of her head. "I wanted to do something special for you."

"Thank you."

I pull back so I can search her eyes. She blinks back the wetness as she stares up at me. There's a look swimming around in her eyes. Happiness. But something else that I can't put my finger on lurks there as well. It's been bothering me all week.

Pushing it aside, I say, "I hope you're hungry."

"Starving. I didn't get a chance to eat lunch because it was so busy," Natalie remarks.

I raise both brows and tease, "What? No time for French fries? How's that possible?"

She smiles, and whatever had been haunting her expression disappears. "It was a marathon session of studying at the library."

I nod, thinking about the first time we studied together on the third floor. Okay, maybe I'm not thinking so much about the studying as what happened during the break.

I clear my head of that image. "Why don't you sit down and I'll bring out our plates."

"Okay."

She takes a seat and picks up her glass of wine, taking a small sip. I set a plate of pasta and garlic bread in front of her. There's a bowl for salad on the side.

Even though I know Natalie is surprised and happy about the dinner I've prepared, I still sense something off with her behavior.

Is she worried that I'm not serious about her?

She doesn't need to be. I've never made a commitment like this, and she knows it. If I wasn't interested in being with her, in furthering our relationship, I would break things off.

I want Natalie.

I get that being with me is a lot to handle. Natalie doesn't care for the attention she receives for being my girlfriend. She likes moving around campus anonymously. She hates the puck bunnies that are always hanging around, but I've done absolutely nothing to encourage their behavior. I keep girls at a firm distance because I don't want her to feel like she has something to worry about. I'm not Reed fucking Collins. I would never cheat on her or hurt her the way he did.

If we're happy together, then that's all that should matter. The rest is nothing more than white noise. We'll make it work.

Once we've both eaten, Natalie rises from her seat to clear the dishes from the table.

"Sit down, I'll do that later. I'm taking care of everything tonight, and that includes KP." When she starts to argue, I point to her half-filled glass of wine. "Enjoy your beverage. I'll be right back."

I grab both of our plates and the salad and dump everything in the sink. I bought a fancy chocolate cake at the store. There was no way in hell I was even attempting to bake a dessert. I'm well aware of my limitations.

Pasta was enough for one night. And the fact that it turned out decent—I'll take that as a win.

I sit down and top off her wine.

"This was really nice," she says.

I smile. "I'm glad you enjoyed it."

"No one has ever cooked dinner for me, so thank you," she adds quietly.

I snag her fingers with mine. This is it. Do or die time. "I know we haven't been together long, but I want you to know that I really care about you." I squeeze her hand to emphasize my words. "I want this to work out between us. I'm thinking long-term." My gut twists with nerves. I have the same feeling I get right before I jump onto the ice for the first time during a championship game. Like I'm so excited that I might throw up. "Next year I'll be in Milwaukee, and I want you there with me."

Once the words are out, I exhale a breath. Relief pumps through me. I expect her to say something, but she doesn't. She just stares at me from across the table.

Not knowing what to do, I blurt, "I love you, Natalie."

With my heart in my throat, I wait for her to say those three little words back. Every second that slowly ticks by feels like agony.

Chapter Forty

NATALIE

I love you.

Those words ricochet through my brain like a bullet. All the pasta I've just eaten feels like it's going to make an unexpected reappearance. I flatten a hand over my belly in an attempt to stop that from happening.

How am I supposed to respond?

I know what I want to say.

I want to jump up and tell him that I love him too, but I can't do that. John McKinnon's words have been rattling around in my head for the last couple of days, and I hate to say it, but I think he might be right.

Brody would be better off focusing on hockey and finishing out his senior year before moving on to Milwaukee. He doesn't need the distraction our relationship has become.

Even though my heart feels like it's being torn to shreds, I say carefully, "Brody, I care about you a lot."

His body grows impossibly still, and he blinks as if he didn't hear me correctly before repeating hoarsely, "You care about me?"

"Yes." I nod. All of a sudden, my chest feels heavy, and I can't breathe. It's painful to draw in air. "A lot." I slide my fingers from beneath his and tuck them into my lap. I keep my gaze focused on his. "But this relationship is moving really fast." I gulp and force out the rest. If I don't do it now, I'm not sure if I'll be able to push the words out at all. "I'm not ready for this."

"You're not ready for...*this?*" He repeats, his eyes widening. "*For us?* For a relationship?" His voice elevates with each question hurtled in my direction.

I want to bury my face in my hands and cry. But I can't do that. I have to finish this off. Unbeknownst to Brody, he's given me the perfect excuse to pull the plug.

"I didn't realize you were thinking long term." I shake my head. "I have no idea what's going to happen next year. I don't know where I'll be. I could be here or anywhere else in the country. I have to go where I can find a job. And with you going to Milwaukee..." I allow my words to trail off as if the outcome is obvious.

"Even if I'm in Milwaukee and you're somewhere else, we can still make this work."

I shrug. "Long-distance relationships are difficult. Most of them don't survive the first six months. Why would we bother setting ourselves up for failure?"

He takes his hands from the table and crosses his arms over his chest. Hurt flashes across his face. "I thought we were on the same page," he mumbles.

"I'm sorry. I'm just not ready to make that kind of commitment. There's so much going on right now. So many unknowns."

He sucks in a breath and blows it out slowly before nodding. "Okay. We can slow things down a bit. I didn't realize I was moving so fast."

My eyes drop to the table. I have to make a clean break. And I can't watch the anguish fill his eyes when I say the words. I just can't. The pain already flooding through me is excruciating. Any moment, I'm going to crumple to the floor and blurt out the truth.

"I think it might be best to take a break. There's no point in us getting involved only for you to leave at the end of the year and head to Milwaukee." I force my gaze to his. "We both know that once you're in the NHL, there'll be many women throwing themselves at you. Are you really going to be able to resist that temptation?" I wait a beat. "Do you even want to?"

Brody's jaw slackens. He looks like I've just slapped him.

"Are you being serious right now?" he whispers. "That's what you think of me?"

I tilt my head. "Come on, you've spent your entire life whoring around. You couldn't even tell me how many women you've slept with."

He shakes his head. "I can't believe you're throwing that in my face. I was trying to be honest with you." His whiskey-colored eyes fill with pain.

"And I'm just trying to do the same."

He reaches across the table. Desperation is written in every line of his face. "What's going on with you, Natalie? Where's this all coming from?"

The tears are so close to the surface that they burn the backs of my eyelids. I'm not sure how much longer I can keep the emotion in check.

I shrug. "I've just been thinking about it a lot lately, and I don't think a relationship is going to work between us in the long run. I don't want to waste either of our time."

Looking upset, he draws back again. "Well, I appreciate your honesty."

"I'm sorry. I really am. You're a wonderful guy. I hope you know that."

He snorts as he gets to his feet. "Sure. I'm a great guy. Just not for you, right?"

"That's not what I said," I whisper desperately.

"You didn't have to."

Panic floods through me, and I shoot out of my seat. Even though I know what I'm doing is best for Brody, it's not easy. The last thing I want is to hurt him, but that seems to be the only way.

"Brody, wait—"

"I'm going to take off." He picks up his jacket and shrugs into it. "I'll see you around, okay?"

I nod miserably.

There's nothing more to say.

He slams through the door and the tears I'd been holding back leak from my eyes.

"I love you, too," I whisper into the silence, knowing he'll never realize how I truly feel about him.

In order to break his heart, I had to break my own.

"Have another beer, bro," Sawyer says. "It'll help dull the pain."

He tosses me a can of Miller Light. I catch it with one hand from the couch I'm sprawled on, pop the top, and take a long swig. I can't imagine anything dulling the pain rampaging through me, but I don't say that because I already feel like the world's biggest pussy.

Tonight turned out to be an epic fail. I told Natalie that I loved her and she, in return, told me she needed to slow-track our relationship to the point of nonexistent.

It's almost laughable. Except I might just cry.

I really thought Natalie and I had something special. How did I misread the whole situation? It doesn't make any sense. I keep going over it in my head, but nothing adds up.

What I do know is that I'm going to wring Luke's neck when I see him. This is all his fault.

Make her dinner, he said.

Then you can talk, he said.

Where the fuck did that get me, other than a boot up the ass?

I'm so lost in my own misery that it takes a moment to realize that bright, fuchsia-colored fingernails are trailing lazily across my arm.

"Hey, Brody," a voice coos in my ear. "I haven't seen you around for a while."

I glance over at the blonde with the tight shirt hugging all her curves. I narrow my eyes, trying to remember her name. She's one of those girls that's always hanging around at the house.

I give her a brittle smile, trying not to recall the reason for that. "Been busy."

She clicks her tongue as her eyes coast appreciatively over me. "Where's your girlfriend?"

"Don't have one of those." Maybe that's where I went wrong. I've always lived my life by a strict set of rules. This was the first time I allowed myself to break them. And now look at me. I'm a fucking mess. All because a girl dumped my ass.

Never again, I vow silently. *Nothing* is worth this kind of pain.

Without invitation, Blondie settles herself on my lap and runs the palms of her hands over my chest. "That's too bad," she purrs, although there's nothing in her voice to suggest that she thinks it's bad at all. "Maybe I can help take your mind off her."

I lift the beer to my lips and take another swig. I'm not interested in what this girl is offering.

Just as I open my mouth to tell her that, I hear, "What the hell are you doing, McKinnon?"

I slant my eyes in the direction of that screeched out question.

Zara.

Luke is standing behind her. On closer inspection, it actually looks like he's holding her back. His brows are drawn sharply together as he glares.

He has the fucking audacity to glare at *me*?

Ha!

Just wait until I give him a piece of my mind. He'll be sorry he ever gave me that sage bit of advice.

Motherfucker.

The girl on my lap smiles coyly and gives Zara a little wave with her fingers. Luke tightens his hold on his girlfriend as she growls and steps forward, trying to wiggle out of his grasp. I have a feeling that if Zara gets her hands on the female perched on my lap, all hell will break loose.

"If you don't get your skanky ass away from him, I'm going rip every damn hair extension from your head!" Zara yells.

Looping her arms around my neck and shoving her tits in my face, Blondie leans toward Zara and sneers, "Try it, bitch."

Cursing a blue streak that would make a sailor blush, Zara struggles to free herself from Luke's hold. She's not going anywhere, but that doesn't deter her from trying. "I swear to God, Amanda, when I get my hands on you, you're going to wish you never glanced in his direction!"

Amanda.

Right.

Blondie-With-the-Toddler- Voice.

Although, there's no baby voice in sight this evening. More like hissing and spitting.

"You should probably go," I tell her. The truth of the matter is that I had no plans on taking her up on the offer written in her big green eyes. There's only one girl I'm interested in, and she kicked my ass to the curb about an hour ago.

Amanda gives me a full-on pouty lip.

But it does absolutely nothing for me.

Nada.

"Are you sure?" Ignoring Zara, who is still swearing and struggling about ten feet from where we sit, Amanda strokes her fingers over me.

"Yup, I'm sure."

Screwing this girl isn't going to dull the razor-sharp pain inflicted by Natalie. If anything, I'll just feel worse in the morning.

"Fine," Amanda huffs.

Taking her sweet time, she wiggles her ass against my junk before standing and stretching like she has all the time in the world. She sticks her tits out and shoots a sexy smile at Luke. "When you get tired of psycho Tinker Bell, you know where to find me."

Oh no she didn't...

My lips tremble with a smile. Zara's eyes flash with rage as she once again tries to lunge at Amanda. "I swear to God, bitch, you come near him, and I'll mess you up!"

Gritting his teeth, Luke locks Zara more firmly against his body and murmurs something in her ear. The fire in her eyes slowly dies as he kisses the side of her face.

Once Amanda is gone, Luke says with a bit of humor lacing his voice, "Can I trust you to make good choices or should I just keep you tucked in my arms for the time being?"

Zara grumbles something about "kicking that girl's ass" under her breath. Which I don't doubt because Zara is one tough chick. I think Luke has met his match with that one.

Luke chuckles and kisses her again before loosening his hold. "Chill out, babe. It's all good. You have nothing to worry about."

Just as Zara relaxes against him, a smile curving her lips, her eyes settle on me and she's back to scowling. "What are you doing with Amanda? Seriously? Three hours ago, I let you into my apartment to cook dinner for Natalie and now you're here," she jerks her thumb in the direction Amanda sauntered off in, "whoring it up with that overused vag?"

Part of me doesn't want to talk about what happened with Natalie. It's still too fresh. But if I don't tell them, then I look like the bad guy. The whoremongering asshole. And you know what? I'm not.

"Didn't work out," I bite out. "Natalie gave me my walking papers."

"Get the hell out of here." A shocked look crosses her face. "You're lying."

"I'm not." I sigh, and everything in me deflates.

Looking as confused as I feel, Zara crosses her arms under her breasts. "How did you manage to fuck up? Because she really liked you."

I snort. "I made the girl dinner and told her that I loved her. So... you tell me how I managed to screw it up."

It's almost comical the way both of their eyes widen. "No kidding?" she breathes.

Embarrassed by what I've just admitted to my friends, I hoist the beer to my lips and take a drink, trying to wash away the humiliation. It doesn't work.

"Dude..." Luke shifts uncomfortably from one foot to the other. "That sucks."

"Yeah...that's a major understatement," I mutter.

"But that doesn't make sense." Zara frowns as she shakes her head. "Natalie likes you. I know she does. Honestly, all of the years you two spent dancing around each other seemed like some kind of bizarre mating ritual. I wasn't surprised when you finally got together, just that it took so long to happen."

I shrug. I've thought the same thing. Minus the bizarre mating ritual part. "Natalie dumped me, Zara" I repeat quietly. "I don't know what else to tell you. She said she wasn't ready to get serious."

Only now do I realize that her strange behavior this past week makes perfect sense. I knew something was up with her.

Unfortunately, I didn't know just how right I was.

Chapter Forty-Two

NATALIE

"You just decided to break up with him?" Zara asks as she throws herself onto the desk chair in my bedroom and stares at me in an unnerving fashion that would break a lesser woman. "Just like that?" She snaps her fingers to add emphasis to her words. Not that she has to. I get it. She's annoyed with me. My friend doesn't understand why I would do something so extreme.

I fidget nervously with the hem of my shirt and glance away, avoiding eye contact at all costs. Zara has known me since the fourth grade. I'm afraid if she searches long enough—hard enough—she'll figure out that I'm lying. I need to shut down this line of questioning before it gets out of hand. "Yep."

Brows furrowing, she shakes her head. "Why would you do that?"

Zara wants answers, and I have the feeling she won't rest until she unearths them. She's annoyingly tenacious like that.

I force my gaze back to Zara's confused one and feed her the same line I fed Brody last night. "Because it seems better this way. He's leaving for Milwaukee after graduation. He'll have a lot going on with acclimating to the NHL and travelling during the season. And let's face it, long-distance relationships rarely work out in the end. There doesn't seem much point to getting attached or prolonging the inevitable."

Most people would agree with everything I've just said. Those are legitimate roadblocks to any budding relationship. But already I can tell that Zara isn't buying it.

That's reconfirmed when she says, "I'm calling bullshit."

"What?" I sit up a little straighter on the bed and clasp my fingers in my lap to still them.

"You heard me, I'm calling bullshit. We've been friends for twelve years, and I know when you're trying to BS me. You have a tell." She tilts her head. "Did you know that? Anytime you try avoiding a situation, you glance away and start fidgeting." She twirls her finger in my direction. "And that's exactly what you're doing now." She crosses her arms over her chest. "So, let's just cut the crap. I want to know what's really going on."

I bite my lip and shake my head. "I can't tell you," I whisper. Talking about it won't change anything. I wish it could.

Rising from the chair, Zara closes the distance between us and sits down on the bed next to me. Her voice softens. "Why?"

I shake my head and look down at my fingers, which are tangled together. I almost snort. She's right about the tell. I glance at her as a fresh wave of resolve washes over me. I'm trying to do what's right for Brody. In the end, that's all that matters. "There's no point in rehashing it, Zar. This is the way it has to be."

"Explain to me why it has to be this way, because I don't understand." When I remain silent, she continues. "I could tell at your birthday party that you were falling for him. What happened between then and now?"

Brody planning my birthday dinner is what finally pushed me over the edge. That night changed everything for me. For us.

I wish she would just drop the subject and let it go, but I know that's not going to happen. Blowing out a breath, I say, "A couple of days ago, Brody's dad stopped by the apartment to have a little chat."

Her eyes bug out. "Well, I certainly didn't see that one coming."

I give a mirthless chuckle as sadness swamps me. I'm all but drowning in it. "Yeah, me neither."

"I take it that Brody doesn't know about it?"

"No, and I can't tell him either. It would only cause problems between them, and I don't want to do that."

"What did he say?"

Even though I'm trying to keep my fingers still, I can't. They continue twisting together in my lap. "He told me that Brody needed to focus on finishing school and his NHL career. He said I'm a distraction Brody can't afford right now." I peek over at Zara. Her jaw is hanging open. "He brought up the fights with Reed and getting thrown out of practice."

Anger kindles in her eyes as she snaps her mouth closed. "And naturally, this is your fault?"

I shrug and force out a breath before admitting, "Yeah, I think it probably is. At least some of it." I remember the library and the sexy study breaks we took or when he wanted to skip practice so he could make love to me instead. Without me, none of those situations would have occurred.

Her brows snap together in irritation. "Did you really just take the blame for that?" Instead of her ire being directed at Brody's father, it's aimed at me. "Give me a break, Nat. Brody is a big boy, capable of making his own decisions. If he chooses to do something—be it good or bad—that's on him. Not you." Disgust fills her voice. "His father had no right to put all that on you."

Part of me agrees with what she said. Brody is a twenty-three-year-old man capable of making his own decisions and accepting the consequences of them. But if me being in his life leads to bad choices, isn't it in his best interests if I back off?

"Brody has lost enough, Zara." I can't get into the specifics with her because they aren't mine to share. I add, "There's a lot riding on this season. I don't want to see him mess anything up with Milwaukee."

Putting two and two together, her voice fills with contempt. "His dad told you to dump him, didn't he?" It's not really a question. We both know that's where the conversation was inevitably leading. "He made you feel like all this was your fault and then told you to take a hike." Zara looks ready to blow a gasket.

"Yeah," I admit reluctantly. Even though talking with Zara doesn't change the situation, it feels good to let it out.

Jumping off the bed, Zara paces the length of the room. She looks as upset about everything as I am. "What a jerk! I can't believe he asked you to do that." Her eyes harden as she whips around to face me. "Brody has no idea what happened between the two of you. He thinks you don't care about him."

I bury my face in my hands as I remember the looks of pain and confusion that flashed across his face when I told him that we were moving too fast and that I wasn't looking for anything serious. Letting him go was one of the hardest things I've ever had to do. "Please, Zar. Don't make me feel any worse about this than I already do."

"Well, it's true," she accuses. "You broke the poor guy's heart." She pauses for a beat. "Brody deserves to know the truth. About everything."

"That's not fair," I whisper brokenly. "Can't you see that I'm only trying to do what's best for him?"

"Did you ever think," she says carefully, "that maybe *you're* what's best for him?"

I stare silently as her words filter through my brain.

I worry my lower lip between my teeth as I rush across campus. I've been dreading my ten o'clock finance class for obvious reasons. I haven't run into Brody since he left my apartment a few nights ago. After a little more than a month together, his absence from my life has left a huge void that feels impossible to fill.

Just as class is about to get underway, I slip into the room and take a seat in the back row. As I take out my materials, I glance around, searching for Brody. Now that we're no longer together, I expect everything to morph back to the way it used to be. Which means Kimmie should be parked next to him, chattering away.

My eyes settle on Kimmie, but he's not there.

It takes a few more minutes to realize that Brody isn't anywhere in the small lecture hall. But he's got to show up, right? This is one of his borderline classes. After fifteen minutes slowly trickle by, it becomes apparent that he isn't going to show up at all.

My dread turns into concern. It's not like Brody to skip class. I may not have realized it before, but Brody's grades mean a lot to him. He did really well on the last finance test and was able to raise his grade to a low B, which gives him a little bit of breathing room. We may have broken up, and he might not want to see me, but I have a difficult time believing he would jeopardize getting benched.

As soon as Dr. Miller dismisses us, I fly through the door and out of the building. I slide my phone from my bag and stare at it, wondering if I should reach out and make sure everything's okay. But I can't imagine that Brody wants to hear from me. For any reason. So, I reluctantly slide the phone back into my pocket and keep moving.

Zara's words have been churning in my head since our talk. Did I make the right decision in letting Brody go? Should I have told him about his dad's visit?

I don't know.

It may not seem like it, but what I did came from a good place. I want only the best for Brody. If anyone deserves success, it's him. The last thing I want to do is stand in the way of that.

As I haul ass past the union, trying to decide what my next step is, my eyes get snagged by a familiar face. His presence is so unexpected and out of place on campus that I grind to a halt. I blink, half-wondering if I'm hallucinating. Our gazes stay locked as my dad rises from the bench he's seated on and gives me a tentative wave in greeting.

I hitch my bag higher on my shoulder and force myself to close the distance between us. I haven't spoken to Dad since the restaurant incident with his fiancée.

I don't understand what he's doing here, of all places.

"Hello, Nat," he says when I stop a few feet from him.

"Hi." I shift uncomfortably from one foot to the other, wishing there was a way to fill the lengthening silence now stretching between us. I hate that this is what it's come to.

"Do you have some time for us to talk?" There's a hopeful note threading its way through his voice.

It's on the tip of my tongue to lie, to tell him that I'm on my way to a class...but I can't. As angry as I still am, he's here. Making an effort. Can I really brush that off?

Maybe hashing things out is exactly what needs to happen. We've both had some time to cool down. More than that, I hate that we're not talking. Before the separation, we were close. The yawning gulf that exists between us is painful.

I nod. "I have a little bit of time."

His lips lift in relief. Some of the tension seeps from his body as his shoulders relax. "Good. Do you want to go somewhere else or," he points to the bench he had been occupying, "sit here and talk? I'll do whatever's easiest for you."

I glance around. Tons of people are rushing past us on their way to class or stopping at the union for lunch. This is the last place I want to have a heart-to-heart conversation with Dad. I think we need a little more privacy than this area affords.

I point in the direction I'd been rushing. "There are some tables near Hamlin Hall, at the edge of campus, where we can talk." I shrug. "It's more private."

"Okay, that sounds good," Dad agrees.

We fall in line with one another and walk in silence. There are no two ways about it—this sucks. Our relationship is no longer easy and effortless the way it used to be. Instead, it's strained and stifling.

We reach Hamlin Hall, which has a large assortment of tables scattered across the front lawn where students can eat lunch or study. Picking one that's away from other people, I plunk my bag down on the metal top and take a seat. My dad slides across from me. He fidgets for a few minutes before resting his elbows on the table and threading his fingers tightly together. He stares down at them as if he's gathering his courage.

If I weren't so nervous, I'd smile. Guess I'm not the only one with a tell.

"First of all, I want to apologize for what happened at the restaurant," Dad says, looking me in the eyes. "In hindsight, I realize that inviting Bridgette to have dessert with us and not telling you about it was the wrong way to go about things. It never occurred to me that you might feel ambushed, and I'm sorry for that."

I shake my head and ask, "How did you see that situation playing out?" I mean, did he seriously think his homewrecking fiancée would sit down with us and all my anger and sadness would just disappear? Or that I'd just magically be over it?

He opens his mouth and snaps it shut again, shrugging his shoulders. He taps his fingers against the metal tabletop. "I don't know," he finally murmurs. "But not like that."

I lean toward him as anger and hurt bubble up within me. Ever since he walked out, these feelings have been my constant companion. They're exhausting. Instead of losing my temper, I inhale a deep, calming breath and slowly release it. "I understand that you've moved on, Dad, but I haven't. I'm still processing the fact that you and Mom aren't getting back together." I gulp and force out the rest. "My family has splintered apart, and you're moving on with your life like it's no big deal."

"I'm sorry, Nat." His hand slowly slides across the table until he's able to slip my fingers into his. When I don't pull them away, he squeezes them tight. "You're the last person I ever want to hurt. You mean everything to me."

You'd think after ten months that the pain of their separation wouldn't feel so fresh, but it does. I don't want to get emotional about this, but it's hard to keep the tears at bay.

Even though I know it's not going to happen, I can't help but say wistfully, "I wish there was a way for you and Mom to work things out."

Again, he squeezes my fingers. His eyes become shiny and full of emotion. It's difficult to witness. And yet it feels good. Kind of like ripping off a Band-Aid. "I wish it could be that way, too. Deciding to leave wasn't an easy decision. I spent years thinking about it, Nat. *Years*," he emphasizes. His gaze searches mine for understanding. "This was way before Bridgette ever came into the picture." His shoulders collapse under the weight of his words. "I should have left earlier. But you were still living at home, and maybe I was hoping your mother and I could work through the problems we were having."

Everything about this moment feels raw and painful. As much as I appreciate his candor, it's tough to hear. Tough to digest and accept. I glance away, unsure how to respond.

"I understand this has been a rough year for you and if I could go back and change that, I would. I hate that any of my decisions have caused you pain." Dad gulps, his voice breaking with thick emotion. "I miss hanging out with you and hearing about everything that's happening in your life. I'm missing out on so much right now. I want us to be close again."

"I want that, too," I whisper. Even though I'm still angry with him, I've missed Dad being a part of my life.

"I know my relationship with Bridgette is a sore spot for you. But I'm hopeful that given enough time, the three of us can get to a better place."

Even though I can't imagine that day ever coming, I keep those thoughts to myself. He's here, and he's trying to fix our relationship. I feel like I have to at least meet him halfway and be open to the idea. No matter how painful the notion is.

"I told Bridgette that we need to slow things down," my father says, catching me by surprise.

My eyes fill with unshed tears that he'd actually do that. That Dad would put my feelings above his own. "And how did she take that?" Is it terrible that I hope she threw a hissy and told him to take a hike?

Probably, but I don't care.

"She understood. She doesn't want to get in the way of our relationship." He smiles just a bit. "I think she was just a little overeager to meet you." He shakes his head and admits, "I should have put a stop to it, and I didn't. That's on me."

As much as it pains me to admit it, even privately to myself, maybe the woman isn't *all* that bad. Although I reserve the right to withhold judgment for a later date.

"I want us to spend time together," Dad says.

Even though it's childish and I'm not proud of myself for it, I ask, "Alone?"

The corners of his lips hitch upward, and he sighs. "Yes, alone. Until you're ready, I won't mention Bridgette, okay?" He glances at our entwined hands. "But you need to understand that I love her, Nat. At some point, I'm going to marry her. If you're not ready for that, we'll hold off." He gives me a hard look. "For the time being."

I'd prefer he come back home and try to work things out with Mom, but I get it—that's not going to happen.

I nod. "Okay."

"Good." He glances at his wristwatch. "Are you sure I can't treat you to lunch? I have some time before I need to get back to the office."

For the first time since running into Dad, I remember my concerns regarding Brody not showing up for class. I shake my head. "No, I'm sorry. There's something I need to take care of." As I rise from the bench and scoop up my bag, I ask, "How did you know where to find me?"

Whitmore's campus is large and sprawling. Trying to find someone here can be like playing a game of *Where's Waldo*.

"Your friend Brody told me where I could find you."

I freeze. "Brody?"

"Yeah, he came to see me at my office. I have to admit that I was surprised at first, but he helped me to understand how hard you've been hit by all this." Dad clears his throat. "I'm embarrassed to say that I hadn't realized just how affected you were by the divorce. I thought because you were older, it would be easier for you to deal with. But that's not the case, is it?"

I shake my head. No matter how old you are, when your family splits up, it hurts. But that's not what I'm focused on at the moment. My knees give out, and I fall back onto the bench. "Brody came to see you?" I can't believe he would do that.

He nods. "Yeah, he did."

"When?" I can barely force out the word. My heart beats erratically under my breast.

"Yesterday," Dad says. "We talked for about thirty minutes."

Brody stopped by the day after we broke up? That doesn't make any sense. Why would he do that?

Tears fill my eyes. I couldn't stop them from falling if I tried.

"Nat?" Concerned, Dad asks, "What's wrong?"

I shake my head and wipe the moisture from my eyes with the back of my hand. "Nothing."

"That young man really cares about you," he comments. "Is he your boyfriend?" He watches me carefully from across the table. I'm sure he's trying to figure out what's going on.

"No," I whisper. "He's not." Saying those words feels like being knifed in the heart. Pain floods through every part of my body. For the second time, I bolt from the bench and gather up my bag. "I have to go, Dad. I'm sorry."

He rises with me, his face marred with concern and confusion. "Are you sure you're okay?"

My mind is so filled with Brody that I can barely concentrate on what he's saying. "I'll be fine." I'm no more than a few steps away from him when I spin back around and blurt, "Is it possible for me to borrow your car?"

"Sure." He doesn't even hesitate, just fishes the keys from his pocket and throws them to me.

I catch them in my hand and start walking backward. "How will you get back to work?"

"I'll Uber it."

The edges of my lips lift. "Do you know how to do that?"

"I'll figure it out." He shrugs. "How difficult can it be?"

I smile. "Thanks, Dad."

He points toward the street. "I'm parked up a block on Denison. Now, get moving. I'll see you later when you drop the car off. Maybe then you can explain what's going on."

"I will!" With those words shouted over my shoulder, I take off running.

I only hope that when I find Brody, he'll hear me out and give me a chance to explain. Maybe it's too late for us to get back together, but he needs to know that my feelings run so much deeper than I let on.

Chapter Forty-Four

NATALIE

I throw my dad's Honda Accord into park and cut the engine. Butterflies swarm my belly, giving me a nauseous feeling. On the way over, I rehearsed everything I wanted to say. I had the whole spiel worked out in my head. But now, as I sit in front of Brody's house, I can't remember a single word.

I'm concerned that he won't give me the chance to explain myself. And I can't really blame him for that. Even now, two days later, the look of pain that flashed across his face when I told him that I didn't have the same kind of feelings for him leaves me cringing.

Coming here feels like a huge risk.

A mistake.

But...

I can't *not* tell Brody how I feel. I can't let him think that I don't care about him, because I do. So much that it hurts my heart.

I squeeze my eyes tightly shut and suck in a deep breath before expelling it slowly.

Okay. I can do this. I can—

Knuckles rap loudly on the driver's side window.

My eyes fly open, and I stifle the rising scream in my throat. I raise my hand and press it against my chest. My gaze locks on the guy standing next to the car. His brows pull together as he contemplates me.

"Natalie? What are you doing here?" he asks.

I gulp and roll down the window. "Hi." I'm so nervous, I can barely speak. "I came to talk with Brody."

Luke straightens to his full height and folds his arms across his chest. Something in his eyes hardens. Luke and I have always been friendly. But right now, he's eyeing me like I'm a bug splattered across his windshield. I get the feeling that if it were in his nature, he'd tell me to go fuck myself.

"That's not really a good idea," he says.

"Why?" Already I feel like I'm going to come out of my skin. His words only ratchet up my misery.

"Because Brody has a lot going on right now." The disgust filling his voice is palpable. It makes me wince. "He doesn't need you messing with his head. You've already done a good job of that."

My mouth tumbles open. Guilt and anguish rush through my veins. I protest weakly, "I didn't—"

"Yeah, you did," he cuts me off coldly. "Whether you realize it or not. You did."

I gulp and try to explain with, "But—"

Unwilling to listen to anything I have to say, he shakes his head and takes a step away from the vehicle. "Brody's in Milwaukee, checking out housing for next year. He won't be back until Sunday night. The best thing you can do for him is leave him alone and move on."

Everything within me collapses.

I thought the worst possible scenario was sharing my feelings with Brody and then having him tell me to go to hell. But this...not being able to put my feelings out there at all, is so much worse. He needs to know that our relationship wasn't one-sided like I led him to believe.

Forgetting about Luke, I lay my head against the steering wheel and stifle the tears that burn my eyes.

What am I going to do?

What I have to tell him needs to be said in person, not over the phone.

"Natalie?"

My head lolls to the side until I'm able to meet Luke's eyes. His fingers now rest on the doorframe, and his concerned face fills the window.

"I need to talk to him." A sob rises in my throat. "I need to explain what happened."

"He really liked you," Luke says begrudgingly. "I've never seen Brody so into a girl. And you..." he trails off.

I squeeze my eyes tightly shut as if that will block out the pain. It doesn't work. I'm all but steeped in it. "I know," I whisper. "I know what I did. I never meant to cause him any pain."

"But you did," he says.

There's no arguing with that comment. "I thought I was doing the right thing by letting him go."

Curiosity fills Luke's voice. "Do you still feel like it was the right thing to do?"

"No."

"You're one of the few people Brody has opened up to and shared his life with. I hope you realize that." Another dagger slices through my heart. Luke and Zara make the perfect pair. Neither one of them hold back any punches.

"Of course, I do." As if I didn't already feel like shit, his unvarnished words only make me feel worse.

Luke sighs and straightens. "Brody and his dad are staying at The Park Hotel in Milwaukee."

When I stare, he shrugs and arches a brow. "Now you know where he is. I guess the next move is yours to make, isn't it?"

Lifting my head, I nod and start up the engine.

Chapter Forty-Five

BRODY

"Any thoughts about the last condo we toured?" Dad lifts the scotch to his lips and takes a healthy drink. "Pretty nice, wasn't it?"

We flew in late last night and met with the Mavericks' defensive coach this morning for breakfast. He and the old man played together in Chicago before Dad was traded to Detroit. Then we spent the rest of the day with Dana, the realtor who is showing us around Milwaukee. We got back to the hotel about an hour ago and stopped at the bar to have a drink.

I nod, but I'm not really paying attention to what he's saying.

I thought this trip to Milwaukee would help take my mind off of Natalie. I could focus on the future and put a little distance between us. All I did was sulk around the house. I caught a glimpse of her on campus yesterday, and it nearly brought me to my knees. I just wanted to grab her and...

I pinch the bridge of my nose.

What? What was I going to do?

Shake some sense into her?

Demand that she acknowledge her feelings for me?

No. I couldn't do either of those things.

Until I can wrap my mind around the truth that her feelings for me don't run as deep as the ones I have for her, I need to steer clear. And getting out of Dodge seemed like the best way to do it.

But all it's done is slam home the realization that once I graduate this spring, I'll be moving on with my life. I won't see Natalie anymore. I won't run into her on campus. Or at a party. Or in class.

That chapter of my life will be over.

Someone needs to explain to me how I'm supposed to walk away from her. From the one woman who actually makes me feel alive.

"Brody."

I jerk out of my thoughts and back to the present. "Yeah?"

Dad eyes me over the rim of his crystal tumbler as he takes another drink. "You need to get your head out of your ass and focus on what's important."

I break eye contact and stare sightlessly out the wall of windows overlooking the busy street. It's been gray and rainy for most of the day, which matches my disposition perfectly. "I am, Dad."

He raises a brow. "This is exactly why I didn't want you getting involved with someone at this stage of the game. You don't need some girl fucking with your head."

Irritated by his words, I drag my fingers through my hair and snap, "Can we not do this right now?" Dad is the last person I want to discuss Natalie with.

"You're better off without her, Brody. I tried telling you that before, but you refused to listen." He stabs a finger in my direction. "You keep it light. No relationships."

It takes a moment for his words to sink in. My brows furrow. "What are you talking about?"

After our discussion at brunch where he told me to cut Natalie loose, I've gone out of my way not to mention her. And I sure as shit didn't tell him about our breakup because I didn't want to hear yet another rendition of the *I-told-you-so* lecture.

I need that like another freaking hole in the head.

"That girl broke up with you, didn't she? That's why you're in such a pissy mood?" Dad places the tumbler of scotch on a coaster. "Listen, the best way to get over one woman is to get under another. Go out tonight and have a little fun. You're in the perfect city for it."

Those words send my temper skyrocketing. "How do you know that Natalie dumped me?"

His eyes flick around the bar before settling on mine again, and he shrugs. "I don't know. You must have mentioned it the other day."

Even though I shake my head, I keep my eyes focused on his. He's lying. "No, I didn't."

He sits back, putting distance between us. "Sure, you did."

I lean forward and rest my forearms on the glass table. My voice sharpens. "*No, I didn't*. After what happened at brunch, there was no way I would tell you anything about her."

"If you didn't mention it, how else would I know?"

There's something he's not telling me. I feel it.

"I don't know," I mutter. But an idea is taking shape in my brain. One I don't want to believe could've happened. I think about the days leading up to the breakup, recalling the odd sensation that something wasn't right between Natalie and me and being unable to pinpoint exactly what it was. The last time we made love, there was a strange intensity behind it. Desperation had poured off of Natalie in thick, heavy waves. And she wrapped herself around me afterward as if she couldn't bear the thought of letting go. At the time, I hadn't given it much consideration. I hadn't understood because I'd been flying high.

In retrospect, her behavior makes sense. All of the puzzle pieces now fit together perfectly.

I narrow my eyes. "What did you say to Natalie?"

A look of annoyance flickers across my father's face. "What are you talking about?"

"You spoke to Natalie, didn't you?" As I release the accusation into the air, I know it's true. Christ, I'm such an idiot. Why didn't I see this before?

He blusters before glaring and pointing a finger at me. "I told you not to get involved with anyone! I told you that it would be nothing but a distraction and you wouldn't listen." He shakes his head and grumbles, "Getting into fights with a teammate and kicked out of practice, looking like shit on the ice...That girl needed to go, and I took care of the problem before she could fuck up anything else for you."

Uncaring of the patrons around us, I slam my fist on the table as rage burns a hole through my gut. "You had no right to interfere in my relationship!"

Several people in the vicinity turn in their seats and gape. But I'm beyond the point of caring. Let them stare.

"I had *every* right!" Dad thunders. "You weren't listening."

"I'm twenty-three years old, for God's sake! I'm more than capable of making my own decisions. You never should have involved yourself in my relationship with Natalie. It had nothing to do with you."

He throws his arms wide. "What should I have done, huh? Stood idly by and let you fuck up everything we'd been working years for?" He shakes his head. "I wasn't going to do that. This girl has you jacked in the head. Someone had to step in and save you from yourself."

God-fucking-damnit!

"Natalie is the best thing that's ever happened to me," I growl. "And you ruined it." The chair scrapes back as I come to my feet. I can't sit here for another moment and listen to the shit he's spewing.

"Sit your ass back down, Brody," Dad grits from between clenched teeth. "We're not done talking."

A muscle ticks in my jaw as I try to control the rage rushing through my body. My father and I have always been on the same page. After Mom died, it was just the two of us. But this time, he's gone too far, and I'm not sure if I can forgive him for it. "We're done."

He rises so that we're eye level. "Sit down," he snaps. "And let's discuss this like adults. Since you keep telling me that you're twenty-three years old and can handle your own life, start damn well acting like it."

I lift my chin. "Sure, let's sit down and discuss how you went behind my back and ended my relationship."

He rolls his eyes. "Don't you think you're being a bit melodramatic? What you had was nothing more than a fling. You let your heart get involved, and it got bruised. In a couple of days, you'll move on. End of story."

I ball my fists and take a step toward him. "It was more than that, and you damn well know it."

He raises a brow. "Do I?" He reaches out and settles a heavy hand on my shoulder. I want to shake him loose, but don't. "I didn't force her to do anything. I put the decision in her hands, and she chose to break up with you. It was the right call to make, and she understood that."

My heart twists because there's a sliver of truth to his words. Natalie could have told me what Dad wanted her to do, but she chose not to. She hid it from me and broke my heart.

"It's for the best, Brody," he says quietly. "Further down the line, it would've only led to more heartache."

Fury boils up within me, and I slap his hand away. "Fuck you, Dad."

His eyes widen as I walk past him. "Where are you going?"

"I'm packing my bags and catching a flight back home."

I have to see Natalie and figure out where her head's at. The truth of the matter is that I love her, but I don't understand how she could have walked away from me. If the situation were reversed, there's no way I would have done the same. Nothing and no one could have ever forced me to turn my back on her.

Chapter Forty-Six
NATALIE

As the cab pulls up to the curb in front of The Park Hotel, I throw a wad of bills at the driver and tell him to keep the change. Was it really six hours ago when I raced home from the hockey house and searched for flights to Milwaukee on my laptop? Before I could overthink it, I pressed *purchase* and printed off the plane ticket. Then I grabbed an overnight bag, stuffed some clothes in it along with a toothbrush, and called a taxi to go to the airport. Three hours later, I lifted off, bound for Milwaukee.

If I'd thought I was nervous driving over to Brody's house earlier, it's nothing compared to what I felt during the two-hour flight north. I barely had time to concoct a plan in my head before the stewardess told us to buckle up and prepare for landing. Without luggage to wait for, I ran through the airport and found a cab.

And now here I am.

Huffing and puffing like a lunatic.

Repositioning my bag on my shoulder, I walk through the revolving glass doors and head toward the posh check-in desk at the other end of the lobby.

A woman dressed in a tailored gray suit with perfect makeup

smiles. "Welcome to The Milwaukee Park Hotel. Will you be checking in with us this evening?"

I suck in a breath, hoping to settle my careening nerves. Now that I'm actually standing here, I'm shaking in my shoes. "No, I'm not. One of my friends is staying here, though, and I was hoping you could tell me what room he's in?" I end the sentence on a hopeful note.

I'm not above begging and pleading, if that's what it takes.

If she refuses to give me the information, I'm screwed. What am I going to do? Camp out in the lobby and hope Brody walks through at some point? I glance around, taking it all in. This is a pretty swanky place. They'll probably kick me out within fifteen minutes.

Her face turns sympathetic, and she shakes her head. "Oh, I'm sorry. I can't do that. It's against hotel policy for us to give out any guest information."

My spirits nosedive. "Is it possible for me to leave a message?"

"Absolutely, but I can't do anything more than that," she adds firmly as if I might argue.

"Okay." I sigh and root around in my purse for a pen and a piece of paper. Of course, I can find everything else under the sun but that. Feeling like an idiot, I glance at the woman behind the desk. "I'm sorry. Could I use a piece of paper and a pen?"

"Certainly."

Just as she reaches under the long stretch of glossy counter, a deep voice says, "That won't be necessary, Abigail. I'll take care of this."

My belly spasms as I spin around and find Brody's father a few feet from where I'm standing. He's the one person I was hoping to avoid and the first I run into.

That's the kind of luck I'm having.

"Of course, Mr. McKinnon," Abigail says. "Please let me know if there's anything else I can assist you with."

"I'll be sure to do that," he says, his eyes never deviating from mine. "Natalie, what an unexpected surprise."

And not a happy one, if his stoic expression is any indication.

I straighten to my full height, which is still a good six inches shorter than him. I allowed this man to intimidate me once, and I refuse to do it again.

"I'm here to see Brody," I say, keeping my voice firm.

His gaze flicks to Abigail, who is busy helping another customer. "Perhaps we can move this conversation somewhere else?"

He doesn't wait for me to respond and simply walks away, leaving me to trail reluctantly after him as he takes a seat at one of the groupings of chairs and couches scattered throughout the enormous lobby.

He settles on the couch, and I'm forced to choose between the chairs flanking it. Feeling ill at ease, I sit on the very edge. "Look, Mr. McKinnon, I know you don't like me." I have no idea if what I'm about to say will make a damn bit of difference, but I have to try. His mind was made up before he ever met me. "But I love your son."

He leans forward and rests his elbows on his knees, loosely knotting his hands together in front of him. "I can appreciate that you have feelings for Brody, I really can. But I know what's best for him. I've been in his position. I understand what he needs to do to be successful. And that's staying focused on finishing his degree and preparing for the NHL."

My tongue darts out to moisten my lips. "I'm not trying to get in the way of that."

"Natalie, you're young." His tone is placating, as if I'm a child. "You're going to fall in and out of love several times before you find the right man. What are you? Twenty-one or twenty-two years old?"

"Twenty-two," I whisper.

A patronizing smile touches his lips as he shakes his head. "You can't possibly know what you want out of life and who you want it with." He allows those words to sink in. "And neither does my son. You're the first girl he's ever been involved with. How long do you think that's going to last? Two months? Four? Maybe, if you're lucky, six?"

Just as I open my mouth to respond, a deep voice cuts in, "I don't know how long it's going to last, but that's for Natalie and me to figure out. Not you."

I shoot to my feet and spin around. As soon as I do, our gazes collide. Everything in me tightens. It's only been a couple of days since I've seen him, but it feels like forever. The urge to throw myself into his arms floods me, but I don't make a move.

I can't.

Not yet.

Not until we've hashed everything out between us.

"Brody," I whisper. My heart feels like it's sitting in the middle of my throat, making it impossible to breathe.

His golden eyes coast over me before skewering mine with intensity. "What are you doing here?" he asks softly.

"I had to speak with you." There's so much pent-up emotion bubbling beneath the surface of my words. It's difficult to keep it contained. It's all I can do not to blurt out my feelings. To beg for Brody's forgiveness.

He raises a brow. "And it couldn't wait until I got back?"

I shake my head. "No." It's silently that my eyes plead with his. I just want him to give me a chance to explain. To make it right.

Brody turns to his father. That's when I notice the bag hoisted over his shoulder. "I can handle the rest of the weekend myself." His voice turns cold and hard. "I won't be needing your help."

John pales as he quickly gets to his feet. "Brody—"

"I'm serious," Brody snaps. "I'll handle it from here on out. I don't need you to hold my hand or decide what's best for me. I'm more than capable of making those decisions for myself."

It looks as though John will argue, but at the last moment he jerks his head into a tight nod. "If that's what you want."

"It is," Brody confirms.

"Then I'll change my flight and head back tonight. Keep the appointment in the morning with Dana and let me know if you come to any decisions.'

Brody rolls his shoulders and relaxes his jaw. "Thank you," he says gruffly.

John glances away for a moment before his eyes come back to rest on his son. Emotion seeps into his voice. "I was only trying to do what I thought was right. That's all."

"I tried telling you what was best for me and you didn't want to hear it. I won't be ignored any longer. I'm tired of you making all of the decisions and steamrolling over the ones you don't agree with."

By the humbled look on his face, I don't think John McKinnon is used to his son taking control of his life. I get the feeling that it's going to be difficult for him to step back and give Brody the breathing room he so desperately needs.

John shoves his hands into the pockets of his black slacks and shrugs. "Fine, I'll back off."

Brody releases a pent-up breath. "Thank you."

"I'm going to head upstairs and make a few calls. Then I'll be out of your way."

"I'll contact you when I get back to town."

John nods. "Sounds good."

Ignoring me, his father walks away, heading to the bank of glass elevators. Once we're alone, Brody pins me with his eyes. My body vibrates with nerves. I have no idea how this conversation will go and that scares me to death.

The man standing in front of me is my everything, and I pushed him away instead of holding him close the way I should have.

I point to the grouping of furniture. "Can we sit and talk?"

"Sure." His whiskey-colored eyes stay locked on mine as he drops down onto the chair next to me.

I suck in a deep breath, unsure of where to begin. I've traveled all this way to tell him how I feel and the words that need to be spoken are stuck in my throat. Tears fill my eyes, and I have to blink them away. Brody reaches over and scoops me out of the chair, hauling me onto his lap. Surprised by the movement, I stare at him with wide eyes.

There's a slight twist to his lips as his arms snake around my body and press me close. His voice is low and just like always, it strums something deep inside me. "Jesus Christ, Davies. You're killing me over here. Just say the damn words and put us both out of our misery."

The thick tension that had choked the life out of me dissolves.

Believe it or not, I giggle. Tears splash onto my cheeks and stream down my face. I swipe at them with the back of my hand. "I'm sorry, I have no idea what you're talking about."

He smirks and shakes his head. My heart flips over in my chest. Did I ever think he would look at me like that again?

I wasn't sure. I was so afraid I'd lost him.

Before I can open my mouth and say anything, his fingers attack my ribs. I shriek with laughter so loudly that it causes people to turn and glance our way. But I don't care about the unwanted attention. I only care about the man holding me in his arms.

"Say the words, Davies. Or we can sit here all night long, and I'll tickle you until you pee your pants."

He'll do it, too. But that's not why I'll say the words. I'm going to tell him everything that's in my heart because it's the truth and he needs to hear it. He needs to know just how much I care about him.

"I love you, Brody," I say between gasping breaths. "I love you so much."

His eyes go soft and his fingers still. I loop my arms around his neck and tug him close so that I can press a kiss to his lips.

"I love you, too." He leans his forehead against mine but still holds my gaze. "You mean everything to me. You know that, right?"

"Yes." How could I not? Even before he told me the night he surprised me with dinner, he showed me in a hundred different ways each and every day. It kills me that I caused him one moment of pain. "I'm so sorry for hurting you," I say with sincerity. "I thought letting you go was the best thing for you."

A shadow passes over his eyes. "I know what my dad did. I'm sorry he put you in that position."

I exhale a breath, relieved that everything is out in the open. "I should have told you right away. But...I was afraid it would cause problems between the two of you. He's all you have."

"Don't worry about my dad. We're solid. He needs to learn to back off, that's all. We'll be fine." He sobers, becoming more serious. "Just promise you'll never keep anything from me again. If there's something that needs to be discussed, we'll sit down and hash it out. These last couple of days without you..." He shakes his head and grimaces. "They were a killer. I don't want to go through that again. Promise me."

"I promise, Brody." I drop my gaze. "I'm so sorry."

"The only thing that matters is that you're here in my arms where you belong."

I sigh and lay my head against his strong chest.

He's absolutely right.

This is exactly where I belong. With him. Always.

"Good. Now that we've straightened that out, we can move on to the next order of business." He shifts me around in his arms and gets to his feet.

I frown. What's he talking about? "We have business?"

"Damn right, we do." With me held securely in his arms, he walks with a determined stride toward the elevators. "You're going to make the last couple of days up to me."

Holding back a grin, I arch a brow instead. "Oh, am I?"

Heat flares to life in his eyes. My tummy trembles in response. I don't know how he does it. All it takes is one look, and my panties melt.

"Yep, and you're going to start by doing that little swirly thing with your tongue that I love so much."

I burrow against his strength, feeling more content than I ever have. "I thought you liked when I..." leaning toward him, I whisper in his ear.

He groans. "Fuck, baby...you know I love that, too."

"Yup, I do." I slant my eyes at him as a smug expression settles on my face. "I guess it's a good thing for you that I've finally learned what to do with my mouth."

He swears harshly under his breath and I chuckle as he stabs the button for the elevator half a dozen times.

Chapter Forty-Seven

BRODY

"What do you think so far?" Dana asks as she walks toward the bank of floor-to-ceiling windows that line an entire wall. "Gorgeous, isn't it?"

I glance around the condo she's showing us. It has everything I'm looking for—tall ceilings, spacious rooms, and a professional-grade kitchen. Without any furniture to break up the emptiness, it looks like an ocean of polished hardwoods as far as the eye can see. I thread Natalie's fingers through mine, and we gravitate to the windows overlooking Lake Michigan.

It's one hell of a stunning view. Definitely something I could get used to.

Natalie's breath catches as her eyes fasten onto the deep blue water.

Yesterday, when Dad and I were out looking at real estate, Dana had flirted shamelessly with me. There'd been several instances when her fingers had lingered a beat too long on my arm or she'd stood a bit too close, her breasts grazing my bicep. Toward the end of the afternoon, she'd proposed meeting up for drinks to discuss the places we'd toured. Sure, it might have started out innocently enough downstairs in the hotel bar, but I have no doubt she would have suggested moving the conversation to my suite.

Today, with Natalie by my side, she's all business.

"And the amenities at the Remington are amazing," Dana continues. "Two parking spaces in a heated garage, a concierge on duty twenty-four hours a day, seven days a week, dry cleaning services, a car service, as well as housekeeping for a very reasonable fee." Her eyes shift between Natalie and me, trying to gauge our interest. "This is one of the most luxurious and sought-after buildings in the city."

"It's beautiful," Natalie murmurs, her gaze still trained on the whitecaps rolling inland.

When I say nothing, Dana clears her throat. "I'm going to head down to the lobby and speak with the manager about throwing in free housekeeping for a year. Why don't you take a few minutes to look around, and I'll meet you down there when you're finished?"

I give her a polite smile. "Sounds good. Thanks, Dana." I'm glad she's giving us a little space to talk privately. I want Natalie's opinion on this place.

Once Dana leaves and the quiet settles around us, I step behind Natalie, sliding my arms around her waist and drawing her against me so that there's no space between us.

Never again, I tell myself.

Never again will I allow there to be space between us.

"What do you think?" I murmur in her ear. "Pretty amazing, huh?"

"I love it," she says, turning her face so our eyes can lock. I thought she'd be more excited about helping me find a place, but she's been subdued the entire afternoon. "But it doesn't matter what I think. It only matters if you like it." Even though she glances away, I glimpse the sadness clouding her eyes. "You're the one who'll be living here."

I press her closer and whisper, "Well, I was kind of hoping we could live here together."

Her eyes widen and fasten on mine. "What?" she croaks out, looking surprised.

Yesterday Natalie told me that she loved me.

I love her, too.

I might not have said the words when I first realized it, but the feelings have been there for a while, growing stronger each and every day. After what we've been through, I don't plan on ever letting her go again. I may not know exactly how my future will unfold, but no matter what happens, I want Natalie by my side. That much I'm certain about.

When she says nothing in response and continues staring, my heart kicks painfully against my ribcage.

Fuck...Maybe I've blown my wad too soon. Maybe I should have played it cool and given us a little more time to be a couple before mentioning the plans that have been simmering in the back of my mind.

Nerves prickle along my skin as I give voice to my emotions. "Look, I know we haven't been together long, and maybe I'm pushing a little too hard, but I want a future with you, Natalie. When I move here in the spring, I want you with me."

"Are you sure?" She searches my eyes as if the answers she's looking for will be written there.

I cup her cheek in the palm of my hand. "Baby, I couldn't be more certain about anything. You're it for me."

She turns and twines her arms around my neck. Her breasts flatten against my chest. "I want that, too."

I grin, feeling like the luckiest bastard in the world. "It's always been you, Davies. Even when you were hating all over my ass, it was you."

"I never hated you," she mutters with a smile that trembles around the corners of her lips.

I cock an eyebrow at such a blatant lie. "Sure, you did, and we both know it."

"Fine, so maybe I did." The smile fades as she grows serious. "But that was before I got to know the man you truly are. The one I've fallen in love with. You're so much more than I ever realized and now... now I can't imagine a life without you in it."

"You'll never have to," I promise solemnly. Because I can't help myself, I angle my head and sweep my lips across hers. Right away, she opens as if greedy for what only I can give her.

Always...Always so greedy. And I fucking love it.

I pull away just enough to ask, "So...any interest in christening this place before we put in an offer?"

She bursts out laughing like I'm joking around. "Brody…"

"I'm completely serious, Davies." Breaking apart, I drag her to the master bedroom, which, if I remember correctly, has a plush area rug we can take advantage of. "Let's go make this place ours."

EPILOGUE

Brody

Two years later...

The door to the condo opens and in strolls my wife.

Yup, that's right.

My wife.

We've been married for two months. Oh, you better believe I locked that shit down. As soon as I wrapped up my first season with the Milwaukee Mavericks, we got hitched and took a two-week honeymoon in Bora Bora. The place we stayed in was ultra-secluded, which is a polite way of saying that there was a whole heck of a lot of naked beach time going on.

Goddamn, I miss seeing my wife frolicking in the water with nothing more than a sunhat. Come hell or high water, we'll be heading back to the island for two weeks every year if I have anything to say about it.

Because I'm in the running for a husband-of-the-year award, dinner is already plated and waiting on the terrace for Natalie. It's just something simple—salad and spaghetti. During the off-season, I like to try my hand at some new recipes. Although I'm not under any illusions that I'm some kind of wizard in the kitchen. But, by the number of BJs I've received lately, I'd have to say that my culinary efforts are very much appreciated. And since I'm quick on the uptake, you bet your ass I'll continue to have dinner waiting for my wife after she puts in a long day at the office.

Now, would I love it if she didn't work and we could spend more time together—naked and in bed, preferably? Hell, yeah. But a career in personal finance is what Natalie wants. And all I want is for my woman to be happy. We make this relationship work by supporting each other. That's never going to change.

"Hey, babe," I say as she joins me in the living room. "Dinner and a glass of wine are already waiting for you on the terrace."

Natalie flashes me a grateful smile and slips off her heels before pulling the rubber band from her hair so that the shiny strands fall in a thick curtain around her shoulders.

An arrow of lust shoots through me as I watch her. But it's more than that. So much more than I ever could have expected when I caught my first glimpse of her across a crowded lecture hall.

How the fuck did I get so lucky?

I have no idea, but I'm going to hold on to it with both hands and never let go.

"Have I told you how much I love you lately?" she asks.

"Nope." I point to my lips. "Give me some sugar, sugar."

She smirks and saunters over, twining her arms around my neck and pulling my face down to meet hers. "I love you," she whispers huskily before feathering her mouth against mine.

I immediately open and her tongue sweeps inside. The simple caress gives me an erection. Dinner is now the last thing on my mind. I want to pick Natalie up and carry her to the bedroom. I think the spaghetti will be just fine heated up in an hour or so. And if it's not, we'll order takeout.

Been there, done that.

"I love you, too," I growl.

Unable to wait a moment longer, my fingers attack the buttons of her shirt. She looks sexy as hell in a silky white blouse and tight pencil skirt that hits right above her knees. And let's not forget the black heels.

Professional Natalie is hot as fuck.

Since me ripping off her clothing is a nightly occurrence, I know exactly what I'm going to find beneath her corporate wear—black thigh-high stockings and sexy undergarments. I'm impatient to see which matching bra and panty set she picked out this morning.

The image of Natalie standing in the middle of our living room with the late afternoon sun pouring in wearing nothing more than her underwear, stockings, and heels is enough to make me sport some major wood.

No matter how many times I have her, it's never enough. My addiction only grows stronger.

Thank God, she's just as needy as I am.

This whole thing between us may have started out as some kind of BS relationship, but it's evolved into the most important one in my life.

Once I peel the blouse from her body, I unhook the skirt and shove it down her narrow hips until she stands in front of me exactly how I imagined.

This girl is a wet dream come to life. And she's mine. She will *always* be mine.

I groan and fall to my knees, staring up at her with open adoration. "Fuck, baby, you look hot."

Natalie smiles. Her hands stroke over my cheeks, her fingernails scraping along the five o'clock shadow darkening my jawline. I expect her to say something to the effect of, *take me to bed or fuck me right here, you big stud.*

But she doesn't.

Instead, she says, "I spoke with Amber today."

I blink. "Huh?" If I don't shut down this conversation pronto, my boner will deflate faster than you can say *stepmother*.

"She's expecting again," Natalie says, continuing to stroke my face with her fingers.

I groan. The process of softening has now commenced. "Really?" I grunt, hoping all is not lost. "Do we really have to discuss this right now when I've got you exactly where I want you?" She needs to throw me a bone. I've been slaving away over a hot stove all day making her dinner…Okay, not really. But still, I deserve a reward for my efforts.

Her shoulders tremble with silent mirth. "I thought you'd want to know that you're going to have another sibling."

I shake my head, trying to rid the image of just how that baby got in my stepmother's belly. I almost shudder. "We have more pressing matters to attend to at the moment, if you know what I mean." Which I'm sure she does. "I think you could have waited an hour or so to share the good news," I grumble. Leaning forward, I feather a kiss over her lace-covered pussy.

Her fingers tunnel through my hair. Gah...I love when she does that. "Well, I thought you might want to know that they won't be the only ones with a baby in seven months."

Wait...What?

My movements still as my eyes arrow to her brightly shining ones.

"I'm pregnant," she whispers with a growing smile.

"How did this happen?" The question shoots out of my mouth before I can stop it.

Natalie cocks a brow. "Do I really need to explain that to you, Brody? I mean, I can, but I thought..." She shrugs.

"No," I chuckle. That's my girl, always a smartass. Of course, I wouldn't have her any other way. This is the woman I fell head over heels in love with. "I meant, how did this happen since we were using protection?"

She shakes her head and nibbles on her bottom lip. For the first time during this conversation, uncertainty flickers in her dark eyes. "I forgot to take my pill a few times when we were on vacation." Her voice lowers, some of her happiness dimming. "Are you upset? I know we talked about waiting a few years before starting a family."

Still on my knees, I wrap my arms around her hips and pull her toward me until I can lay my head against her belly. How did I not see this before? Natalie has always had a perfectly flat abdomen. Now there's a slight roundness to it. Not that anyone would notice, but I see her naked every night and didn't think anything of it.

"Are you kidding me? I'm fucking thrilled." And I am.

I turn my face so I can meet her eyes again. So she can see the truth of my words.

"Really?" she whispers, still looking unsure. I hate that I've taken away even a moment of her joy.

"Of course, I am. I love you. And I love that we created this baby on our honeymoon. It makes it even more special."

I lay a kiss against her belly and rise to my feet. In one swift motion, I sweep Natalie off hers and carry her to the bedroom. She beams at me, and there's so much love shining in her eyes that it makes me feel like the luckiest man on the face of the earth.

Yeah, we'll definitely be ordering takeout in roughly two hours.

Three, if I have anything to do with it.

Now, if you'll excuse us, you bunch of nosy bastards, I'm going to make slow love to my gorgeous wife. And maybe, just for shits and giggles, I'll have her explain how babies are made. Because the thought of all the demonstrating she'll have to do gets me all hot and bothered.

CAMPUS PLAYER

Demi

"Morning, Demi!" Gary, one of the stadium custodians, calls out with an easy smile and wave as he saunters toward me. "Up and at 'em bright and early this morning, I see."

My heart jackhammers beneath my ribcage from the twenty-minute run as I flash him a grin. "Always!"

"You have a good one! I'll see you tomorrow!"

Since I've already moved past him, I holler over my shoulder, "Same place, same time!"

Even with *The Killers* pumping through my earbuds, I almost hear the deep chuckle that slides from his lips. Our morning greetings are a ritual three years in the making. I've been running through the wide corridor that leads to the stadium football field since I stepped foot on campus freshman year. This will be something I miss when I graduate in the spring. Five days a week, I'm up at six, logging in a four-mile run before returning home, jumping in the shower, and heading off to class.

At this time of the day, the stadium is still relatively quiet, with only a few people wandering the hallways. There's something both serene and eerie about it. I've been here on game days when there are thirty thousand fans packed shoulder to shoulder, rooting on the Western Wildcats football team. Three-fourths of the stadium filled with black and orange is an amazing sight to behold. Football is a religion at Western. Unfortunately, the same can't be said for the women's soccer team. We're lucky if there are a couple of hundred spectators in the stands.

I've come to terms with it.

Sort of.

I keep my gaze trained on the light at the end of the tunnel and push myself faster. As soon as I burst out of the darkness, bright sunlight pours down on me, stroking over the bare skin of my arms and shoulders. It's late August, and summer is still in full swing. A whistle cuts through the silence of the stadium, and my gaze slices to the field. Nick Richards has been head coach of the Wildcats for the last decade. He also happens to be my father.

Two days a week, the guys are up at six in the morning for yoga. Dad is a big believer in flexibility. Even though I'm winded, a smirk lifts the corners of my lips. Watching two-hundred-and-eighty-pound linebackers contort their bodies into Downward-Facing Dog, the Warrior II Pose, and the Cobra is enough to bring a chuckle to my lips. Some of the guys actually like it, but most grumble when they think Dad isn't paying attention. Little do they know that he sees and hears everything.

My father catches sight of me and flashes a quick smile along with a wave in my direction. He has a black ball cap pulled low and aviators covering his eyes. There's a clipboard in one hand as he paces behind the instructor.

When I point to the field, he shakes his head. He might make the guys do yoga, but he refuses to participate. Something about old dogs and new tricks. Every once in a while, I'll tell him that he needs to get out there and set a good example for the team. He usually shoots me a glare in return.

Every Wednesday night, Dad and I get together. Our weekly dinners became a thing when I moved out of the house and into the dorms freshman year. He's busy coaching football, and my schedule is packed tight with school and soccer. Getting together once a week is the best way for us to stay connected. It doesn't matter if we're in the middle of our seasons; we always make time for each other. Especially since Mom lives in sunny California. After eighteen years of marriage, she got fed up with being a distant second to the Western University football program. She packed up her bags and walked out. I hate to say it, but Dad didn't notice her absence for a couple of days. Which only proved her point. Now she's remarried, learning to surf, and is a vegan. I visit for a couple of weeks during the summer before soccer training camp starts up at the end of June.

Even though it's only the two of us, our weekly dinners are set for three people.

I tell myself to stare straight ahead and not glance in his direction.

Don't do it!

Don't you dare do it!

Damn.

My gaze reluctantly zeros in on him like a heat-seeking missile. Long blond hair, bright blue eyes, sun-kissed skin, and muscles for miles. And he's tall, somewhere around six foot three.

I'm describing none other than Rowan Michaels.

Otherwise known as the bane of my existence.

My dad discovered the talented quarterback the summer before we entered high school and took him under his wing. Which has been...aggravating. In the seven years since, Rowan has become an irritatingly permanent fixture in my life. He's the brother I never wanted or asked for. He's the gift I wish I could give back. He's the son my father never had but secretly longed for.

On a campus with over thirty thousand students, one would think that avoidance would be easy to accomplish. That hasn't turned out to be the case. Somehow, we ended up in the same major—Exercise Science. I get stuck in at least one class with the guy each semester. This time it's statistics, which is a requirement. Three times a week, I'm forced to see him. And then there are the weekly dinners at Dad's house.

Every Wednesday, Rowan shows up without fail.

It's so annoying.

No, *he's* annoying!

Our gazes collide, and electricity sizzles through my veins before I immediately snuff it out and pretend it never happened.

I am not attracted to Rowan Michaels.
I am not attracted to Rowan Michaels.
I am not attracted to Rowan Michaels.

Maybe if I repeat the mantra enough times, it'll be true. That's the hope I cling to. I've made it through the last seven years trying to convince myself of this. I only have to get through our final year together, and then we'll go our separate ways—me to graduate school or maybe to the Women's National Soccer League, and Rowan to the NFL. He's one of the most talented quarterbacks in the conference. Hell, probably the country. There is little doubt in my mind that he'll be a first-round draft pick come next spring.

Trust me when I say that Rowan Michaels fever is alive and well at Western University. His fanbase is legendary. The guy is a major player.

Both on and off the field.

Girls fall all over themselves to be with him. They fill the stands at football practice, show up at parties he's rumored to be at, and basically stalk him around campus.

It's a little nauseating. Don't these girls have any self-respect when it comes to a hot guy?

I wince at that unchecked thought.

Fine...I'll begrudgingly admit it; he's good-looking.

I shake my head as if that will banish the insidious thoughts currently invading my brain. Enough about Rowan. It's time to focus on the reason I'm at the stadium at this ungodly hour. I rip my gaze from him as I hit the cement staircase. After half a flight, all thoughts of the blond quarterback vanish from my mind. How could they not when my quads, glutes, and calves are on fire, screaming for mercy as I force myself to the nosebleed section. By the time I finish, my legs are Jell-O, and I still have a two-mile run back to the apartment I share with my best friend off-campus.

I give Dad a half-hearted wave before leaving. It's the most I can muster. His lips quirk at the corners as he shakes his head. He thinks I'm crazy. At the moment, I can't argue with his assessment of the situation. Although, it's the extra training I put in that helps me run circles around the other team in the second half of the game.

The jog home feels like it will last forever. By the time I unlock the apartment door, I'm ready to collapse. I beeline for the shower and jump in before it's fully warm. My skin prickles with goose flesh, but it feels so damn good. Twenty minutes later, I'm dressed and ready to take on the day. My hair has been thrown up in a messy bun, and I'm making a protein smoothie that will fuel me for my morning classes.

Just before taking off, I poke my head into Sydney's room. I know exactly how I'll find her, and that's buried beneath a small mountain of blankets. She doesn't disappoint. We met the summer before freshman year in training camp and have been besties ever since. She's the yin to my yang. The peanut butter to my jelly. The Thelma to my Louise. Where I'm more introverted and cautious, she's loud and boisterous. She's been known to leap without necessarily looking at what she's jumping into. Every so often, it gets us into trouble. Sydney and I have lived together since sophomore year. I gave up trying to cajole her ass out of bed for a six o'clock run after the first week of us cohabitating when she nearly took my head off with an alarm clock.

"It's that time again," I sing-song obnoxiously, "rise and shine."

There's a grunt and then some shifting from under the blankets that tells me she's alive.

When I chant her name repeatedly, each time escalating in volume, she growls, "Get the fuck out!"

"Awww," I mock, "that's so sweet. I love you, too."

Sydney snorts before a hand snakes out from beneath the blankets to give me a one-fingered salute. Then she grabs a pillow and tosses it in my general vicinity. It falls about five feet short of its mark.

I stare at the dismal attempt. "If you're trying to cause bodily harm, you'll have to do better than that."

"Piss off."

"All right then." I shrug. "See you after class." With that, I close the door behind me.

My farewell is met with another indecipherable mouthful. If this weren't something we went through on the daily, I'd worry she was in the midst of a stroke. Sydney is definitely not a morning person. She's more of an early afternoon person. Another thing I've learned over the years? The action of waking up to a brand-new day is a gradual process.

She's like a bear rousing prematurely from hibernation. It's not a pretty sight. She's lucky I don't take her insults personally.

I grab my backpack from the small table crammed into the breakfast nook area along with a coffee before heading out the door. The apartment I share with Sydney is located three blocks from campus, which is highly sought out real estate. We're fortunate Dad is friends with the guy who manages the building. It's probably one of the only perks of having a father who is a head coach of a college football team.

You'd think there would be more, but you'd be wrong. Honestly, being Nick Richard's daughter is more of a hindrance than anything else. People assume you receive special treatment on campus, from professors, or that you have an in with all the football players.

Or worse...

Much worse.

After a bunch of ugly—not to mention untrue—rumors circulated freshman year, I've done my best to distance myself from the Wildcats football team. They're a great bunch of guys, but I don't need all the ugly gossip and speculation that comes along with being friends with them.

As I reach Corbin Hall, the mathematics building for my stats class, my gaze is drawn to a clump of students standing around outside the three-story, red-brick building. In the center of that crowd is Rowan. I don't have to see him physically to know that he's close. The muscles in my belly contract with awareness. It's like a sixth sense. One I wish would go away. He's the last person I want to be cognizant of.

As I jog up the wide stone stairs to the entrance, my gaze fastens on him. A smirk twists the edges of his lips, and my eyes narrow before I drag them away and yank open the door to the building. Relief rushes through me as I step inside the air conditioning and disappear from sight.

"Hey, Demi, wait up!"

I turn at the sound of my name before slowing my step. The dark-haired guy jogging to catch up smiles before falling in line with me.

Justin Fischer.

He's a baseball player and teammates with Sydney's boyfriend,

Ethan. We've been seeing each other for about a month. It's still casual at this point. With school and soccer, I don't have a ton of time to invest in a relationship. He seems to understand that and isn't pushing to be more serious.

When he leans in for a kiss, I angle my head. At the last moment, he tilts in the opposite direction, and we end up bumping teeth instead of locking lips. With a grunt, I pull away and chuckle. My fingers fly to my mouth to make sure I haven't chipped a tooth.

Maybe I've been reluctant to admit it to myself, but that kiss sums up our relationship perfectly.

Awkward and a step out of sync with each other.

"Sorry," he murmurs with a slight smile. I search his face and wait for any telltale sign of sexual chemistry to ping inside me. Unfortunately, my insides remain completely unfazed, which is disappointing but not altogether unexpected. I had a sneaking suspicion when we first got together that it might turn out this way.

"No problem," I say, hoisting my smile and brushing aside those thoughts.

"I haven't seen you for a couple of days," he remarks as we turn a corner and continue walking.

"It's been busy." Which isn't a lie. School might have recently started, but the academics at Western are rigorous. And being a Division I athlete is more like a job. If you're not ready to put in the work, don't bother showing up. There's no half-assing it around this place.

"When's your next game?" he asks.

"Tomorrow at six." My gaze flickers in his direction. Not that I expect him to come, but...

Fine, so maybe I do. If he wants to be my boyfriend, then he needs to show a little support.

His dark brows draw together. "That sucks. I've got a mandatory study hour I have to attend."

I shrug off the disappointment. It's another nail in the coffin of this relationship as far as I'm concerned. "That's cool. It's not a big deal."

"But I'll see you tonight?"

Oh. Right.

Tonight.

Well, damn. In a moment of weakness, I threw out an invitation to join our Wednesday evening dinner. It's one I now regret. If only there were a gracious way to rescind the offer.

"If you're busy, I totally understand—"

"Are you kidding? No way." With a grin, he shakes his head. "I wouldn't miss it for the world. I'm looking forward to meeting Coach Richards."

Great. So this is more about my father than me? Exactly what every girl wants to hear.

I force a brittle smile. "Awesome. He's excited, too."

That might be something of an overstatement.

Justin nods toward the end of the corridor. "I better get moving. Professor Andrews is a real stickler for punctuality."

"Yup. See you later."

This time, when he leans in, our lips align perfectly. The kiss is nothing more than a fleeting caress. There and gone before I can sink into it.

And I'm left feeling...absolutely nothing.

I bury the disappointment where I can't inspect it too closely before giving him a wave as he takes off. For a moment, I stand rooted in the hallway and watch as he disappears through the crowd. There's nothing to distinguish Justin from the thousands of guys who look exactly like him on campus. He's of average height and build with dark hair and espresso-colored eyes. He's nice enough. Although, if I'm completely honest, he's a little self-absorbed. He talks about baseball all the time. If Ethan hadn't introduced us, he's not someone I would have looked twice at. We don't have a ton in common.

As much as I hate to admit it, this relationship has probably reached its expiration date.

Now it's a matter of pulling the plug.

Ugh. I hate breakups. Although, it's doubtful this will end up destroying him. I'll have to make it through tonight and figure out the rest.

With a sigh of resignation, I head to the classroom and find a seat tucked away in the far corner of the small lecture hall. A lanky guy I recognize from a few of my other classes settles beside me. He flashes a dimpled smile as we empty our backpacks.

The tiny hair at the nape of my neck rises seconds before Rowan enters the room. It's like my body knows when he's within a thirty-foot radius. I glance at him from beneath the thick fringe of my lashes before shifting away. Air becomes wedged in my lungs as I wait for him to take a seat. And it won't be next to me because I'm—

"Hey man, would you mind moving?"

Surrounded on both sides.

Damnit. I'm hoping the cutie next to me will tell Rowan to go take a flying leap.

What? It could happen. Not everyone at this university is enamored of the football-playing god. Although I realize the odds aren't stacked in my favor. Rowan is the most recognized athlete on campus. People fall all over themselves to accommodate him.

It's a little sickening.

Okay, maybe more than a little.

"Sure, no problem, Michaels." The guy next to me hastily packs up his books before vacating the desk. Unable to ignore him any longer, I glare as Rowan slides onto the seat next to me.

"Did you really think you could evade me that easily?" Laughter brims in his deep voice. A voice, I might add, that does funny things to my insides.

"One can always hope, right?"

"Oh, answering a question with a question." He leans closer, eating up some of the much-needed distance between us. "I like it."

I roll my eyes as his lips stretch into a satisfied grin. Irritation bubbles up inside me when sexual tension blooms at the bottom of my belly. Or maybe that tension has settled a little lower.

It's definitely lower.

I'm tempted to swear like a sailor. How is it possible that I feel nothing for the guy I'm actually dating, and yet my pulse skitters out of control for someone I don't even like? It's so freaking ironic. It's been this way since we met, and nothing I do stomps it out. I can try to fool myself into believing it's not there, but that doesn't make it any less true.

It's a relief when Professor Peters takes his place at the podium and clears his throat. Once he's captured everyone's attention, he delves headfirst into the probability of dependent and independent events.

Grateful for the excuse to ignore Rowan for the next fifty minutes, I open my textbook and concentrate on the lesson. Just as the blond boy fades into the background, his bare knee bumps into mine. Electricity ricochets through my entire being. I glance at him to see if he's noticed the strange energy we always seem to generate and find his ocean-colored gaze fastened to mine.

My guess is that he does.

Damnation.

Want to read more? Buy Campus Player here -) https://books2read.com/u/mYAxqV

THE GIRL NEXT DOOR

Mia

Summer before freshman year of college...

"Get your butt over here," my best friend squeals from the window where she's taken up sentinel, "you *need* to see this!"

That's a negative, Ghost Rider. I'll take a hard pass. I have zero interest in spying on a yard full of drunken classmates who are partying it up at my neighbor's house. Reluctantly, I glance up from the toes I'm painting with a pale pink polish. Coney Island Cotton Candy, to be precise.

When our gazes lock, Alyssa waves me over. She's practically vibrating with excitement. Kind of like a schnauzer.

"Everyone is over there!"

"Not true," I mutter, lacquering my baby toe with an impressively steady hand. "W*e're* right here." And that's exactly where I plan to stay.

"Yeah, that's kind of the problem." She steeples her hands together before shaking them at me. "Please?" she begs. "Can't we go over there for a little bit? *Just a little*? That's all I'm asking."

That's all she's asking...ha!

I'm calling bullshit.

Alyssa knows I'd rather chew my arm off than crash one of Beck

Hollingsworth's parties. I didn't mention it to her, but Beck shot me a text earlier this afternoon with all the details. If she even suspected an invitation had been issued, she would have dragged my ass across the lawn that separates our properties as soon as the first guest pulled into the drive.

No, thank you.

It's obvious from all the commotion coming from next door that the entire senior class has shown up to celebrate our newly graduated status. If we didn't live on a quiet cul-de-sac tucked away in a gated subdivision, I'd expect the police to make an unannounced visit and shut down the festivities.

Then again, no one wants to mess with Beck's father, Archibald Hollingsworth. He's a high-priced attorney with a fleet of underlings working for him. He's one of those overly tan guys with blindingly white veneers you see on television yapping about if you've been injured, you need to call them—they fight for the little guy! The dude is everywhere. Billboards. Commercials. Newspaper and magazine advertisements.

The local police have tangled with Archibald several times over the years because his son is a magnet for trouble. Let's see, there was the time (or five) when he was picked up for underage drinking. When Beck was fifteen years old, he *borrowed* his parent's brand spanking new Range Rover and did a little off-roading. And the police were involved when he super glued the locks on the high school building doors for senior prank day.

Instead of hauling Beck to the station every time he's picked up, they drop him at his front door and don't bother talking to Archibald about it. Beck is on a first name basis with a number of guys on the force. A few showed up to his graduation party in June.

It shouldn't come as a surprise that Beck always figures out a way to circumvent the obstacles standing in his path. His parents. School. The law. It's as irritating as it is impressive. Maybe one of these days, he'll use his powers for good instead of evil.

"Come on, Mia!" Alyssa whines, all the while flashing sad puppy dog eyes at me.

Double whammy.

My bestie knows I have a difficult time resisting puppy dog eyes.

I wiggle my toes from the bed and grumble, "I can't go anywhere until my nails dry." I'm doing my best to prolong subjecting myself to the aggravation of being anywhere near Beckett Hollingsworth. The guy drives me bat shit crazy.

And that's putting it mildly.

"Great! So...five minutes?" She swings away before pressing her face against the screen as her voice turns dreamy. "I bet Colton is already there."

Ugh.

Colton Montgomery is Beck's righthand man, so it's not a wager I'm likely to win.

Against my better advice, Alyssa has been crushing hard on Colton for more than a year. Not only is he popular, but he's a football player. Heavy emphasis on the *player* part. If Alyssa were smart, she'd find a nice guy to fall in lust with, but she has tunnel vision when it comes to the blond-haired, blue-eyed heartbreaker.

Colton has it all going on. Brains, brawn, and more than likely, a one-way ticket to the NFL after college.

The only problem is that he's aware of his own appeal.

His ego is as massive as other parts of him.

Or so I hear.

And not from Alyssa since he refuses to sleep with her. I can't decide if the situation is amusing or sad. The more Colton keeps Alyssa at a firm distance, the more determined she is to have him.

Last football season, Alyssa dragged me to every game. Even the away ones. My greatest fear was that Beck would assume my ass was in the stands in support of him. His fan club is already legendary without adding me to the ranks.

When it comes to the ladies, Beckett makes Colton look like an innocent babe. He goes through girls like most people go through underwear. Speaking of panties, the girls at our high school are always happy—hell, I'd go so far as to say thrilled—to drop theirs for him.

It's ridiculous.

He's a chronic user and abuser.

There should be a warning label slapped across his forehead.

Beware. Toxic to the female species.

But you know what?

That wouldn't stop these bubble-headed chicks from spreading their legs wide for him. I've stopped trying to figure out the appeal. All right, I'm well aware of what the attraction is. As much as I've tried to pretend I'm immune to his charms, I'm not. I just do a damn good job of burying them deep down where they never see the light of day. If I didn't, Beck would annihilate me in a heartbeat, and I have zero desire to end up a casualty on his hit list.

Given the choice, I'd rather flip through Netflix and find a movie to watch rather than be dragged over to Beck's bash.

Doesn't sitting around in pajamas and stuffing our faces with pizza sound way better than watching a bunch of our classmates get sloppy drunk, engage in way too much PDA, puke all over the place before alcohol poisoning sets in?

I won't bother posing the question to Alyssa. There is no way she'll willingly opt for sitting home instead of stalking her crush.

Would you like to guess what Colton will be doing while I wipe drool from Alyssa's chin?

You guessed it. He'll be flirting with every vagina he thinks he has a chance of penetrating.

Honestly, it's one of the most masochistic things Alyssa could do. I have no idea why she insists on putting herself through this kind of agony. Apparently, my job as her best friend is to support her decision to inflict untold amounts of mental anguish onto herself. I'd slap her upside the head if I thought it would knock sense into her.

My prediction for the evening goes a little something like this— Alyssa will have a few drinks, moon over Colton, before dissolving into a puddle of tears while that manwhore makes out with other girls in front of her face. Then I'll drag her home and she'll end up knuckle-deep in a gallon of triple chocolate ice cream.

But that's what friends are for, right?

Don't worry, I've already made my peace with it.

"Fine," I grumble with a scowl, hoping she understands the depth of my reluctance. "But let it be known that I won't be staying for more than an hour. So you better make good use of your time, girl."

She swings around to face me, bouncing on the tips of her toes as she claps her hands together with excitement. "Yay!" As soon as she gets the affirmative, she beelines for my closet, which is half the size of my room.

I have the kind of closet most girls my age can only dream about. Shoes, purses, clothes, jewelry. It's all there and organized.

"Cue the montage music while I find something schmexy to wear!" she squeals.

"What you have on is fine." I roll my eyes and yell, "It was good enough for me, wasn't it?"

From within the depths of my closet comes a snort.

For the next ten minutes, I'm treated to an impromptu fashion show. At the rate Alyssa is going, we won't make it to the party any time soon.

Take your time, girlfriend. I'm totally good with that.

A dozen outfit changes later, Alyssa settles on a black knit tank and white skirt that showcases her sun-kissed legs to their best advantage. Alyssa has been taking dance classes since she was three years old. She's toned with long, lean muscles.

"Damn girl, you look hot." Not that her crush will appreciate the effort. Alyssa needs to move on. I'm thinking a twelve-step program would help kick the Chase Montgomery habit.

"I would gladly live in your closet if you'd let me." She grins before doing a little twirl. "It's my happy place."

A reluctant smile quirks my lips.

My mother is a card-carrying shopaholic and has the Amex Black Card bills to prove it. She buys clothes like our house burned to the ground and nothing could be salvaged. Even with racks and racks of space, my wardrobe is bursting at the seams. Three quarters of the stuff has never seen the light of day. Alyssa is lucky we're roughly the same size so she can borrow whatever she wants.

Now that she's dressed and ready to mingle, her eyes narrow as she takes a hard look at me. Wordlessly, she spins around and races back inside the closet only to resurface a handful of minutes later.

"Here you go," she says, tossing two garments at the foot of my bed.

I glance at the shimmery gold tank and dark wash jean skirt that resembles a folded-up napkin. The skirt is cute as hell, but I would strongly advise against going commando while wearing it unless you're looking to flash everyone your goodies.

Since that's not my usual style, the price tag is still dangling from the pocket. I have no idea what my mother was thinking when she picked it up.

Unsure why she's throwing clothes at me, I point to the small pile. "What's that about?"

"You need to change." She gives me a look that says—*duh* before clapping her hands together. "Chop-chop."

Changing my clothes was not part of the plan. I'm fine with going in my pajamas. It's not like I'm looking for a hookup. Or anything else, for that matter.

I shake my head and fold my arms across my chest. "No, thank you."

Her gaze rakes over me as she points at my T-shirt. "Is that a coffee stain on your boob?"

With a frown, I glance at my chest and inspect the dark spot marring the fabric of my right breast. My guess is that she's right. Caramel Macchiato, to be specific. "Possibly."

Her lips flatten. "I refuse to go anywhere with you looking like *that*."

"Great!" I stretch out before stacking my hands behind my head. "What kind of movie night does it feel like to you? Romcom? Horror? Psychological thriller? Angsty tearjerker?" A benevolent smile curves my lips. "You can choose."

Alyssa stomps her foot on the carpeted floor. "Mia!" she wails at a decibel that could shatter eardrums. A few neighborhood dogs howl in response. *"You promised!"*

Promised?

No, I don't think so.

I scrunch my nose and tap a finger against my lips. "I don't believe I ever *promised* to do anything. *Reluctantly agreed?* Yes. *Was browbeaten into capitulating?* Definitely. But *promised?* Not in this lifetime."

When she straightens to her full height, I groan, knowing exactly what's about to happen. *"Mia Evelyn Stanbury*! Do I need to remind you who was there when—"

Argh.

This is the portion of the evening where Alyssa trots out every damn thing she's ever done for me until I relent. And she'll start with Harper Hastings. The girl who bullied me relentlessly in seventh grade because Xander Rossi asked me to the movies instead of her. After months of Harper's meanspirited attacks, Alyssa waited for the girl after school. My bestie let it be known that if Harper didn't cease and desist, she'd spread the good word that the other girl was a known bra stuffer. It must have been true, since Harper immediately backed off and I never heard a peep from her again.

"Yes, yes, Harper Hastings," I mutter, not appreciating the direction this conversation has swerved in.

Alyssa folds her arms across her chest as a smug smile twists her lips upward. "Harper Hastings is only the beginning, my friend." She arches a brow. "Need I continue?"

Silently we glare before I fold like a cheap house of cards. "Fine, I'll change." I straighten before scooping up the skirt and top and shaking them at her. "It's only because I love you and you're my best friend that I'm even willing to step foot next door."

An angelic smile spreads across her pretty face before she blows me a kiss. "Love you, too. Now kindly move your assets."

"An hour," I remind. "That's all you get."

Looking unconcerned, she waves a hand. "No worries, that's more than enough time to work my magic."

What she means to say is that it's more than enough time for Colton to ignore her, all the while hooking up with another girl. Part of me almost wishes he would sleep with Alyssa. Maybe then the rose-colored glasses would come off and she would realize what a douche the guy is.

In one fluid motion, the stained T-shirt is stripped from my body and replaced with the shimmery gold tank. Then I slide off the comfy shorts I've been lounging in and yank on the tiny rectangle of material that doubles as a skirt.

I step in front of my floor-to-ceiling mirror that's propped against the wall and stare at my reflection before attempting to tug the skirt further down my thighs, but it's useless. There's not a spare inch of material to be found.

What the hell was my mother thinking when she picked this up? Was she mistakenly shopping in the toddler section? That's the only reasonable explanation.

I turn around and bend over, touching my toes before peering over my shoulder to the mirror. It's as I suspected. My thong is on full display. Actually, it doesn't even look like I'm wearing underwear since the material is wedged between the crack of my ass like dental floss.

Lovely.

Not to mention uncomfortable.

"Is there a second option to consider?" My gaze slides to Alyssa's in the mirror. "One where my ass isn't hanging out?"

"'Fraid not. I'm seriously loving the whole—is she or isn't she wearing panties guessing game you've got going on." She winks. "Play your cards right and maybe you'll get lucky tonight."

I narrow my eyes as my lips thin. "Believe it or not, I'm perfectly content being unlucky."

"That, my dear, is only because you don't realize what you've been missing."

"Heartache, STI's, and the possibility of an unplanned pregnancy?" I flutter my lashes and smile. "You are so right."

Ignoring my comment, she tosses a pair of gold sandals at me before sliding her feet into black leather ones that strap up her legs, giving her that whole Grecian goddess vibe. She looks amazing. But then again, when doesn't she? Alyssa has long blond hair and dark blue eyes. Her skin has a natural sun-kissed glow that darkens under the summer sun.

It almost offends me that Colton refuses to fuck my friend.

What the hell is wrong with him?

"Ready to go?" she asks, checking her reflection in the mirror one last time.

I slip the sandals on before rising to my full height. "As I'll ever be."

Five minutes later, we've traversed the lawn and are walking around the side of the Hollingsworth mansion. All sixteen thousand square feet of it. Needless to say, Archibald has turned ambulance chasing into a lucrative art form.

With every step we take, the sound of drunken laughter and the pulsing beat of music grows louder, assaulting our ears. As soon as the party comes into view, I wonder why I let Alyssa talk me into this.

It's complete chaos.

As much as Alyssa would like to convince you otherwise, I'm not a complete dud. I like to party as much as the next girl. But Beck enjoys taking his antics to the next level. He's not content to have a low-key get together where people sit around and chill.

This party is moments away from becoming one of those teen movies where all hell breaks loose and the host wakes up naked the next morning in a dumpster five states away next to a goat.

Over to the left, a few people are holding a guy upside down while he performs a keg stand.

Chants of—*chug, chug, chug* permeate the air.

It wouldn't surprise me if one of these drunken idiots is found floating face down in the pool come morning.

It begs the question of why Beck's parents would leave him alone without supervision. He might be eighteen years old and technically an adult, but he needs an adultier adult to keep him in check. Someone who can put the kibosh on his hijinks.

Good luck with that. His older brother, Ari, is out of the country for the summer.

Archibald and Caroline, his parents, must have realized this was inevitable. Every time they go out of town, Beck throws a huge bash. Depending on the amount of damage, he gets grounded anywhere from a couple of days to a couple of weeks. The threat of conse-quences—hell, actual consequences being enforced—are in no way a deterrent.

Believe it or not, before our parents left town for a long weekend in New York, Archie asked me to keep an eye on their son. His actual words were—*make sure no one dies.*

As if I exert that much control over Beck?

Yeah, right. Beck doesn't listen to anyone, let alone me.

Exactly what am I supposed to do?

Tattletale?

Facetime his parents so they can get a first-hand glimpse of the ensuing pandemonium?

As much pleasure as that would give me, it's not going to happen. I might be a lot of things (a rule follower and a goody-goody, if you listen to Beck) but there are lines that can't be crossed and snitching is one of them.

This will be one more antic Beck gets away with. I suppose that's the beauty of being Beckett Hollingsworth. He doesn't give a shit about anything other than football.

The Neanderthal sport is his life.

By the time Beck was a freshman in high school, he'd already drawn the attention of Big Ten college coaches. They couldn't wait to get him on their roster. If he could have gone straight to the NFL after graduation, he would have. But that's not a possibility. Players aren't eligible to enter the draft until after their sophomore year of college. Beck's father has taken it one step further by insisting he wait until senior year because—and I quote—*no damn son of mine is going to be a college dropout.*

Beck will be proof positive that C's really do earn degrees.

As my gaze drifts over the thick crowd of glassy-eyed stares, it collides with bright green ones. A little zip of electricity sizzles its way through my veins as our gazes fasten. The muscles in my belly tense with awareness. Once I realize what's happening, I tamp down the reaction. My life has been filled with a thousand little moments like this one. Moments I like to pretend never transpired.

For all I know, it's gastritis from the sushi I picked up at the gas station last night.

Anything's possible, right?

Instead of glancing away, I hold his stare and scowl. What I've learned is that it's better to brazen out these situations than turn tail and run. Beck's perfect cupid's bow of a mouth lifts into a knowing grin before he crooks his finger.

A gurgle of laughter bubbles up in my throat.

I don't think so, buddy.

I'm not like the bubbleheads he usually toys with. I have a working brain and I enjoy using it to make good decisions that won't come back to bite me in the ass. Unlike Beck, I have a healthy amount of self-preservation.

I press my lips into a tight line before emphatically shaking my head.

A wolfish grin spills across his face, giving him a boyishly handsome appearance. With dark tousled hair, sharp cheekbones that scream his Russian heritage, and thick eyebrows, he's a danger to females everywhere. I won't mention the chiseled body that looks like it was carved from stone. Broad shoulders and a tapered waist complete the package.

It's almost a relief when a bikini-clad girl steps between us, severing the connection. Now that his sharp gaze is no longer pinning me in place, I'm able to exhale all the air from my lungs.

Alyssa grabs my hand. "There he is," she whisper-yells excitedly over the babble of voices and music. "Oh my God, he's so freaking dreamy."

I regard the crowd of newly minted high school graduates before finding Colton.

Sure, I'll admit it. He's as hot as Beck. Instead of short dark hair, he's golden blond. It's buzzed on the sides and left long on top, so he's constantly pushing it away from bright blue eyes. He's tall and brawny. If I hadn't gone to school with him since elementary, I'd suspect he flunked a few grades. Even his muscles have muscles.

Girls are already circling around him, vying for his attention. The guy is like a rock star picking out groupies to sleep with at the end of the night.

"He's okay," I mutter, wanting to downplay his attractiveness.

"You're so full of shit, your eyes are turning brown. He's way better than *okay* and you know it."

"Ewww." I scrunch my nose. "That's gross."

"Focus!" She snaps her fingers in front of my face.

I make one last-ditch effort to sway her. "You can do better than Colton. He knows exactly how hot he is and takes full advantage of it every chance he gets. Find someone like," I stand on my tiptoes and pick through the mass of bodies before zeroing in on the perfect guy for Alyssa, "Landon Mathews. Not only is he good looking, he's a sweetheart."

Alyssa's expression turns thoughtful as she assesses the tall guy with inky-black hair and unusual blue-green eyes. He's standing around with a bunch of football players, laughing at something one of them said.

"He's definitely yummy," she admits.

For one glorious moment, my spirits soar. Maybe she'll drop this whole Colton Montgomery nonsense and go after someone more attainable. Landon is a great guy. He's as hot as his friends, but he's not a total asshat. Unfortunately, he doesn't get nearly the same amount of hype that Colton or Beck do since he's been labeled a good guy.

I mean, who wants to date a nice guy when you can have one who treats you like total crap?

Said no one ever.

Except...there seems to be way more truth to that statement than most females are comfortable acknowledging. Whether they realize it or not, these girls have been conditioned to crave unattainable jerks.

It's disturbing on so many levels.

"Added bonus," I continue, "he knows you're alive!"

"Um, excuse me, Colton knows I'm alive," she grumbles.

"Are you certain about that?"

She bites her lip as we glance at the guy in question who is— surprise-surprise—surrounded by a bevy of scantily clad girls competing for his interest.

Uh-oh.

Alyssa's got that look in her eye. The one that tells me not to bother trying to talk her out of her plans.

She confirms it by saying, "Wish me luck, I'm going in."

It was worth a try.

"Good luck."

One of Alyssa's best qualities is that she's not a quitter. That girl can be as tenacious and persistent as a terrier. And sometimes, just as yappy.

In this instance, it's a negative.

When she's a few steps away, I cup my fingers around my mouth and yell, "Maybe you should take off the panties so you can flash him your puss. That way he'll know you're a sure thing."

She whips around with a grin. "Excellent idea!"

My jaw drops when she shimmies out of her panties and tosses them in my direction.

"Christ, girl! I was joking! That was sarcasm!" I glance at the wadded-up material I now clench in my hand. "What am I supposed to do with these?"

She shrugs. "Keep them as a souvenir?"

Gross.

"I don't think so." I stalk to a garbage can and pitch them. When I turn around, Alyssa is pushing her way through the crowd, moving steadily closer to Colton and his harem.

If nothing else, this should be entertaining. It takes a moment to realize I'm alone at a party I didn't want to attend in the first place. I slip my phone from my back pocket and glance at it.

Fifty minutes and counting.

This is shaping up to be the longest hour of my life. Maybe I should head inside and grab a drink. By the number of drunken idiots I'm surrounded by, my guess is that the booze is flowing freely. I maneuver my way through the crowd and into the kitchen before taking in the scene.

If Beck's mom saw all these people sitting their asses on her polished-to-a-high-shine marble countertop, she would probably have a conniption. She's kind of a germ-o-phobe. There's a half-naked girl stretched out on the island with a lime clenched in her teeth as one of the football players slurps tequila from her belly button.

I'm no aficionado on hygiene, but that definitely doesn't seem sanitary.

A few people greet me as I make my way to the keg and take my place in line. I'm in the middle of chatting with a girl from my French class when she turns an unflattering shade of green and bolts to the nearest bathroom with her hands slapped over her mouth. All thoughts of a refill are abandoned as she pushes her way to the back hall. I really hope she makes it in time. Caroline will be furious if she finds out someone has thrown up on her marble floors.

Once I have a frothy cup of beer in hand, I head to the patio to check on Alyssa's progress.

Am I a terrible friend for hoping she's already been shot down and has thrown in the towel for the night?

Probably, but I can deal with that.

Instead of finding a dejected Alyssa crying in the corner, I'm amazed to discover that she's clawed her way to the front of the pack. Who knows, she may actually have a shot of getting picked from the crowd.

This could be a real game changer for her.

Guess that means I'm stuck here. I look around the patio, searching for a place to park my ass. The Hollingsworth property is about an acre in size, which is the same as ours. The space around the pool is gated with a black iron fence and tall arborvitae that spear into the dark night sky. Toward the back of the gate is an unoccupied lounge chair with my name on it. I'll hang out there for forty minutes before dragging Alyssa's panty-less ass back to my house.

Before I can take three steps, a deep voice cuts through the raucous noise of the party.

"Well, well, well. Look who decided to make a cameo appearance tonight."

I swing around, knowing exactly who I'll find.

Beck.

As difficult as it is, I try not to notice how delicious he looks in plaid board shorts that hang low on his hips, showing off the cut lines of his abdomen before disappearing beneath the waistband. The chiseled strength of his arms and chest are enough to bring most girls to their proverbial knees.

The operative word in that sentence being *most.*

I, however, am not one of those idiotic girls.

"Coming here tonight wasn't my idea. I was dragged under duress."

"Yeah, I figured you would have better things to do than hang around with a bunch of wasted assholes."

He's got me there.

"You know me too well." When my throat grows dry, I lift the red Solo cup to my lips. Before I can take a sip, he snatches the drink from my fingers and brings it to his mouth. I watch his throat constrict as he drains the contents.

"Rude much?" My fists go to my hips. "What did you do that for?"

He shrugs. Even though it's a slight movement, his muscles ripple and attraction bursts to life in my core. "You shouldn't be drinking."

"Excuse me?" My eyes pop wide as laughter tumbles from my mouth. "Are you being serious right now?" I wave a hand toward the drunken mass that surrounds us. It's not even eleven, and already people are passed out on loungers. "Look around, dude, everyone is shitfaced." Hopefully, there are a few designated drivers among this group or Uber will make a hell of a lot of money tonight.

As soon as Beck smirks, I know his answer is specifically designed to piss me off.

"That might be so, but everyone knows you're a good girl. And good girls don't drink. I wouldn't want the society to revoke your membership. You've worked so damn hard for it."

My eyes narrow to slits. The attraction that had flared to life so quickly is extinguished by his teasing.

I hate when he calls me that. And he knows it, which is precisely why he continues to do it. Beck loves nothing better than to crawl under my skin. He's like a rash I can never quite get rid of, no matter how many steroids I use.

It's irritating.

"I'm not a good girl," I growl before stabbing a finger at his ridiculously hard chest. "And *you* are not my keeper. I can drink if I want to." In a haughty voice, I remind, "I'm the one who was requested to babysit *your* ass. Not the other way around."

He crowds into my personal space. Instead of retreating, I stand my ground. I refuse to let him intimidate me.

"Babysitter, you say? Hmmm...I could definitely use one of those tonight." His fingers trace a path down the center of my chest, lingering in the valley between my breasts. "Should we take this elsewhere and you can demonstrate everything your service entails?"

His nearness does funny things to me and clouds my better judgment. Instead of pushing him away, I'm tempted to pull him closer.

My body wavers before sanity crashes down on me and I bat his hand away. "Go to hell."

"See?" He laughs as if I've proven his point for him. "A good girl through and through."

"I'm not as good as you think." The words shoot out of my mouth before I can rein them back in. To be clear, they are a total lie. I *am* as good as he thinks. Probably better. I have to be.

"Is that so?" He steps closer until the tips of my breasts brush against his bare chest. "Sweetheart, I'd love nothing better than to test that theory but we both know you'll always be Mia Stanbury, little miss perfect."

And he'll always be Beckett Hollingsworth. The guy with little-to-no impulse control who can't walk down the school hallway without finding trouble. The same one who can't be left alone in his own house for a night without inviting a hundred of his closest friends over for an impromptu party.

We are opposites in every sense of the word.

"Shut up, Beck." I've never met anyone who has the power to turn me on and piss me off at the same time. If he ever cranked up the charm, I'd be toast. He's capable of melting the panties right off a girl with one well-aimed look. I've seen it happen with my own eyes. I refuse to be one of those ridiculous females. I won't be used and tossed aside like dirty Kleenex.

I don't realize that I've become trapped in my own thoughts until his fingers settle under my chin, lifting it so I'm forced to meet his bright gaze. "What's the matter? Truth hurt?"

"There's nothing you can say that will hurt me." If only that were true.

His face looms closer until it fills my vision, blotting out the party. My world shrinks around us until it only encompasses Beck. My breath gets clogged in my lungs and burns like a fire before spreading to the rest of my body. Any moment I'm going to self-combust.

What am I doing?

I should pull away, but I'm powerless to do anything other than stare into his eyes and fall under his spell.

"Beck, baby!" a loud female voice booms over the rowdiness of the party, "over here!"

Even when she continues to bleat like a sheep, our gazes remain locked for several long heartbeats and I almost wonder if he'll ignore her. But she's persistent and continues to repeat his name until he severs the connection between us and swings around.

As soon as I'm released, the air rushes from my lungs and my body sags with relief. Or maybe it's disappointment. I tamp down the emotions so I can't inspect them too closely.

What would have happened if we hadn't been interrupted?

Nothing good.

This is *exactly* why I avoid Beck at all costs. Even though we're constantly sniping at each other, there's an undercurrent of attraction that hums beneath the surface. No other guy has ever provoked these kinds of emotions in me. I want to slap him almost as much as I want to kiss him.

Sanity returns with a rush as I focus on the statuesque blond twenty feet away. Ava Simmons is wearing a teeny tiny bikini that leaves very little to the imagination. Once she has Beck's full attention, she reaches around and unties the strings that hold the tiny triangles in place. The material floats to the cement at her feet. She lets him—and everyone else in the vicinity—ogle her perky breasts before running and jumping into the pool.

People cheer, and more girls ditch their tops, following Ava into the water.

A grin slides across Beck's face as he glances at me. A challenging light enters his eyes as he jerks his dark head toward the pool. Water sloshes over the edge of the azure-colored tile as more bodies dive in.

Oh, hell no.

My heart pounds as I throw my hands up in a *what can you do* gesture. "Sorry, didn't bring a suit."

His grin turns predatory. "Doesn't look like you need one."

Yeah...not going to happen.

"As fun as that seems, I'll pass," I wave an arm toward the pool, "but don't let that stop you from mingling with your guests. Ava's waiting." Topless. From the corner of my eye, I see her breasts bobbing like inflatable safety devices.

When his focus is drawn to the people splashing around, I follow suit. It's so much easier to stare elsewhere than hold the intensity of his gaze. Even when that option includes watching a bunch of topless girls I've known since elementary school. I don't check out the guys loitering in the area, but I'm sure most are sporting wood. Honestly, if it weren't for Alyssa, I would get the hell out of here before it turns into a raging orgy.

Beck steps closer and my gaze snaps to his. "Sure I can't persuade you to go for a swim?"

"Nope." I shake my head.

"That's too bad. This would have gone a long way to prove you're not the good girl I always pegged you to be."

Before I can summon up a pithy retort, he runs and dives headfirst into the water. I catch a glimpse of plaid as he disappears beneath the surface.

A mixture of relief and disappointment bubble up inside me until I'm nearly choking on them. It's the latter emotion I'm having a hard time accepting.

With a huffed-out breath, I stalk to one of the many loungers that surround the pool and settle on top of a plush cushion. I glance around for Alyssa, hoping she's given up on Colton so we can head home. It's not too late for the evening to be salvaged with pizza and a movie. Instead, I find her in the pool.

Topless.

Sucking face with Colton.

Great.

As much as I want to take off, I can't leave her here alone. God only knows what will happen if I do.

With a groan, I squeeze my eyes tight and prepare myself for a long night.

Want to read more? Buy The Girl Next Door here -) https://books2read.com/u/4EPQPg

ABOUT THE AUTHOR

Jennifer Sucevic is a USA Today bestselling author who has published nineteen New Adult and Mature Young Adult novels. Her work has been translated into German, Dutch, and Italian. Jen has a bachelor's degree in History and a master's degree in Educational Psychology. Both are from the University of Wisconsin-Milwaukee. She started out her career as a high school counselor, which she loved. She lives in the Midwest with her husband, four kids, and a menagerie of animals. If you would like to receive regular updates regarding new releases, please subscribe to her newsletter here- Jennifer Sucevic Newsletter (subscribepage.com)

Or contact Jen through email, at her website, or on Facebook.

sucevicjennifer@gmail.com

Want to join her reader group? Do it here -)

J Sucevic's Book Boyfriends | Facebook

Social media links-

www.jennifersucevic.com

https://www.instagram.com/jennifersucevicauthor

https://www.facebook.com/jennifer.sucevic

Amazon.com: Jennifer Sucevic: Books, Biography, Blog, Audiobooks, Kindle

Jennifer Sucevic Books - BookBub

https://www.tumblr.com/blog/jsucevic

https://www.pinterest.com/jmolitor6/